CW01664165

fierce VOW

KOZLOV EMPIRE BOOK THREE

MONICA KAYNE

Copyright © 2023 by Monica Kayne

All rights reserved.

No part of this publication may be reproduced, distributed, or transmitted in any form or by any means, including photocopying, recording, or other electronic or mechanical methods, without the prior written permission of the publisher, except as permitted by U.S. copyright law.

The story, all names, characters, and incidents portrayed in this production are fictitious. No identification with actual persons (living or deceased), places, buildings, and products is intended or should be inferred.

ISBN 978-1-7782704-3-7

Book Cover by Opulent Swag and Design

Editing by Nina Fiegl

Editing & Proofreading by Krista Dapkey

Interior graphics by AJ Wolf Graphics

First edition 2023

This book is dedicated to all the readers who never fully grasped their kinks until a morally grey book boyfriend growled, 'Good girl,' and STFUATTDLAGG, and suddenly everything clicked into place.

AUTHOR NOTE

Fierce Vow is a dark mafia romance with mature themes and profanity. Please check my website for trigger warnings.

https://monicakayne.com/trigger-warnings

1

ALYONA

"It's not you, it's me."

I meet Marcel's gaze, his words a sucker punch to my gut. Is this guy for real!? He's using the most overused line in the history of breakups on me. And to add insult to injury, he can't even look me in the eye. He keeps fidgeting with his cell phone on the tabletop, his eyes pinging around the dimly lit Parisian bar.

He clears his throat. "I've really enjoyed our time together," he mumbles, "but I think it's better if we part ways here."

Leaning back in my chair, arms crossed over my chest, I don't bother to hide my sarcasm when I ask, "Aren't you going to suggest we stay friends?" Since he's clearly a fan of clichés, I thought he might want to use the second-most overused line in the breakup handbook.

Marcel looks aghast, as if I've suggested we rob a bank together. What is this guy's problem? We've been seeing each other for a few months, I thought it was going well enough.

He's a French painter that I met at a fashion industry party on the Rue de Turenne. He pursued me in the beginning, doing all the legwork. Showered me with compliments and flowers. It was pleasant enough, the sex was ... satisfactory, and I enjoyed his company, but I wouldn't say this is a major heartbreak.

It's not like I was looking for love with him, or any of the men I've met in my seven years in Paris.

No, I already lived through love once before and barely survived. Never again.

Still, I crave companionship, and a girl's gotta get laid now and then. But I'm getting mighty sick of the it's-not-you-it's-me line. Maybe French guys are commitment-phobes? Then again, the last guy I dated was Italian, and before that a Brit, and they both fed me the same bullshit line. So maybe it *is* in fact me.

"No." Marcel's mouth sets into a grim line. "I don't think we should remain friends. It's just ... too complicated."

Ouch.

I reach for my martini and polish it off in two large gulps, reveling in the liquid burn. "In that case, it's been a slice. I'll leave you to pay the bill." Snatching up my purse from the seat beside me, I rise to my full height of five nine, allowing him to appreciate the length of my legs, accentuated by four-inch Louboutins, and my little black Prada dress. I don't work in the fashion industry for nothing. I know how to use my assets, and judging by the wistful sigh Marcel releases, he seems to agree.

Just not enough to keep me around.

"Au revoir, Marcel. Good luck working through your mommy issues in therapy."

"Alyona," he says, apologetically.

But when I glance back at him over my shoulder his eyes widen with alarm. "There's nothing else to say," I assure him.

The look of relief on Marcel's face is palpable. He closes

his eyes, exhales a sharp breath, and then hurries off to find our waiter.

Like all my breakups, this one comes out of the fucking blue, right as things were settling into a comfortable rhythm. Dump Me Debbie, that's me. I usually make it a few months before they inexplicably find something wrong with me. Just like Leo had.

I step out of the brasserie onto the sidewalk. It's a gorgeous spring night, and Paris is bursting with energy—tourists crowd the streets and young lovers stroll arm in arm. *Well, isn't that just perfect?* A walk would do me good, help me blow off some steam. I choose a route along the Seine, heading towards the seventh arrondissement, the chic neighborhood where my flat is located.

I've had my place since I first moved here at eighteen. Well, *fled* might be the correct word. At the time, my only thought was to escape New York and the man who had nearly destroyed me, but I've slowly built a life here. I learned French. Made friends. Now I have a fulfilling career as a buyer for a luxury fashion brand, and I live in the city with the world's best pastries. What else do I need?

Yes, I miss my brother and friends in New York, but the ocean separating me from Leo Kozlov makes it all worthwhile.

As I cross over the Pont des Arts bridge, a handsome man with sparkling green eyes and an olive complexion flashes me an interested smile. In the past, I might have returned that smile, but not tonight. Maybe not ever again. There's only so much rejection a lady can take.

Jolting me from my bleak thoughts, "What is Love" blares from my phone—the world's most ridiculous ringtone, which is assigned to my sister-in-law, Rowan—finally giving me a reason to smile. "Why are you calling me from your vacation? Shouldn't you be making a baby?" I say by way of greeting.

"Welp, since you asked, I wore Yulian out last night, so he's still sleeping. It's six in the morning here."

"Yeah, didn't need to know that," I add with a laugh, dodging the tables of a crowded sidewalk cafe. "So what's Fiji like? Everything you dreamed of and more?"

"It's pretty awesome," she confirms. "And the best part of it is that I get Yulian all to myself for the next two weeks. In an hour, we head to a more remote island for the full off-the-grid experience. No cell service!"

My eyes widen in surprise. My brother is not the type to step away from his work. I mean, bratva leaders don't exactly work a nine-to-five. And my brother runs security for the Kozlov Bratva, the Russian mafia that controls the East Coast of the US.

The bratva that we grew up in.

Except I turned my back on the brotherhood long ago. After it took both my father and mother from me much too early, I swore I'd never be part of that underworld.

"Damn, girl, he must really be serious about making a baby." Yulian and Rowan definitely need a few weeks of no distractions, no work emergencies, nothing but lube and an ocean view.

She snorts. "He is. Anyhow, I just wanted to say goodbye before we sign off. Is everything good with you?"

I conceal my sigh as I round the corner of my block. "Yeah, everything is great." This is not the time to share my latest breakup sob story. It just gets Rowan all worked up.

Turns out I'm a great catch on paper, but that's where it ends. God knows Marcel is just the last guy in a long list of bailers. Not that any of them mattered—none except for Leo. My brother's best friend and one of the only people who truly knew me, the real me. But even that wasn't enough apparently.

"Well, I won't keep you. Have an amazing time. Relax. And

don't worry about a thing," I say, digging in my purse for my keys. "Just enjoy and make me a little niece or nephew."

"On it!" she squeals.

I smile to myself as I push the key into my front door. In nine months there could be a baby. A baby I'll love like my own. Maybe there is something to look forward to.

ONCE INSIDE, I go to disengage the alarm, but there's no red light flashing on the wall. Shit, I must have forgotten to turn it on this morning. It's something that happens more regularly than not.

Truthfully, I never wanted this damn alarm system in the first place. Yulian had this place wired like Fort Knox one day while I was at work, that stubborn *mudak*. No prior discussion, no warning. I came home, and there it was, a brand-new alarm system with the code sent to me through an encrypted server.

It's just another example of my brother's over-the-top protective tendencies. Shortly after I bought this flat with my inheritance money, he purchased the other three units in the building to prevent anyone else from moving in. Multimillion dollar units just sitting empty. It's insane, really.

Not that Yulian and I ever talk about it. Nah. I let him do what he needs to for his peace of mind with me living halfway across the world.

On one hand, I get it. Being eight years older, Yulian has always looked out for me, and before Rowan, we were each other's only family, having lost our father when we were teens, and our mother in our twenties. But his worry is misplaced. The most dangerous thing that's happened to me in months is tripping over a wayward cobblestone in my stilettos.

Exhausted, I kick off my heels and make my way to the

kitchen. The familiar creaks of the wooden floorboards underfoot are comforting. Everything in Paris is old. Worn. It has history, something else I adore about this city.

My only goal tonight is a cup of tea, pajamas, and trashy reality TV. Maybe I'll treat myself to a bubble bath. I pour water into the kettle, and turn it on, leaning against the counter. That's when the door to my bedroom catches my attention. It's open an inch. Barely anything noticeable, but I always shut my bedroom door. It was part of Leo's training, a security measure he said.

The hairs on the back of my neck rise. Something feels off.

The shrill whistle of the kettle only adds to my growing anxiety. I make my way to the kitchen drawer, searching for a weapon. You don't grow up in a bratva household without learning self-defense. My hand wraps around a small paring knife. Pausing, I also reach for a compact pocketknife that I keep in my junk drawer beside the fridge. Just in case, I tuck it into the waistband of my skirt.

Creeping towards my bedroom, I push the door open and turn on the light, ready to face an intruder. But there's no one here. No open window, no furniture out of place, not even a stirring of the air. Releasing a sigh of relief, I chuckle to myself, feeling foolish for letting my imagination run wild. I blame Marcel. That asshole threw me off my game.

Switching off the light, I'm about to head back towards the kitchen when a gloved hand materializes out of the dark, covering my mouth as a large body pins me against the wall from behind. A chill of terror sends my pulse into overdrive.

"Don't make a sound," an accented male voice murmurs in my ear. His arm is cinched tightly around my chest, making it difficult to breathe. "I won't hurt you if you make this easy. I just need you to come with me."

Despite the terror, I resist the urge to scream. It would be a waste of energy when I need to focus on fighting back. And although my hand is still gripping the paring knife, I don't need a blade for my opening move. In one swift motion, I shift my weight and push my free hand against the wall. Slamming my elbow back into his stomach, he grunts loudly, and I attempt to wriggle from his hold, but he recovers quickly, wrapping one arm around my neck to keep me in place. "We can do this the easy way or the hard way, your choice."

"The hard way," I choke out before plunging the knife back. I can't see what I'm aiming for, but I know I've hit my target when the knife sinks into the soft flesh of his thigh, and he loses his grip, grunting in pain.

I spin on my opponent, finally getting a good look at him. Well, sort of. He's wearing a ski mask—a balaclava—and his mouth is puckered into a tight knot, his dark eyes narrowed into a scowl. He's wearing all black, so I can't see the blood I imagine is seeping out of his wounded leg.

With a menacing growl, the intruder reaches into the back waistband of his jeans. The clicking of his pistol resounds through the room, sending a chilling jolt down my spine.

"Put down the knife and walk towards the door," he orders.

Adrenaline surges through my blood, but I'm not the type to take orders from a brute like him. Unless it's in bed. "Fuck off."

"My orders are to take you in alive, but that leaves a lot of room for interpretation, don't you think?"

His orders? What? This isn't a petty robbery or random attack. I've been targeted. "What are you talking about? Who wants me?"

"If you think I know or care, you're stupider than you look. Now fucking move already."

"Okay, okay." I toss the knife aside and raise my hands in the air. He's angry and armed; I'll have a better chance of escape if I convince him that I won't fight anymore. "I'll go with you. Just please don't hurt me."

"Move." He gestures towards the door with his gun, and I bow my head, slowly shuffling through the hallway towards the front door, his pistol pushed into my spine.

The pocketknife burns a hole in my waistband, but I need him distracted before I can make a move for it. I can already sense my attacker's impatience; he keeps glancing out the window, as if checking for someone outside. The getaway car. Fuck.

My hesitation angers him. "What's the hold up? Open the fucking door."

"I'm just getting on some shoes, jeez." I shoot him a dirty look over my shoulder, but he stops me from turning fully, burying one hand deep into my hair.

"Not gonna fall for that one, princess." He kicks my heels towards me, the ones I'd abandoned earlier. "Hands up, and put these on. And don't you dare do anything stupid when we walk out of here."

I nod, slipping one heel on. I make a move to put on the other shoe but deliberately lose my footing and fall to the side. "Shit," I exclaim. He reaches out to steady me, and in that brief moment, I retrieve the knife from the back of my skirt. In one move, I press down to release the blade and drive it into his upper arm, causing him to falter and drop his pistol.

"You fucking bitch," he howls.

"Yeah, so sorry about that," I taunt. The sensitive flesh of the upper arm really is a shitty place to get stabbed. He scrambles for the gun, but I get there first. I reach for his pistol lying on the ground and point it straight at his chest. "Who sent you? What do you want with me?" I ask, hysteria edging into my voice.

His smile is demonic. "You'll find out soon enough. It's not going to stop with me, others will come for you."

As much as I need answers, I don't think I'm going to get them from him, which means he's of no use to me. I lift the gun, press down on the trigger, and release a bullet between his eyes. In the quiet aftermath, my breath comes in quick gasps and my palms break into a clammy sweat, the adrenaline now replaced by a shivering cold sensation throughout my body. The full horror hasn't fully sunk in yet, but a numbness has taken over. Am I in shock?

I leave the body lying on the foyer floor as I escape to the kitchen, heading straight for the freezer where I keep my emergency cigarettes. My shaking hands pull a Gauloises from the pack and press it between my lips. The first drag feels like heaven. It makes me light-headed and dizzy, but it calms my fried nerves. I take another long pull and think about what to do. My options are limited. But I do know I need to get this dead body out of my home, and then I need to figure out what the fuck is going on.

Yulian. I have to call my brother. Anxiety ripples down my spine as I realize the one person who I can count on to sort this out has turned off his phone and, for the first time in his life, is unavailable to me. Fucking great.

My mind flips through other options. Of course I can call Andrei Kozlov, the Kozlov Bratva pakhan. I know he'd do anything for me. We're childhood friends, grew up together, and he's a solid guy. As solid as gangsters come. But I know if I call Andrei, he'll call in the troops. I'll have bratva swarming this place in no time. With one man in particular guaranteed to show his face.

Leonid Kozlov. Andrei's younger brother, sworn-in *vor*, and the one person I'd be happy never to see again. Fuck that. I'm going to pull up my big girl panties and deal with this on my own. Retrieving my phone off the kitchen counter, I flip through my contacts before I find the man I'm looking for. Gianni Mero. Local gangster for hire. It's the one underworld contact my brother insisted on. Just in case. I never imagined I'd have to use this number, but desperate times and all that. Because when you call Gianni, things are bad.

Gianni answers on the first ring, his voice gruff like sandpaper. "Alyona Nikitin." My family isn't as high-ranking as the Kozlovs, but my last name still buys me respect.

"I need a cleanup crew," I say, sticking to the code words.

"I see. Are you harmed?"

"I'm not," I say. But am I alright? Far from it.

"I'll have a crew there in fifteen minutes."

I hang up, not even questioning how he knows my address. I stub out my cigarette in the sink and run cold water over the ash. The noxious smell rises up, nearly making me gag. The cigarette did its job and calmed my nerves, but being an infrequent smoker, it also made me feel sick.

Or maybe it's the dead guy on my hallway floor.

Despite the cold sweat sliding down my spine, I know what I have to do. Marching towards the foyer, I steel myself as I peel the bloodied balaclava off his face, hot sticky wetness coating my fingertips.

Sweet Jesus. Tattoos of monasteries and skulls crawl up his neck.

Russian prison tattoos.

I throw my back against the wall.

An echo of his accent comes back to me now. It's Eastern European for sure, but he didn't sound Russian, and it's an accent I'm familiar with considering it's my family's lineage. Whatever his origins, one thing is clear. My troubles extend way beyond a shitty breakup.

2

LEO

"Stop ... please. I did it, it was me." A desperate sob works up the man's throat, and I stand back, relieved that he's finally admitting what I already know. He held out longer than I'd expected. Bankers are usually quick to squeal, but for some reason, Gerhart here did not.

But everyone has their breaking point, and I eventually found his.

"I wish you would have admitted to taking the money sooner," I tell him as I stuff a gag in his mouth. I'm not interested in anything else he has to say. "I wouldn't have had to resort to this level of ... ugliness." His face is a canvas of bruises and cuts, and I'm sure he's nursing broken ribs. The chair he's strapped into is the only thing keeping him upright.

Looking down at my bloody knuckles, I frown. "This isn't my usual line of work," I confess.

Much to my father's disappointment, I was never a typical vor. My brothers embraced the brutality of our world, but I preferred using my brains to my fists. My computer skills to my knife skills. I learned early on that everyone has deep dark secrets—finding and exposing what others want to keep quiet makes me a much more dangerous adversary.

Like with my friend Gerhart here, the Swiss banker we trusted to launder our money who'd given in to temptation. He swiped a cool three million from the brotherhood, probably thinking we wouldn't notice. But I noticed. And now he must suffer the consequences, because you don't get away with cheating the bratva and live to tell the tale. We've got enforcers for this kind of thing, but sometimes, like now, I volunteer for the job just to see if I still have it in me.

"I know why you did it," I say, shaking my head, my voice echoing off the walls of the bank vault. "Stupid, but I understand." I grab the photos from my bag, leafing through them until I find the right one: Gerhart and a beautiful blonde entwined in each other. "I'd like to think you took the money for love. That, at least, I get. Love's one hell of a drug."

It'll take you to the highest of highs and the lowest of lows. I should know.

He nods desperately, as if he could sway me with a heartfelt plea. But we both know the truth.

"Let's cut the crap. You didn't steal for love; you stole for pussy. Katarina, right? She wanted to be wined and dined. Whisked off to Dubai for a weekend, the Caribbean the next. Expensive tastes." Gerhart scowls and stiffens against the binds. Of course he doesn't want to be reminded of his weakness. No man does.

"The thing I don't get ..." I say, throwing the pictures on the floor so they scatter in all directions. "Why cheat on your wife?" I let that question hang as I pick up one picture in particular. It's of his family. Big smiles all around at his daughter's high school graduation. I hold it up to his face, devastation crossing his features. It always comes down to the sins of the father. "She's a lovely woman, your wife, I can tell. She loves you, and you fucked it up. For what?" I heave out a sigh for the shame it is and once again take the seat across from him.

"I was in love once. With my best friend's little sister. Cliché, right?" I smile wistfully. "She was the one person in my life who believed I could be something other than a cold-blooded vor. That I was capable of more than just darkness. Guess I proved her wrong." I force down the guilt, reminding myself that loyalty to my family came at a cost. Like everything.

Gerhart maintains his scowl, guess he's not in the mood for story time. But fuck him, this is my version of torture. "But the difference between us? I know what I lost, what I had to turn my back on. And I still feel the loss every fucking day." Every time I look in the mirror.

I rarely talk about Alyona and what we had. Because when I do, when I allow her to take up too much real estate in my mind, I spiral. Pushing her away was the hardest thing I've ever had to do. But there is no rewriting the past, so I focus on the one thing I can control. Her future.

"Well, Gerhart, our time here is up," I say, sounding more like a therapist than a vor. His eyes widen in horror, and he tries to squirm out of his bindings, a futile effort given his battered state. I'm almost regretful our chat has to come to an end—it's not often I can talk so freely. "So, here's what's going to happen," I say, preferring to be straightforward about these things. "I'm going to shoot you in the head. You'll die instantly. Tomorrow morning, someone at the bank will find your body, usually a janitor or a member of the staff. Your wife and kids won't learn about the mistress. They'll think it's a bank robbery gone wrong. Tragic, but at least they'll never learn what a dirty dog you are. But we know the truth, don't we?"

He releases a pitiful wail, but his pleas fall on deaf ears, I've heard enough. I glance down at my phone, swiping a few times to make sure the money Gerhart took is now back in our offshore account where it should be.

The black metal of my Sig looks dull under the shitty fluorescent lighting. "It's been real, my friend." I pull the trigger, not wanting to stretch out the moment. It's a clean shot, right between the eyes, he's dead within seconds.

THE BIKE RUMBLES beneath me as I rev the engine, the vibrations lulling as I turn near the private airport in Geneva. My bones ache. Hours of standing on the cold concrete floor of the bank vault will do that to you. But in less than nine hours, I'll be touching down in New York.

I park in front of the hangar doors, my Jetstream visible inside. Dismounting, I pull the helmet over my head, and hand it off to one of the men standing by. He'll load the black Kawasaki in the hold of the plane.

Damn, it's a pretty bike. Might need to acquire one in red when I get home.

What's another bike when you have forty already?

Whatever fills the void.

As I sling my bag over my shoulder and head towards the waiting jet, my cell buzzes from inside the bag. It's late here in Switzerland, meaning it's the dead of night back home—never a good sign. But when I check my phone, it's not my brother Andrei calling.

"Matis, what's happening?" I demand. A phone call means something's gone wrong, and I pay Matis handsomely to ensure that never happens. "Is the ass wipe still in the picture?"

"No, no," Matis's distinct rasp comes through. "The little merde dropped her like a hot potato. Nearly shit his pants when we had our talk. She really picks some losers." He laughs before breaking into a coughing fit.

They pick her, but I don't bother correcting him. "So what's the issue?"

"The problem is ..." Matis hesitates, which I don't like. He's usually very direct. "Alyona called Gianni. I don't have all the details, but ..."

He doesn't need to finish the thought. You don't call a man like Gianni Mero unless you require his expertise in body disposal, cleanup, or erasing a murder.

My chest tightens, anxiety coiling around my throat. "Just tell me, is she hurt?"

"No, no, not at all. It seems she did the hurting."

I pause, considering this. I know what she's capable of—I trained her myself—but it's been years. "Keep an eye on the situation," I order. "I'll be in Paris in just over an hour. And, Matis, you better have some answers when I land."

3

LEO

Motherfucking Paris traffic is going to be the death of me. It's almost one in the morning, yet the area around the Champs-Élysées is jam-packed. I blame the tourists, they all buy into this "city of love" bullshit, especially at night.

My only saving grace is the bike. Like a true Parisian, I drive like an asshole, weaving in and out of traffic to get to my destination faster. When I finally pull up behind Alyona's flat, Matis is waiting for me, leaning against the hood of his car.

"You made it here in record time," he comments dryly, glancing at his watch.

"A private jet helps." I stow my helmet on the bike's back seat and cut to the chase. "What do you know?"

Matis flicks his cigarette away, springing off the hood of his car. He's not bratva. He's actually an ex-cop, but all that matters to me is his loyalty, ability to follow orders, and connections. Which is why Gianni tipped him off about Aly.

He shrugs carelessly in that nonchalant French way of his.

"An intruder got into her flat, someone who was trying to abduct her ... there was a tussle, she killed him, but she's not saying much more than that." He pauses, already lighting another cigarette.

The breath catches in my throat. "Abduct her!"

"It would seem so." Matis shrugs again, making me itch to throttle him. He's way too relaxed for this situation. "One more thing. The guy's covered in tattoos—Russian prison tats for that matter. Gianni's men are dealing with the body, but he'll send pictures and anything else he finds."

Jesus fucking Christ. Russian prison tattoos were popular among bratva members in the 1990s and 2000s, indicating the number of years they had served, their crimes, and their rank within the organization.

So this wasn't a random break-in. She was targeted. My blood runs cold. "Text me the moment you have anything," I bark over my shoulder.

I might be the last person Aly ever wants to see again, but she doesn't have a choice. I'll deal with her anger—I have for years—but I'm not allowing her to face this threat alone. Hell will freeze over first.

I saved her life once though it cost me everything. And if need be, I'll do it again.

MY KNOCK REVERBERATES throughout the hallway but there's no answer. I shift my weight from one foot to the other and consider crashing down the door. No one else lives in this building, I made sure of that, but I figure it'll get our reunion off to a bad start.

It's not like we haven't seen each other at all these past seven years. Our families are closely connected, we grew up together. In the years since we broke up, run-ins couldn't be helped. Weddings, funerals, any big family event. She usually avoids me like the plague, even if I can't tear my eyes off her.

I knock again, harder this time. Finally, footsteps approach, and the door swings open. Alyona stands rooted to the spot, staring at me as if I'm her worst nightmare come to life.

And maybe I am.

But that doesn't stop me from soaking in her very presence. All I can hear is the thunderous pulsing of blood in my ears. Even after a shit sandwich of a night, she still possesses the same devastating beauty I've damn near memorized. Long, silky black hair, still damp after a shower, high cheekbones, piercing blue eyes, and full, sensuous lips—although, at the moment, those lips form a disapproving pout.

Her stare is cold enough to freeze my balls. If she's surprised to see me, she doesn't show it, the only thing that's clear is her unhappiness. If only I could find her as distasteful as she finds me. Because all I see is perfection.

She clutches her fuzzy robe tightly around her body, as if it's armor against my presence. "What are you doing here?" she snaps, her words laced with acid.

I flash her a smile which only deepens her frown. "Rumor has it you could use some help." I don't bother waiting for an invitation into her flat—I know it won't come. I push my way past her, and as I do, I'm enveloped by warm vanilla and jasmine. It's a scent wrapped up in so much memory it makes my bones ache.

"You heard wrong. I'm fine. I've sorted it all out myself, so you can leave." She holds the door open and gestures in the direction she wants me to go.

"I'm not going anywhere, Aly. Like it or not, I'm here to stay."

Her cheeks flush, irritation flickering in her eyes as she

slams the door behind me with more force than necessary. I know she's tough, but beneath her bravado, she's shaken up. Who wouldn't be?

"Let's not do this, okay?" she pleads. "As you can see, I'm fine. There was a break-in, but I handled it. You don't have to pretend to care—"

"I'm not pretending, Aly. Someone came here tonight to abduct you and I need to know why."

Even though she's trying to put on a brave face, I notice how her shoulders sag with exhaustion, and every protective instinct within me surges. I want to scoop her up and shield her from everything bad in this world. Even if that's impossible. Even though I couldn't protect her from my own flesh and blood.

Without saying a word, she stalks into her kitchen, grabs a bottle of red wine, and fills a stemmed glass right up to the top. She gulps down half the contents in three seconds flat. She doesn't offer me a drink or a seat, but at least she's not screaming bloody murder for me to get out. *Yet.* There's still plenty of time for that.

My eyes sweep the apartment; there's not a book or a knick-knack out of place. It's spotless. Gianni's team did an impeccable cleanup job, but I'm sure the memories of what took place here still linger.

"How do you know what happened?" She narrows her eyes, crossing her arms over her chest. "I didn't involve the Kozlovs for a reason. I'm not interested in their help, and I'm *definitely* not interested in yours."

I advance on her, the space between us shrinks until we stand inches apart. Her eyes meet mine, unblinking. I am keenly aware of every detail of her face, every flicker of expression that crosses her features—the delicate arch of her brows, the lush fringe of her lashes, and the gray flecks that dance in her irises.

"It's too late, I'm involved." Aly needs to know that I won't take a chance. Not when it comes to her safety. She has every reason in the world to hate me, but that doesn't mean I'm going to back off. "Either tell me what happened here tonight, or I'll find out from someone else. But either way, I'm not letting this go."

She crosses her arms and scowls at me. "Why do you care? I'm nothing to you. You made that very clear a long time ago."

The undercurrent of vulnerability in her voice causes my stomach to tighten. She's not nothing to me, far from it, but how could I tell her the truth? Instead, I offer her a half-truth. "Your brother's not here to deal with this, so I will. We both know Yulian would gut me like a fish if I don't protect you with my life. Whether you want my protection or not."

"Good," she snaps, "I'd love for him to finish you off." I nearly smile at that. I bet she would.

"This is not a game." I level with her, running an aggravated hand through my hair. "I need to know everything that happened tonight."

She slams back the rest of the wine and sits down on one of the dining room chairs. I sit across from her. "There's not much to tell. I came home after a sizzling-hot date where he fucked my brains out and I came three times, and there was someone in my flat." She blinks up at me innocently, but I keep my expression flat. "He was wearing a ski mask. I couldn't see his face. He wanted me to go somewhere with him, but I wasn't willing. He had a gun, but I had a knife. And only one of us is standing here alive, so ..." She shrugs.

Atta girl. Always knew she had it in her.

My phone buzzes with a text from Matis. Opening up the message, I find pictures of a bloody naked body, his body a patchwork of stars, churches, spiderwebs, and playing cards. All intricate designs that hold symbolic meanings within the Russian criminal underworld. I slip the phone into my back pocket. The pictures aren't pretty, and she's been through enough tonight.

"What did this guy say? What did he want from you?"

"Fuck, Leo, how am I supposed to know what he wanted? My killer shoe collection? Who knows? And now this conversation is over. You can leave. I killed one man tonight, I don't mind raising the body count." She releases a ragged breath, exhaustion weighing down her features.

My phone pings with another text.

> Matis: He had an injectable sedative cocktail and restraints on him. Everything points to abduction. Not a random attack.

My hands white-knuckle the dining room table so hard I'm sure it will splinter. Aly doesn't live in our world, she escaped it long ago and never looked back. I made sure of it. So why her? Is it about Aly's connection to our family, or is there another angle at play?

"What's wrong?" she asks, voice trembling. "Why are you looking at your phone like that?"

"You're not safe here." I don't sugarcoat the truth; it won't do her any good. "Until we know what's going on, you can't stay here."

"Forget that. I'm not upending my life. Can't you just assign security to me?"

I shake my head. "That's not enough. You need to come with me."

"No way in hell am I going with you anywhere." She's up and out of her seat, heading to her bedroom, presumably to lock herself away, but I can't allow her to do that.

Moving quickly, I gather her in my arms, stopping her from running. This position has the unintended consequence of bringing her body flush against mine, and fuuuck, that feeling is everything. The soft curve of her ass presses into me, and even though she's glaring daggers at me over her shoulder, I have to will my dick not to get hard.

"Leo," she chokes out, her pulse throbbing against her delicate neck, "let me go."

"Not until you agree to go into hiding."

"I ..." She squeezes her eyes closed as if she's gathering patience. "I can't do that. I have a life. I have a job. I can't just walk away from all of this."

All of what? Fuckboys and vapid fashion parties?

"You can and you will." Releasing a frustrated snarl, she tries to wrench herself free from my hold, but I only tighten my grip around her waist. "Somebody is after you, and until we know more, you're not safe. Not even with security, because if it's the Russians, a guard won't stop them. These are people that use any method necessary to get their way."

"I'll pack up and go to the Alps or something. Lay low at a little villa." This time, there's less conviction in her tone. "Just not with you."

Unfortunately, yes with me.

She flinches when the needle pierces her skin. She wrenches her head back and I see her eyes widen in alarm, then darken with deadly intent. "You're a fucking dead man, Leonid Kozlov" is the last thing she says before her eyelids flutter shut and she falls limp in my arms.

I WAIT until we're at cruising altitude before I call Andrei, my oldest brother and the Kozlov Bratva pakhan. There's no way I can avoid having this talk with him, but I know there will be questions. Questions that won't be easy for me to answer.

He picks up after the first ring. "You still in Switzerland, *brat*?" Last he heard, I was paying a visit to our banker friend, not stalking the younger sister of our oldest friend.

I clear my throat. "No, that's taken care of. Another matter came up that I had to deal with."

"Oh yeah?" I hear him whisper something, probably to his wife, Georgia, considering the late hour, then there's rustling as he changes locations. "What's up?"

There's no easy way to say this, so I just spit it out. "Alyona was attacked tonight."

"Jesus. Is she okay?" His voice is laced with worry. Alyona is one of us; she's practically family. Like her brother, Yulian, she grew up in our home alongside me, Andrei, and our middle brother, Daniil. Her papa was an *avtoritet*, right-hand to our father, the pakhan. Andrei cares for her like a little sister—if only I shared the familial sentiment.

I glance at the aisle across from me where she's sleeping on a couch. Those long, dark eyelashes resting on her pale skin. Flawless, just like always. Right now, she's a picture of peace, a sleeping angel, but the cocktail will wear off eventually, and I have no doubt hell's wrath will pale in comparison to the storm she'll unleash on me when she wakes. She promised as much just before the lights went out.

Drugging her wasn't my finest moment, but it had to be done. She was not going to come willingly with me, and hiding out in the Alps wouldn't cut it. Whoever is after her has the resources to track her down unless she's expertly hidden. And that duty now falls to me.

"She's shaken up and has a small gash on her forehead, but it's not too bad considering."

"What the hell happened?"

"Some psycho broke into her place and was lying in wait when she got home. Attempted to abduct her." Andrei hisses a curse on the other end of the line. "She fought him off, managed to kill the guy, then called Gianni's crew to clean up, which is how I was alerted to this whole shit show."

"Fuck me." Andrei sounds as livid as I was. He despises being caught off guard, and we've truly been blindsided. "Where is she now?"

I stir the ice in my two fingers of Macallan and glance out the window towards the twinkling lights of France below. "She's with me on the jet."

Andrei releases a grunt. "All this after I insisted Yulian take a holiday and turn off his fucking phone for once in his life. He's going to have an absolute conniption." He exhales heavily. "Can I talk to Alyona?"

"She's sleeping." Not a lie. At least not entirely.

"I suppose I'll see her soon enough. When are you landing?"

"Soon. But we're not coming back to the States."

I'm met with hard silence. "Care to explain?"

"I'm taking her off-grid, to a place she won't be found. I don't like this, *brat*. The man who came for her was covered in Russian prison tattoos. He's a vor or at least connected with one of the brotherhoods." Everyone in our life is a target for our enemies. We're constantly worried about Andrei's wife and daughter, Georgia and Anya, along with Bianca and Rowan, the wives of Daniil and Yulian. They have 24/7 security. I always assumed Alyona being so far removed from our world made her a neutral party. Looks like I thought wrong.

I down another gulp of whisky, hoping to melt the fear coiling in my gut.

"You need to come home so we can figure this out together." His voice is terse, betraying his irritation. But he softens a little to add, "You know Kira will go ballistic if you don't bring Aly home."

It is true, our sister and Alyona are super close, even though Kira didn't grow up under our roof. My brothers and I weren't even aware we had a sister until three years ago. Our mother had a child out of wedlock, a secret so tightly guarded that our father only revealed it on his deathbed four years ago. Days after she was born, Kira's father, a ruthless bratva rival, stole her from my mother and had her raised abroad. After a very dramatic reunion that nearly saw all of us killed, Kira is now an integral part of our family and our brotherhood.

She's also Alyona's best friend.

"I'm taking her somewhere safe until we know more. Dima's already on the case gathering intel," I say, referring to my best hacker. "I respect you as pakhan and my older brother, but I won't take a chance with her."

Andrei's dark laughter filters through the line. "I find it hard to believe Aly would go anywhere with you willingly."

Alyona's contempt for me is no secret within my family—her icy stares at every gathering have made her feelings clear. Most assume she had an unrequited crush on me, and I'd rather keep it that way. "Maybe not, but it's for her safety. And Yulian would approve." Mostly.

Letting out a huff of air, I slump back into the seat and glance over at Aly's unconscious form. Without a frown, she resembles the girl I fell in love with as a teenager; the girl who'd spent hours curled up on the couch with a book or clinging to me on the back of my bike. The girl whose face turned an adorable shade of pink when she asked me for sex lessons at the start of that fateful summer.

The line falls quiet, the only noise coming from Alyona's soft puffs of breath. "You better be fucking sure about this," Andrei mutters. He doesn't argue further. He knows when I make my mind up, I'm a brick wall. Unbending. Even to his authority. "As soon as we know what we're up against, I expect you to bring her back to New York. Where are you taking her now?"

"Let's just say we're going to be on the move."

"*Ty sumasshedshiy,*" Andrei bites out.

But he's wrong. I'm not crazy. Crazy is the bender I went on after I turned my back on her; the ensuing years I've spent trying, and failing, to fuck her out of my system; the aimless bike trips I go on looking for absolution that I never find.

A satisfied grin curls my lips. This is, in fact, the sanest I've felt in years.

4

10 years ago

ALYONA

THE PARTY DOWNSTAIRS is in full swing—the bass line is thumping, and the distinct sound of girlish laughter floats up to my quiet refuge in the library. When the pakhan is out of town, the boys don't waste time throwing a rager. I'm used to it by now. I don't mind, although I have no desire to join them.

Still, I can't help but wonder what I would find if I went downstairs. Would Leo be talking to a pretty girl? Would he even realize if I made an appearance? I see how girls look at him—sending him flirty smiles and making heart eyes at him. Not that Leo seems particularly interested in anyone. I should know, I tend to watch him closely. He's hard to miss. Despite being the youngest of the Kozlov brothers, he's also the largest. At eighteen, he's already over six feet tall and has muscles in all the right places.

A year ago, my family moved into the Kozlov's East Hampton estate. Yes, we have our own wing of the house, but still. Thank god for boarding school or I would have to see him all the time, and honestly that would be hard knowing he sees me as a fifteen-year-old kid. Just his best friend's little sister, and the daughter of his father's right-hand.

For one night, I'd like to forget all that and have him see me as something else. Not likely, though, considering our age difference and Leo's loyalty to Yulian. I've never had a boyfriend, so there're no boys in my life for Yulian to scare away, but I imagine if there were, my brother's intimidating presence would be enough to send them running.

I reposition myself on the cozy armchair, trying to focus on the book in my hands, *Fifty Shades of Grey*. I wasn't expecting to like it, but a friend lent it to me, and I admit it's kind of like book crack.

Despite the sounds of the party that continue to filter towards me upstairs in the library, I manage to get sucked into the scene where Christian takes Anastasia's virginity. My cheeks flush and my heart beats a little bit faster. Holy shit, is this what sex is like? I'm so engrossed that I don't notice the door creaking open or the heavy footsteps approaching until it's too late.

A pair of motorcycle boots appear in my line of sight. I lower the book as my eyes travel upwards, taking in Leo's tall, muscular frame. His dark hair is pulled back into a ponytail, and he's wearing ripped jeans and a fitted white T-shirt that shows off his sculpted arms. Yulian always jokes that Leo should have been born into an MC family instead of the bratva because of his style.

"Knew I'd find you here," he smirks, but it's not condescending. It's more conspiratorial. Butterflies erupt in my stomach at the little smile he offers me. He's not like the other boys my age. I'm not even sure if I'd describe him as cute. He's something else entirely with that sharp-as-a-blade jawline and the masculine indent in his chin. But it's his eyes that get me. Dark. Intense. Like they can see into my soul.

He flops into the chair directly across from me, his eyes snagging on the book in my hand. "Whatcha reading?"

Shit. Fuck. Shit. My cheeks heat, and I casually toss the book aside, out of his eyeline. "Nothing, whatever," I choke. "Just something I found to pass the time."

He eyes me knowingly but lets the matter drop. "Not interested in joining the party?"

"Nah." I shift my position on the chair. "Anyhow, Yulian would flip if he caught me drinking." I'm about to smile, and then I remember my braces, so I settle for a closed-mouth grin.

"You don't have to drink to have a good time. You can just come hang out. Play pool. Dance. I bet you don't get to have too much fun at that fancy all-girls boarding school your papa sent you to."

"School is fun for me." I shrug. "And twice a year, the school holds a dance with all the all-boys school across campus. It's alright." What I don't mention is how I never get asked to dance. How I'm always overlooked, especially by the older boys.

"Good. There's nothing wrong with letting loose once in a while."

I chuckle at that. "There's no letting loose with Sister Agnes reminding us to act piously from the sideline of the dance floor. Kinda ruins the vibe."

He barks out a laugh. "Nuns are good at ruining vibes. That's why we throw parties here. It's not about getting smashed, at least not for me, I just like to let loose without authority breathing down my neck." He runs an agitated hand through his dark hair, weariness settling around his eyes. "Shit's getting intense now that I've graduated high school and have started training ..." He's quiet for a moment. "No more carefree student life."

I nod. Leo is eighteen, he'll be expected to train for the next few years before taking the vor oath. Pakhan insists that they go through training like any other soldier. No special treatment when it comes to his sons, or my brother.

Leo is lost in thought, entering bratva life must be weighing heavy on him. I snake a foot out from underneath me and use my toe to nudge his thigh. His very firm thigh. "Why aren't you downstairs taking part in the festivities? Go have fun."

His eyes soften. "I came to find you, Aly-cat." *Aly-cat.* He's the only one who calls me that. A little spark flares within my core, and I have to remind myself to *chill out.* He views me as a sister, nothing more. "It's been a while since we caught up, and I won't be around this week while you're home. Papa is shipping me off somewhere for training," he says with a frown.

Still, the fact that he sought me out when he could have his pick of fangirls falling over him, does something mushy to my insides. I can't fight the smile that breaks out on my face, braces be damned, or the blush that's furiously moving down my neck.

"I don't really have any exciting news," I shrug, racking my brain to come up with something—anything—that would make me sound more interesting. "I joined the school newspaper. I'm going to be writing about fashion and style. I don't know much about it, even though my mom is a total fashion plate," I admit, "but I'm interested in learning more ... even if I have to wear the most hideous school uniform day in and day out."

Something heavy smashes below—the party is clearly taking a turn for the rowdy. He lets out a sharp sigh rubbing his temples. "Shit," he mutters. "What are those assholes doing? No breaking shit in the house. Is that too much to ask?"

"You should probably go downstairs and see what's going on." I don't want him to feel like he has to stay up here and babysit me. I know he's just being nice, stopping in to say hi. "The girls are probably protesting your absence by smashing things."

"You think so, huh?" His piercing gaze locks onto mine. "Well, what if I'd rather spend my time with you? None of those girls at the party have anything interesting to say. They're not smart or special, they don't read books or write newspaper columns like you do."

For the first time, I sense a glimmer of something. It's not attraction—that, I'm sure of—but rather a feeling that sends shivers down my spine. I'm blushing so furiously I have to look away. No guy has ever complimented me like that. And for those words to come from Leo, I'm not even sure how to process it.

Another crash from downstairs rips through the air. This time, loud yells accompany the sounds of something heavy and no doubt expensive hitting the hard floor.

"What the—" Leo is up out of his seat, the muscles in his jaw twitch as he grits his teeth, clearly agitated. "Seems like we're the only two sober people in this house. I better go deal with whatever is happening down there."

I try not to slump in my chair or let my shoulders droop in obvious disappointment. "You should."

"Enjoy your book, Aly-cat." He winks.

Winks! Fireworks spark inside my chest and a smile breaks out on my face, until my gaze drops to the book on the table beside me.

The wink was about *Fifty Shades*—he knows I'm reading smut!

"I hear it's ... memorable." He gives me a little smile before leaving.

My cheeks heat. I can die now. The floor can open up and swallow me whole. I silently pray, but it doesn't happen, and I spend the rest of the night wondering if he'll ever see me as more than an awkward fifteen-year-old with braces and saucy taste in books.

5

ALYONA

My eyes snap open, and instantly, I know one thing without a doubt. I'm on a boat. A big one. The gentle rocking sensation beneath me is the first clue, as is the faint hum of the engine.

Damn. How long was I out?

And what exactly happened?

And most importantly—what the fuck am I doing here?

Sitting up in this foreign bed, my head pounds with a relentless throb that won't let up. The dull ache only worsens under the onslaught of sunlight streaming through the curtains.

I dig through my memories, trying to piece together the course of events. The memories are slow to surface, but when they do, horrifying images rush back into my consciousness—the attack, nearly being abducted, taking a man's life. A man covered in foreboding tattoos.

Tension knots my muscles. I killed a man. Maybe it was in self-defense, but still. This is bad. My hands shake, my breaths come in shallow and fast as another memory surfaces.

Leo. At my door. Insisting I was in danger, that I come with him. The dull prick of a sedative being injected into my veins. *Christ, that man.* He wrecked my life once before and now seems hell-bent on a repeat performance. He'd better be on this boat so I can throttle him. Or then again, maybe it's best if he's not. Because nothing good can come from us being in close proximity for any length of time.

With a groan, I heave myself off the bed and stumble towards what I hope is a bathroom at the far end of the room. My legs are like jelly, but I make it to the door, relieved to discover it is in fact a washroom.

I do my business, grateful to find the bathroom fully stocked with a toothbrush, toothpaste, comb, and face wash. I'm still in the silk pajamas I'd changed into last night after scrubbing my skin until I was near raw, trying to erase the sheen of violence. Oh well, they'll have to do until I can convince Leo to turn this boat—no wait, *yacht* around.

Stepping out of the room, I follow a long narrow hallway towards stairs that lead up to the deck area. Ouch. The light assaults my eyes when I step out into the fresh air and sunshine. I wince, wishing I had a pair of sunglasses. It must be around noon, and being out on the open water, there is nothing to block the furious rays.

My Lord, where the hell has he taken me?

It's not long before I spot the man I'm searching for. Lounging beneath a canopy with a breakfast spread before him, I wish time had taken a toll on him, but the opposite is true. He's more muscular, more inked. A rugged five-o'clock shadow adorns his chiseled face, emphasizing his full lips and perfectly straight nose. He may not be as pretty as Daniil or as classically handsome as Andrei, but he's *more*—bolder, sexier, fiercer. He's cut his dark hair short, not like the thick mane of shoulder-length hair he had when we were together, but with the more conservative cut, Leo looks like a modern-day Greek god.

His lips curve into a smirk as I march toward him. He knows what's coming, he expects me to be furious with him. But judging by the relaxed set of his shoulders, and the amused glint in his eye, he's not the least bit concerned. Typical. He was always water to my fire, calm to my storm.

"Melon?" He raises a plate of fruit as I stride toward him. His eyes sparkle with classic Kozlov charm that draws everyone and everything into his orbit like planets dancing around the sun.

I don't bother to respond or even sit down. In a burst of rage, I grab a piece of fruit and fling it at his head. He dodges it.

"So that's a no?"

"You drugged me, you abducted me, you went against my wishes and—"

"And I saved your life," he interrupts cooly, popping a grape in his mouth.

"No you didn't. I saved my own life. You just swooped in at the end to play savior in Yulian's absence." This is about duty to my brother, nothing more. Leo would do the same if it was Rowan or any other woman associated with the brotherhood.

"Sit. Have a coffee." He pushes a mug my way and pours the brown liquid into it before reaching for the cream, adding two splashes, and then half a sugar. Exactly how I like it.

"I'm not here to debate with you. I'm here to tell you that you had no right to take me anywhere against my will, and you need to turn back this ridiculous yacht right now." I stop and look around, trying to find any landmark in the distance. "Where the fuck are we?"

He strokes his chin thoughtfully, eyeing the expanse of crystal-blue water surrounding us. "We're cruising the Mediterranean. What else do you really need to know?" He shrugs casually. "I'm not here to debate with you either, but I have no intention of turning back."

"Let me be clear," I say, teeth clenched together. "I don't want to be here." I grab a croissant from the breakfast spread and fling it at his smug face. "And I certainly don't want to be here with you."

I'm about to reach for a platter of fruit to dump on his head when powerful fingers clasp around my wrist, stopping my outburst. I still. His touch like fire on my skin. "Have the captain, or whatever pirate you found willing to do your criminal bidding, turn this yacht back to shore."

I'm about to yank my hand from his grasp when Leo leans forward, his face right beside mine. "Let's get one thing straight, Aly. I don't need your permission or your compliance when it comes to your safety. What I say, goes." This is Leo the predator, the high-ranking vor raised in a family of criminals. "If you want to fight me or rebel, I'll tie you to the bed and leave you there for the remainder of our ... *adventure*. So you decide. Enjoy a pleasant vacation on the Mediterranean or spend the next week bound to the bed as my captive. To be honest"—his eyes flash with heat—"the second choice has a definite appeal."

How dare he? As if I'd ever allow that to happen.

Without thinking, I rip myself from his hold and grab a fork off the table, attempting to shove the tines into his thigh, but he's too quick. He deftly moves out of my way and has me collared by the throat before I can blink. Not so hard that I can't breathe, just hard enough to make his point.

A traitorous shiver drips down my spine. It's like my body has a Pavlovian response to his scent, his heat, his voice—it all sends me hurtling back to a time when he was my entire world. My everything.

But those days are long behind us. Now all I see when I look at him is the man who chose his vor stars over a future with me. Because the one thing I made clear to him is that I'd never tie myself to a man in the bratva. The senseless death of my father when I was just seventeen changed how I saw everything. He was killed over what? A property dispute, a run-in with a rival mob? Seeing how it destroyed my mother, her heart irrevocably broken, confirmed one thing: I couldn't let that be my story. I would steer my own course, shape my own fate, away from the harsh world of the bratva.

Leo knew this from the start.

He studies my face, a muscle in his jaw ticks as he takes in the small scrape on my forehead. The only outward sign that I was hurt in last night's attack. Then he leans in towards me, his lips grazing the tip of my ear. "I'm not like that jackass you killed yesterday. I'm quicker, sharper, stronger. Better. Remember Aly, I taught you everything you know."

"Get away from me," I hiss, enunciating each word.

"Gladly." With the utterance of that single word, his hand glides downward, the gentlest of touches trailing the curve of my neck. Finally, he loosens his grip and adjusts his posture, standing upright. The loss of his touch is both a relief and a curse. A reminder of how alive I feel with his hands on me. "I'm not here to argue with you. Not when it comes to your safety." The chair beside me scrapes along the floor, his message loud and clear. "Sit," he quietly commands again.

I'm about to tell him to fuck off when my stomach rumbles loudly. It's been nearly twenty-four hours since I've had a proper meal, and I'm feeling less than stellar. Without asking my opinion on the matter, he piles a plate high with pancakes, double bacon, and melon. Not the eggs or the sausage, because he knows I don't like them. Just like he remembered how I like my coffee.

Something twists in my chest at the memory of him

bringing me breakfast in bed when we were alone in the Kozlov mansion the summer I turned eighteen. *Our* summer.

We were so entwined, so obsessed with learning all the little details of each other. I know he's right-handed except when he boxes, and that he'd rather drink filter oil than black coffee. While I'd like to erase my brain of all this useless information, I can't. But the one thing I can do is eat and save my energy for a chance at escape. Or perhaps pushing Leo overboard.

"Fine," I relent, lowering my body onto the offered chair. "And for the record, I don't appreciate being collared like a dog."

"Noted," he adds with raised eyebrows. But I don't miss his lip twitch of amusement.

We eat in silence for a while. The food helps to settle my nerves and regain enough composure that when Leo finally peels his gaze off the plate in front of him and levels me with a satisfied look, I can resist throwing a fruit platter his way.

"Where is my phone," I ask, breaking the silence. "I need a way to contact the outside world."

"Somewhere safe. There might be a tracking device on it, or worse. You can't take a chance by using it."

"What?" My eyebrows shoot up to my hairline. "You can't just rip me from my life and expect me to cut off all contact with everyone I know."

"I can and I will." His voice is hard, unrelenting. He's become the vor he never wanted to be. "I know you don't like it, but being out on the open water, constantly on the move, is the best way to keep you safe. Your brother would agree." I roll my eyes. Right. This is about Yulian. He's not doing this because he cares about me. "Consider this a vacation." He clears his throat. "With your fake fiancé."

My heart stills in my chest. "I'm sorry, I clearly misheard you."

"You didn't."

"You're very clearly out of your mind, Leo. Mentally unwell," I say, pointing to my head. "I'm thinking it might be a head injury." Because it'll be a cold day in hell when I'd consider touching that man for any other reason than to throttle him.

But Leo isn't fazed. He leans back in his seat, threading his hands behind his head, a lazy grin on his face. "The staff can't know our true identities or our real reasons for being here. We'll pose as a wealthy American couple. I spontaneously popped the question during our trip to Paris, and here we are, on a spur-of-the-moment trip, celebrating our impending nuptials."

"Jeee-sus." I have to close my eyes for a minute to try and absorb everything Leo's just thrown at me. My mind spins in a million different directions, and none of them are good. "This won't work. I can't do it."

"Aly." There's sympathy in his gaze and it makes me feel exposed, vulnerable. A feeling I hate. "You've been through a lot. You killed a man, and even though you handled it like a goddamn rock star, I'm going to guess that's the first life you've ever taken." I look away from him, not wanting him to see the emotion building in my eyes. "There's no shame in that. You made the choice to leave a life full of threats and danger behind, you shouldn't have to be pulled back in. Let me handle this for you. I'll keep you safe."

Tears threaten, but I won't let them fall. I haven't cried since my mother died two years ago, and I'm not about to start now. I shrug, feeling defensive. "Just because of his tattoos? We can't assume it's bratva after me. We don't know anything for certain."

Leo regards me like a puzzle he's trying to figure out as he runs a thumb down the centerline of his lips. Those damn lips I thought I'd never tire of, but now they just inspire bitterness. "Tell me," he says thoughtfully, "have you crossed paths with anyone involved in organized crime recently? Dated someone connected? Dealt with them through business?"

I frown. "Of course not." He knows more than anyone else how strongly I feel about living a normal life, with a normal job, and friends that don't reach into their back waistband every time a car slows too close to the curb.

"Well then, based on the little information we have, it's a safe assumption that whoever is after you is connected to one of the brotherhoods in Russia." He cocks a brow, daring me to argue with him. "You know as well as I do that these people are dangerous. They don't fuck around. So until we know what's actually going on ..." He spreads his arms wide, head tipped up to the sun, basking in the Mediterranean glory all around us.

I roll my eyes in irritation. I'm glad he thinks this is going to be a grand old holiday. "Don't pretend you're doing me any favors by taking me against my will, forcing me on to this yacht, and having us pose as a goddamn couple. This is a ridiculous idea even by your standards."

He leans back in his chair, assessing me with a narrowed gaze. "And what would you suggest?"

I huff out a breath and cross my arms over my chest. "Not being stuck here with you, pretending to be your fiancée, for one."

"You've made that clear. What else?"

"Fine. What about the Kozlov compound? It's fortified as hell, surrounded by guards. Why not take me there?"

He sits back, a muscle pulsing in his cheek. "As safe as the estate is, it'll be the first place anyone expects you to go. And if this threat is as serious as I think it is, it'll bring unnecessary risk to Georgia and the baby."

Oh my god, Georgia and Andrei's baby daughter, Anya. My chest squeezes, and I suddenly feel like the shittiest human in the world. As much as I want to downplay what happened, how can I bring that danger to the door of the people I love?

"Of course I wouldn't want to do that." My brain spins out thinking of solutions that don't include being trapped on a yacht with Leo. I could demand that he track down my brother and Rowan, but he's on a remote tropical island with no cell access. Not ideal.

The heavy realization that being here *is* the safest bet sinks like a stone in my belly. Why him? Anyone but him.

I force down the lump in my throat. "Fine. We stay on this boat as long as it takes for you and your people to manage this threat, or whatever it is you need to do. But the moment Yulian is back in play, you hand me off to my brother."

He raises his hands innocently. "I wouldn't dream of making you stay in my presence a minute longer than necessary. But in the meantime, the stateroom closet is stocked with clothes that should fit you. And I did pack a few of your"—he smirks before continuing—"necessities. Top bedside drawer."

"Seriously, you packed up my shit?"

Leo looks way too freakin' smarmy. "Didn't want you to go without. And don't worry Aly, you'll barely see me. Lots of work to keep me busy."

I pick up the last piece of bacon and bring it to my lips, my eyes narrowing. "Good," I say and mean it. I'll avoid him at all costs. Just like I have for the last seven years. "And Leo, one day you'll need to explain to me why we couldn't pose as siblings or friends even."

His dark, intense eyes meet mine, flashing with something I can only describe as possessiveness. "I don't think that would be believable, do you?"

Since I can't answer that question truthfully, I don't answer it at all. Instead, I throw my napkin down onto my now empty plate and give him my best steely glare. "Just so we're clear, there will be no physical contact between us, don't even think of pulling any PDA shit. And obviously separate suites."

"Obviously, except ..." He shrugs. "We don't want the yacht staff to get suspicious, so we need to keep up the illusion of a shared bedroom. I'll sleep on the couch."

I rub my temples, hoping to wake up from this nightmare. "Who even owns this yacht?"

"I don't know. I secured it through a rush deal organized by a third-party broker. The less information exchanged the better. But it's ours for as long as we need it."

Here's to hoping it's not long. I push away from the table and stand, exhaustion seeping into my limbs. "I need a shower and some clean clothes," I announce.

Leo nods. "Meet me here in an hour. I'll introduce you to the crew."

"Great." I don't even bother smiling or thanking him or doing any of the things a halfway decent person may think to do. Instead, I turn and stride away, flashing a middle finger salute over my shoulder with my head held high.

SOMETHING STRANGE HAPPENS in the shower.

I cry.

Something inside of me shatters. Like an internal dam ruptured, emotions I've kept tightly restrained for years pour out of me, my salty tears mixing with the shower spray. Reality sucker punches me. The reality that I killed a man yesterday. He deserved it, but that doesn't make it any less horrifying that I took someone's life. The reality that someone dangerous is after me. The reality that I'm stuck on this boat, pretending to be engaged to someone who once upon a time told me he did not love me back.

The gods have a shitty sense of humor.

And try as I might to fight him, to act the tough chick, I'm scared. Something I'll never admit to Leo, but here, alone, with the water pounding down on my back and sobs heaving my chest, my fear is real.

Emerging from the shower with a towel draped around me, I survey the stateroom. Sure, it's impressive with its rich mahogany panels and floor-to-ceiling windows, but luxury feels like a cage when you're not there by choice.

Sitting on the bed, I slide open the bedside table drawer where Leo put my personal effects.

Shit.

He didn't.

A vein in my head throbs. *Jesus, this man is on thin ice.*

Reaching into the drawer, I find my daily multivitamin, various over-the-counter meds, an e-reader, and, ugh, my birth control pills. Fine, I can live with that. It's what comes next that turns my cheeks ten shades of red—my hand wraps around something silicone and unyielding and no. Just no.

He packed Bob ... my Battery-Operated Boyfriend. Actually, if we're going to get technical, it's a bright-purple rabbit vibe for extra clit stimulation. Because that's what I need to get off, and Leo of all people, knows that. I bring Bob fully out of the drawer. And hot damn, there's a sticky note attached to it.

I approve ☺️

A hot wave of humiliation washes over me, making my cheeks flush further and my fists clench. This may be his idea of a joke, but that man will pay! I don't know how, and I don't know when but I will find a way to get my revenge.

I storm into the stateroom's walk-in closet and stop in my tracks. There are rows upon rows of designer clothes, accessories, and shoes arranged neatly in their own little cubbies. This is clearly someone's stuff, a very wealthy woman, judging by the racks full of Chanel and Prada, displayed like trophies.

I work for a luxury clothing brand, and I even find this collection impressive if a little risqué for my tastes. But I can't just wear someone else's clothes! It's entirely possible that Leo stole this yacht. I'm about to put my pajamas back on when a shimmering golden bikini, hanging from one of the swimwear racks, catches my eye. It's Dolce & Gabbana. I'd noticed it in last month's *Vogue*, and damn, it's even more stunning up close. The fabric glimmers and shines, catching the light in a way that calls my name.

Finally, at twenty-four, my body has grown a little more generous. A few graceful curves have emerged. Mama always told me that one day I'd fill out and be a head turner. A bitter laugh leaves my lips. It didn't quite happen that way, but I've definitely left the gangly girl with a nothing-to-speak-of chest and braces far behind. That girl that was hopelessly in love with her older brother's best friend.

For reasons I don't want to examine too closely, I want Leo to see how much I've changed. How much of a woman I am now. Which means, the gold bikini it is. I say a silent thank you to whoever's wardrobe I'm raiding.

Once I've changed, I stand in front of the full-length mirror and admire my reflection. The string bikini top is made from a soft, buttery fabric that feels amazing on my skin. The cups give my small breasts a subtle lift while the bottoms have ties on either side with a cut that shows off the flare of my hips.

Satisfied with my choice, I scan the shelves for footwear. *Well, hello.* I settle on a pair of strappy, metallic sandals with towering heels and a pair of oversized sunglasses perched on my head.

I take one last look at myself in the mirror. The bikini is flashier and sexier than my typical wardrobe, which tends to be all black and conservative, but screw it. I look smokin' hot, and I'm damn well going to make sure Leo knows it. He might've forced me into close quarters with him, but that doesn't mean I have to make it easy on him. This is my sweet revenge, served on a shimmering gold platter. I'll show him exactly what he threw away.

Eat your heart out, asshole.

6

ALYONA

I FIND Leo exactly where I left him, basking in the sunlit top deck dining area. He's on the phone, but when he spots me approaching, his gaze sticks to me like a magnet, lingering on the sway of my hips. Can't deny that I may be sauntering a little more than usual.

He promptly ends his call as I reach the table. I catch the way his eyes trail down the length of my body and then back up again. The vein in his temple ticks like he's annoyed. And if that's the case, then well done, me.

"I see you were able to find something that met with your stamp of approval," he says, jaw tight.

"Oh, this old thing." I make a sweeping motion in front of my body. "As you suggested, I made myself at home. I'm curious though," I say, leaning casually against the deck railing. "Be honest. Who did you steal this yacht from?"

His chuckle is rugged and masculine, evoking a familiar shiver down my spine. His deep voice was always a turn-on. "I didn't steal it, like I said, it's a rental. When you're willing to pay top dollar, people become very accommodating."

"If you say so," I say, lips twitching. "But I don't think the owner will be very happy after he realizes I've raided his wife's —no, make that mistress's—closet."

Leo waves a hand in the air like it doesn't matter. "Wear what you want. I'll replace it when this is all said and done."

When this is all said and done. What does that even mean?

I'd like to believe this will all be sorted out quickly so my life can go back to the status quo—back to Paris, back to my job, back to ... well, I suppose that's it. Most of my friends are work colleagues, if I am going to be honest, and other than making time for a few bad dates, my life is pretty boring, even if I'm in one of the most exciting cities in the world.

Shit. Which reminds me. "My boss! She's going to lose her mind if I don't show up at work."

Leo rises to his full height beside me. It's rare for me to feel dwarfed, but he manages to make me feel small, petite even. I used to love that. Now, not so much. He casually checks the time on his watch. "Already taken care of. You emailed her this morning saying there was a family emergency back in New York and you're taking a leave of absence. Pauline was very worried; she sends her regards. Nice lady," he adds.

I huff out a bitter laugh, unsurprised but still annoyed. "You hacked my email."

He shrugs, not apologetic at all. "It had to be done. We didn't need your boss calling the cops when you didn't show up for work."

"Hmm, let's tally up your federal offenses over the last twenty-four hours, shall we? Impersonation, kidnapping, unauthorized email access, grand theft yacht ... should I go on?"

He crosses his arms in front of his chest, causing his biceps to bulge enticingly. "Actually, I have something to add to your list. We're going by false identities. Your name is Alison Henderson, and I'm Leonardo Walker. We live in New York. I'm a Wall Street dude."

I burst into laughter. "Who in the world would believe that you work on Wall Street!?" His beefy build and canvas of tattoos is more rock star than stockbroker, but if he thinks he can sell that cover story, I won't stop him. "And why are you the only one with the job? What about me?"

His face breaks into a wicked smile. "Good point. Hmm, let's think about it." He gestures with his chin at my bikini. "Stripper?"

A small smirk forms on my lips as I rest a hand on my hip. "Why not? There must be a pole somewhere on this floating prison. I'd be happy to put on a show ... for anyone that's not you."

All humor fades from Leo's expression. "Not happening. On this boat, you're mine. I'm the only one you'll put on a show for. So if you want to dance for me, by all means. There's nothing I would enjoy more." My brow creases in irritation. As if I would dance for him. As if he has any say in what I do with my body. Just him shutting down that idea makes me want to walk around here in the nude.

"By the way, if we're supposed to be engaged, where's my ring?"

"Oh, we'll get to that soon." He chucks me under the chin in a gesture that has my teeth on edge and wanders ahead.

As we climb the stairs, I notice he's changed as well. No longer in his standard ripped jeans and fitted white shirt, he's wearing chino shorts and a button-down pale-pink linen shirt. The ensemble is so not Leo—I've definitely never seen him wear anything remotely resembling shorts and definitely not ones that are two sizes too small on him.

Now that I've noticed the way the fabric hugs that fine ass of his—well, I can't *un-notice* it.

"Looks like I'm not the only one who had to dip into someone else's wardrobe," I mutter.

"You checking out my ass, Aly-cat?"

Busted. "I'd rather eat worms," I say with feigned sweetness as we enter onto the bridge of the yacht. "Just hard not to notice you stuffed into a pair of khakis. I thought you were allergic to preppy styles."

"Like you, I didn't exactly come prepared." He stares at me intently, his eyes blazing, before he moves closer and murmurs into my ear, "And I thought you were allergic to string bikinis." The rough pads of his fingers brush against my back, and a warm tingle runs down my spine. It's so fast, so light, I'm not even sure it happened. Before I can spin on him, he breezes past me, his flip-flops—*flip-flops!*— tapping lightly against the polished teak floor.

I slide my sunglasses up to my forehead, taking in my surroundings. The bridge, the yacht's command center, is spacious and modern, with huge windows offering a panoramic view of sun and sea.

As we enter, a line of poised crew members stands at the ready. A silver-haired man steps forward first, introducing himself with a Scandinavian lilt. "Ms. Henderson, I'm Captain Karl Hansen. Pleasure to meet you." He offers his calloused hand, all seriousness and authority. "My crew and I are at your service."

"Thank you," I say. "And please call me Alison." The name sounds odd from my lips, but I get why we need to keep our identities under wraps.

"Of course. First, let me introduce our chief steward."

A lively woman that looks to be in her mid-thirties steps forward to shake our hands. She has warm brown skin and a friendly smile. "Bonjour, I'm Genevieve," she says, her voice tinged with a French accent. "I'm in charge of making sure the food and service meet your expectations. Any culinary or other preferences, please let me know."

It's on the tip of my tongue to tell her we won't need anything special because we're not staying long, but Leo intervenes, throwing a casual arm around me. "We should probably mention that Alison here loves a green smoothie in the morning. Spinach, wheatgrass, broccoli—whatever you got, throw it in. Oh, and a raw egg, too." His eyes sparkle. "For protein."

My smile is brittle. I despise smoothies, they're like drinking baby food, and Leo knows how I feel. He's also touching me, something I strictly warned him against. Well, two can play that game. I straighten, subtly shaking his arm from my shoulder. "And we should probably tell Genevieve about your ... little problem?"

Leo eyes me with interest. "And what would that be, honey?"

"Oh, you know. Your issue ..." I wink at him. "Down there."

He tugs at his collar, lips pressing together in a thin line. I'm starting to enjoy this. I let Leo sweat it out for a few more moments, then add, "I meant his heart. Leonardo has high blood pressure. So no salt in his food. Nothing. No cream, no butter, nothing fried of course. Actually, best to serve him a vegan diet."

"I don't think that's necessary," Leo says, jaw clenched.

He lives for steak and fries. I'm not even sure he knows the true meaning of vegan. "But, honey-bunny, I'm worried about you."

To her credit, Genevieve doesn't bat an eyelash. "Whatever you need, my team is here to make it happen."

"That's so kind of you." I'm about to ask if there are any little blue pills on board because my fiancé forgot his at home, but the moment my lips part, Leo seizes the back of my neck and crashes his mouth onto mine.

My pulse falters. His kiss is not sweet or gentle; it's deep and unrelenting—possessive. The world around us blurs into insignificance and my knees weaken. I raise my hands to his chest intending to push him away, but when his tongue brushes mine, my mind becomes too addled to do much of anything.

With a final nip to my lower lip, he is the one to break the contact first, his gaze gleaming with victory.

Fuck me. And I fell it for it, hook, line, and sinker.

I rear back, ready to give him hell, but his eyes flash in warning. We're still surrounded by the crew, still expected to act the role of a head-over-heels couple. So I do what I have to do. I grit my teeth and smile at the next person who steps forward, still feeling unsteady.

The man in front of me is tall and fit with sandy-blond hair that's artfully tousled and bright-blue eyes that glitter as they roll lazily over my body. I don't know what to make of his appreciative stare—and right in front of my pretend fiancé no less. But the feel of Leo bristling beside me has me smiling and holding out my hand.

"I'm Jack, the first officer," he says, a broad smile spreading across his handsome face. Damn. He's more GQ model than weathered sailor. "I assist Captain Hansen and manage the deck crew. I'm sure you'll see a lot of me this trip."

Picking up on the distinctive inflection in his speech, I ask, "Is that an Australian accent I detect?"

"Guilty as charged. Born and raised in Brisbane, though I've spent the last few years overseas, working on yachts like this one. It mellowed the accent a bit."

"My family were huge fans of the *Crocodile Dundee* films," I confess. "I know it's so cringey, but it gave me the travel bug." I huff out a laugh. "Made me want to visit Australia."

"You definitely should. I'd be more than happy to help you plan an itinerary, even show you the sights—"

"Perhaps on our next adventure, love," Leo interjects.

I shoot him a *what the hell?* look, but he avoids my eye.

A few other crew members step forward, but I don't pay too close attention, mostly because I'm fascinated at the way Leo is glaring at Jack. Is he just playing the part of a jealous boyfriend, or does he still feel some claim over me? That kiss sure seemed like he did, even if it was just to shut me up. The realization brings a satisfied smile to my lips.

It seems I've found a way to get under Leo's skin—some harmless flirting with Jack. I'm not interested, and I'd never go out of my way to make a real boyfriend jealous, that's not my style, but Leo isn't a real boyfriend.

Not anymore.

He's just some guy who broke my heart.

7

LEO

"This isn't good. We should have more intel by now." I rest my forehead against the window. My brother Daniil's words barely register in my brain, my attention fixated on Aly by the pool below, chatting away with Jack, the Aussie first mate. Ever since we met him yesterday, he's been buzzing around her under the guise of being helpful, but I know what that fucker is about.

A sudden burst of laughter pulls my gaze. It's Aly. Her head's thrown back in the kind of laugh that reveals her perfectly straight white teeth. She seems so unburdened and carefree, unlike when she's with me, that I consider reaching for my Sig in the desk's top drawer.

That bastard has no right to make my girl laugh like that. Even if she's not actually my girl. Not anymore. Still, possessiveness surges within me, and I have to clench my jaw to keep from pounding on the window and shaking my fist at them. There was a time when I was the one eliciting those happy looks from her, basking in the glow of her affection. But those days are long gone, replaced by bitter glares and tense silences. And I only have myself to blame.

I really should find another office to work from; this one is going to be a problem. It overlooks the sundeck Aly seems to enjoy most for reading and lounging. And so far today, I've done little more than stare at her splayed out, gorgeous and golden in the sun, replaying our kiss from yesterday in my head rather than doing any actual work.

Fuck. That kiss.

I hadn't planned for it to happen. Just felt like the best way to get her to shut her mouth at the moment. I had no idea it would be like a sucker punch to my gut.

Her soft body against mine was familiar yet entirely new. Curves that hadn't graced her eighteen-year-old form pressed against me. Her breathless sigh as she relaxed into my touch made my dick hard. Christ, nothing good is going to come from fantasizing about her lush mouth, and—

"Are you even listening to me?" Daniil's irritated voice filters into my consciousness.

"Of course I'm fucking listening," I say, jabbing at the remote control in order to shut the blinds. Watching her is only getting me worked up. "You're just telling me what I already know."

That we haven't found anything. That whoever is after Aly covered their tracks well.

A ripple of unease slides under my skin. I've had Dima and his hackers working on this since the moment Matis called me. But even the sharpest black hats have yet to bring me anything useful, which may be the most alarming part of this.

"Jeez, what crawled up your ass? Oh wait, I know. Is Aly giving you a hard time?" Daniil's smug tone irritates the fuck out of me. Probably because he's right.

He's the only one who knows that Aly and I were together the summer she turned eighteen. He doesn't know how serious it was, that I was ready to leave the brotherhood behind. That was our secret, but he knows our story runs deeper than others believe. He's somehow managed to keep that fact to himself.

I credit some of his good sense to marrying Bianca over a year ago. Daniil finally seems to have mellowed out. Though their union started off rocky—an arranged marriage between our family and the Colombians— now that the dust has settled, it's clear they're a perfect match.

It's cool to see my brothers and Yulian happy and in love, but it is also a painful reminder of everything I lost when I pushed Aly away. Because there's no one else for me. She's it, but since I can't undo the past, I'll remain alone.

"It's not about Aly," I grumble, swallowing the lie. "I don't like being blindsided. Not knowing which direction the threat is coming from."

My jaw tightens. I'm in charge of intel for this brotherhood; I'm the one with the network of contacts and hackers around the world. The fact that I haven't been able to deliver any useful information weighs heavily on me.

I grab the files Dima pulled together about Aly's abduction off my desk. "Here is what we know so far. The kidnapper was Russian, but we can't pin him to any specific bratva. He was sent to abduct her and bring her somewhere, alive. He wasn't working alone. Security cameras show a getaway car outside of Alyona's flat, but whoever was waiting, bolted at the first sign of trouble." I let out a heavy sigh and slump back in my chair, buried in a mountain of worthless paper. "My hackers are trying to get an ID on the car and license plate. But they sure as shit didn't rent the vehicle from the local Avis. The car is untraceable." Although I've refused to accept that as an answer. I've told my men not to sleep until we have a hit on the car. Along with the dead mudak, it's our only lead.

Daniil scoffs. "What I don't get is why they'd hire an amateur to go after a high-value target. Aly took him down with a pocketknife."

I clear my throat, a swell of pride filling my chest. "She actually has skills. I taught her to fight."

"Oh, did you now?" Daniil sounds way too amused. "And when was that?"

"Before ..." Before she hated me. Before I took her virginity. Before I tore out her heart and walked away. "Before shit got weird between us."

"Do you ever plan on telling me what really happened between you two?" His tone is light, but behind those words is real concern.

I steady my voice and keep to the script I've recited a million times. "There's nothing to tell. She wanted more, and I couldn't give her what she wanted." That's only part of the truth. The rest of it will be buried with me.

When we were younger, Andrei and Daniil could never understand the resentment I had towards our father, but I had decided never to tell them—or anyone—the full story. Not only because they would be forced to take sides, but because if it ever got back to Yulian, the fallout would be devastating. It would start a civil war. It's why I've kept my mouth shut all these years. To protect the people I love.

That and the shame. Because even if my hand was forced, I let her down. I let myself down.

Daniil is quiet on the other end of the line. He may not entirely believe me, but at least he has the good sense to drop it. "The one thing we know for sure is that the source is connected to Russia. So that's where we start. Andrei and I talked about it last night. He's tied up, but I'll fly to Moscow and see what intel I can gather on the ground."

Daniil and I were born in the US, but with Russian-born parents, our roots run deep. Beyond the business interests that my father maintained in Russia, we also spent time there training and visiting relations on my mother's side. She died when I was a boy, and after her death, Russia felt like the one true connection I had to her.

We still maintain ties to the bratvas in Russia, so it's a good place to start.

"I'll start making discreet inquiries with contacts," Daniil continues. "Anyhow, it'll give me an excuse to send Bianca to live at the estate in East Hampton. It's safer than the penthouse until we figure out what's going on."

"I'm sure Georgia will be thrilled for the company." My sister-in-law has taken this year off her teaching job to be at home with Anya. I've never been one for babies, but my niece, with her mother's dark hair and gray eyes and Andrei's fiery personality, has me wrapped around her little finger.

As Daniil talks of his plans for Moscow, I pull back the blinds and peek out of the window. What can I say, I'm a glutton for punishment. What I see has my teeth on edge. Aly's arm is linked with Jack's, they're talking like old friends as they head towards the yacht's interior. At the very last moment, Aly looks up, catches my eye and smirks.

Hot irritation flares beneath my collar. That woman knows exactly what she's doing.

Has she realized I've been watching her like a lovestruck schoolboy for the last hour?

Correction. For the last seven years.

Something tells me if she did know the depth of my obsession, I would not still possess both of my testicles.

I DON'T LEAVE the office all afternoon while I try—and fail—to catch up on work. I need to follow up on what's happening with our Swiss accounts now that Gerhart is out of the picture, get an update from Matis, as well as look into a triad boss that we hope to work with in Shanghai, but so far all I've managed to accomplish is pacing the ridiculous nautical-themed office and staring out the window for any sign of Alyona ... or Jack for that matter. There's something about him that rubs me the wrong way. Sure, it could be that I don't like the way he looks at her—like she's an ice-cold drink and he's parched.

My gaze wanders out the window towards the sun setting in the distance. It casts a soft pink glow across the sky—a reminder that it's nearing the dinner hour. As an engaged couple, we'll be expected to dine together. They may not think anything of a rich American businessman spending his vacation working—the French think we're heathens as it is—but no one is going to buy our cover story unless we're seen spending some time together.

Picking up the house phone, I dial Genevieve's line. She answers promptly. "Monsieur Walker, how can I help you?"

"We'll take our meal on the upper deck this evening. I'd like to start with chilled champagne. It's Alyo ... Alison's favorite."

"Of course, monsieur. We will have everything ready by eight sharp. Is there anything else?"

"No vegan food. I'll take high blood pressure over being miserable." Genevieve releases a little laugh and agrees to a new menu.

The next words burst from my lips without approval from my brain. "Can you put out some candles or shit, maybe flowers. Make it feel romantic."

"*Bien sur.* We always do. Especially when a couple is

enjoying time away together," Genevieve gushes, clearly thrilled to play Cupid.

If she only knew.

"Please let Alison know to dress up tonight." This may not be my brightest idea, but in for a penny, in for a pound.

I hang up the phone and slump back in my chair, wondering what the fuck I'm playing at. Aly's going to have my balls when she sees how thick I've laid on the romance tonight. I could blame it on our cover, but we both know I'd be lying.

I should keep her at arm's length—treat her like I would anyone else under my protection—but instead, here I am, ordering fine champagne and candles. Next, I'll be scattering rose petals all over the bed.

A smile grows on my face. I'm asking for trouble, and I have a feeling that's exactly what I'm going to get.

8

8 years ago

LEO

There's nothing more depressing than the rituals and customs of a Russian Orthodox funeral. Earlier today, we'd stood in the front pew—my brothers flanking me and my father at the end of the row—as the priest led the congregation in prayer. Reciting passages from the Bible, his voice resonated through the church adorned with golden icons and the soft glow of candlelight.

But I barely registered any of it. My focus was entirely on Alyona sitting beside her mother, Mina, both of them quietly sobbing, their shoulders shaking with each tearful breath. Her grief is like a bullet to my chest. Yulian sat on the other side of his mother, his face pale and solemn, his eyes glued to his papa's casket.

Much like Yulian, my father remained stoic, a clenched jaw

and serious expression, masking the sorrow pressing on his soul for his loyal *avoirtet*. But I didn't miss the way his hands curled into fists when the last rites were read.

Back at my family's secluded East Hampton home, hundreds have gathered to pay their respects to the Nikitin family and, by extension, to my family as well. I haven't caught a glimpse of Aly through the crowd of mourners, but I imagine she is busy shaking hands and receiving condolences.

It was barely a week ago that my father called Yulian and I into his office and told us the tragic news. Kiril had been killed protecting my father in a shootout with a rival mafia. Yulian took the news like the vor he was raised to be. His sorrow morphed into rage. Unsure of what else to do, I got shit-faced with my best friend, then allowed him to unleash his pain on me in the boxing ring, his grief materializing in forceful blows.

Aly was away at boarding school. Her mama left right away to pick her up, and while we've been under the same roof for the last few days, she's been holed up with her mama and Yulian. The truth is, I don't know how to console her. Unlike Yulian, a shot of vodka and a pair of boxing gloves won't cut it. So I've stayed away even though I know she's hurting. Alyona was close to her papa, he called her his *zaychik*, his little bunny, and doted on her, always bringing her Matryoshka dolls from his trips to Russia. I wonder if she still has the collection?

Nearing the late afternoon, the guests have finally thinned out, my brothers and Yulian are off smoking in the garage, and I know it's time to face Aly. I'd spied her slipping out of the room about an hour ago and I know just where to find her.

The hallway leading to the library is quiet, as expected, all the guests are holed up in the other wing. Swinging open the heavy wood door, I find Aly's long form huddled by the bay window, and she's nursing something that is definitely not juice.

Her head snaps around, eyes wide and startled by my unexpected presence. "Leo, oh my god," she exclaims, placing a hand over her heart, "you scared me."

"Whoa, didn't mean to scare you," I blurt, nervously rubbing the back of my neck. We're both frozen for a beat, just taking each other in. Even with red-rimmed eyes, I can't rip my gaze from her. "I can leave you alone if you'd like."

"No, of course not," she says, rising from the window seat. "It would actually be nice to have someone to drink with." She holds up a tumbler of amber liquid.

I clear my throat, stepping farther into the room. I feel like a total jackass and at a loss for words. So I go with the trite shit I've heard from others all day. "Aly, I ... I'm sorry—"

She starts shaking her head before I can get the words out. "No, please don't. Not you too." I'm not sure what she means, but keeping my mouth shut seems like the best course of action. Her gaze snaps to the window, looking off at the distant sea, while she brings the tumbler of ... what? Whisky maybe? ... to her lips and takes a hearty gulp, causing her to cough.

"Shit, that's strong," she announces, pounding her chest. A chest that's a hell of a lot fuller than the last time I saw her. I feel like a fucking asshole. The day of her father's funeral, and here I am, eyeing up her perfect curves.

Over the past year, she's blossomed, ditched the braces, and started styling her hair so it falls in a glossy black wave down her back. Even in her somber funeral dress, her legs seem to go on forever, and my mind takes a detour, imagining them hooked over my shoulders while I—

Stop. Jesus. What the hell is wrong with me?

Aly's always been in my life, but something has shifted lately. I can't help but notice her, like really *notice*. She's got this spark that sets her apart from all the other girls I know. Plus, she's a knockout—smart, fierce, and drop-dead gorgeous.

It's like I've got Aly goggles on. Every family gathering, every holiday, she's the only thing in my sight line. Hell, she's all I jerk off to.

But there's a big fat line between my fantasies and real life. Aly's off-limits—too young, too innocent, my best friend's kid sister. I can't go there. Ever. I shove those thoughts aside, focusing on what she needs right now—a friend.

I snag the Stoli from the mini fridge in the corner, then sidle over to her. "Switch to vodka, trust me," I suggest, unscrewing the cap and passing her the bottle as I hop up onto the window seat.

She eyes me with uncertainty. "What? You're not going to give me a lecture about underage drinking like my brother?"

A wry smile tugs at my lips. "Nah, it's your dad's funeral. You get a free pass today."

She seems to agree, taking the icy bottle from my grasp, swigging from it like it's the nectar of the gods. Like anybody with Russian blood, she puts away a good few ounces, not even hiccuping when she's done.

"I meant what I said earlier. I'm sorry I didn't come and find you when you first came home. I just ... fuck." I bite out a curse, my emotions all over the damn place. "I'm not good at this stuff, Aly."

"It's okay." She joins me at the bay window, sitting so close our thighs touch. The heat from her skin and her scent, like ripe peaches, is distracting. "I know Papa's death brings back difficult memories of your mom."

I turn to look at her, her face a picture of quiet sympathy. How is Alyona the one comforting me when she's experiencing such a devastating loss? But she's not wrong. Even though I was a child when my mother took her own life, the memory of her death still haunts me. On days like today, it feels more present than ever.

"She's on my mind a lot," I admit with a helpless shrug. "I hope she found happiness wherever she is; happier than she was here."

Kids have a sixth sense. Even as a young boy, I could tell our free-spirited mother was wilting under the bratva's rigid rules and constant threats. The tightening of her freedom. My father, busy with his empire, grew more and more distant, and all of it weighed heavily on her.

"I've made a decision," Aly says, looking down at the vodka cap she's spinning between her fingers. "I want out of this life. The bratva, the brotherhood, whatever you want to call it. I don't want it to be my future." Her eyes widen as if she fears I might misunderstand her. "I mean, your family will always be important to me, but I don't want to be like Mama today, a vor wife mourning a husband who was destined to die the minute he took the oath." Her watery eyes meet mine. "And I want to make a life of my own. Have a job. All of that."

I nod in understanding. "I hope that for you, too. Shit, I wouldn't even mind that for myself."

"Really?" Her head tilts in interest. "What would you want to do?"

"I dunno," I say with a shrug. But that's not true, I know exactly what I'd do. When Aly's eyes meet mine, so big and earnest, waiting for my answer, I decide to be truthful. "I think being a video game designer would be a cool job. Or maybe a virtual reality developer. Something with computers and tech." There. I said it. I've never told another person that except maybe my dog, Bones, but yeah, he doesn't count.

She bumps her shoulder gently against mine. "I think you'd be great at whatever you put your mind to."

"Thanks. But being the direct heir to the pakhan, it's tough to walk away from my family obligations." More like impossible.

"You never know. It's the modern world, people break with tradition all the time. And, no offense, but you're third in line to the throne. Surely that buys you a little more freedom."

My lips curl into a cynical grin. "None taken. But Papa doesn't see it that way. Would you like to be the one to discuss it with him?" Serge Kozlov is as traditional and uncompromising as they come. He's made it clear that his children are expected to join the family business. It isn't a choice, it's an obligation.

She snorts, familiar with how rigid my father can be. "Hard pass."

"What do you want to do?" I ask, screwing the top back on the vodka bottle when I notice a red flush working its way across Aly's delicate cheeks.

"Probably something to do with fashion. You know how I love combing through *Vogue* and *Elle* and all those magazines. I could see myself as a stylist or a buyer. There's just something about working in that world that excites me."

"I'm not sure if you've noticed, but you're beautiful enough to be a model."

She scrunches her nose, as if she doesn't believe me. I take that moment to study her. She really is breathtaking with eyes a deep blue nearing sapphire, subtly upturned at the corners. Cheekbones that are high and broad, tapering down to a slender nose. And her lips, plump and full, have starred in some of my hottest fantasies.

Her cheeks flush, a sign she's caught me staring at her lips. I quickly lift my eyes to meet hers. I hadn't meant to perv on her so obviously.

Suddenly, the atmosphere shifts. The air is charged, heavy with anticipation. Of what, I don't know. "Did you really mean what you said earlier ..." Aly's hoarse voice breaks the silence.

She looks up at me through thick dark lashes. "About a free pass today?"

"'Course I did. Anything to feel something other than pain." First-hand experience is the most ruthless teacher, and I know all about the power of diversion, the desperate need to feel something—anything—other than the searing slash of pain.

"Would it be selfish to ask to feel good? So my memory of today isn't all sadness and loss?" Her words nearly send me tumbling from the windowsill. I could blame the booze, but her stunning eyes are clear, completely alert. And they're trained right on me.

Maybe I'm reading this all wrong, maybe she just wants to take a sauna or something, get a massage ... but that's not the vibe I'm getting. Maybe I should talk her out of whatever idea is brewing in her head, but I don't want to. So, instead, I say, "I don't think it would be selfish."

Her voice doesn't waver when she asks, "What if you kissed me? Then I'd also remember today as the day I got my first kiss."

Shit.

Desire floods my system, impossible to block out. A grunt leaves my throat as I try—and fail—to ignore the spark of heat in her eyes as she looks up at me. This is ridiculous. I should say no. I should tell her it's a terrible idea, her brother is my best friend and would probably beat my face in if he knew I took advantage of his emotionally vulnerable sister. But she doesn't look vulnerable right now. She looks damn sure of herself, and how can I deny her?

No, more than that. I don't want to deny her.

I reach out and tuck a strand of silky dark hair behind her ear, enjoying the way her breath catches in her throat. "You sure, Aly?"

She nods, a hint of shyness coming through in her expression. "I'm sure ... I just don't know what to do. Will you show me?"

My throat goes dry. Screw it, I can't pretend the idea of being her first kiss isn't enough to make me instantly hard. I shoot a cautious look at the closed door, confident that no one's coming in here anytime soon. I clear my throat and push to stand. She watches me closely. My fingers instinctively find her chin as she blinks up at me, vulnerability etched across her face. I'm on the verge of crossing a line that should never be crossed, and I can't find it in me to care.

"You know, I want this as bad as you do," I say.

"Really?" Her cheeks turn a shade of pink as her gaze drifts down to my lips. My thumb skims over her mouth, a mouth I'm sure is going to taste like the sweetest ripe fruit. Like perfection.

Her pulse flutters in her throat as I tighten my grip on her chin and run my tongue over her lower lip. This kiss is like jumping off a cliff, exciting and terrifying all at once, because after this, there is no turning back. I'll know what she tastes like forever.

My lips capture hers. What she lacks in experience, she makes up for in sheer enthusiasm, opening herself up to me so perfectly. I devour her, running my tongue along her full lower lip then sucking it into my mouth. She releases little moans as my tongue brushes against hers, her skin silky and soft beneath my hand, still cupping her jaw.

Her hands find my arms, fingers digging into my skin like she doesn't know what to do with all this need, all this pent-up desire. And damn, I feel it too. If it was any other girl, I'd be balls deep in her right now. But not Alyona. This kiss is all we can share.

So I make it count.

I grab her ass and lift her onto me. Her arms wrap around my neck, and her legs instinctively find their way around my waist. "You're such a good girl," I praise her, and she arches against me. "Your body knows exactly what to do. What it needs."

Her response is a whimper from the back of her throat. She's desperate for it now, shimmying her hips, eagerly seeking relief. "More," she begs.

And I'm so tempted to give her the more she is craving. One hard circle of her clit, and I bet she'd go off like a rocket in my hand. I imagine her face flushed, back arching as my fingers brush against her throbbing clit, and it's so fucking tempting, but ...

But that's not what she asked for.

She asked for a kiss, that's all.

Her first kiss. So that's what I give her.

9

LEO

The moment Alyona steps onto the main deck, she comes to a dead halt and her hand shoots up to cover her mouth. Her eyes ping-pong around, absorbing the scene in front of her. It's a lot. Some would call it sensory overload. "What. The. Fuck," she mutters.

Genevieve may have gone a little overboard. Resting my ankle on my knee, I sit back in the chair and enjoy the look of bewilderment on Aly's face. "What? Not to your taste?" I feign offense.

There's champagne chilling table-side in a silver bucket that glimmers under the fairy lights strung crisscross above us. A layer of rose petals so thick you'd think a flower shop had exploded covers every surface, and rows upon rows of candles line the dining area, their flames dancing in the shadows, even though I'm sure it's against fire code.

This is not romance, it's romance on steroids.

Aly approaches, still looking at me like I'm mentally unwell. "Should I be concerned? Are you feeling alright?"

I raise my whisky glass in cheers. "Perfectly fine, thanks. Nice outfit," I shoot back.

She blinks innocently, but there is nothing innocent about her chosen attire. She's wearing a snug-fitting white T-shirt that exposes her midriff, minuscule denim cut-offs, and rhinestoned cowboy boots.

I don't have to question whether she knows the effect her outfit has on me; her defiant smirk says it all. She lowers herself into the seat across from me. "I dressed up, just like you requested. Since we're posing as an American couple, I thought I should look the part." Liar. She just didn't like me telling her what to wear. "But this"—she gestures at the petal explosion all around us—"is disturbing."

Her glossy hair tumbles around her shoulders, but it's her lips I can't tear my eyes from. Full and lush, they're painted a vibrant, bold, take-no-prisoners kind of red. It feels personal.

I just shrug nonchalantly, popping an olive into my mouth. "Maybe this is what a man does when he's head over heels. Maybe you need to find a man who truly understands the meaning of romance."

"Oh please. Like this flower disaster is romantic." She crosses her arms in front of her chest. "And I've been with plenty of romantic guys. Paris is the city of love."

Except it hasn't been for her. I've made sure of that.

"Okay." I raise my eyebrows. "What's the most romantic thing anyone's ever done for you?"

Holding eye contact, she reaches for my glass and takes a long hard swallow. I'd say she's buying herself some time. "Took me dancing."

I take my drink back, positioning my lips directly over her lipstick stain, chasing the taste of her on the glass. Dancing guy? I remember that loser. He took her to one lousy salsa dancing class and nearly shit his pants when Matis told him to get lost. Broke up with her by text if I recall. "If it's dancing that you want, I'm sure Genevieve can arrange for that. Would be nice to slow dance under the stars, wouldn't it?"

She rolls her eyes, her lips setting into a thin line. "Not with you." Running a finger over the rim of her water glass she adds, "You know what's *not* romantic?"

I pause with the glass halfway to my mouth and brace for impact. She leans forward. "Packing my vibrator."

A breath I didn't realize I was holding escapes my lungs. "I disagree. I think it was a very romantic gesture. I'm making sure your needs are taken care of."

Truth is big romantic gestures are not my thing. I'm a believer in the small things. Like how Aly and I used to drag blankets up to the roof of the estate to watch the stars or go for spontaneous motorcycle rides along the coast. Just her and I and the open road. Fuck candles and roses, it didn't get more romantic than that.

But that was then, and this is now.

"Not sure I'm going to need Bob," she answers lightly. It takes me a minute to catch on that Bob is her battery-operated boyfriend. "Jack seems pretty nice after all."

A snarl escapes from my lips as my hand clenches into a fist, crumpling the napkin under my grip. "Are you trying to provoke me? Because I warn you, butterfly, that's a very dangerous game to play. On this boat you belong to me." Not only on this boat. In my heart, in my soul. Just not in this lifetime, my father made damn sure of that. "And if you need a reminder of how your body still responds to me," a slow smile grows on my face as I watch her nipples hardening beneath her thin shirt, "I will be happy to provide one."

A beat passes, and I wonder if she'll argue. But instead, her stained-red lips twist in amusement. I have a feeling I just played into her hand. "So easy to rile up, Leonid. What happened to that easygoing boy I once knew?"

"Long gone," I say. Left the day Alyona flew to Paris, and I got my vory stars. Silence fills the space between us until it's interrupted when a server appears by our table.

"Good evening. My name is Becky, and I'll be serving you tonight." A young woman with blonde hair in a neat bun introduces herself before reaching for the bottle of Veuve chilling in the ice bucket beside the table.

"Nice to meet you, Becky," Aly offers. "I don't think we've seen you before."

"This is my first trip out. I'm still getting my sea legs," she admits, her smile wavering as she goes about her task. Sweat beads form on her forehead, and her grip on the champagne bottle is unsteady. Aly and I exchange a look; something is not right.

"I think I might be ..." Becky swallows thickly while attempting to work the cork out of the bottle. "A little seasick."

With a loud bang, the cork escapes the bottle, ricocheting off the canopied sun cover and landing with a thud on the deck. The champagne gushes out in a fountain, dousing the table and drenching Alyona, who jumps up and starts to pat at her sopping clothes while Becky looks on mortified. But more than mortified, Becky looks green.

"I'm ... I'm so sorry," she stammers as she lunges towards the side of the boat, retching into the water below.

Aly abandons her napkin to the floor and approaches the sick woman to hold back her hair and murmur words of comfort. My chest squeezes. This is the Alyona I grew up with. The girl with a tender heart who wasn't afraid to show the soft side of herself instead of hiding behind the steel shield she holds up all the time now, pretending nothing can ever hurt her again.

When the sounds of retching stops, Aly escorts Becky back into the cabin as a flustered, wild-eyed Genevieve comes bounding up the stairs, a look of frozen horror etched on her face.

"Oh, *mon dieu*," she mutters, her eyes closing in a slow blink. "I'll have this all cleaned up for you and back to—"

"It's okay." Alyona's voice echoes from behind Genevieve, who startles before turning around. Aly's got two bottles of beer in one hand and a bag of chips in the other. "I got it covered."

Genevieve bites her lip, looking terribly apologetic. "We ruined your romantic evening."

I bark out a laugh, because oh, the irony of it. "Not at all, we're good," I assure her. In fact, I can't think of anything more romantic than swigging a beer and sharing a bag of chips with Aly.

FIFTEEN MINUTES LATER, Aly is changed into yoga pants and a T-shirt with her hair piled into a bun on the top of her head. I'm still wearing clothes that are two sizes too small for me, but I've abandoned my jacket and tie and popped the first few buttons on the dress shirt.

Now we're sitting on the ground cross-legged, our backs pressed against the bow of the ship, a perfect view of the vast, star-studded sky. Neither of us has said much, but the mood has changed. It's less charged, more relaxed.

Aly expertly twists the cap off the beer bottle and hands it to me. She then does the same with her own bottle and raises it in a toast. "*Za tvoye zdorovye*!" I respond, clinking my bottle against hers.

When she takes a swig, the tendons in her neck work as she swallows, and fuck, the view makes my dick twitch. In fact, being near Aly in general is making my damn dick ache. I've been sleeping on the couch in the office—not an easy feat for a man my size—because I find the little sleep sounds she makes arousing. Well, that and she made it clear we would not be having a slumber party.

"Oh my god," she gasps, pulling the bottle from her lips with a satisfied sigh. "I needed that."

The full moon casts a white light across the water, making it sparkle like glinting diamonds. As beautiful as it is, that's not the most breathtaking view afforded to me. Not even close.

"I hope that wasn't the only pair of cowboy boots in the closet. They suited you." As did the crop top and itty-bitty jean shorts.

Alyona turns towards me with a smile, the first genuine smile I've had for a damn long time, and a tingle works its way up my spine. Her blue eyes sparkle, crinkle at the corners, and her cheeks bloom with a soft blush. "I'll see what I can find," she promises. A wince crosses her features momentarily. "Poor seasick Becky. Talk about an occupational hazard."

We exchange a look, and like when we were younger, that's all it takes for both of us to explode in a fit of laughter. When we get going, we really get going. Alyona throws her head back, her body shuddering. I haven't laughed like this for as long as I can remember, and it feels good to let loose, especially since things have been so tense.

A warm rush spreads through my chest. A tangible reminder of how much I've missed the easy banter, the inside jokes. This is what we were, what we had.

"Know what that reminded me of?" Alyona chuckles, wiping away a tear. "The time when you decided to open a bottle of champagne using a sword that Christmas after Papa died. Only you ended up slicing the curtains in half, and the champagne showered everyone in the room. I swear, I thought your father was going to kill you."

"I thought he was going to kill me, too," I say, bringing the bottle to my lips.

"It wasn't your smartest move," she admits, taking a chip from the bag between us. "But it did make me giggle for weeks just thinking about it."

I still smile at that memory. It had been months after Alyona's father died, and she had barely cracked a smile the whole Christmas holiday, but I was desperate to change that.

The kiss changed everything for me. She was on my mind constantly, other girls tried to get my attention, but they may as well have been invisible. The day she walked into Christmas dinner looking so beautiful but so sad, I knew I would do anything in my power to make her smile. I thought of dumb shit to cheer her up like dressing up Bones, the family dog, as Santa and teaching him to howl "Jingle Bells," which came out sounding more like a yowling cat.

"Remember Bones?" I ask her. "I swear once that dog learned how to sing, he never stopped."

Alyona snorts, her upturned nose wrinkling in amusement. "That poor long-suffering pup. Growing up with the three Kozlov boys."

"Are you kidding?" I exclaim. "That dog had the best life of any pet I know. He roamed around like he owned the estate, kind of like we used to." And then because I am feeling bold, I say, "I miss laughing with you. I miss the kind of fun we used to get up to."

She sighs deeply and stares out at the sea in front of us. "Yeah. Me too." She pauses for a moment, her brows drawing together. "Sometimes I forget to have fun. I'm young, I'm in my prime, my life shouldn't be so damn serious. Even more so now that some psychopath is after me."

It's the mention of her age that suddenly clues me in. "Hey, it's going to be your birthday soon."

She shoots me a dirty look. "Don't remind me. I'm going to be so annoyed if I have to celebrate on this boat." When I pull a mock-offended face, she hits my arm. "It's not you. Well, not entirely. But I want to be with my brother, Rowan, Kira, and get back to ... normal life."

"Is that what you really want?"

"I ... I don't know what I really want anymore." Her eyes meet mine, the air between us is heavy with everything we are not saying. It's then that she reaches out, her finger tracing down the scar bisecting my chin.

"Where'd you get this?" she asks.

"When we were ambushed by the Antonovs. It's not the only war wound I walked away with, but it's the most visible." It's been nearly three years since Kira's father, our family's greatest foe, ambushed me, my brothers, and our men when we thought we were saving Georgia after she was abducted. Turns out, Georgia ended up saving us, but not before an epic battle ensued, one that nearly killed Georgia, and left my brothers and sister, Kira, in rough shape. At the end of the day though, we're all still standing.

"Right," she replies, still not breaking eye contact. The energy shifts around us, and I can't look away, even if I wanted to. Heat blasts through my veins, and it takes everything in me not to lean forward and—

"Sorry to interrupt, mates!" A voice I've come to associate with nails on a chalkboard carries over the sea breeze. It's big, it's brash, and it's unmistakably from Down Under. Jack appears on the edge of the deck, and despite his words, he doesn't look sorry at all. "The deck crew spotted a pod of dolphins playing off the starboard side of the boat. I thought Alison would be interested in watching."

But the only interest I can see reflected in his eyes is directed at my fiancée. Fake or not, I don't like it. I stand, turning on this jerk who somehow thinks it's acceptable to disturb a couple having a private drink. "Thanks for the tip, buddy, but we're in the middle of something. How about you give us some privacy."

"'Course. Never meant to intrude." His words of apology don't match the glint in his eye. Recognizing that hardened look all too well—it's one I see in other criminals, in other bad men, like me—I make a mental note to ask Dima to dig into his background.

I'm on the verge of telling him to get lost, but a second thought stops me. This is a perfect chance to remind this dipshit that I'm her man. At least I am on this boat. "No worries, brother." I clap him on the back harder than necessary. "On second thought, if Aly wants to see the dolphins, why not?"

Alyona stands, the look on her face says *What the fuck are you playing at?* but she doesn't push the issue. Instead, she strolls by me and tells Jack to lead the way.

"Yes, Jack, lead the way," I echo, sounding too cheery, causing Aly to throw me another questioning look over her shoulder.

"What?" I whisper as we head towards the upper deck. "I like dolphins, too."

She snorts. "News to me."

Jack leads us to the starboard railing where a few other crew members have gathered. It's dark here, most of the overhead lights extinguished, there's only a few deck lights illuminating our path, and of course the stars twinkling overhead.

Jack settles on the other side of Aly, so she's sandwiched

between us. He leans down and murmurs into her ear, "Just keep your eyes on the water, they can pop out at any moment." But unlike Aly who is scanning the surface for signs of activity, Jack Off here hasn't looked towards the water once. His eyes are solely focused on her.

Fucker.

But I'm just as guilty. She's captured my full attention with the hopeful way she's staring out at the water even though the dolphins have yet to make an appearance. Tendrils of dark hair have escaped her bun, flowing in the breeze, her eyes sparkling. I don't question my next move, probably because it feels so natural, and it's what any fiancé would do. Especially a man looking to stake his claim.

My arm fastens around her waist to bring her taut ass flush against my now hardening dick. I will it to behave, but the fucker has a mind of its own when it comes to her. Aly's breath hitches in her throat and her body tenses against mine. I'm sure she's about to shove an elbow into my ribs when a splash in the distance pulls our attention out towards the water. Saved by Flipper.

A pod of dolphins appears below us, leaping and playing in the water a few feet away.

"Oh my god," she breathes, her eyes wide while she drinks in the scene below. "They're amazing."

"Aren't they?" Jack agrees, but the mudak hasn't even glanced at the water once, his eyes are still roving over the woman in my arms. I'm about to knee him in the nuts. Instead, I do one worse. I give him a show.

Leaning down, I let my breath dance over the nape of her neck, followed by a brush of my lips that summon tiny goose bumps in their wake.

"What are you doing?" she whispers, but it comes out a little breathy, a little undone, just the way I want her.

"Just enjoy the show."

She swallows audibly, but instead of pulling away, she relaxes against my chest.

Her body seems to like me a lot more than her mind does, so I use what I can to my advantage. My lips brush behind her ear, her favorite spot. Her breath catches in her throat, and her head rests against my pec. I'm sure it's part booze and part dolphin magic, but to feel her soften against me is fucking intoxicating.

This isn't about Jack Off anymore, and it's not about me staking my claim. Touching her just feels right. For the first time in a long time, everything in my world aligns. Like pieces of a puzzle have snapped back into place. It's a feeling I'll chase forever.

With her body still flush against mine, we watch in silence as the dolphins splash around. Jack talks quietly with his colleagues but steals glances at Aly now and then.

"It's like they're putting on a show for us," Aly murmurs.

Jack is quick to jump in. "Or they're showing off for the beautiful girl watching them."

I roll my eyes. What a charmer with these stale-as-shit lines. Just for that, I trail my fingertips over her arms, and a subtle shiver runs through her. She's not just playing a part right now, her body is responding to my touch.

"What do you think, butterfly?" I ask her, deliberately using her pet name, letting it hang in the air between us. Aly's eyes flicker back to mine, a knowing smirk tugging at her lips.

"I think they're more interested in showing off for each other than for any of us," she responds, her body brushing against mine. Whether it's to keep warm in the evening breeze, or for some other reason, I don't care.

I make sure Jack is watching when I lean down, my lips ghosting over her ear, "I don't give a fuck about the dolphins.

Holding you is the highlight of my day. Fuck, the highlight of my year."

She doesn't say anything, just keeps her eyes on the water, but her body leans further into mine, and that's all the response I need.

A few minutes later, the dolphins have had enough of our attention and head off in another direction. With the show over, members of the staff slowly disperse, but Jack stays rooted to the spot. I look up and give him a big, fake smile. "Those dolphins are really something, aren't they?"

His tone is light, but his eyes are ice when he answers, "Smart too."

"Oh, don't give them too much credit now. Not as smart as you think they are."

"Maybe you're underestimating them." His smile is gone, as is the pretense that we're talking about anything other than him and me right here. Fierce competitors.

Aly sighs and steps away from my chest. I miss her warmth immediately, but I'm guessing she's done with the pissing contest we're having over here. In any other situation I'd solve this issue with my fists or a gun, but that's not going to fly here.

"Anyhow," I say in dismissal, "thanks for the hot tip on the dolphins. We'll catch you later."

Jack looks from Aly to me and then back again. "Yeah, sure. Enjoy your night."

The moment Jack stalks away, I can sense the spell is broken. Aly pivots towards me, hands on her hips. "Seriously, Leo, was that really necessary?"

"It was. It was very fucking necessary," I respond.

She blinks up at me, as her pulse pounds in her throat. "No PDA, that was part of the rules."

I reach out and run a thumb over her bottom lip. The red stain is still holding on, as stubborn as she is. "I don't give a fuck about the rules." As her gaze locks with mine, my skin sizzles as if I'm standing too close to a roaring fire. I bend so my mouth is directly beside her ear. "I needed to touch you."

Her eyes flicker shut for a moment, lips parting slightly as if to let out a breath she's been holding for far too long. "Leo," she begins, her voice shaking as she opens her eyes. She swallows hard, and I can see her struggle, caught between what she should say and what she wants to say.

My hand moves from her lip to cup her cheek, thumb tracing circles on her flushed skin. I don't know what I want from her, I just know I can't be in such close proximity to her and not touch her perfect skin.

Finally, she shakes her head, loose strands of hair framing her face. "I can't do this," she says, her voice barely above a whisper.

Her words slice through me, leaving a cold emptiness that's far worse than the heat of rejection. And with that, she retreats, leaving me standing alone in the darkness.

10

ALYONA

There was a time in my life when I thought Leonid Kozlov could do no wrong. That the sun rose and fell at his bidding. That time is past. *Like way past.*

He was out of line last night. But the worst part—so was I. Because the minute his hands dared roam over my skin—and they sure did roam, touching, exploring, making me feel things I hadn't felt in a long time—I was a goner. I melted into him. And that kiss he dropped along my neck while I was pressed against his firm body rippling with— Nope, not going to go there.

I've spent so much time trying to forget him—the way he could make me burst out laughing with one perfectly timed eyebrow arch, the way he'd happily leaf through fashion magazines with me while I pointed out the latest styles. He made me feel safe, like I was the only one in his world.

Last night proved to me this isn't going to work unless I set some firm boundaries. If we're going to do this fake engagement thing, he doesn't get to kiss me or touch me just because he wants to. Because Leo's touch sets me on fire. It makes me want things I shouldn't, and that messes with my head.

Slipping on the most demure dress I find in the closet—a white linen summer sheath paired with cork-wedge heels—I step out of my suite and head upstairs towards Leo's office turned makeshift bedroom. I assume this is where he's been holed up every night, because I sure as hell haven't invited him to sleep in the stateroom with me.

I am a big enough woman to admit I'm part of the problem. I teased Leo about Jack, and it got him all fired up. Yeah, Jack's flirty, but it's harmless, and I'm definitely not interested, even if I let Leo think otherwise. What can I say, the ego boost felt good, and I enjoyed getting a rise out of Leo. But now it's time to stop playing.

Just as I'm about to knock, a voice on the other side of the door stops me in my tracks. It's a voice I recognize buzzing through the speakerphone, and she is furious.

"On a yacht?! You basically abducted her in the middle of the night, and now you're forcing her to stay with you? Leo ... what exactly is wrong with you?"

God bless Kira. The youngest of the Kozlov siblings and one of my closest friends and fiercest defenders, as evidenced by the shit she's now raining down on her brother. I know I shouldn't, but who in their right mind would be able to resist eavesdropping on this conversation? Certainly not me.

"I did what I had to do to keep her safe. I don't need you busting my balls. Trust me, Alyona's done enough of that already," Leo shoots back defensively.

"Well, can you blame her?"

Leo mutters a curse I don't quite catch. "I owe it to Yulian and the brotherhood to treat this threat as serious, to make sure—"

Kira's laugh slices through his words like a knife. "Who are you trying to convince? 'Cause I don't buy it for one minute. Chartering a private yacht, blowing off your other duties to be her personal protector. What are you really after?"

A tight knot forms in my stomach as the tension on the other side of the door buzzes like a live wire. I don't know what Kira's getting at, but it feels like she's dancing around that one topic I've begged her not to touch with a ten-foot pole.

My history with Leo.

Kira's the one person that knows the full truth. Maybe it was easier to talk to her because she didn't see us grow up together, or maybe it was the two bottles of rosé we polished off on the patio of Café de la Paix when she came to Paris last year. But I told her everything. Like *everything*. The whole sordid tale of love, rejection, and heartbreak. And she pinky promised never to breathe a word to another soul.

Leo lets out a sound that's part sigh, part growl. "Kira, I love you, but you don't know what you're talking about. The history between Aly and me is complicated. I ... I care for her." He hits the brakes mid-sentence, going silent. It feels like an eternity passes before he finds his voice again. "But right now I need to act in the best interest of the brotherhood."

"Is that what you did all those years ago when you chose the bratva over her?"

My hand flattens against the door and my blood pounds in my ears. Holy shit, what is Kira thinking, spilling secrets I entrusted to her?! Knowing her, she's probably been itching to give Leo hell ever since I told her how we ended. I get that she's concerned, but I really wish she'd let it go.

"Did she tell you that?" Leo's voice is strained.

"Oh, you mean the part where you shattered her heart, trampled all over it, and then fed it to a wood chipper for good measure?"

I'm on the brink of pounding down this damned door, when Leo's voice slices through the air.

"I made the only choice I could to keep the people I love from getting hurt," he admits, his voice raw. "It was the hardest thing I ever had to do, and it cost me everything."

Resting my palms on the wall above my head, I struggle to draw in my next breath. What does he mean the people he loved would get hurt? I did get hurt! He broke me. Could he mean something else? My mind spins, tossing his words about like a Rubik's Cube, frantically trying to solve the riddle. Because the only truth I know is that Leo Kozlov did exactly what he promised he wouldn't.

He discarded me like trash on the floor.

He told me he didn't love me, never had. That we were a mistake.

I spiraled into a dark place after that, and the only escape was distance. So, three days after he broke things off, I packed up my life and moved to Paris while he pledged his loyalty to the Kozlov Bratva. He became a vor, the one thing I could never accept in a partner.

I stiffen, my back pressing into the wall as I slide down onto the cold floor.

"I'm sorry, I didn't realize," Kira says, her voice softer now. "You've never opened up about what happened with you and Aly."

"It's not something I find easy to talk about. With anyone."

"I don't know what to say." Kira exhales a heavy sigh. "But the two of you alone for days on end ... how's that working?"

Leo scoffs. "Once Daniil is back from Russia, we'll have a better understanding of the situation. Until then, nothing else matters. This is the safest place for her to be."

The faint sound of a clock ticking fills the silence. "It's not safe for her heart. Keep that in mind."

Exactly what I confessed to Kira two bottles in, I don't remember. But there's a flicker in the back of my mind, a sliver of memory hinting that I may have confessed a truth so raw, I can barely admit it to myself.

The fact that I've never truly gotten over Leo.

"Why would you say that?" Leo prods, a new tension in his voice.

And that's my signal to make my presence known before Kira spills any more of my secrets. *Thump, Thump, Thump.* "Leo, can we talk?" I call out.

"Kira, I need to go. We'll catch up soon."

"Remember what I said," she reminds him.

Seconds later, Leo swings open the door, his gaze latching onto mine. A storm rages in his deep-brown eyes, holding me captive. I squirm under his scrutiny but do my best to keep my expression neutral. If he suspects that I eavesdropped, he doesn't mention it, and I'm certainly not about to confess.

Instead, I flash him a breezy smile and stroll past him into the office. "Am I interrupting something?" I ask, perching on the edge of his desk.

Three heavy beats pass before Leo answers. "Nah, Kira was just checking in, wanted to make sure everything was okay. I'm sure she would have wanted to speak with you."

I cross my arms in front of my chest. "I bet a lot of people would like to speak with me, but considering you took my phone, I guess that's not happening."

He smiles, but it feels forced. "Safety first."

"Whatever." I swallow, making a conscious effort to avoid his gaze, because every time I meet it, I lose my bearings. I swear, his warm brown eyes are like a trap. "So ... any news about my situation?"

He gives a slow shake of his head. "No news from Brooklyn. What happened to you seems to be an isolated incident.

No one's made a move on the Kozlov Bratva or anyone linked to us. I suspect it's personal. Whoever's after you is after you for a reason."

A shiver creeps up my spine. "I'm being targeted?"

Resting his hands on the back of a chair, he leans forward, lines of frustration etched on his face. "We don't know anything for certain yet," he admits. "Daniil's in Russia trying to dig up answers. Once we know what we're dealing with, we'll head back to New York. You just need to tolerate me for a few more days, then I'll be out of your hair." His jaw clenches and releases. "That is what you want, right?"

I clear the lump in my throat. "Yes, of course that's what I want."

His eyes dark, Leo runs a fingertip over the scar on his chin. "What did you come here to talk to me about?"

I part my lips, only to clamp them shut again. If we're only going to be here for a few more days, it hardly seems worth it to dive into the whole PDA drama. Besides, Leo was only getting touchy-feely with me to make a point in front of Jack. I'll make it easier on everyone by avoiding the first mate altogether.

"Just checking up on things," I say, easing off the desk. Then, words I hadn't planned on escape. "I appreciate it, you know. You being here ... doing all this." Even if Leo's presence is about his loyalty to the brotherhood and Yulian, he's kept me safe. And that's not nothing.

A flicker of surprise crosses his features, before he nods, the movement slow and deliberate. It feels like there is more for us to say, especially after how we left things last night, but I can't find the words.

I'm halfway to the door when Leo's voice rings out. "Aly?" My name tumbles from his lips like a plea. I pivot, looking back at him. His lips part and close in a silent battle with his thoughts. Just when I expect something profound, he catches me off guard. "We need to go shopping."

"Shopping? Seriously?" My eyebrows shoot up in surprise.

"Hell yeah. Look at me!" He gestures down to his outfit, another too-tight polo shirt and beige shorts—it couldn't be further from Leo's usual biker-dude look.

Positioning my hip against the door, I arch an eyebrow at him. "And how exactly do you propose we go shopping? Unless there's a mall somewhere out here in ... wait, where exactly are we?"

"Heart of the Mediterranean," Leo replies, his eyes crinkling in the corners. "We'll be docking in Lipari tonight, an island off Sicily's coast to refuel. There're a few shops we can hit up."

A worried frown creases my forehead. "Is it safe for us to leave the boat?"

"I'll make sure it's safe." He crosses his arms over his chest looking like a superhero come to life with his bulging muscles and chiseled jawline. "And it will be under the cover of night."

My first impulse is to tell him no, but a different part of me, the part still grappling with what I overheard, with the raw vulnerability in Leo's voice—pipes up instead. "Alright, let's do it."

"By ready at nine," he says. "Maybe we'll go dancing afterwards."

I narrow my eyes at him, but I can't help the smile that forms on my lips. Or the flutter of excitement between my legs. "Don't push it."

He grins back at me. "But that's what I do best."

I SPEND the afternoon in the yacht's home theater immersing myself in nostalgic nineties rom-coms, but instead of getting lost in the on-screen romance of *Notting Hill*, my mind is preoccupied, replaying the conversation I overheard earlier between Leo and Kira.

Who would force his hand to end things with me? And why wouldn't he just tell me if that was the case? We knew his father and brothers would be angry when Leo refused to take the vor oath, but he was prepared to stand up to them. We were going to forge our own life, even without his family's approval, believing they would ultimately accept our choice.

When Leo broke up with me—dismissing our relationship as nothing more than a summer fling—I took his words at face value. But deep inside, doubt always lingered. Maybe there was more to it that I didn't see at the time?

Confronting him is just too damn daunting. Some things are best left in the past. Especially memories so jagged they can still knock the air from my lungs. It's time to accept he had his reasons for doing what he did. I may never know those reasons, but I'm ready to let it go. Mostly.

What I need to stop doing is feeling all fluttery every time his arm brushes against mine or he stares at me from across the room. No more of that. I'll keep my head on straight and treat him like any other friend.

Are we friends, though?

Can we ever just be friends?

Who knows, but my brain is fried just thinking about all this, so I decide to settle in and watch Hugh Grant attempt to charm Julia Roberts, when there is a knock on the theater door.

"Come in," I call out. Somehow, I'm not surprised to see Jack standing in the doorway.

"You can't watch a movie without popcorn," he says,

holding up a giant bowl in his hands. "It's actually against yacht rules."

I straighten in my seat and smile at him. He's obviously trying to win my favor, but I appreciate the thought. And I do love popcorn. "Thank you," I say, taking the snack from him.

"Mind if I join?" he asks, already settling into the seat next to me. As usual, he's looking handsome with that tan and athletic build. I'm sure most of the ladies he encounters love being doted on by him, but I'm not one of them. And I intend to make that clear.

"Your fiancé sure works a lot for a guy on holiday. Must suck for you." His hand delves into the popcorn at the same time as mine. I pull my hand out from the bowl like it's on fire, not wanting to make contact.

"Yeah, well." I shrug. "He's a busy man with a busy job. You know how it is."

"Oh yeah." He smirks. "I see it all the time. A powerful, rich dude wants to impress his woman, so he rents a mega yacht and then neglects her the whole time. Common story."

My jaw tightens. He's certainly making a lot of assumptions about my relationship. Well, my fake relationship. "His work is demanding, but he's trying his best. We're actually going on a date tonight."

"Oh really?" Jack lifts his eyebrows as he sinks further down into his seat. "Big plans?"

"Yes, in fact. We might go dancing."

"Happy to hear that. I hate to think of a beautiful woman like you being neglected."

I roll my eyes. "Puh-lease. You probably say that to all the girls."

A grin stretches his lips. "Just the pretty ones."

Do his super cheesy lines actually work? I get it, he is used to all the bored housewives on the yacht spreading their legs for him, but that won't be me.

"Just to be clear, I'm not looking for anything else. I'm in love with my fiancé." I pause for a minute and look him square in the eye before delivering what I hope he takes as a dismissal. "Thanks again for the popcorn."

He takes the hint and stands. "Well then." Jack tosses me a wink. "You know where to find me if you need me."

Like hell. I plan on giving him a very wide berth.

11

7 YEARS AGO

LEO

As I STEP OUTSIDE, I'm greeted by thumping bass music, the flickering light of tiki torches, and the raucous laughter of my brother's barely legal guests.

Fucking Daniil. You leave him alone for a week, and he's throwing a bash to rival the hottest Coachella after-party. I push my way through the throngs of half-drunk dudes and the bikini-clad women that love them. Half the party is splashing in the pool, tanned bodies glistening in the moonlight.

"Hey, bro!" I call out, trying to catch my older brother's attention over the music. He's surrounded by a group of his friends, all of them holding beers, a joint passing between them. When my brother spots me, he grins, beckoning me over with a wave of his hand.

"You made it in time for the party," he says, offering me a

hit off his joint. I shake my head, I'm not in the mood to get fucked up tonight. I just got back from a week in New York where Papa had me working as a foot soldier, protecting cargo coming through the ports. It was shit work, which I guess is the point. Papa makes us train from the bottom up. We earn our stars like any other vor.

I'm tired, worn-out, and all I can think about it is seeing Alyona.

"Papa's been gone less than six hours, and you throw a rager to kick off summer," I say, shaking my head, but a smile plays on my lips. That's Daniil. Party or die trying.

"Might be our last summer of freedom, I'm gonna make the most of it." He takes a hit from the joint and passes it to one of his friends. As usual, my mood dips when we talk about being sworn in to the brotherhood. It's our destiny, our future, and we've never questioned it. Daniil bought himself some time before taking the oath, having convinced Papa that a university education in business management would benefit the bratva's operations. But he's nearly done with his studies.

"You should blow off some steam, grab a drink," Daniil suggests, pointing to the bar set up beside the pool.

I don't care about partying. My eyes keep scanning the crowd for her, not that I imagine she'll show. Alyona's never been into our parties, but a small part of me hopes tonight is an exception. She just graduated high school, maybe she'll feel like celebrating.

"Dude, you're so fucking obvious." Daniil laughs, knocking me in the chest with his elbow. I narrow my eyes at him, but I can't be too pissed since he's right. He'd caught me texting with Alyona a few weeks ago, and eventually pried the story out of me how we kissed, just the once, the day of her father's funeral, and how we've been texting back and forth while she's been at school.

Aly hasn't mentioned the kiss again, and neither have I. I'm not going to push it with her, even if she's been on my mind constantly. Aly is off-limits, but we've settled into a chill friendship. We text about everything from the latest Marvel movie to what she's having for dinner. Sometimes we talk about deeper stuff like her Mom's declining health, but overall, it's pretty casual.

Still, I can't help but wonder about this upcoming summer. For the first time, we'll be living together for several months. My father, Andrei, and Yulian will be away in Russia for most of the summer—a fact I try not to dwell on too much. That leaves just me, Aly, and Daniil residing at the Kozlov estate. Alone.

"I'm not fucking obvious," I grumble, "I'm cool as a cucumber." I grab the beer from his hand and down it in a few gulps.

"Yeah, whatever you say." Daniil's tone turns somber. "She's been with her mama all day. Mina's not doing well again."

"Shit." I shake my head. Mina has been on a downhill slide since her husband died. First it was the pills to help her sleep, then the ones to calm her down, then the ones for pain. We don't talk about it, my father in particular just calls it "the sickness" and tells us there's nothing to be done. I know Yulian and Alyona have tried their best to get her help, but so far nothing's worked.

It's heartbreaking for everyone.

I'm about to return the half-empty beer to Daniil and head inside when he lets out a low, long whistle. "Well, twist my nipples and call me Alice!"

"What the hell—?" But before the words slip through my lips, I turn and see for myself. Alyona is walking towards us with a brilliant smile on her face, her long legs exposed by the slit in her slinky black dress. She's always been stunning, but tonight? She's straight-up fire.

"Fuck me," I blurt, earning a chuckle from Daniil.

"Dude, I'm not gonna tell you how to live your life, but I will remind you that she turned eighteen last month. Fully legal."

"Not helping," I bite out. "She's our best friend's little sister. Off-limits."

Daniil snuffs the joint underfoot, sighing, "Just saying she's old enough to make her own choices. And it seems like she knows what she wants."

Her eyes lock with mine across the crowd, her stare unwavering and undeniably fixated on me. Christ. This girl has turned me inside out. I brush my hair from my face, a low flutter in my gut suggests that after tonight, nothing is going to be the same.

"Hey," she says, approaching us, smoothing down her way-too-short dress. "I hope it's okay that I came. I just needed a change of scenery."

"'Course. It's more than okay." Daniil jumps in. "Stay here, I'm getting you a drink."

Daniil heads off, leaving us alone. Our eyes meet, and I swear my lungs forget their job. I've always been a sucker for her baby blues, and tonight, with the hint of mascara and eyeliner she has on, I'm already lost in their depths.

"Is that a new tattoo?" Aly asks, breaking the awkward silence. She's pointing at the new ink of a Chinese dragon I had done recently.

"Yeah, what do you think?" I ask, holding my forearm out for her to take a closer look.

Her fingers skim my bare skin, sending shivers up my arm. "It's really cool," she says. "Doesn't the Chinese dragon symbolize power and strength? It's perfect for you." My head snaps up, thrilled by her unexpected compliment.

When I meet her eyes, there's no trace of the once-shy teen in her stare. Her eyes flash with something I've never seen before. Lust. Holy shit. The perfect angel is ready to dance with the devil. That look alone should send me running, but it doesn't.

Instead, I tell her exactly what I'm thinking. "Shit, Aly, you look ..." I try not to let my eyes linger as long as they do on her lips, on the swell of her tits in that tight dress, on all that bare leg. I fail miserably. "Amazing."

So much for not perving on her. She flicks a glance to the grass, a blush tinting her cheeks before her eyes reconnect with mine. I draw in a deep breath, letting it escape as a soft hiss, because now there is no denying it. She's flirting with me.

Daniil joins us again, pushes a drink into each of our hands —beer for me and some girly concoction for Aly—and tells us to enjoy ourselves before sauntering up to a pair of brunettes that have been eye-fucking him all night. I know how my brother's evening will end, I'm just not sure about my own.

I nod my chin towards the swings hanging from a branch of the great oak tree on the edge of the property. She offers me her hand, and I lead her through the crowd so we can be alone.

"And here I thought your wild parties were all about sex, drugs, and rock and roll." She smirks, taking a seat on the swing beside mine. "Apparently, you prefer to swing."

I laugh. "First time for everything," I drawl, taking a slow sip of my beer before placing the can down at my feet. "Have to admit, I've been thinking about you these past few months."

She twists the swing so she's facing me. "I've been thinking about you, too. More than you know." Our eyes clash, and the simmer of attraction bubbles into something far more electric.

"Oh yeah?" I give her my full attention, despite the chaotic scene in the distance which includes a borderline orgy raging in the pool. "What is it you've been thinking about?"

Her tongue swipes over her full bottom lip, and my cock throbs in response. With no hint of hesitation or uncertainty, she says, "I've been thinking about that kiss. What happened between us. And I think I'd like it to happen again, but I want more this time."

A groan escapes my lips. Because what she's suggesting is going to be my fucking downfall. "Yulian—"

"Yulian is not here," she interrupts. "And it's none of his business what we do, anyhow."

"I think Yulian would find it very much his business what happens between us, but fuck ..." I trail off. I'm not made of granite, and I've been on my knees for Aly since our first encounter. I haven't so much as touched another woman, the taste of her still branded on my lips.

"I'm not asking for a happily ever after or anything. I just want you to ... to teach me." She raises her eyebrows, looking at me to fill in the blanks.

"Teach you ...?" She's not saying what I think she's saying, is she? "I need you to say the words."

She reddens slightly but still manages to get the words out. "I want you to be my first time. I want you to teach me. Show me what I'm missing." Her eyes dart over to the bodies writhing in the pool, her half-lidded gaze a silent challenge. "Or maybe I can find a hot manwhore who'd be willing to—"

"Fuck no." Protectiveness wells up inside of me. Coming to my senses, I stand up and grab ahold of the swing's ropes above her head. "None of those assholes are good enough for you," I say angrily. "You want to learn what feel's good, you come to me."

"That's what I'm doing." She leans back and wraps her legs around my waist, bringing my hard cock flush into her core.

Her dress rises, bunching around her waist, exposing me to the intoxicating sight of her pussy covered only by a tiny scrap of lace.

"Did you come here to seduce me?" I gather her hair in one hand and force her head back so she's looking up at me. "Because you knew you could? Because I'm weak for you?"

"I'm sick of being the good girl, the dutiful mafia daughter. I'm living my life on my terms now, no one else's. And I know what I want."

Whatever resolve I had, or thought I had in her presence, completely snaps. One hand makes contact with her bare hip while the other tugs the rope of the swing so I have her right where I want her.

Every inch of my body sings with anticipation, but it's not about me right now, it's about her. My fingertips trail down from her hip towards her inner thigh, tracing small patterns, just brushing the seam of her pussy every now and then.

She sucks in a sharp break. "Leo," her voice is tinged with desperation. "You need to touch me."

"I am touching you."

"No, like touch *touch*."

"And you need to learn patience," I say through gritted teeth. I take pity on her and allow my hand to connect with her clit, delivering a light slap. She yelps and wide accusatory eyes land on me, but as the sting fades, a look of half-lidded pleasure remains.

"Oh my god," she grits, "that was ..."

"Hot," I say, finishing that sentence for her. "Has another man ever touched you here?"

"Just fingers, that's all, but it wasn't very good. We both didn't know what we were doing."

I chuckle low in my throat. That won't be her experience with me. With my body blocking her from view, I feed one thick finger into her hole, satisfied that she's nice and slick for me. "We'll start with one finger and work you up from there."

I circle her clit with my thumb as my finger plunges inside of her. She's so ripe for the taking. I can feel how wet she is for me, her tight heat wrapped around my finger is pure heaven. I might be more experienced, but I'm barely hanging on with my dick straining against the fabric of my jeans. She releases a low moan as I work my finger in and out of her while circling her clit. Before I can suck in another breath, she opens her eyes wide and announces, "I'm close."

"What a good fucking girl," I growl against the crown of her head. "So responsive. Coming so quickly for me."

"Leo ... I need ... oh god," she grits out, because I know what she needs before she does. And I'm giving it to her.

Pushing in deeper, I work my fingers in and out of her a few times, and then I stay deep, swirling inside of her as my thumb brushes over her tight bundle of nerves, strumming out a perfect rhythm. She goes off like a Fourth of July firecracker, her pussy contracting hard around me. Her gasps turn into loud moans, and I bend down and cover her mouth with my own, swallowing her cries.

Our breaths mingle in the space between us as she drifts back to reality. Bringing my soaked fingers to my mouth, I suck her juice like it's nectar from the gods. It certainly tastes like it. Her salty tang dancing on my tongue is just a tease. I can barely wait to taste her properly, but for that, we'll need to go inside.

"Ohmygod." She barks out a surprised laugh, her cheeks flushed, her blue eyes dancing like she's made a new discovery. "I had no idea it could be like that."

I pull her off the swing and smooth down her dress. Not that anyone is paying attention to us, but Aly is mine now. Both her pleasure and her pain is mine to give or deny her.

I've always been dominant in bed, I like being in charge,

but something about Aly has awakened a primal side of me. I need her under my control. I tilt her face up so she's looking directly at me when I say, "From now on, your pretty little pussy submits for me and only me. No one else gets to touch you like I do."

She blinks but doesn't avert her gaze. "The same goes for you, then. There's no one else while we're ... doing this."

"Goes without saying. And Aly, I'm just getting started tonight." I swat at her ass under her dress, kneading her flesh.

Her eyes darken with lust. For a virgin, and an inexperienced one at that, she doesn't seem intimidated in the least. She strides towards the house, tossing a beckoning glance over her shoulder.

My laughter is husky as I trail behind her, fully aware of the dangerous game I'm playing. I'd follow this woman into the depths of hell. And who knows, maybe that's where she's leading me.

ALYONA

I had no idea how Leo would react to my request for sex lessons. Honestly, I expected more pushback, more "but think of your brother"—which, incidentally, is the last thing I feel like thinking about—but once I threatened to get my lessons elsewhere, something snapped in Leo.

And now here we are, he's leading me upstairs to his room, and I don't know exactly what happens next, but I do know I am *here for it.* I'm not the person I was six months ago. After Papa was killed, the predictable, safe world I once stupidly believed in imploded before my eyes. Good or bad, anything can happen, so why should I follow anyone's rules but my own.

I'm doing what I want when I want. And without a doubt, what I want—what I've always wanted—is the man looking at me like I'm his next meal. Kissing Leo at Papa's funeral was not enough. The memory of that kiss sustained me for the rest of my semester at school. It lit me on fire. Consumed me. And what's about to happen now, as Leo opens his bedroom door and leads me inside, is the only cure.

The air is heavy and charged, like the atmosphere before a storm, as Leo pulls me into the solid expanse of his chest. Tension ripples between us. The door closes with an audible thud behind us, leaving only the sounds of our breaths.

"Last chance to run from me." He smiles as he brushes his thumb down my cheek, swiping over my bottom lip. His brown eyes appear midnight black. "Because once we start, I'm going to consume you. I know you're a virgin, but I'm going to take you how I need you."

Moisture gathers between my legs. This is what I need from him. "I'm not running." To prove my point, I step back from him and drop the dress from my shoulders. It pools by my feet, the air cooling my skin. My bra and panties follow suit.

"You are unreal," he breathes. Leo's gaze is searing as he takes me in, like he's discovering a hidden masterpiece even though that's far from reality—my body is more straight than voluptuous, my breasts firm but small.

His lips crash down on mine, his tongue gently flicking into my open mouth. This kiss is way more erotic, way more urgent than the first time he kissed me. It's a promise of something to come. His hands come up and encircle my breasts, pinching and pulling at the nipples, making them swell and ache and stand at attention. He breaks the kiss to stand back and admire his handiwork, the pink points of each breast extending out to him like arrows.

I grab at his shirt, a silent plea for him to do something. "Why are you still dressed?" My voice comes out husky.

He chuckles and plants a kiss on my neck. "Because I like this—you, naked, hungry for my cock, desperate for me to show you how to use it. Is that what you want, Aly? To be my perfect little slut?"

His words should offend me. I should be kneeing him in the balls not salivating for him to get naked and take me any which way he wants. "Yes," is all I can manage to say.

Noticing my pleading expression, he swallows hard, dropping a tender kiss on my lips. "Alright, I can see I've teased you enough. Now ... I'm going to make you feel good, butterfly."

Butterfly? He's never called me that before, but it's warm and possessive coming from his lips. And something tells me it's a name reserved just for me. He fists my hair, tugging my head backwards so my neck is exposed to him. And with that, he inhales against my skin, breathing me in deep, before his lips trail past my collarbone, further down my body. Now he gives me what I need. Suckling my tits, using his tongue, lips, even a little teeth as he devours the right peak before doing the same on my left side.

My toes curl and my body begins to shake as Leo continues his erotic assault, back and forth, practically swallowing each breast until I am ready to lose *my ever-loving mind.*

"See, butterfly, I told you it was worth the wait. Now I'm going to eat your pussy until you come and then feed you my cock, and you're going to love every second of it."

As much as I want his mouth on my pussy—because oh god, that sounds like heaven—I also can't wait another second for him to take me. I've been anticipating this moment for so long, thinking about what it will feel like to have Leo inside of me.

Once more, I clutch at his shirt. My nipples, sharpened to

tight points, press against his firm body. "I need you inside of me. I can't wait any longer."

He glares down at me. "But you're not ready," he argues. "You need to be soft, wet—"

I bring his hand down between my thighs so he can feel how soaked I am. "I'd say this is wet enough, wouldn't you?"

He practically shakes as I squirm against his fingers. He grunts in surrender, and I hold his face, leveling our stares. "I'm ready for this. I want it more than I've ever wanted anything."

Like a dark Prince Charming, he murmurs, "Your wish is my command."

He begins to undress ... first his pants come off, revealing sculpted legs. Legs I've ogled a thousand times since he's always walking around in workout wear. But it's his upper torso that makes my pulse race. Smooth unblemished skin pulls tight over his chest. Muscular shoulders and pecs narrow to a solid, ridged abdomen. And when he sheds his boxer briefs, his eager cock glistens with beads of pre-cum at its taut head.

Holy shit.

His cock is thick and ridged, it curves against his stomach, and it's just ... What am I going to do with that!? I gulp. "I'm not sure I can handle that."

"Don't worry, baby." He smiles. "I'll make sure it fits perfectly." He uses his grip on my hand to lead it down to his cock, wrapping my fingers around his length. He shows me how to stroke him from base to head. Demonstrates the speed he likes and how hard to grip him. Once I get into the groove, he removes his hand from mine and lets me continue on my own. I can't get over how smooth he is, like silk wrapped around stone. Why is that such a turn-on?

"Like that?" I ask, finding my own rhythm, exploring the underside of his velvety hard length.

Leo's moan in my ear is one of strangled pleasure. "Ease off or I'm gonna come all over you. And while that's in the cards, I want to fuck you first." He removes my hand and fists his cock, swiping his thumb over the moisture on his tip, and then brings it up to my mouth.

"Open," he commands, and I do as he says. I wasn't sure I'd like the taste but knowing that it's Leo's essence is the ultimate turn-on. He stares at my mouth as his distinctive salty flavor lingers on my tongue.

"Are you on the pill?" he asks, dark eyes boring into mine. I nod. My mother made sure of it. She has a real hang-up with the idea of me getting pregnant before marriage. "I'm clean. I've never fucked without a condom. Ever. But I don't want a barrier with you. I need to feel your bare pussy squeezing me."

My thighs clench, his dirty talk is beyond arousing. And then I say something I didn't realize I wanted until the words are out of my mouth. "I want to watch. I want to see you take me."

His pupils dilate, and a visible shiver courses through him. He's still for what seems like an eternity. Then a wolfish smile grows on his perfect lips. "You dirty, dirty girl. I had no idea you were capable of being such a vixen. But now that I know, I'm going to take full advantage."

Just like that, he has my hands restrained behind my back in his grip, as he leads me to his bed. It's big with crisp gray sheets and smells like Leo, a spicy scent I can't put my finger on, but I'm sure if I found a way to bottle it I could sell it to horny ladies everywhere. Men too.

He sits on the edge of his bed and positions me on his lap facing outward towards a large mirror affixed to the door of his closet. His hulking body cradles mine, my back to his chest, his arms wrapped around my middle. He positions his legs between mine, so my inner thighs are draped over his firm outer thighs. When I look up into the mirror, I'm spread wide, completely exposed to his reverent gaze. "This is the most perfect pussy I've ever set my eyes on. Stunning."

My face flushes as he rubs my clit in slow, sure circles. Fighting to keep my eyes from rolling up in my head, I begin to squirm in his lap. "Leo, it's too much, I can't—"

"You can," he commands, though he must take pity on me, because his fingers abandon my clit, and drop lower to my entrance. As I watch, my legs spread out as wide as they'll go, he feeds me one of his fingers. "Fuck, that's hot," he bites out, his big frame shuddering against my back. "Let's see if you can take two."

Both of our eyes are glued on the mirror, entranced, as his fingers enter me again. The stretch is unmistakable, it comes with a sharp bite of pain, but as soon as Leo's thumb swipes up over my clit, the pain morphs into something softer, something that spurs a wave of desire within me.

"Leo." I squirm on his lap, our sweaty bodies now glued together. "I'm ready."

He kisses my shoulder and adds a third finger, and oh god, the burn is real, but so is my arousal, rippling through my veins.

"You're ready," he confirms, nearly panting. "Watch closely" is his last instruction before his hands hook under each of my arms, raising me up a few inches before lowering me. I gasp as the tip of his cock lines up perfectly with my wet, swollen flesh. "This might hurt." My back flush against his chest, he slides one arm around my waist and then flexes his hips, pushing inside of me.

I cry out because there is pain, but it's tempered by the view of us joining together. He hisses, "Aly, talk to me."

But words are beyond me right now. The feel of Leo inside me is sharp and deep. It's too much and yet not enough. And having a front-row view of him filling me sends my head spinning. Leo looks even bigger in this position, not fully seated inside of me. Holding still, his labored breaths fill my ear.

"I'm good, really good," I somehow manage to say. The bite of pain between my legs has softened into a feeling of being stretched, of being full of Leo, and even though I can see the smear of red on Leo's cock, with every flick of my clit, I'm floating, the pleasure winning out over any other sensation.

"Thank fuck," he chokes before slamming me back down on his cock, impaling me fully. "Touch yourself."

I reach down and strum my clit, mesmerized by the view in the mirror of Leo buried inside me, his left hand squeezing my right breast, his other hand grasping my knee, holding on like it's the only thing stopping him from floating up into space.

"This is so fucking hot," he groans, transfixed by the sight of us joined. "You're doing so good, Aly. Taking me so fucking good. I'm going to flood your tight little pussy with my cum." His words of praise coupled with the way he's thrusting up into me is all that's needed to drag me to the point of no return. A moan slips past my lips as I start to quiver, his hand tracing a path down my body. Heat touches the hollow of my neck as he whispers against my flushed skin, "Come for me, butterfly."

Leo's hand replaces my own, circling my clit with a deftness that my fingers don't possess. Swirl, swirl, flick, rub ... I can't begin to catalog exactly what he's doing, I just know that as he thrusts upward, I have to close my eyes, and give in as waves of sensation escalate. My back arches as my climax hits, and I cry out.

"Look at me as I fill you," Leo commands. Heat pools low in my belly at the sight that meets me. He looks so big behind me, so dominant, as he pulls my hair to the side, panting against my skin before I feel him release himself inside of me. I'm desperate for all he has to give me.

Once the waves subside, I sink back against him, my body

loose, exhaustion creeping into my bones. I can't help but wince as he gently lifts me off his cock but leaves me in his lap, legs wide.

"Are you sore?" he murmurs, his sturdy arms cradling me from behind.

It's pretty obvious, so I don't bother trying to sugarcoat it. "Yes."

"Good." His eyes flash with something hot and possessive. "Look at what a mess we made." He swipes between my legs, showing me his cum mixed with my virgin blood. I don't know if I should be mortified or turned-on. Could it be possible to be a bit of both?

"I bled all over you," I say, attempting to close my legs, but his hands are in the way, holding me wide open.

"Don't you dare get embarrassed by what you just gave me." He gently swivels my face towards him, so our lips are practically touching. "Thank you, Aly. That was incredible." Fuck. He's not wrong. "I'm going to take care of you now," he promises, lifting me up into his arms.

Despite my earlier bluster, what we shared was super intense and I'm feeling vulnerable right now. But Leo doesn't allow me to spiral. He kisses my head, cradling me to his chest like I'm precious, before he lowers me onto his bed. "Rest, I'll be right back."

As I close my eyes, he disappears into the bathroom, and the sound of running water fills the room. Moments later, he's back with a glass of water, aspirin, and a warm wet cloth that he gently applies between my legs. I hiss. Without the racing hormones to distract me, fire erupts between my thighs.

Leo whispers comforting words in my ears, telling me the heat will soothe the bite of pain, which it eventually does. Moments later, he's lying beside me, and I'm gathered into his arms. "Did you enjoy your first lesson, butterfly?"

"Yes," I admit, smiling in the dark. And then I have to ask. "Why, *butterfly*? Where did that name come from?"

"Because you've reinvented yourself. Emerged from your chrysalis a whole new woman. The old Aly wouldn't have asked me for sex lessons. But this new creature, she's something else." He nuzzles into my neck, sending shivers coasting down my spine.

"I like that," I admit, my eyes feeling heavy. "Can we do this again?"

His laugh is a low rumble in my ear. "Yeah, that can be arranged."

Lulled by his heartbeat under my ear, I drift towards sleep. His fingers threading with mine is the last thing I'm aware of before I go under.

12

LEO

At 9 p.m. sharp, Alyona materializes on deck. She's breathtaking in a light-blue silk dress with a halter tie around her neck, and fuck, I'm not even convinced she's wearing a bra with the way her nipples are standing at attention through the barely there material. Her jet-black hair, styled straight, is slicked back from her face.

"You look amazing," I blurt out. "But where are the cowboy boots?" Her cowboy-chic outfit took center stage in my fantasies last night.

"They weren't all that comfortable," she responds, a shy smile playing on her lips. She runs a hand down her dress, and I notice a steady flush creeping up her neck. "You don't look too bad yourself. If you overlook those too-tight pants."

With a parting smirk, she strides down the gangplank towards the dock, and I have to take a minute to breathe, not only because of the chinos clinging to my thighs, but because watching the sway of Aly's ass is making my dick lengthen against the zipper.

Man, I really need some new clothes.

Aly however, is a different story. Given the chance, I'd happily buy her the entire yacht's wardrobe, because not a single day has passed when she hasn't looked like a queen. Then again, I am biased. She could wear a paper bag and I'd probably be bowled over.

Aly strolls towards the harbor area without looking back, knowing I'll follow her lead. And I do. There's something different about her today, a new energy I can't quite put my finger on.

Earlier, when she was in my office, she thanked me for keeping her safe. My jaw nearly dropped to the floor. This is the woman who nearly clawed my eyes out, who was throwing random shit at my head a few days ago.

And now? Well, I can't say we're the best of friends, but she doesn't seem quite as hostile. Whatever her reasons are, I'm just grateful for it.

"You gonna hurry up or what?" Her voice breaks through my thoughts. She's standing, waiting for me to catch up, on the edge of the harbor, one hand perched on her hip.

"Just enjoying the view," I tell her, a suggestive eyebrow raised. She throws me a mock scowl, but there's no sting in it. It's almost ... teasing.

We stroll past the bustling cafes and bars dotting the port area, veering towards the winding streets that head into the old town. I wouldn't dare reach for her hand, but I do offer her my arm like any gentleman would. After a moment's pause, she takes it, and we walk together, looking like any other loved-up couple on holiday.

"You've been to Lipari before?" Aly asks me.

"A few times over the years. Mostly for business. We have

connections with the Cosa Nostra in Sicily, but Kira drags me here if we can spare a day or two. There's something about this island that feels off the grid." My familiarity with Lipari has worked out in my favor; I have contacts with the best shopkeepers on the island.

Aly's lips curl into a soft smile. "I'm glad Kira forces you to take a break now and again. You've all been working so hard since your papa died. May he rest in peace."

A sick feeling crawls up my spine. Even in death, my father doesn't deserve her respect. "We've modernized the bratva," I admit. "It's not like when our fathers ran it. We've expanded the legitimate side of the business, and we use the casinos for laundering. Online is the new battlefield, and cybercrimes are my domain." I smile bitterly. "I did go into tech after all, just on the other side of the law."

My gaze flicks to her face, trying to gauge her reaction. When I was with Aly, I dreamed of being a video game designer or something else equally cool. But, of course, that was not an option for the pakhan's son.

Aly twists her head to look at me, her voice sincere. "I guess it's all worked out for you in the end. How does the expression go? All's well that ends well."

I press my lips together. "I wouldn't say that."

"No, seriously, you should be proud. If there is an organization that needs modernizing, it is the bratva. Presumably with cybercrimes, there's less violence. Or at least, I assume there is," she adds with a shrug. "I don't keep on top of bratva business."

Pride is the last thing I feel but admitting that is a confession I'm not ready to make.

Soon enough, we close in on Giuseppe's tucked-away shop. I rap twice on the door, pause, then knock twice more. It's after business hours, but he's opening as a favor for me. I didn't tell him the reason for my visit, but I think he'll be pleased by the money I'm about to drop.

How Aly will take it is another question entirely.

A moment later, the door swings open to reveal Giuseppe. He's a short man sporting an impressive white mustache that reaches down to his chin. The first time I met him, he struck me as a real-life Geppetto, the toymaker who brought Pinocchio to life.

The shop is small, and while nothing special to look at, Giuseppe is known as the finest jeweler in the region. It's not like I'm a regular client, but Kira is, and she's hauled me in here more than once. And let's just say Giuseppe has a soft spot for repeat customers with deep pockets.

Giuseppe greets me heartily, before dipping to plant a kiss on each of Aly's cheeks in true local style. He lets loose with a torrent of Italian, welcoming her to his modest shop. I bet she hasn't a clue what he's saying—I can barely keep up, and my Italian isn't half bad. But her eyes find mine, and she gives me an amused shrug.

Once Giuseppe finally gives her some space, her gaze sweeps across the room in surprise, taking in the glass-encased jewelry and displays. "I thought we were going clothes shopping? Why are we here?" she whispers.

"I had a personal shopper pick out the clothes and deliver them here earlier." I point to two massive paper bags in the corner. "But when you're passing by the finest jeweler in Southern Italy and your fiancée is without a ring, you stop by and get her one."

Her hands fall to her hips and she fixes me with a narrowed gaze. "You lured me here under false pretenses."

"Did I?" I scratch my chin, a small smile on my lips.

"I didn't agree to ring shopping. I just agreed to help you

find some damn clothes that fit. I'm sick of seeing your ass shrink-wrapped in Dad pants."

"So you admit you've been checking out my ass?"

Her lips twitch. "Don't deflect. And a ring is hardly worth the money if we only have a few more days on the yacht."

"There are no guarantees." I shrug. "The least we can do is take a look around since Giuseppe kept the shop open for us." Our gazes clash, but I'm not backing down. Even if it's fake, even if it's just for a short while, I want to see her wearing a ring I bought for her.

Finally, she leans in, jabbing a finger into my chest. Her eyes hold a naughty glint. "Remember this moment when I choose a four-carat beast."

Giuseppe takes that as his cue to step between us. Like the Italian grandfather he is, he takes Aly's cheeks between his palms, even though he has to reach up a good few inches. In Italian he asks, "Who is this lovely woman? I've never known you to have a girlfriend. You always come in here with your sister."

"She's not my girlfriend," I answer, "she's the woman I'm going to marry. My fiancée."

The smaller man claps me on the back, a grin splitting his face. "You're getting married! Congratulations are in order. She's very beautiful, I can see why she captured your heart."

"She is very beautiful," I agree, drinking in the curve of her neck, the swell of her breast, those legs that go on and on. "But she's much more than that. She's strong, beautiful, brave. I'm a lucky man." I mean every word I say.

Aly is oblivious to our conversation. Her eyes sweep over every detail of the shop. From the glass cases, brimming with glittering baubles, to the quirky wrought-iron chandelier, casting a moody light over the room.

"Perhaps you two will return to Lipari for your wedding. We will throw you a beautiful celebration here," he chuckles.

I smile to myself, picturing getting married in one of the many ancient stone churches on the island. Only our closest friends and family there. Aly walking down the aisle towards me in a simple white dress with wildflowers in her hair. Happy. Glowing. In love.

The fantasy digs a painful cavity in my chest, reminding me of all that can never be. The what-if game is a terrible thing to play.

What if I found another way?

What if I went to war?

What if, what if, what if.

But *what-if* doesn't change reality. So instead, I smile politely at Giuseppe and say, "Maybe, we will see."

At Giuseppe's urging, Alyona wanders around the shop, admiring the various rings, necklaces, and bracelets displayed, commenting on his fine designs and the quality of his craftsmanship. I do my best to translate for Giuseppe, who seems pleased just watching her wander around and gush over his creations.

After a few minutes, Giuseppe takes her left hand into his own. Murmuring to himself, he scrutinizes the slender expanse of her fingers, while Aly looks on with interest. I don't know what he is doing, but after a thorough inspection, he releases her hand, reaches into one of the cabinets and pulls out a single ring, presenting it delicately between his two fingers. "This is the one," he declares, nodding decisively.

Aly swallows visibly as Giuseppe slides a brilliant diamond solitaire onto her finger held aloft by a sleek platinum band. The cut of the diamond catches the light, a prism of colors dancing around the room. Giuseppe, confident in his selection, retreats to the back of the store, plunging us into a heavy silence.

"If you want something bigger ..." I try to make a joke of it.

"It's perfect," she says quietly, shaking her head. Her gaze remains fixed on the ring sparkling like a beacon on her finger. "But ... this is crazy Leo, this diamond is ... you can't spend this kind of money to prove a point to the yacht crew."

But it's not about the money. She knows the money is nothing for me. She's getting cold feet, because this cuts too close to the bone. Once upon a time, this is what we would have done together ... ring shop in a charming little jewelry store like this one.

Even though I can admit that this is all kinds of fucked-up, I'm still desperate to see her wearing my ring. I lean in close to her, my breath brushing her lips as I murmur, "Are you really going to tell me what I can and can't do?"

She huffs, her shoulders hitching up towards her ears. "Be reasonable," she says, but her eyes drift down to my lips and linger. The air between us crackles with intensity so volatile a single spark could ignite it.

"I'm buying it," I say with finality.

Her brows furrow, a sign that she's about to argue with me, so I do what any possessed man would do. I swoop down and capture her lips in a devouring kiss.

The kiss is a storm—violent and consuming. The moment her tongue slowly dances with mine, I am lost. I swallow up her taste, her smell, her very being, desperate for more of her. My hand moves to cup her jaw, and I flick my tongue into her mouth again, then pull back to suck on her bottom lip because I know she loves it when I do that. Her hands dig into my shoulders, and she releases a soft gasp of pleasure.

Fuck. Hearing her pleasure has my cock throbbing in response.

This is nothing like the kiss we shared a few days ago, that was for show in front of the crew. This one is pure, unfiltered desire. It's like I need her lips more than my next breath.

When she pulls away, I'm snapped back to reality. We're both breathing hard and fast, my hand still wrapped around her jaw, when I say, "You gonna argue with me some more, butterfly? Because if so, we should probably get a room."

"You're impossible," she snaps, but there's no real fight in her words. Her cheeks are flushed and as her finger traces her swollen lips, I know I've affected her. She liked that kiss. Not nearly as much as I did, though.

And my point is made—I'm buying that ring, and I want it on her finger.

Moments later, Giuseppe reappears. He doesn't bother with pleasantries; instead, he snatches Aly's hand and admires his handiwork. "Perfect for her, isn't it?" he says, absolutely sure that we feel the same way. Presenting his open palm to Aly, he looks my way to explain, "I am going to polish it and make a small alteration for fit. It'll be ready in an hour."

Then, in painstakingly slow Italian, as if addressing a child, he says to Aly, "*Congratulazioni per il tuo prossimo matrimonio.*" Congratulations on your upcoming marriage.

I'm about to translate for her when Aly leans forward and in *perfect fucking Italian* says to him, "Thank you for your hospitality. You have a lovely little shop, but sadly, Leo and I won't be coming back here for a wedding. I'm actually just using him for his body."

She punctuates her words with a wink and then, with a sway of her hips that has me swallowing hard, she saunters out of the shop.

I stand there, stunned into silence for a moment before shocked laughter rumbles in my chest.

Well played, Alyona. Well played.

Giuseppe claps me on the shoulder. "You're a lucky son of a bitch," he says before closing the door behind me.

13

ALYONA

The nightmare always starts the same. My parents are fighting, their voices angry. Sharp. They think they're whispering, but I can still hear them with my ear pressed to the door. I catch snippets. Words like, "needs to know," and "it'll only get harder."

The words swirl and echo in my brain like a bad song. Who are they talking about? They hardly ever fight, but when they do, like now, it's scary. Mama's crying and Papa's voice is all wrong. It doesn't sound like him—the Papa who gives me sweets and calls me *zaychik*, his little bunny.

Something crashes and breaks, and I jump back from the door. Mama's voice gets louder now, like she's really scared, and then something else breaks. It's too much—the yelling, the crying, the smashing stuff. I can't stand here a moment longer.

I run to my favorite place, the tree house. Crammed with dolls, books, and my silly cartoon drawings, this is where the world makes sense. The loud voices fade away, replaced by the soft rustle of leaves and the smell of worn-in wood.

My breathing eases and my body calms down. It feels safe in this place, and I get lost in my book, forgetting about the chaos I just escaped. Everything is better until the first rumble of the storm.

Lightning flashes in the sky, followed by the loud crash of thunder. The tree sways violently in the wind, and I know I shouldn't have stayed, but it's too late for me to leave now. Worst of all, nobody knows where I am. I could die out here. Alone.

I hide against the wall, but the rain sneaks in anyway. It's so icy cold, it glues my clothes to my skin. But what's scarier is the lightning. It flashes, wild and bright, followed by the intense boom of thunder.

I squeeze my dolls tight, curl into a tiny ball and rock, trying to imagine myself somewhere else. Somewhere warm, and safe, where the wind and the rain and the lightning can't reach me.

It feels like I'm here forever.

It's Yulian who finally comes for me. When he scoops me up, I'm barely awake. I manage to peek at him. His eyes look scared, too, and he's crying. His shouts for help mix with the thunder as I bury myself into his chest.

BOOM!

Jolting awake, I hastily swipe the sleep from my eyes as a cold tremor works through me. Heavy rain lashes against the windows so loud it drowns out the frightened whimper that slips from my lips. I pull a pillow over my head, hoping to hide from the storm raging outside that's reflecting the one of that memory. The nightmare is a memory triggered every time the sky rages and the wind howls and lightning streaks the sky.

Like now.

I hate this; I wish I wasn't like this. While I no longer seek refuge in closets like I did as a child, a wild storm like this still has the power to knock the wind from my lungs. My skin is cold and clammy, my eyes squeezed shut, nausea twisting my belly as I sink inwards, retreating to the place where nothing or no one can reach me.

Just as I'm slipping away, strong arms draw me tight against a warm familiar body. Like it's the most natural thing in the world—my face burrows into his chest, the thud of his heart humming in my ear. One of his hands skims over my hair and down my back, soothing me. A barrier against the chaos in my head.

"Breathe, Alyona. Just breathe. I'm here. I've got you."

I suck in air through my nostrils, counting to four silently, holding the breath for another four-count before letting it escape, and then repeating. It's a technique called box breathing, a trick my therapist taught me to combat the panic.

"Good girl," Leo murmurs. "Keep on going."

It takes three more rounds before the tremors subside, before my heart stops thudding wildly, and I find the strength to peel my eyes open. When I do, Leo's worried gaze meets mine. His forehead creases, lips pressed in a thin line as he studies me closely.

"You're okay, I've got you." His breath fans across my lips while his calloused hand draws soothing circles on the bare skin of my lower back. My terror fades with every sweep of his palm.

"You remember," I whisper, a statement not a question.

"'Course I remember. I remember everything about you." His eyes ghost over my face with a look so tender I feel like I might shatter from the inside out.

"I stopped having them for a while," I admit. "I was seeing a therapist in Paris that helped me work through my panic attacks. But once in a while, when it's storming out, the memories come back full force."

Leo goes silent for a long moment. I can't read his expression so I'm not sure what's going through his mind. "You never talked about what happened that night," he murmurs. "When you were a girl."

That night has always been difficult to discuss, but somehow, in the tranquility of the stateroom, with rain still pattering against the window, the words just spill out. "I was seven or eight, and my parents were fighting. Yelling, throwing things. It wasn't like them at all, I was so scared. My tree house was the only place I could think of to run to."

He's quiet, contemplating my words, his hand idly caressing my back. "Why were they fighting?"

"I don't know," I admit, "but it was my father who was angry, my mother was ... upset. He was mad at her for some reason. I never told my parents I ran to the tree house because of them. Some things are better left unsaid." As soon as the words leave my mouth, I realize I could be talking about Leo and me as well. But if he sees it that way, he doesn't say anything. He just continues rubbing those delicious circles on my bare skin. "Anyhow. It was a long time ago."

"Doesn't make those memories any less powerful."

"Maybe not." I sigh and slide my palms up his solid chest. This is definitely breaching the no-touching rule I established, but right now I can't find it in me to care, because his body pressed to mine is the only thing grounding me. "I just want to forget it all right now. I don't want to think about anything."

He chuckles, a sound that is low and rich. "That's funny, I haven't managed to forget a single thing about you."

"Oh," I say, licking my lips. "What exactly is it that you remember?"

His hand dips lower, settling just above my ass crack, and

oh wow, a shiver races up my spine. "How you take your coffee, your brand of toothpaste, how much you love to listen to live music." He pauses, his lips dipping to my ear. "How you like to be fucked rough the first round and sweet the second."

His words set my pulse on fire. His scent, his power, his proximity—they eclipse everything else. The storm is a distant rumble in the background, barely noticeable compared to the excitement thrumming beneath my skin. The flutter of excitement in my core. Our lips are half an inch away from each other. I could lick him without moving a muscle.

Would that be so bad?

Yes, yes it would. God, Alyona, get a fucking grip.

I attempt to wiggle out of his grasp, towards my own side of the bed, but he doesn't let me. Keeping me caged into his powerful frame, his voice is husky in my ear. "Where do you think you're going?"

"I just ... I think this may be a bad idea."

Of course it is. If I knew what was good for me, I'd push his hand away, demand he stop touching me, order him to get the hell out of this bed, just like I should have stopped that kiss earlier in Lipari.

But I don't.

Instead, I plaster my body against his, because it's too hard to resist this pull any longer.

He huffs out a laugh, a dimple forming on his left cheek. Why does he have to be so damn handsome? And shirtless. Heat emanates from his broad, half-naked torso like a furnace.

"Let me make you feel good. Let me help you feel something other than fear." The storm has died, but his fingers continue making those small hypnotic circles just below the waistband of my sleep shorts. "Do you want me to go?"

He responds to my silence by gently weaving his hand through my hair, nudging my head back so I'm looking into his eyes. Moisture floods between my legs. *Yes, please go.* "No." Why aren't my words cooperating with me?

He chokes out a curse. "Do you want me to touch you?"

I exhale a ragged breath as he gently runs the back of his hand down over my burning skin. "I ... I don't know."

"If I dip my hand between your legs, will I find you wet for me?" Without waiting for a response, he glides his hands down the length of my thighs and then palms my ass to pull me on top of him. Even through his shorts, I can feel his cock hard as steel, like a pole between us.

"Holy shit, Leo." My words spill out, hoarse and desperate, his big body spread out beneath me. Pleasure trickles down my spine as his cock swells against my core. All the tension and fear still coiled in my body could be relieved by one intense orgasm that I know first-hand he can provide.

But it's not a wise choice.

"I don't want to fuck you, I ... I still hate you," I say, desperate to put him off any way I can. Those words aren't really true anymore, though.

"You don't have to fuck me," he says, his gaze molten. "You can hate fuck my face. Grind on my tongue. Soak me in your cum. I promise it'll be just the distraction you need."

Uh, yeah it might. I used to love riding Leo's face. Almost as much as I enjoyed choking on his cock. "Did you come here because you knew I would be weak and vulnerable? Ripe for the picking?"

My words are the knife in the chest I intended them to be. He pulls away as quickly as if I burned him with fire. "Is that what you think? Because if you believe that's who I am, even for one second, I'll leave."

As a vor, he may have blood on his hands having done unspeakable things, but deep inside, I know who he is at his core. The real Leo.

"No," I answer honestly, my voice ragged.

"Then what are you waiting for?" He swats my ass. "Hop on."

Shit. Am I really going to do this?

But with the way my clit is pulsing and the wetness that has pooled at my entrance, I don't think my body is giving me a choice. I've never gone from cold fear to burning need so damn quickly, and I take that as a good sign.

Leo lies back and centers himself on the bed, his expression filled with wonder.

"This doesn't change anything between us," I warn him. "And neither does that kiss in Lipari."

"Just ride my face, butterfly. That's all you need to think about right now."

I rise to my knees, peeling my sleep camisole up over my body, and wiggling out of my sleep shorts. Leo's gaze is lit like fire, glued to me the whole time.

"Fuck, Aly, you're even more beautiful than I remember. You are fucking perfect, a goddess." Electric sparks scatter across my nerves, igniting them. I teeter on the edge, craving his words of praise and worrying that I won't ever be able to recover from them. "Now let me eat you," he growls.

But I want to savor this moment, get him as worked up for me as I am for him. Straddling him, I tilt my hips, rubbing against his clothed erection until my clit throbs and my nipples are hard as cut glass, scraping against the smattering of dark hair on his chest. Beneath me, Leo's muscles quiver, and his eyes snap shut, a needy groan leaving his lips.

I like him like this. Desperate, wanting, a beast fighting to be released from his cage. I'm just as affected, but I know if I keep this up, I'll be begging him to throw me down and fuck me into the mattress.

Which sounds like heaven, but the few brain cells I have

that are still firing remind me his cock needs to stay out of the equation. Because Leo's dick is a thing of beauty. And I don't say that lightly. It's big, thick, ridged, and more than that, he knows exactly what to do with it.

"Aly," he gasps. Sweat beads on his forehead, and arousal darkens his gaze. "Either impale yourself on my cock or impale yourself on my tongue, but you're going to need to pick one. Now."

Without further discussion, Leo seizes my hips and hauls me so I'm straddling his face. Then he gets to work. My brain barely has time to catch up before his two thumbs spread my lips wide, and his tongue delves into my folds. *Holy hell.* That tongue. It possesses magic, always has and apparently nothing has changed.

"I need more," he demands, roughly hammering my hips down so my pussy is smothering his face. His overnight stubble provides the perfect friction between my legs.

My back arches in delight. "You're still really, really good at this."

"And you still taste like fucking heaven." He reaches up to cover my breasts with his big hands, finger pinching my sensitive nipples. "Grind on me, baby. Drench me in your cum."

He rocks me forward on his face, and then his tongue is inside me, deep, fucking me like his cock would. Tasting me. Sucking and licking around the sensitive flesh, making me whimper because the feel of him beneath me couldn't be more perfect. It's so good it hurts. My cunt is swollen and needy, desperate for release.

Always so in tune with my body, Leo must sense I'm ready to go off, and just like that, he sucks my clit between his lips. *Hard.* It's too much. I grab at his hair, pulling his dark strands as my thighs tremble around his head, but I don't want to lower my full weight onto him. It would be too— *Smack*!

"Leo!" I cry out. The sharp sting of his hand on my ass still burns. "What was that for?"

"Stop holding back. Sit. On. My. Fucking. Face."

"I am!" I scream.

"Like this!" With two hands grabbing each ass cheek, he slams me down so hard I lose my bearings and fall onto his face.

I squirm in delight as he eats me like a man possessed, and it feels like seconds before my climax overwhelms me. Stars scatter across my vision as I float somewhere high above. I'm not entirely sure if Leo can breathe under me, but he doesn't push me off.

Instead, he offers gentle licks, and finally, when I give him some room, whispers of praise. "So incredibly beautiful," he says, his voice a soft murmur against my skin.

I still feel too good, floating on the high that only a delicious orgasm can offer. The best orgasm I've had in ... oh, seven years.

Once my thighs stop shaking and I regain control over my limbs, he releases me. Boneless, I tumble over to my side, still stunned by what just took place.

My gaze is drawn to the ring on my finger. Forget the orgasm—how on earth did tonight end with me wearing his ring? I quickly correct myself: his pretend ring, one for appearances' sake only. Yet, in this moment, its weight on my finger feels incredibly real, as does its significance.

Beside me, Leo's chest rises and falls with heavy breaths. He sweeps his tongue leisurely across his lips, his eyes closing as he savors the last traces of me.

My eyes drift lower to see his hard-on straining against his shorts. Whoa. I doubt he could walk comfortably without some relief. But I can't be the one to provide that.

Coming all over his face tonight was a reminder I certainly did not need. The mistake of allowing him into my bed is magnified tenfold now that the orgasmic glow has faded.

Because every man that came after Leo paled in comparison. He was my first, but he's also the only man to ever make me come. Many have tried, and all have failed.

I can't bear the thought of making small talk with him, so I close my eyes and pretend to be asleep. Maybe he'll go away and leave me to my stewing thoughts. But he doesn't go anywhere, just runs an exploratory finger up and down my arm that causes a sweet ache in my chest and the world to fade to nothing but his touch. I open my eyes a crack and catch him staring at me like he is cataloging each of my features, committing them to memory. Maybe he knows that this is a one-time deal, that I won't make the same mistake twice.

Even if the sex was incredible, us hooking up is definitely a mistake.

Turning my back to Leo, I silently dismiss him, but he doesn't seem to care. His arm, firm and strong, wraps around me as he spoons me from behind. I could just tell him to leave but ... Maybe I can just enjoy this feeling for a little while longer. But seconds turn into minutes, and I can't find it in me to move. Somehow, the warmth radiating from his body, his familiar scent, the power of my release—together, they act as a potent drug, and it's not long before I'm drifting to sleep.

Moments before I go under, I'm vaguely aware of a kiss on my forehead. A hand brushing down my cheek. And then his voice whispers in my ear, "You're still the only one. Always have been, always will be."

14

ALYONA

THE MIDDAY SUN beats down hard on my back as I lie face down on a lounge chair. A soft ocean breeze attempts to offer relief, but it's just a tease against the overwhelming heat. It's another idle day in paradise with nothing but time to get wrapped up in the thoughts swirling in my head.

Last night was unexpected.

The ring.

The sex.

Pulling me back from the edge of a panic attack.

Memories flicker into my consciousness of strong arms wrapping me from behind, the heat of his skin searing into my body. How he dragged me onto him and forced me to ride his face. The way his tongue worked my sensitive flesh, lashed over my clit, made me come so hard I may have entered another dimension.

When I woke up, he was gone. The only thing left of him was his musk on the sheets. And I may or may not have buried my head in the linen and inhaled deeply, reveling in the sweet smoky scent that is Leo's and Leo's alone.

But he hasn't made an appearance on deck today, and it's left me spinning. Are things going to be weird between us? Did I let it go too far?

I groan and bury my head in my folded arms. Three days ago, I woke up on this yacht hating him and now ... the bitterness I once felt is losing its grip. I don't know if it's because he's kept me safe or because I can still see glimpses of the old Leo, the one that cares, that I can talk to about anything.

Or because what I overheard him say to Kira ... information that I'm still grappling with. *I made the only choice I could to keep the people I love from getting hurt.* I may never know what that means, but it has thrown a wrench into my I-hate-Leo narrative. And now I'm wearing his engagement ring on my finger. A ring I adore, and one he insisted very sharply I wear.

Everything is getting messy.

When we find the shitheads who are after me, I swear I'm going to castrate each of them with rusty nail scissors for forcing me back into Leo's orbit. If it wasn't for those *mudakys,* I wouldn't be here feeling confused and vulnerable. I would be in Paris, living my perfectly pleasant, uncomplicated life.

"Hope you're wearing some sort of protection." A deep male voice disrupts my train of thought. I push up onto my elbows and slide down my sunglasses, revealing Jack standing over me. "It's hard to tell with the breeze off the water, but the sun is strong this time of day," he clarifies.

Right, sun protection. I sit up fully, adjust my bikini top, then rise from the lounge chair, uncomfortably aware of his gaze tracing my form. "Thanks for the reminder." I give Jack a tight smile. "I put it on this morning, but I'm probably due for a reapply."

A playful smirk flutters across his lips watching me reach

for the bottle of sunscreen on the small table next to my chair laden with drinks and a paperback Genevieve lent me.

"So, did your man finally show you a good time last night?"

I bristle at Jack's veiled suggestion, the implication that Leo is a shitty fiancé.

"Actually, we had an excellent evening. Leonardo took me to a jeweler friend in Lipari." With a playful flick of my wrist, I let the honking engagement ring catch the light. "I'm now an officially engaged woman."

Jack whistles and grabs my hand for a closer look at the ring. "Quite the rock you got there. You sure he isn't trying to make up for something?" He says it in a joking way, but it's annoying nonetheless.

I narrow my eyes at him. "Don't you have somewhere better to be?"

"Nah." He leans back against the railing. "I'd say I'm right where I'm supposed to be. Making myself useful." He plucks the lotion out of my hand and motions with his finger for me to spin around. "Let me help with your back."

I hesitate for a moment. I don't want Jack to get the wrong idea, but there is no one else around, and it really is near impossible to apply sunscreen to your own back, and sunburns suck so ...

"Fine," I agree, turning. "But no funny business."

He makes a *harrumph*-like sound from the back of his throat. He sweeps his hands upwards, spreading the sunscreen over my shoulders, settling into a rhythm that feels a lot more like a massage than an efficient spreading of the cream. "Where is he now? If I had a fiancée even half as hot as you, I wouldn't neglect her for one second."

I roll my eyes so hard I nearly pull a muscle. "Yeah, well, I don't see a ring on your finger. And you don't strike me as a one-woman kind of guy."

He snickers. "Yeah, maybe not. Although if you were single, I'd have to reevaluate."

"Puh-lease."

I'm about to tell him hands off when another voice slices through the air, seething with fury. "Get your filthy fucking hands off my fiancée."

Startled, I whip around so quickly the lotion bottle slips from Jack's grip, hurtling through the air. I don't know why I feel like I was doing something wrong, I wasn't, but the atmosphere is charged with very aggressive, very male energy. When I look up, I find Leo's eyes flashing dangerously, his lips drawn into a thin line.

"No bother, mate." Jack straightens to his full height and squares off with Leo. Stupid man. "I was just helping Aly with her lotion since there was no one else around to do it."

"I am fucking bothered, *mate*," Leo mimics, dark energy coming off him in waves. "I'm the only one who gets to touch her."

Leo's words of possessiveness set my teeth on edge. What right does he have over me?

Not wanting things to escalate further, I jump in between them. Jack has no idea what Leo is capable of. Hell, I have no idea what he's capable of. He was once laid-back, but years as a hardened vor means he doesn't blink at the prospect of brutality. And right now, he looks ready to murder someone. Jack in particular.

"Didn't mean anything by it, just trying to be helpful." Jack raises his hands and backs up slowly, correctly interpreting the murderous glint in Leo's eyes.

"Next time you want to be helpful, stick your finger in an electrical socket."

Jack throws a hard look over his shoulder before disappearing inside the yacht, leaving Leo and me to face off. He's vibrating with anger, but fuck him, I'm angry, too. "That was completely uncalled for. I am capable of taking care of myself. And furthermore"—I stand my ground, head tipped up, shoulders squared—"despite this ring, I'm not yours. You gave up that privilege a long time ago."

It's then I notice he's dressed in formfitting swim shorts … and that's about it. The material stretches across his muscular thighs, emphasizing every bulge and ripple of his powerful legs. But it's his upper body that makes my mouth go dry.

His broad tan shoulders and rippling biceps are on full display, along with a patchwork of scars and tattoos. A lot of them. Way more than he had before he took the oath. Ink depicting a menacing black eagle clutching a blood-red rose creeps up his neck, and over his right shoulder is a snarling wolf with piercing blue eyes emerging from a field of dark shadows, symbolizing his loyalty and ferocity.

But over his heart is a tattoo that makes my mouth go dry. A delicate butterfly, its wings adorned with vibrant hues of blue and purple, flutters gracefully. Its presence a secret language etched into his skin.

I swallow heavily. Am I the butterfly inked on his skin? It couldn't be, could it? No, of course not. I bury that thought, locking it away within the depths of my soul.

"As long as you're wearing my ring"—he thumps his chest—"you're mine to protect. I won't sit by while that mudak has his hands all over you."

We lock eyes, tension thick between us. "Why? Are you worried that I liked it? That I craved more from him?" I didn't. Jack kinda creeped me out, but after last night, Leo needs a reminder that he can't slap a ring on my finger and act like a brute.

His hand reaches out and covers my jaw, his thumb rubbing

against my bottom lip. I'll bite it if he comes any closer to my mouth. "Alyona, don't push me," he growls.

Even though I promised myself I would stop provoking Leo, I can't help it. I want to see what will happen when his perfectly composed facade drops away. "He's sexy, don't you think? In those little white shorts, all tanned muscular legs and—"

Without warning, Leo's hand is at my waist, pulling me to him as he sinks into the lounge chair. Before I know it, I'm face down, deposited over his knee. In one brutal move, he rips off my bikini bottoms, yanking them around my knees. "I warned you, Aly. I told you not to push me."

Oh, hell no. I thrash and fight him, but he's too strong. With one hand flat in the middle of my back, he has me pinned into place, and that's when he delivers one sharp slap to my ass.

Heat shoots through me so hard and fast that I have to bite my lower lip to keep from releasing a little moan. Still, this is ludicrous. He can't get away with treating me like a child. "Leo," I cry out. "If you do that again I will murde—"

Another slap, this one delivered to my other cheek. It stings, but an involuntary shudder ripples through me. "Anyone can see us," I argue, but he rains down another smack, which has me tensing and squirming in his lap. And that's when I feel it, the weight of his thickened cock pressing into my abdomen.

Like me, his breaths are coming hot and fast. Instead of anger, there's choked lust in his voice. "You deserve this, Alyona. You deserve to be punished for what you do to me. How you make me feel."

Those words should send murderous rage through my bloodstream, but I'm past that point, bent over and bare, my skin alight—all I feel is deeply turned-on. Like I might explode all over his hands if he applies pressure any lower.

This time, the words that escape my lips are a desperate plea. "Please."

He deals another smack, this time closer to the apex of my thighs, closer to where I need relief. "Is this what you need from me?" he growls.

Another smack sends a shock of pleasure to my clit. My limbs are taut with anticipation. A delicious ache spreads through my body. "More," I beg. My breasts have fallen out of my bikini top and are now rubbing against the hair on Leo's bare legs—the feeling so overwhelming it robs me of my sanity.

One hand drops between my legs, strumming a perfect rhythm over my clit, while the other administers another stinging blow. "I think this is what you really need, isn't it, butterfly? One hand delivering pleasure, the other delivering ..." *Smack*. "Pain." He adjusts me on his lap so my head is lower to the ground, and he has a perfectly level view of my throbbing cunt. "I am going to give this pussy the relief it needs, but first"—I release a strangled moan and squirm on his lap—"tell me who it belongs to."

Is he serious? Forget it. "It belongs to me," I fire back.

Smack. He braces a hand on my back as he delivers another forceful slap against my swollen clit, and I fight to keep myself steady. His two fingers push into my entrance, and the sound of my wetness fills the space between us. He keeps rubbing and teasing me—his touch unleashes a tsunami of desire that threatens to swallow me whole. When he abruptly pulls his fingers away, leaving me feeling empty, I whimper.

"Try again," Leo bites. "And this time, I want the truth, or you don't get to come."

I wish I had the strength to fight him, to say anything other than what he wants me to admit, but I'm past the point of being able to resist him. "You, Leo. You own this pussy. You are the only one—"

The words aren't even fully out of my mouth before he pinches my clit, making lights explode behind my eyes and sending a wave of pleasure coursing through my entire body. Another slap lands on my clit, lurching me forward, but this time, the mix of pain and pleasure pushes me over the edge.

I cry out, chasing the delicious high that only Leo and his evil hands can deliver.

"Fuck, baby," he groans. "That was the hottest thing I've ever seen."

The cold, hard reality snaps me back to the present. I push myself off his lap, hurriedly pulling my bikini back on. The repercussions of my reckless words hum under my skin. What have I done?

I just admitted the one thing I kept guarded from him, from the world.

That I'm still his.

Try as I might to deny it, Leo Kozlov still owns me fully and completely.

15

LEO

The whisky just doesn't burn the way I need it to. Fuck this fancy stuff with its smoky-smooth drawl, I need something with enough bite to dull the ache, and this shit isn't cutting it.

I scan the dismal array of half-empty bottles on the office bar cart. Bingo. Tucked away in the corner is a bottle of vodka coated in a thick layer of dust. It's more like a bottle of hooch, but I grab it anyhow, twist off the cap, and take a long swig, relishing the burn as it slides down my throat. Papa would turn over in his grave if he saw me now, drinking this swill straight from the bottle, splayed out on the ugly beige couch shoved into this closet of an office.

The thought makes me smile. Good. He doesn't deserve my allegiance. He doesn't deserve anything from me, but a middle finger straight in the air.

To taste her again was pure magic. To bury my face in her beautiful pussy and have her writhe on me was nearly enough for me to die a happy man. But it wasn't just about the sex. Holding her, feeling her body relax and her breathing steady during the storm was an unexpected reward. I hadn't planned for what happened next, but I sure as shit didn't avoid it when the opportunity presented itself. Because I'm a weak man when it comes to her.

I grasp the bottle tightly in my hand and take another hearty slug, the raunchy burn exactly what I was looking for. Maybe if I drink enough it'll help keep me from knocking down the door to her room and fucking her like the animal I am. Like the animal she makes me.

It took everything in me to drag my sorry ass out of her bed early this morning after spending half the night just staring at her sleeping. *Pizda.* Who have I become? A man who is so desperate for a taste that I force her to wear my ring under the flimsiest of excuses. A man who laid her over my knee and spanked her bottom red for allowing another man to touch her. A man who had no issue with making her come face down in my lap after delivering her punishment.

All of my perfectly laid plans went to hell in one jealous moment. I had planned to set work aside and spend the day with her by the pool. Instead, I let anger get the best of me, and I paid for it—after she took her orgasm on my fingers, she stormed off the deck without another word.

My phone rings in my pocket. A welcome distraction from my raging thoughts. Seeing Daniil's name on the screen, I pick up right away. "*Chto ty uznál?*" I ask, desperate to know if he has any new information.

My brother lets out a low whistle between his teeth. "Whoa. Are you into the sauce already, *brat*? Isn't it a bit early for that?"

Shit. I only speak Russian when I'm well on my way to buzzed, but right now, I don't feel the booze. Just numb, which was the point. "I'm fine," I mutter, switching back to English, determined to keep my words from slurring.

He chuckles darkly. "I'm not worried about you. I'm worried about Alyona being trapped in a confined space with you."

An irritated grunt bubbles up from my throat. "You don't have to worry about her, she holds her own better than any vor I've known."

"Yeah, I don't doubt that." Silence on the other end of the line. "But you're not just any vor, and she's not just any girl."

"Thanks for the reminder, now I assume you called for a reason?" My eyes track up to the ceiling, and I ease back on the couch, a wave of disappointment settling over me.

Daniil snorts. "You sober enough to talk business?"

Maybe. "Yes." I relinquish the bottle of vodka to the floor. An espresso and shower are what I really need, but I settle for a bottle of water from a side table. "What have you learned?"

"The man who was hired to abduct Alyona is named Alexander Luzkov, a Latvian national who moved to Moscow in his twenties. He was thrown in prison in the early 2000s for running low-level scams with the Kuznetsov Bratva." That explains the stars on his shoulders and spider webs on his knees—tattoos you only earn from hard years in the Russian prison system. "He was released from prison fifteen years ago, and that's when his trail went cold. He became a ghost, unaffiliated with any of the known bratva families. No registered bank account or digital footprint. He operated completely under the radar."

"What do you mean? Dima couldn't find anything on him?" I ask, my hands curling into fists. If our best hacker is coming up empty, it's a bad sign.

"He's still working on it but so far, nothing. The guy's identity has been wiped from the system. I've met with all our connections, no one has any idea of who he could be, which only means one thing." My jaw tenses, a sick feeling spreading from my chest outward. I know what Daniil is about to say, but I want to hear him say it anyhow. "He's protected. He's working for the highest echelon of society—oligarchs, politicians, someone who has the means to exist outside of any system."

Gangsters are powerful in Russia, but they are no match for those that work for the state. Power and money, often interchangeable, come to those with connections to the Kremlin. A shiver of dread seeps into my veins. This is more serious than I imagined. I'm haunted by the feeling that there's a piece of the puzzle we're missing. Something I'm not seeing.

"Daniil," I bark into the phone, "give me a few hours. I need time to look into this."

Because if someone important is after my Aly, they will have to get through me first.

THREE HOURS LATER, I have gone down a steep, sticky rabbit hole chasing the identity of Alexander Luzkov. We have some of the best hackers and computer nerds in our pocket, but they can't always make the connections that I can. Having grown up in the bratva, I understand the web that is criminal networks. Between my hacking skills and knowledge of organized crime networks, I can find a needle in a haystack.

Daniil is right, after leaving prison fifteen years ago, Luzkov hasn't been spotted in Russia. So the question is, who was he in prison with? Did he make a connection there that could have lured him out of the country? Slowly, I've narrowed down my search to three main suspects: a Croatian arms dealer, an Albanian enforcer, and a Russian drug dealer who has since left the country and set up a mini empire in Hungary. My Spidey sense tells me one of these men is the key to finding who Luzkov works for.

I exhale slowly and lean back in my chair. The screen before me flickers with activity, the data whizzing by in a blur as I run the information through an encryption program before sending it to Daniil and Dima.

My thoughts drift back to the encounter earlier today—Jack Martin. Something about the first mate doesn't sit right. Is he just a creep or something more? Either way, I fire off an email to Dima, asking for a comprehensive background check on him. I want every dark secret from his past unearthed.

My thoughts are disrupted by a knock on the door. "Come in," I call out.

A moment later, the door creaks open and Genevieve pokes her head in. "Sorry to interrupt." She holds up the tray in her hands. "Since you've been holed up here all day, I figured you must be hungry for dinner."

"Thank you, come in," I gesture, shifting in my chair. "You can put the tray down on the side table over there." She enters, stepping over the vodka bottle on the floor without a second look. Once the food is on the table, she straightens and asks, "Is there anything else I can do for you?"

"Actually, there is." I clear my throat. "Where is Alison now?"

"In the gym, I believe."

"Good. I need you to deliver something to our room," I say, holding up a package. My gift comes with no strings attached. I planned to give it to Aly regardless, but it can't hurt to butter her up after what happened earlier.

Genevieve takes the package from my hand and promises to deliver it straightaway, just as my cell phone rings. With the door closed firmly behind her, I answer Daniil's call. "Did you look at the information I sent?" I ask.

"Yes. That's what I called about." He releases a slow breath. "This only opens the door to more possibilities, not less. I just spoke to Andrei. He's going to meet me in Moscow. None of us are safe until we get to the bottom of this."

Relief fills me. Daniil's more than capable, but I welcome the all-hands-on-deck approach.

"*Spasiba, brat,*" I say, a rare tremor in my voice. Not that he needs my thanks, but I want him to know this means something to me. "I wish I could be there with you."

"No, you need to be looking after Aly, at least until we get ahold of Yulian." There's a strained pause at the other end of the line. With his voice pitched low, Daniil asks, "You gonna survive her?"

I tip my head in thought, it's a question I don't know the answer to. She has me all turned around. The moment I entered her flat feeling like my chest would cave in with worry, I was lost to her. Tasting her has only reawakened my addiction. "I don't know," I answer honestly. "I really don't know."

But I do know one thing. As long as we're trapped on this boat together, I'll take whatever she's willing to give me. And when this is all said and done, I'll let her go.

I've ruined her once, I won't allow myself to do it again.

16

ALYONA

Goddamn, I hate running. It's not a good sign when I voluntarily get on a treadmill and pound the pavement so to speak, trying to outrun my twisting thoughts. Beads of sweat travel down my body, pooling under my sports bra, but no matter how high I crank up the speed, my thoughts flit back to the one place I wish they wouldn't.

The fact that Leo spanked me. And I liked it. No, I loved it. I thought hate fucking his face was as good as it gets. Turns out the raw energy of being tipped over his knee and punished was way beyond anything I'd experienced before.

There must be something wrong with me. I went from furious at Leo to wet and needy in, oh, five seconds flat. I'm still trying to digest it all. Leo's jealousy. My own petty games, taunting Leo about my nonexistent attraction to Jack. The butterfly tattoo flitting above his heart, which may or may not mean a thing. All the feminism abandoning my body when he threw me over his knee, only to send me soaring like a firework.

Screw it. I slam the red button on the treadmill, coming to an abrupt stop. After guzzling water, I towel off and head back to my stateroom. Well technically, *our* stateroom. Thank the gods he knows better than to make regular appearances. Other than last night, he's slept in his office, only coming in for showers and to get his clothes.

As I enter back into the room, I notice a nondescript package lying on the bed. I tear it open, and pull out a cell phone. Although it's not mine, there's a little note stuck to the front.

I've set up a secure line. Expect a video call from Kira soon.

The note is not signed, but it's clearly from Leo. No mention of what happened earlier. But really, what is there to say? Anyhow, I'm too excited about being allowed contact with the outside world to complain.

I take a seat in the elegant armchair by the window. I only have to wait a few minutes before the video call rings and Kira's face comes into view.

"Look at you!" Kira's sweet smile brightens the entire screen, coaxing tears to my eyes. It feels like a lifetime ago since I last spoke to my friend, before my life spiraled into chaos. I hadn't fully grasped how lonely I feel, being so far removed from everyone and everything familiar. Yet seeing her now brings all my swirling emotions into sharp focus.

"Georgia, get your butt over here," Kira bellows over her shoulder at her sister-in-law and my friend. "You need to see how ... glow-y Alyona looks."

What!? I glance in the dresser mirror. I am looking rather

flushed, and I dunno, dewy, but it must be from the workout. Or maybe time spent in the sun.

"How are you? I've missed you both so much," I exclaim when Georgia's face comes into focus, her head pressed against Kira's in a contrast in colors. Georgia's raven hair to Kira's honey-blonde locks.

"We miss you, too!" Georgia croons. "Are you okay? Seriously, Aly, what is going on?"

I bite my nails, a terrible habit I dropped long ago, except when I'm stressed. Like really stressed. "I don't even know. It's been a crazy week."

"Of course, you were nearly abducted!" Kira cries. "Although kudos to you for unaliving that mudak who came after you."

A shiver blasts down my spine. "I'm still processing the trauma of that day, but honestly, there's so much else happening, my mind can barely keep up."

"Oh, you poor thing." Georgia frowns. "I can't imagine how terrifying that must have been. I hope you can at least relax now that you're safe on the yacht."

I blow out an exaggerated breath. Fuck, if she only knew. "I guess. It's a bit messed up having to pose as Leo's fiancée and all."

My two friends exchange a look. Georgia's eyebrows press together. "Sorry, what did you say?"

I shift in my seat. It almost sounds more ridiculous when I say it out loud. "It's part of our cover with the yacht's crew. We're posing as a rich, newly engaged couple." I hold up my finger with the sparkler to the camera so they can both take in the lengths that Leo is going in order to sell our story.

Kira's jaw drops. "Whoa. That ring is serious business. Is it real?"

I gulp. "Yes."

Beside Kira, Georgia looks like she's fighting a smile. "So, what's all included in this fake engagement? Hand holding? PDA? Hot al-fresco sex in the Mediterranean sun?"

My face glows with embarrassment. I didn't plan on telling my friends the details of what's going on between us, but I'm afraid my face says it all.

Kira elbows her sister-in-law with a frown. "What is wrong with you?"

"Okay, I was kidding about the sex. But seriously, what's involved in pretending you're engaged?"

I shrug, feeling oddly self-conscious. "First of all, let's be clear, this was not my idea. Second, it's nothing like that. A little hand holding here, a peck there, just so we're believable."

Memories of writhing on Leo's face surface before I push them down and force a neutral expression on my face.

Kira tilts her head to the side. "And that's not weird for you guys to be ... touching and being all lovey-dovey?"

While Kira knows all the gritty details of our tumultuous past, Georgia assumes it was a hookup that didn't pan out—a narrative I'm happy to maintain.

I clear my throat. "Not as weird as you'd think." I'm not ready to share everything that's happened between Leo and I when I can barely figure it out myself. "Anyways, what happened between Leo and I was so long ago. I barely think about him," I lie.

"If you say so," Georgia mumbles at the same time as Kira says, "Uh-huh," in a way that suggests neither is buying what I'm selling.

"Fine," I concede, sitting back in a huff. "I do think about him sometimes, but only because the sex was so good." I take a moment to brush an imaginary piece of lint off my workout pants while my friends stare back at me. When the silence gets to be too much, I add, "And maybe ... he's the only guy to ever deliver the big O."

Georgia's eyes nearly bug out of her head. "As in— Oh god, oh shit ... I'm going to—"

"Yeah, that O," I interrupt.

Both women are quiet for a moment. Stunned maybe. Georgia looks slack-jawed when she says, "Okay, this is news I was not prepared for. Aly, what the fuck? You've been with a bunch of guys after Leo, right? Is it a French-guy problem, or a Leo-has-mad-skills situation?"

Leo does have mad skills, but it's also his dominance. His dirty talk. The way he knows exactly what I need. How he gets off on my pleasure. And maybe, just maybe, it's tied to the fact that he's the first and only man to capture my heart. Try as I might to ignore it, the connection is still there.

"It's not a French-guy issue," I mumble, my cheeks reddening. I hate having to admit this. I've been with enough guys that someone else should have blown my mind. Or at least made me come. But nope. "I've dated every nationality under the sun, it's just a me-and-him thing, I guess."

Part of me hoped when I mounted Leo's face that he wouldn't be able to get me there ... but oh shit, he got me there and more. Pretty sure I skyrocketed to the moon.

"I'm not surprised," Georgia adds, raising her eyebrows. "Every time you two are in the same room, it feels like explosives are about to go off. Listen, I know you two have history, which you're both super weird about." She adds a playful eye roll for effect. "But that aside, maybe this is an opportunity to break your orgasm dry spell. I mean, you're stuck on a yacht off the coast of Italy. Enjoy yourself."

I twist his ring on my finger, hating how much I like its weight and everything that it represents. Even though I'm still annoyed at how he dealt with Jack, a small part of me found his possessiveness hot—although I'll never admit that to another person.

"You are a bad influence," I mutter, even though I've been spinning the same idea since I came on his face. Maybe hooking-up is what I need to do to get on with my life. Revive my sexy time mojo. Cause god knows it's been bleak for way too long. I'm in my twenties, I should be in my sexual prime, not feeling empty after every sexual encounter.

"Oh, there's my baby!" When I glance back at the phone, Georgia's nanny is placing her baby daughter in her lap. Anya's cherub cheeks and gummy grin immediately lighten my mood as Georgia drops a kiss on her baby's head.

"Hello, beautiful girl," I coo into the phone. "She's gotten so big. I've missed so much of her babyhood already."

"And that's why you need to move back to New York." Kira grins hopefully. "You can still have your fabulous career *and* be close to your family."

And Leo. Which I'm not sure is a good or bad thing. "I can't think of what's next," I say sadly. "I need to get through this current threat. Whatever it is. I just want this all to be over."

"We all do," Georgia agrees. "I'm sure they'll have answers soon, especially with Andrei joining Daniil in Moscow."

"He is? Leo never mentioned it."

"He only just left. Hang in there, Aly. It was so good seeing you, but I need to put this little one down for her nap."

Georgia waves before slipping off-screen, leaving Kira to stare at me. She narrows her eyes and tilts her head. "You're not just glowing from the sun, are you?"

"Seriously!?" How does she know?

"I can tell," she says, nodding sagely. "Was it good?"

"Just to be clear, we didn't have sex." I consider my words carefully because this is her brother after all. "I sat on his face." Okay. Not that carefully. My skin flushes from head to toe.

"And yeah, it was really, really good." I leave the chair I'm in and flop back onto the bed, holding the phone above me. "But I'm worried about it getting complicated." More than that, I'm terrified of being hurt again, even after seven years. "And Leo pulled a total jerk-off move today, freaking out on one of the crew members who was ... er, helping me apply sunscreen."

"Oh." Kira raises an eyebrow. "I take it this crew member was male."

"And hot," I confirm. "He was also being a total creep, but I was going to handle it before Leo got involved." I nibble on my bottom lip. "Maybe his freak out was part of our cover, but it didn't feel that way."

"He's still protective of you, Aly. And it's not about Yulian, no matter how much you tell yourself that."

I sigh loudly and stare up at the ceiling, debating if I should reveal what I heard. But I want Kira to know the truth. "You know, I overheard your conversation with Leo on the phone the other day."

Her eyes go wide. "Oh, you sneaky bitch!"

"Yeah, well, maybe he shouldn't take personal calls on speaker phone." I flash her a mock-glare. "And perhaps in the future you can avoid spilling my deepest, darkest secrets that I shared with you while under the influence of some very fine French rosé."

She cringes. "I'm sorry, I got a little carried away defending your honor. But if you heard everything, then you heard him say he was forced to end things with you."

I huff out a breath, exhaustion and overwhelm making my brain foggy. "What does that even mean?"

She shakes her head. "I think that's for you to find out."

"I don't know if I want to," I admit. "Some things are best left in the past." Leo was young when he chose the brotherhood over me. We both were. As much as I've held onto my anger like a life raft for all these years, deep down, I know that part of being young is making mistakes.

She smirks. "Georgia is right. The sex can be a distraction from all the crazy shit going down."

The problem is, Leo doesn't inspire all that much hate from me anymore. He inspires something entirely different. And it's this shift that terrifies me. It's like I'm standing on the edge of a cliff, about to fall and hoping the crash doesn't shatter me all over again.

FIFTEEN MINUTES LATER, I haven't moved from the bed. I'm still stewing in my thoughts, staring out the window at the darkening sky, still no closer to answers.

Resisting Leo is futile, I *want* him. How could I not? Sex with him is a near religious experience. I'll need to make sure it stays just sex, nothing more. I'll take what I need and then move on.

Easy. I can do that, can't I?

Who knows? But I do know one thing, I have to protect my emotions, because it's too easy for me to fall under Leo's spell. If it was just sex it would be one thing, but he has a way of seeping into my soul, and I can't afford to lose myself again.

The phone buzzing in my hand startles me. I glance down as a text flashes on the screen.

Sex God of the Seas: How was the call?

I can't help but bark out a laugh. It doesn't take a genius to figure out who the self-appointed sex god is.

Me: I'm sorry, not familiar with this number. Deleting now.

Sex God of the Seas: Another option is Salty Sea Stud.

Me: No. Just no.

Sex God of the Seas: Buccaneer of Booty? Swaggering Seaman?

Me: I am about to throw this phone overboard.

Sex God of the Seas: Ouch.

I smirk. I actually do get a kick out of his bizarre names, but I definitely don't want to encourage his massive ego.

Sex God of the Seas: So … are we good?

I think about it for a minute before typing back my response.

Me: Maybe. I require some groveling.

I've decided to let the spanking go because, well, I enjoyed it thoroughly, and I can't claim otherwise. But going crazy alpha male on Jack was irritating, even if I did provoke him.

Sex God of the Seas: I can make it up to you in another way …

Me: You're not getting out of the grovel. 🤨

Sex God of the Seas: I'm sorry for being an ass.

Sex God of the Seas: I'll back off with the alpha male posturing.

Me: And?

I find myself looking forward to what he's going to say. This is the most playful he's been the whole trip, and I'm weirdly enjoying this text banter.

Sex God of the Seas: Can I show you how sorry I am?

Tempting, but he needs to work a little harder for it.

Me: Try again.

Sex God of the Seas: Fine. I have just the thing.

Me: ?

Sex God of the Seas: It's a surprise. Tomorrow AM. Meet me on the main deck nice and early.

Me: Details?

Sex God of the Seas: Nope.

Me: Fine.

I take a deep breath, my fingers hovering over the keys. But he has to hear this.

Me: And Leo ... no more getting involved in my shit. I can handle myself.

Sex God of the Seas: I know you can. You proved yourself with just a pocketknife.

I'm still surprised at myself, if I'm honest. Never in a million years did I imagine I'd rely on Leo's training in a life-and-death situation. But when it comes down to it, he is the reason I'm not being held captive right now.

Me: I did have a good trainer.

Sex God of the Seas: It was not just fighting if I recall …

A small smile curls my lips. Yeah, his training was extensive, and it certainly wasn't just fighting.

Me: Right. Going to sleep. I'll see you tomorrow.

The little blue dots appear, and then stop. And then appear once again.

Leo: Sweet dreams, butterfly.

17

7 YEARS AGO

ALYONA

Leo stands in front of me, knife in hand, his eyes locked on my own. I wipe my hands on my thighs, trying to swallow down my nerves. "Is this really necessary?"

"You know it is," he responds, with a raised brow. I nod, but I can't tear my gaze away from the blade glinting in his grasp. I don't feel comfortable with knives, no weapons really. Even if it is just for self-defense. As I've reminded Leo a hundred times, most people don't need to learn how to defend themselves with a knife, and since I plan on living life like most people—far from the world that stole my beloved papa from me—this lesson is pointless.

But Leo insisted, and I can't say no to this man. Especially not after the last four weeks—we've barely managed to make it out of bed. If I'm going to be honest, at some point it became less about Leo teaching me, and more about us exploring. Discovering each other. Devouring each other. I had no idea sex was supposed to be like this. *All-consuming.* My girlfriends never talked about sex like it was an addiction, the best high one can imagine. But with Leo, that's what it is.

We've spent most of July living life. Doing what normal people do. Exploring Long Island on his bike, spending hours lounging on sandy beaches, the sun warming our skin, while our evenings are spent around a bonfire, wrapped up in each other and talking under the starlit sky.

Even while we're immersed in our own little world, Leo doesn't lose sight of the bigger picture. Which is why he's dragged me out of bed and down to the training room this morning. He insists that there are bad people everywhere, even outside of bratva life, and that self-defense is a necessary skill. He already insists that I keep my bedroom door shut when I'm not in my room—a precaution, he calls it—a way to spot any sign of intrusion.

I'm not crazy about the idea of knife training but I'm willing to play along if it puts his mind at ease. There's not much I wouldn't do for him.

"Ready, butterfly?" He kisses the side of my head, and my stomach flutters at his show of affection.

"As ready as I'll ever be." I roll my eyes but flash him a cheeky smile, getting into a position a few feet in front of him. Leo crouches down, his jaw held tight, his expression serious, focused. I was hoping to distract him by wearing a tiny sports bra that does amazing things for my boobs and leggings that show off every dip and curve of my ass, but I've come to learn that there is no distracting Leo when he's hell-bent on something.

And right now, he's hell-bent on teaching me how to defend myself with a knife. "First thing. You need to grip the knife firmly. Put your thumb on top of the handle for maximum control." He demonstrates for me.

I hold the switchblade away from my body, my hand trembling a little. I've never held one before, and the weight of it feels strange in my grip. But I do as he says, wrapping my fingers around the handle and positioning my thumb carefully as he watches.

"Good," he says. "Now, watch my movements closely. I'm going to show you a downward strike." He swings his knife in a smooth, fluid motion, making it look effortless, when I know it's not. "It's best used in close quarters, when your attacker is right in front of you. You aim for the head, neck, or chest—those hits will cause the most damage and give you a chance to escape." He nods at the weapon in my hand. "Now you try."

"Leo." I can't help but laugh. "This is overkill. I'm not like you or my brother. I don't live a dangerous life, and I don't plan on it. I'm not going to walk around with a switchblade in my purse."

Leo runs a hand over his face, frowning. "Sometimes danger finds you, butterfly. You know this, we've talked about it."

"But you'll be there to protect me, right?" I give him my best flirty smile, the one I know he can't resist. Except apparently, he can, because he's quick to take a step back.

"Stop right there, vixen. I know exactly what you're doing."

"Oh?" I raise an eyebrow, and bite down on my bottom lip. "How about I make you a deal? I'll take this self-defense lesson seriously, if afterwards you teach me something I actually want to learn."

He smirks. "Oh yeah, what's that?"

"How to deep throat."

His lips tighten, and his eyes flare with interest. I've given Leo blow jobs before, many blow jobs over the last couple weeks, but it's more like me tentatively exploring his cock. I've loved it, I'm pretty sure he has, too, but I want to know how to take him deep. I want him to fuck my throat. I want it to be dirty and depraved. I want to feel like his whore, not his best friend's little sister.

"So what do you say?" I urge him.

He inhales sharply, a pained look crossing over his features. "What are you doing to me?" He flicks the switchblade in his hand, open and closed, open and closed, considering my words. With a final nod of his head, he sheaths his blade and steps towards me, slanting his lips over mine. With a light flick of his tongue, he enters my mouth, driving the kiss deeper with the perfect amount of tongue. His mouth is hot and hungry, a promise of what's to come.

He pulls away, holding me close, studying my face carefully. "I've been holding back, not wanting to scare you. At least not yet."

"I know," I say. "But I want everything with you Leo." I don't even know what I am asking for, just that I crave *more* from him.

His thumb hooks into my mouth, pulling my lower lip down. "This fucking mouth," he breathes, his eyes dip to my lower lip as if he was fighting the urge to suck on it. Or bite it. "There is no more perfect vision in my mind than you choking on my cock. I hope this mouth is ready for me, butterfly." His eyebrows raise in suggestion, his fingers trail from my lips, down over my throat to rest on my collarbone.

Arousal builds in my belly, making my clit throb. Oh man, how am I going to focus on the rest of this lesson? But he's giving me what I want, so I smile at him, even as I feel a flush spread over my skin. "I'd say you've got a deal."

The rest of the lesson can't go by quickly enough. If Leo is anxious for our other lesson, he doesn't show it. He watches me carefully, offering advice and corrections as needed. "Keep your elbow in," he says, guiding my arm into a better position. "And don't forget to follow through with your strike." He's as patient and conscious as he always is about everything. So I give it my all, too.

At first, swinging the knife in the air, pretending an attacker is close to me, feels awkward, but eventually I get into the groove, my movements becoming sure and more coordinated. I may never relish the idea of fighting, but I can reluctantly admit that it is important to be able to protect myself, even in the real world.

Finally, when my limbs feel like Jell-O and I can't maintain proper form, Leo takes the knife from my hand, declaring our first lesson officially over. "You did great," he says, pulling me into a tight embrace. "You're a natural with the knife."

I can't help but puff out my chest a bit, pride warming my cheeks. "Now onto the other lesson."

Leo laughs at my eagerness, but he seems just as happy as I am to go upstairs to his room. We've had the estate practically to ourselves this summer with the pakhan, Andrei, and Yulian in Russia and Daniil partying with friends in LA. Sure, there is staff around, but they are paid to be discreet. Daniil knows of course, but my overprotective brother would flip out so it's better to keep our ... whatever this is ... quiet.

Mama is also here, but she never leaves her quarters. It's the one sore spot in this otherwise magical time. I visit her every day, but it's hard to see her wasting away. We've never been close—she's always been more concerned with status and money than raising her children—but since Papa's death, she's retreated into herself. I've done my best to help her, but it's a battle I'm losing to her demons. And it eats me up inside.

But right now, as we head up to Leo's rooms on the third floor, I refuse to think about any of this. I only want to think about Leo and what we're about to do. He makes it easy when we enter his room and he pushes me down on the bed, stripping his clothes off like they are on fire.

I prop my head up on my hand and watch him, because his body is a work of friggin' art.

"What are you waiting for, butterfly? Get naked," he demands, impatience lacing his words.

Rolling onto my back, I shoot him my best teasing glare. "I thought you could do it for me."

"If I do, say goodbye to your pretty gym clothes."

"Goodbye," I echo as he advances on me. In one brutal pull, my bra comes apart. I didn't know it was possible to rip spandex with arm strength alone, but Leo is like the Hulk when he's all horned up. This is not the first piece of clothing I've lost to his impatience.

I am particularly fond of these leggings, so I scramble out of them on my own as Leo watches, stroking his already hard cock. "Let me shower for you," he says.

"No." I pull him back towards me as I kneel on the bed. "I like it when you're a little sweaty. I like your taste." Like the ocean and the earth, it's a taste that's uniquely his.

"Oh, butterfly," he groans, "you have no idea what you do to me."

"Show me."

"Come." He motions to a pillow on the floor in front of him. "I need you kneeling here."

I get into position, my knees on the pillow, even as he stays behind me.

"Shouldn't you be in front of me?" I ask as he grabs a handful of my hair and pulls gently, so my face is upturned.

"Not for what we're about to do. Put your hands down on the floor behind you. There. Is that comfortable?"

I nod. Even though my arms are a little tired, I'm jacked up on adrenaline and so fucking turned-on I'd happily try any sexnastics position he suggested.

He's straddling me, his cock right above my face. Holy hell, this is new, but Leo gently coaxes me. "Lean your head back, that's right. See how your mouth and throat are in alignment." He runs a finger up over my throat. "It'll make taking me deep easier. Now open." He slowly lowers his cock into my open mouth, only feeding me the tip for now, but letting me play, licking the pre-cum off the head and wetting his length.

"You control how deep you take me," he says, his breaths already coming short and fast. "Just breathe through your nose, and if it ever gets too much, push me away."

I hum my assent, opening my jaw further. Letting him slide in, inch by inch, he edges his length towards the back of my throat. It's a lot, I'm not going to lie, but it's also a crazy turn-on as Leo throws his head back, muffled curse words slipping between his lips. He sounds like he's losing his shit, and I love that I'm doing this to him, that he's barely keeping himself under control because of me.

When the head of his cock finally hits the back of my throat, I freeze, my gag reflex activated. Leo stands above me still as stone. "Breathe through your nose," he urges, his voice husky. "And relax your throat."

Should I push him away? It's uncomfortable, my throat being full and my gag reflex triggered, but I really want this. For both of us.

Breathe. Relax. Breathe. Relax.

I hold him deep for about ten seconds before I have to retreat for a moment. I'm still sucking him, lavishing his beautiful cock with my lips and tongue. He's panting hard, like he's just run a marathon, and hearing him come apart like that makes me want to try again for him.

I suck him to the back of my throat. The second time is

easier. My gag reflex doesn't get triggered, and I am able to breathe more steadily, even enjoying the feeling of my mouth and throat being full of him. The third time taking him deep, I'm able to move my head a little up and down his shaft, which sets Leo off. His muscles ripple, a visible shudder coursing through his torso.

"You suck it so good, butterfly. Fuck, so good." I grasp the base of his cock with one hand as my lips close around his head. Moaning in pleasure, so he can feel the vibrations around his shaft. I continue taking him deep, my hand and mouth work in tandem, as saliva trails down my chin

It's so intense—for me, and judging by his moans and groans, for him as well—I know he's on the verge of spilling down my throat, the taste of pre-cum already filling my mouth.

"Are you going to take my cum?" Leo asks, but he already knows the answer. Like each time before, I will lap up every drop. With him, it's like an addiction. Sensing his need, I increase the tempo.

Grabbing my hair so my mouth is at the exact angle he needs, he starts thrusting, hitting the back of my throat, and then holding it there. But I swear I'm a pro now. Even though tears leak from my eyes, I don't gag, I'm able to breathe too despite my mouth being used for his pleasure.

It's so fucking hot I press my legs together to control the ache. My chest squeezes, my core thrums, and an overwhelming urge to see him undone hits me hard.

"You're so beautiful on your knees, letting me fuck your face like this." Leo is a champion dirty-talker, and he knows it turns me on as much as him. "You're such a good little whore for me, butterfly. And now you'll swallow me down. Every. Last. Drop."

His shoulders brace and his head snaps back as he floods the back of my throat. It's a lot. I try to swallow him down, but some of his release escapes from my mouth and drips down my chin.

I lift my gaze to find a cocktail of desire and amazement written across Leo's features.

"I'll never forget this sight, Aly. Not as long as I live."

Desire spreads from my core, radiating outwards like wildfire. I know he'll take care of me later, for now I just want to be in this moment with him.

Leo helps me off the floor and carries me to his bed. He sits me down, brings me a glass of water, and pulls me into his huge chest.

"Was that okay?" he asks, eyebrows knitted together in concern. "Did I hurt you?"

My throat feels a little raw, but I'm definitely not hurt. I feel ... great. "I'm fine," I assure him. "I actually really liked it. What about you?"

"I fucking loved it, Aly. I'm not even sure I have the words." He pushes me back on the bed and cradles me into his body. This is what I love about Leo, even though this is just about sex or sex lessons—or at least I think it is, we haven't defined our relationship—he still treats me like a cherished object. Like he cares.

He rubs circles on my back, leaning in to drop kisses on my neck and collarbone. A moment ago, I was desperate for release, but now I'm enjoying lying here, being close to him. Inhaling his smell, like fresh clothes and clean sweat, trying to commit it to memory.

Out of nowhere, he says, "Everyone will be home in a week."

"I know." The pakhan, Andrei and Yulian are coming home for one week to attend to business matters stateside, before returning to Russia. I tip my face up towards Leo. "Should we take a break while everyone is back home?" There're no rules against Leo and I hooking up, but since it's just that, a summer fling, there's no need to tell everyone. Especially since Yulian's probably going to freak.

"Maybe," he says sourly. "But I don't want to. Fuck, I'm not sure if I'm capable of staying away from you." He tucks a strand of hair behind my ears. "It's up to you, the ball is in your court. But we'll have to tell Yulian at some point."

I groan. "Why do we have to tell him anything?" My brother is so protective of me. As soon as Leo opens his mouth about us, it'll strain their friendship. I know it will. And Yulian will be all in my face about stuff I don't want him in my face about. "I mean, this is only a summer fling, right?"

Leo pokes me gently in the ribs. "So you're going to fuck me and dump me, butterfly? Is that how it is?"

I giggle. "Yeah, that's how it is." Leo knows I'm not looking for a boyfriend, and certainly not one that is destined to become a vor. "Anyways," I add, "You'll be taking the bratva oath in September, and I'll be ... well, I have to figure that out. But we'll both be busy."

Leo cups my cheek with his hand, studying my face as I study his strong cheekbones, piercing brown eyes, and full lips I can't get enough of. "I'd make time for this. For you," he whispers.

Heat spreads across my skin, but I know it's wishful thinking. "How can you say that? You know how it is when you join the brotherhood, especially the first few years." I pause for a moment before saying, "And you know my feelings about distancing myself from the bratva. We can't continue this once you're a sworn-in vor."

His face falls, and he slumps onto his back. "Fuck, I don't want to think about that right now. I just want to focus on you and the time we have left together."

I lean against him, basking in the little bubble we've

created. One that's starting to feel too good. If I don't cut this off at the end of the summer, I'll fall for this man. Who am I kidding? I already have. But with each day that passes, I only fall deeper.

Leo dips his head to steal a sweet kiss from my lips. "What are you thinking about?"

"I'm thinking about you," I admit, but the truth ends there. "I'm thinking that if we keep up the knife fight lessons, I'll be able to take you down in no time."

He growls, and playfully tackles me against the bed. "I'd like to see you try. And don't think you can scare me out of these lessons. Two times a week, no matter what, I'm teaching you how to defend yourself." Against my ear, he whispers, "And if you're lucky, we'll move on to more deep throating after that. You made me feel so good, butterfly. How can I return the favor?"

My thighs clench together but he pries them apart with just one hand. "Do you want my tongue first or my cock? Or maybe my cock and then my tongue ... and then my cock again?"

"Yes," I gasp, as his fingers dance over my clit. Light, playful movements. A tease.

"Yes to what?" He stares down at me as my eyes roll up in my head, pleasure radiating from my core to every limb in my body.

"Yes to everything, Leo. You know what I need," I whimper, feeling more and more desperate for him as he skims his fingertips down to my opening.

"I do, butterfly. I know exactly what you need." And with that, he replaces his fingers with his cock and sinks inside of me in one hard thrust.

"Oh. My. God," I cry out, lost in the feeling of Leo filling me up so damn perfectly I nearly weep.

"No god here, Aly, just me. Owning your pussy. Branding

it." His thrusts turn merciless, he's pounding in and out of me like his life depends on it. It's too much, too good, and I'm dragged to the edge in no time. Holy shit. I explode, my inner walls clamping down around Leo's cock, milking him so fucking hard I swear I see stars. It's a matter of seconds before his release spills inside of me, like the hot brand he promised.

As we come down from our high, I burrow my cheek in his neck and my eyelids flutter closed. Just as I'm drifting off, Leo murmurs, "I don't care where you go, or what you do in the future. You will always be mine. We're as inevitable as the planets circling the sun. And there's not a force on earth strong enough to keep me away from you."

18

ALYONA

I ARRIVE on the main deck of the yacht to find crew members bustling about, preparing for something. I'm not sure what it is yet, but I'm going to guess it has something to do with the surprise Leo has in store for me. Whatever that is.

It's another ridiculously perfect day. The sun is shining down with relentless enthusiasm, but it only makes my head pound harder. I didn't manage to sleep much last night, my anxieties on overdrive.

And the thought that's screaming the loudest—should I sleep with my ex? Not just any ex, the one that broke me.

It could either be the best or the most disastrous idea I've ever had, but I don't know if I have it in me to resist him any longer. The pull I feel towards him is like a living, breathing entity that pulses and thrums in my veins. So hot that I had to use Bob multiple times last night, hoping to work out all my pent-up sexual energy. With my eyes squeezed shut, I allowed myself to imagine what it might be like to finally give in to the overwhelming temptation to spread my legs for Leo again. It was good—really good. But I know for a fact the real thing is so much better.

I steal a croissant off the breakfast buffet and make my way towards the lounge area. It's there that Jack catches up with me, his hair messily flopped to one side, a sheepish smile on his face. "Aly, do you have a minute?" he asks, falling into step with me.

"Uh, sure." I'm uneasy around him but seeing as we're stuck on this yacht together for god knows how long, I might as well hear him out.

Jack runs his hands through his hair, nervously shifting his weight from one foot to another. "I want to apologize for yesterday. I'm a friendly guy, but I don't mean anything by it. I hope I didn't cause any friction with your fiancé."

I sigh and take off my sunglasses. He needs to hear what I'm about to say. "Jack, you seem nice enough, and I'm sure plenty of the ladies who are guests on this boat appreciate your attention. But I am not one of them."

He dips his head, a contrite gesture. "Understood, and I hope we can still be friends."

We were never friends, but I don't want to make more of this issue than necessary, so I smile and say, "Sure."

"Good, I'm glad." He's still staring at me, though, that flirty little smile ever-present on his lips. "Are you ready for today?"

"I don't even know what's happening today," I admit. I take a step back, crashing into a big hard body. Might as well be backing up into a brick wall.

"That's because it's a surprise," Leo says in my ear as one big arm wraps around my front, pulling me into him. Warmth floods my veins at his familiar touch. "Jack." Leo nods in acknowledgment. I'm grateful he's put the alphahole bullshit behind him. Maybe we could all just be civil to each other. "Everything ready?"

"'Course it is, Mr. Walker." Jack smiles a little too brightly.

"Good, we'd like to get going soon."

Jack takes the hint, backing away to do whatever the hell a first mate does.

Leo spins me around in his arms. His eyes travel over my lips and over my face, like he's trying to get a read on me. My eyelids flutter in the wake of his hot breath caressing my skin. In the brilliant sunshine, he looks like a sea warrior come to life. Maybe Sex God of the Seas is fitting.

I break the silence. "Are you going to tell me where we are going?"

His smile is mischievous. "Somewhere special."

I squint, looking past Leo at the horizon, but we're literally surrounded by water. "So mysterious. I wonder if we're going to be looking for treasure?"

Leo's lips twist to the side. "Something like that. You always loved a good adventure. I think you'll love this, too."

One of the deckhands approaches us with a smile. "Good morning. We're all ready for you," he says, leading us to the tender deck at the back of the yacht. He helps us step from the stern onto a small motorboat, but when he makes a move to join us, Leo stops him.

"I got it covered."

Concern creases the young man's features. "But do you know how to drive one of these—"

Leo's already fired up the small engine, and we're on our way before the poor guy can get his words out. A laugh peels from my throat. "Ah, there's that Kozlov charm, after all. And stupid confidence."

"How hard can it be to drive one of these things?" Leo is clearly in his element, wind whipping through his hair, handsome face turned up towards the endless sky. He's wearing nothing but tiny swim shorts and stylish shades, it's all I can do not to stare at his bronze skin. In his early twenties, he was hot, but as a grown-ass man, he's devastating.

He points to a rocky outcrop in the distance. "That's where we're headed."

"And what is that exactly?"

"A deserted island—basically a big cave with a sandy beach."

I arch an eyebrow, skeptical. "How do you know? Have you been here before?"

"Not exactly. I hacked into the University of Rome's computer system. The university uses it as a research center for geologists studying tectonic activity in the Mediterranean region. That's how I discovered it."

"Putting your hacking skills to good use, I see."

His lips tip up in amusement. "Guess you could say that."

Closer to the island, the clear blue waters shift to a darker hue, and he kills the motor, dropping a small anchor into the water below.

"We have to swim from here." With that, he grabs a waterproof sack, slings it over his shoulders, and dives in, disappearing under the water. When he emerges, he's all slick, and his smile is bright. It might be the most genuine smile I've seen on his face in years, and I swear it makes my heart stutter in my chest.

Standing, I slide the beach cover-up over my head, revealing a white string bikini that I chose for strategic reasons. Namely, to make Leo pant after me.

His eyes blaze over my skin before he says, "Hot damn, Aly. Remind me to send a thank you card to the owner of the yacht."

With a loud whoop, I jump off the side of the boat, slipping into the aqua water. If there was such a place as heaven on earth, this might be it. Hot man bobbing in the water beside me included.

"Feels good, huh?" he purrs, and a shiver travels up my spine. His body gleams, and a particular bead of water catches my eye as it traces a path down the strong column of his neck.

We swim the rest of the way to the island, the waves gently rocking us, schools of tiny multicolor fish dart around my legs, which makes me giggle. The shore is not so much a beach as a sandy, craggy entrance to a cave, surrounded by big chunks of gray rock. From his trusty pack, Leo hands me a pair of water shoes which look like a cross between sandals and football cleats. It's then that it hits me.

"There're probably bats in there," I say, my shoulders hiked up to my ears.

"Maybe," Leo responds without batting an eye.

"Seriously!? This is not what I meant when I said to grovel."

Leo throws his head back and laughs. "Still so easy to rile up, butterfly. I'm just messing with you." He clears his throat. "Bats are nocturnal anyways."

"That doesn't make me feel any better. May I suggest a visit to Prada next time you're looking for an apologetic gesture."

"Why?" Having slipped on his own water shoes, he pulls a flashlight out of the sack. "You can buy your own clothes. Hell, you're given a designer wardrobe every year. I'm giving you a life experience. Can't put a dollar amount on that."

"How do you know where I get my clothes from?" He's right. Working as a fashion buyer, I do get a little inventory from the sample sizes or even gifted some beautiful pieces. But how Leo knows anything about the world of fashion is beyond me.

"I just assumed." He shrugs. Leo is way too smart to just

assume anything—my guess is Kira fills him in on my life. That girl loves to talk. "You ready for this?" he asks.

I bite my lower lip. "As ready as one ever is to go into a dark, enclosed space with no other human around for miles and miles."

As soon as we enter the cave, darkness envelops us like a thick curtain, and the sound of the waves fades to a distant echo. Being in a damp cave that smells of musty earth is creepy, but it's also kind of cool to feel so far away from the world. Like Leo and I exist in a timeless bubble, entirely our own. I like that idea way more than I should.

Leo is ahead of me but turns and waits, holding out his hand for me to take, which I do. This is not PDA for the crew, this is ... well, I'm not sure what it is, but I also know I like the comfort of his big hand wrapped around mine. Just for today, I won't question why that is.

"Hey," he says gently, "I promise once you see the crystals you won't be thinking about anything else."

"It's okay, I kind of like it here," I admit, my fingers brushing over the rough, rocky walls as we make our way through a winding tunnel. "Feels like we can hide out from real life for a bit."

"Maybe we can," he says, his voice a low rasp. "I can be Leonardo, and you can be Alison. Newly engaged lovers head over heels for each other."

My brows shoot up to my hairline. I don't know what game he's playing here, but I am tempted to find out. I don't back down. "Sure, we can pretend," I answer. "So, honey, what's your favorite part of the trip so far?"

"I'd say the food on the yacht is top-notch. And we've had perfect weather."

"We have," I agree, playing along. "The Mediterranean is beautiful this time of year."

He stops suddenly, and I crash into his chest. He dips his mouth to my ear. "Want to know what I've enjoyed the most?" I don't know if it's the husky growl of his voice or the way I'm pressed up against him, but I swallow hard, before answering.

"What?"

"Listening to you fuck yourself with your vibrator last night."

Oh no. No, he didn't. My cheeks burn with embarrassment. "You heard that? That was ... was not for your ears."

He chuckles, and I feel it rumble in his chest. The chest I'm still pressed against. "I was passing by your door. It was impossible not to hear you." Suddenly, the cave is plunged into darkness as Leo switches off his flashlight. I feel his warm breath on my cheek, his hard body aligned with mine. "And guess what, butterfly. I fucked my hand just as desperately as you fucked your pussy. And I made sure to come with you. For old times' sake."

I'm breathless while my pulse pounds in my ears, my nipples hard as a blade, as he holds my waist. I'm one part shocked but also turned-on beyond reason. I'm not even sure how to respond, but Leo doesn't miss a beat. "Tell me, Aly, did you picture me plundering that perfect cunt? Filling you up, making you feel so good. Making you explode all over my hard cock."

With the darkness as my cloak, I'm about to admit to everything. I did come fantasizing about him taking me roughly. Multiple times. I always come thinking about him, Bob might as well have *Leo* written down its side.

But before I can say all of this, he drags me two steps forward, and with one click, his flashlight illuminates the ceiling of the cave to reveal crystal-like icicle formations hanging everywhere. My mind scrambles to catch up. "What the ...?" I gasp. It's magical, and I reach out to touch one of them, feeling the smooth, cold surface under my fingers.

"Stalactites," Leo says. "Mineral deposits formed over thousands, even millions of years."

"Beautiful," I breathe.

"I couldn't agree more," he purrs. But Leo isn't looking up, he's looking at me. His face is inches from my own, his eyes glued to my mouth. "There is one more thing ..."

"And what's that?" I rasp.

My eyes lock with his, and suddenly I can't take a full breath, I'm hanging on his every word. "Tasting you again ... The way you rode my face, drenched me with your perfection. I would gladly spend years floating at sea if that was my reward every night." He wraps his hand around my hair and pulls back, so I can't look anywhere else but at him.

My pulse races, blood drumming a fierce rhythm in my ears.

"Oh, that. I've had better." I attempt to sound casual, but my voice wavers.

He chuckles darkly in my ear. "Well, if it was just okay, I'd better try again and make it a hell of a lot more memorable." The cool air does nothing to relieve the sizzle of my skin as Leo's hand brushes from my waist down to my hip, hovering there. "Tell me you don't feel this." His words are a rough plea against my skin. "What's still between us?"

I swallow. If I tell him the truth, there is no going back. My heart will be on the line, and I'm not ready for that, am I? Instead, I say, "All I feel is your hard-on pressed into my stomach."

"That should tell you everything you need to know."

The air in the cave shifts, causing goose bumps to erupt all over my skin. He moves his hand, tracing a path from my cheek into the waves of my hair. I quiver under his touch, my resolve to keep him at arm's length melts away with just the barest of contact.

His hold tightens, pulling me towards him as a surprised gasp flies from my lips. "Is this what you want?"

If I was a stronger woman, maybe I could resist. But I can't. So I settle for negotiating. "Just for the time we're together. As soon as we're done here, we say goodbye and go back to our regular lives. No strings. No expectations of something more. Just sex."

A shadow passes over his expression, but he doesn't move. He appears not even to breathe as he considers my words. Finally, he gives me a single nod. "If that's what you want."

"It is," I insist.

"What else do you want?" Not skipping a beat, he lowers his hand, cupping me between my thighs. I melt beneath his touch, and a whimper escapes my throat. "More of what you're doing."

"One more thing I want to show you." He drags me forward until we come across a pool of water that glimmers like silver under the beam of the flashlight.

"Holy shit," I breathe, dipping my finger into the cool liquid.

With a small splash, he enters the shallow pool, the water reaching just below his hips. With one firm tug, he pulls me down to sit at the edge, my legs spread wide as his body crowds my own.

Now I get it. If you're going to have sex in a cave with only hard ridges and stone edges, this might be the most comfortable place. My mind stills for a moment. Sex? Is that what we're about to do?

I pull away from him. "Is this part of the groveling? Taking me to a deserted island and fucking me?"

A low growl rises from the depths of his throat as he leans

in to take my mouth, but I turn away, denying him my lips. Unfazed, he loops his arms under my knees, seizes my hips, and forcefully pulls me to him. The hard ground scrapes against my skin, but it only heightens the arousal buzzing in my veins.

"Who said anything about fucking? I just want to taste your pussy again. And no, this wasn't pre-planned but ..." His fingertip grazes the inner edge of my bikini bottoms, causing a shudder to run through me. "I've been thinking about you all the fucking time."

Biting down on my lip, desire washes over me. There's no way I can turn back now. Not with Leo's words echoing between us, making me feel wild and a little reckless.

A naughty grin spreads across his face. "Now, where were we?" With that, he slaps my ass, encouraging me to rise up, which allows him to slide the bikini bottoms down my legs, leaving me completely bare to his perusal. He stills for a moment, then inhales sharply. "Do you want me to taste you again, butterfly?" He runs a finger through my slit, as if testing my readiness. "Do you want me to make you come with my lips and tongue? Maybe teeth as well?"

Words are beyond me now, so I just nod. He knows I need this. I need the relief that only he is able to provide.

"This perfect cunt. Your taste has haunted me for years, Alyona. Seven fucking years." He leans down and kisses between my parted legs, it's wet and sloppy, almost as if he was kissing my mouth. When he looks up from between my legs, his lips swollen and wet, it's so obscene, I nearly spontaneously combust.

Before I've had my fill, he pulls an inch away from my desperate pussy, taunting me by blowing a feather light breath against my core. My eyes snap open. "Leo, stop teasing, just ... lick me."

"So, so needy," he taunts, before his tongue lashes out against my clit, circling my bundle of nerves.

An involuntary moan escapes me as my hips tilt toward his mouth, demanding more. He gives it to me, nipping and biting my clit, devouring me like a piece of ripe fruit. When he presses two fingers into my core, pleasure zips up my spine.

His shoulders strain with tension, and he makes a husky sound of approval as his mouth overwhelms me. "You taste like nectar from the gods, butterfly. I'll never get sick of drinking from this pussy."

Oh, shit. His words. That hot tongue. The way his fingers press into my inner thighs, holding them open. It destroys me. Shatters me like glass. All it takes is one sharp flick of my clit with his tongue, and I'm chanting his name as I come undone.

Boneless, I lift myself up on one elbow, entranced as Leo wipes his wet mouth against the back of his arm. "I want to taste myself on your lips," I gasp, because I can't think of anything more erotic than the taste of us together. A feral glint lights up his eyes, and he pulls me to him, devouring me. His tongue flicks against my own before exploring every inch of my mouth.

I don't think this is hate-fuck territory anymore. Was it ever, really?

It's something more intense. Something hotter. Something neither of us can fight; Leo's heavy breaths and look of lust suggest he's in just as deep as me. Healthy boundaries be damned. The only rational thought in my mind right now is how desperately I need this man.

19

LEO

"I NEED YOU INSIDE OF ME."

My head snaps back, unsure if I heard her correctly, but praying I did. Her blue eyes look midnight gray in the dark of the cave, just as beautiful as she looks in the pure sunlight.

"Don't tempt me unless you mean it," I rasp. "I am not a man to play with right now."

She reaches down and squeezes my already painfully hard dick—hard despite the cold water I'm standing in chilling my bones. "I mean it, I want this."

Christ, this woman. She destroyed me when she was younger; with just one look I would be hungering for her, thinking about her constantly. Now that she's all grown, matured like a fine whisky, she's even more addictive.

But there's something she needs to see first. I lower my shorts, holding my dick in my hand like I'm making an offering at the altar of Alyona. Which I suppose I am. With the low light in the cave, I'm not sure if she can see the metal glinting on the head of my penis.

"You're pierced?" She looks one part shocked, one part intrigued. "When did you get that?"

"A long time ago," I admit. When I was trying to fuck her out of mind, out of my very soul. It never worked. "It'll make you feel good," I say, as I press the hard metal ball against her swollen clit.

"Let me see it," she demands and comes closer. Heavy breaths escape her lungs as she takes in my apadravya piercing, a vertical barbell through the head of my dick. She's quiet for a moment, and I worry that she's turned off. But then she says, "I've never seen one like this before."

"Have you seen many other pierced dicks?" I growl, unhappy with the thought of her handling any other cock in this world but my own.

"Well, no."

"Good." We stare at each other, the seconds feeling like minutes. "I'm going to make you come so hard, you'll forget to breathe." I drag my pierced head over her clit, circling around her entrance and then back up over her bundle of nerves.

She reaches down and replaces my hand with her own, using my cock like a toy, focusing on the spots she needs it most. And fuck, it's hot. I love watching her use me to take her pleasure. But I'm also a man on the verge.

"Baby, you might want to lighten your hold, or I'm going to blow all over you." I bend down and drop a kiss on her inner thigh. "And I'd much rather come inside you."

Her lips form an O, and she drops my cock like a hot potato. A moment later, a wrinkle forms between her brows. "Do you have a condom?"

Like hell I'm using a condom with her. There will never be

a barrier between us. "No condom, but I'm clean and you're on the pill."

She swallows hard. "How do you know either of those things?"

Well fuck, I know everything about her, but it's nothing I can ever admit. "When I packed up your stuff," I say. "And aren't you clean?"

"Yes, but ..." She shakes her head a little. "Are you?"

I force down the lump in my throat and harden my resolve. "I've never gone bare with anyone but you." Random sex lost its luster for me a long time ago. One-night stands—and that's all they ever were after her—were just something I did so my cock didn't explode. It was never something I took much pleasure from. That's why I plan to enjoy the fuck out of this.

"Are we done discussing this?" I ask, pushing her legs apart to sink two fingers inside her. Her eyes roll up in her head, and she lets out a breathy moan, grinding into my hand. Aly is on the edge again; I know she is since her tight little pussy squeezes me like she's about to detonate. So I help her along by scissoring my fingers inside of her until she is mewling in need.

I could make her come like this. It would be so easy. And nothing would bring me more pleasure than watching her face as she unravels. Well, almost nothing. Which is why I remove my hand before she tumbles over the edge.

Her eyes fly open, and she looks at me like I just stole her favorite toy.

"If you're going to come, it's going to be on my cock," I growl, my voice husky with desire. "And now we need to lose this." I loosen the strings that tie her bikini top, the material giving way as the knot comes undone.

A deep, guttural sound emerges from me as I explore her breasts, thumbs tracing over her responsive nipples. She bites her lip, her head thrown back as she basks in the sensations of my rough hands on her soft skin. My teeth press together, a tension simmering in my jaw as she takes hold of my shaft and slides my pierced head along her slit. I don't know how I'm going to hold out for more than a few thrusts. Because to feel Aly from the inside is all I've dreamt about for years. For way too long.

About to explode, I grab at her hips, nearly shaking at the energy it's taking to go slow, patiently feeding her beautiful cunt the head of my pierced cock, giving her a moment to adjust to my size. And then I do her favorite thing—I wrap my hand around her throat and squeeze. Just the tiniest bit. She gasps and throws her head back.

It seems my girl still likes it rough. As tough as she is on the outside, she still wants to be dominated in bed. So I push her down, one hand pressing her back to the hard cave floor. The rocky ground below will only heighten the sensation.

With one hard thrust, I'm deep inside of her. Pushed to the hilt, the feeling so intense it's like I'm levitating. "How does it feel?" I ask, running my tongue up her throat.

"Big," she chokes.

"Good." I swallow. "You're made for me, butterfly. Your body knows how to open for me. You'll take every inch, and you'll love it. Even if you're sore for days."

She nods, her eyes a dark, hazy mass. As I begin to thrust, she clutches the edge of the pool. Just enough to keep her in place as I fuck her like a madman. Giving her everything I have to give.

"How do you make me feel this way?" she gasps. I don't have an answer, so I bend down to kiss her, savoring her perfect taste. I brush my hand over her nipples, tweaking and pulling until I don't think she can take much more. Then I attack her clit with my fingers, moving in circles, fast then slow. The pressure is hard, unrelenting—how she likes it.

I work her clit until she's moaning into my mouth, our lips pressed together but not kissing. Her breath mingles with my own as she pants. It's dirty and it's so perfect, exactly what we always brought out in each other.

When she finally breaks free to drag in a full breath, my head rolls back, and I pull out, eliciting a very unhappy moan from Aly. "Don't worry, butterfly. This is where it gets good."

"It was pretty good before." She glares up at me, perched on her elbows.

I scoop her up, bringing her into the shallow pool with me. She yelps at the cold, but in a moment, she'll understand what I'm doing. "Face the ledge," I instruct her. In front of me, she drops her hands to the rocky ledge as I grab hold of her hips, rocking her perfect ass back so she's presented to me.

"Always so fucking beautiful," I murmur, running my hand along her spine, the perfect expanse of smooth skin, now marked by small cuts and scrapes from the rocky floor. I kiss each one of them while Aly presses her ass against my still rock-hard cock. I know she's trying to coax me back inside her, but I want to take my time.

"Don't worry, baby girl, I'm going to fuck you again soon," I say. And to drive my point home, I slap her ass. Hard. She yelps, but that yelp soon turns into a low moan. "But only when I say you're ready."

As a reminder, I lean over her and bite down on the side of her neck. Again, she cries out and wriggles in my grasp, but I have her caged in, locked between my arms. I love seeing her trapped and vulnerable beneath me.

"Fuck, Leo, now," she gasps.

I give her one more love bite, this one delivered on the other side of her neck. I follow it up with a sweet kiss, my tongue soothing the hurt. And then I reach down and line my dick up with her soaked entrance. "You were always such a good slut for me. I'm going to put you in the exact position I need you in. Head down, ass up, and then I'm going to fuck you like it's our last day on earth."

Through her veil of hair, she looks back at me. The look of need on her face is so intense it blazes up my spine. I line myself up and push inside her, feeding her only my head while admiring how fucking sexy she looks bent over, ready to take everything I have to give her. The barbell on the head of my dick will stimulate her G-spot and deliver the most devastating orgasm of her life. She's in for a thrilling surprise.

"Deep breath," I say gently before slamming my cock inside of her.

"Oh fuck," she cries out, rocking forward as my hands lock around her hips to keep her upright.

"That's right, butterfly. Rest your head on your arms. I'll do the rest." Angling her hips as high as they'll go, I rest one knee on the ledge of the pool at the perfect angle to hammer that secret place inside of her.

I give her slow, hard thrusts, watching her ass jiggle every time I smack into it. Such a beautiful view; her moans music to ears. The feeling of being wrapped inside her again is like no other. I swear I could fuck her blindfolded, and I'd still know it was her. It's a form of alchemy between us. And with every thrust up, my barbell hitting its target, she claws desperately at the stone floor.

Her first orgasm hits almost immediately, as I knew it would. But this is not the one that's going to launch her into space. We're just getting warmed up. "What a good girl you are." I lean over her, allowing her a quick reprieve as I kiss up and down her spine. "You milked my cock so fucking perfectly. And now you're going to soak me in your cum."

"I can't," she sobs. "That was ... too much."

"You can and you will."

I stand up straight, notching her hips back in place. But this time, as I drive into her, I force her upper body down against the unyielding rock, knowing with every thrust, her nipples scrape on the ground. She tries to adjust her position, but I don't allow her to. "Take it," I whisper, my touch harsh, but my words meant to be soothing. "I'll make it good."

She grunts but holds herself in place. When I reach forward to trap her clit between my thumb and forefinger and squeeze, her whole body jolts as if she's been electrocuted. "Oh god, Leo."

"That's right. This is probably a good time to pray." And then I unleash myself inside of her. I can feel the tension in her body mount, the thrusts, my fingers rubbing and squeezing her clit, the way the tips of her breasts scrape on the floor. Her pussy contracts hard, hurtling me towards my own release. But I need to hold off, just long enough for—

"Oh fuck, oh fuck." Alyona bucks up, but I hold her in place, my fingernails digging into her hips. I hammer into that one spot again and again until she screams and comes around my cock, soaking me in her juice. She looks back towards me, her eyes filled with shock.

"It's okay. That was a G-spot orgasm." I reach down between us, where my cock is still flush inside her pussy, and drag my finger through her cum. Bringing it to my mouth, I lap up her taste, and it's exactly what I need to push me over the edge.

A raw energy radiates from my core, seeping into every limb, every muscle of my body before the orgasm slams into me like a tidal wave. I yell out as I release inside of her—the thought that it's Aly and there is no barrier between us makes me come so much harder. It takes minutes before I can stand upright and start to collect my thoughts.

Aly doesn't say anything, and I don't know if that's a good or bad thing. She's exhausted and overwhelmed, I imagine. When she pulls away from me and makes an attempt to crawl out of the pool, I stop her. I knew if we were ever together again, it would be intense, but I didn't expect it to be like this.

"Shh," I soothe. Turning her around to face me, I cradle her into my chest. "Are you alright?" I search her hooded eyes for a sign she's not drowning in regret.

"I don't know what happened ... I let go. It felt like I ..." She looks mortified, and I have the urge to take away all her pain. To hold her in my arms and carry her out of this cave and make it all better.

"You didn't." I nuzzle my forehead against hers. "You squirted. It happens sometimes with a G-spot orgasm, the piercing helps it along."

"Oh," she breathes. "That was ... intense."

"I know." I reach down to the cool water between us, scooping it up and using it to clean between her legs. "Just let me take care of you. Will you?" I ask, before planting a kiss on her lips.

She looks conflicted but then says, "That's not what this is. We agreed it's casual—"

"No." I cut her off. "We agreed that we have an end date. When you are safe, and this is all over, we'll part ways." I nearly choke on the words. Even though I agreed to it, uneasiness fills my gut. "But you and me, we don't do casual. While we're together I'm going to fuck you hard and make you sing, take care of you, and do all the things ..." I don't know how to finish that sentence. Do all the things I've dreamed of doing for years? I settle for, "You need."

Her mouth tightens, and she looks unsure, like she's about to agree to some life-and-death prospect. But I don't care. If I only have this short time with her, I'm not holding anything back.

"Okay," she finally agrees. "But I'm serious, Leo, this won't ever be more than sex. I won't be ..." She stops herself, biting her lip, her eyes cloud over, and it pierces my soul like a dagger.

I know exactly what she's about to say—she won't be destroyed by me again.

If she only knew.

It's a nightmare I also lived through once.

And barely survived.

"AREN'T YOU A SIGHT," I groan. Aly is in the hot tub on the back deck of our stateroom, soaking completely naked. We've only been back on the yacht for half an hour, long enough for me to check any important voice messages and grab us some food. After what I put her through, sustenance is definitely needed.

"Mmm." She sinks deeper into the bubbling water, her expression almost half-drugged. "This is exactly what I needed."

Guilt tightens my throat. I was hard on her today. Rough with her. Even though that's how she loves it—rough and dirty—I should have been more careful.

"Are you feeling a little tender?" I ask, stripping off my swimsuit and sinking into the hot water beside her.

She licks her lips and gives me a lazy grin. "A bit." She seems almost shy now, after all we just did. "I haven't been taken like that in a long time."

"Was it okay?" I run a hand down her cheek, and search

her clear blue eyes, needing to know I didn't hurt her. After seven long years, it was a struggle to control myself.

"It was a lot better than okay." She lowers down into the water and lets her eyes flutter shut. "It was ... well, fuck it. I don't want to give you a big head."

"Too late for that, baby. You know what they say, big head—"

"Big brains," she tosses out with a saucy grin.

"Something like that." With a gentle touch, I guide her face towards mine and brush my lips against hers. I never imagined I'd get a chance to be with her again, even if it is for a short time. I'll take any scraps she's willing to throw me. "So," I say breezily, "Does this mean I get to share a bed with you tonight? The couch in my office is getting mighty uncomfortable for a man of my size."

Her laugh is throaty and warm. "I guess. As long as you're not still a cover hog."

"What!? When was I ever a cover hog?" I am a total cover hog, still love to wrap myself up like a sausage roll, the only difference is now there's no one to steal the covers from. "You're telling stories." And then because I can't help it, I pull Aly onto my lap, enjoying having her close even if my cock twitches when her ass brushes against my bare skin.

"I am not. I would know, we spent enough nights wrapped up in each other." As soon as the words are out of her mouth, I sense the shift. "Anyways," she clears her throat, "are you telling me that girlfriends haven't complained about your cover stealing?"

I pause, my hand reaching out to guide her chin, demanding she meets my eyes. "There hasn't been anyone else," I say, unsure how she's going to take the news, but hey, it's the truth. "I haven't slept in the same bed as anyone since you."

She shakes her head like what I'm saying is impossible.

"How could that be? You've had no girlfriends? No one serious in your life since ...?"

Yep, and here it is. "Not since you." I stare at our hands entwined under the water. "The brotherhood is demanding, like a beast that constantly must be fed. I don't have the time or energy for a relationship." The lie sizzles between us. I could make time if I wanted to. Andrei, Daniil, and Yulian did. But I'm not interested in anyone else. Not when I had everything I could ever want and lost it because I was weak.

And yet, here I am in a Jacuzzi with the only woman I want, and the only one I can never have.

Alyona breaks contact with me, floating over to the other side of the tub and looks out towards the endless horizon. There's no beginning or end point, it's the same vista for as far as the eye can see. Much like my life. No matter what direction I look in, it's endless nothingness.

Until now.

Until Aly showed up like a streak of lightning—the empty void I've lived in is now so obvious it steals the breath from my chest.

"What's the expression ... You made your bed, now lie in it." Aly cocks her head, bobbing in the water across from me. "I hope you're happy, Leo, I really mean it. I hope your position in the brotherhood is everything you wanted." She bites the inside of her cheek, as if it's costing her to say what she's about to. "I was angry with you for a long time, but I've had a realization recently. You were young—we both were—but you were too young to make a decision like that, one that would affect all aspects of your life. I don't understand what happened, but I do forgive you."

My stomach is in knots, my breath shallow. Of all things she could say to absolutely destroy me, it's this. She forgives me when what I did was unforgivable. Self-loathing fills my gut, but I push it down. I can't stand the distance between us, so I approach her, caging her against the side of the tub.

And then I tell her the truth, one that I've kept long buried. "I don't forgive myself. I never will." Not even close. Her eyes search mine, confusion swirling in her irises. I hate that I have to be so cagey, but that's all I can say without opening Pandora's box.

"It was a long time ago, Leo. We were kids. It was barely more than a summer fling—"

"It was a lot more than a summer fling," I spit. Her breath catches when I grab her chin and force her blue eyes on me, pain etched in their depths. "And it doesn't mean that I didn't hurt you. For that, I am endlessly sorry. If I could have made a different choice ..." But there was no choice. I wasn't given a choice. I'm on perilous ground here, because she can never know that, so I veer into safer territory. "Does this mean you won't be shooting me daggers at every family event and holiday from now on?"

She snorts. "I'm sure we can be civil with each other from now on. Yulian will be relieved. He never really understood what the beef was between us. I told him you snapped all my Barbie dolls' heads off when we were kids, and I still haven't forgiven you."

If only it were that simple, I could fix everything that lies in ruins between us. But since I can't, I offer her the one thing I can. "I'm glad we were able to have this conversation. But you know what I'm really happy about, butterfly?" She raises her eyebrows, waiting for me to continue just as my hand snakes under the water, lightly brushing my fingers between her slit. "I'm really, really glad I got to fuck you again. Because you soaking my cock today will stand as one of the highlights of my life."

Despite the steaming hot water, a shiver works its way

through her. She's as affected by me as I am by her. "And I'm not done with you yet. Whatever time we have together, I want to make it count. And that means giving you so many orgasms you won't be able to walk straight."

"Jesus." She bites her lip, her eyes darkening with lust. "That piercing of yours ... is it supposed to do that?"

I bark out a laugh. "Do what? Make you squirt all over me? According to the *Kama Sutra,* this kind of piercing enhances female pleasure." A flirtatious grin dances on my lips. "And it's especially useful for G-spot orgasms."

"I thought the G-spot was a myth, like Bigfoot or a comfortable pair of high heels."

I cock an eyebrow at her suggestively. "Well, you tell me ... was that a mythical orgasm I gave you?"

She pretends to think about it. "No, I suppose that was as real as it gets." She pauses for a moment, her eyes flicking away before they meet mine again. "Why did you get the piercing?"

"After you, every encounter left me feeling empty, unfulfilled. I got the piercing to try and ... I dunno, feel something. Anything more than numb." I run a thumb over my bottom lip. "I got it at the same time I got this," I say, pointing to the butterfly hovering over my heart. She's noticed it, I know she has, despite the fact that she hasn't asked me about it. "When I realized it was all I had left of you."

Her eyebrows draw together, a frown pulling at the corners of her mouth. "Why are you telling me this?"

"Because it's true," I say simply. Maybe I'm an idiot for telling her all of this, but some weird, twisted side of me wants her to know.

She sighs and stands up. Stepping out of the Jacuzzi, she grabs a towel from the ledge and wraps herself up in it. I'm not sure if I killed the buzz we have going, but she saunters towards the bedroom and throws me a beckoning glance over her shoulder.

"You coming?" she asks. "I'm starved." I don't know if she means for food or sex, or maybe both, but it's not like she has to ask me twice, I am right behind her.

Willing to follow her to the ends of the earth.

20

ALYONA

The smell of fresh coffee and something warm, buttery, and inviting wakes me up. I can hear Leo moving around the room, but I linger for several minutes with my eyes closed, letting my mind wander.

Over the course of the last week, Leo and I have found our rhythm. It feels surprisingly normal considering we're exes living aboard a yacht posing as an engaged couple. What happens on the yacht, stays on the yacht—like our own floating Vegas.

After our time in the cave, we entered our stateroom and haven't really left. I spend my days wrapped up in Leo, lying out in the sun, splayed on his chest after a day of swimming. Our evenings are spent dining on the terrace of our stateroom—while barely dressed—before locking ourselves in the bedroom for hours and hours.

The sex is insane. I knew it would be. But it's the rest that worries me. Something feels different—a shift between us. I've tried to convince myself that with the ground rules—no feelings, nothing long term, just sex—there's no danger to me or to my heart. But the lies I tell myself are getting harder to swallow with each passing day. And the crazy thing is I'm too wrapped up in him to care.

Lost in my whirlwind thoughts, I barely register the bed dipping and Leo's big, calloused hand brushing the hair from my face. "I can tell you're awake. Your breathing has changed."

I open my eyes to find Leo's face right above mine. Goddamn, how does he manage to look so handsome first thing in the morning? He's wearing a plain white T-shirt and a pair of board shorts, and with this naturally bronzed skin, he looks like a surfer, like someone who was raised on the water rather than the streets of Brooklyn.

"Happy birthday, butterfly." He kisses me on the lips. "Did you think I would forget?"

I smile wistfully. "I almost forgot myself. It's like we've been living in a time warp." A rush of melancholy hits me, as it always does around my birthday, because my mama and papa are no longer here to enjoy it with me. I usually celebrate with Yulian and Rowan and whatever friends are willing to make the trek across the Atlantic. This birthday will be different.

"What's wrong?" Leo frowns. "Something is bothering you."

"Oh, it's ... you know, sometimes birthdays are tough." I wave a hand in front of my face, but he stops me, covering my hand with his own. "I was hoping Yulian would be back by now. It would at least be nice to hear from him."

"I get it," he murmurs, sweeping my hair back from my face. "I used to dread my birthday after Mama died. No matter how many presents I was showered with or how many other family members joined to make it special, it was never the same. Always felt like she was missing."

This man. Reaching out, he strokes my jaw with his knuckles. How does he always know the right thing to say? "Usually, I can distract myself, but sometimes it catches up with me," I admit. Rolling onto his back, he draws me into his strong chest. "I never imagined I would lose both parents before I turned twenty-five, you know?" My mother's death a few years ago was a long time coming, not that it made it any easier when she finally succumbed to liver failure. I don't want to wallow any longer, so I burrow into him and say, "Let's do something fun today."

He pushes me onto my back and leans over me, bracketing me between two strong arms. "I have some ideas. But first, for your birthday present ..." With that, he plants kisses along my neck, trailing downwards as he peels the covers from my upper body. His hands wander while his mouth focuses on my left breast. Flicking the hard point of my nipple with his tongue, he sucks it deep into his mouth, taking long pulls until I'm panting and breathless.

Just as his hand wanders below the covers, my stomach growls like a monster come to life. Leo pulls away, and I immediately feel the loss of his touch. "Food can wait, my pussy can't!" I attempt to argue.

"Other way around. Your pussy can wait for a few minutes while you eat." He narrows his eyes playfully. "Greedy girl, didn't I give you enough orgasms this week to last a lifetime?"

I smirk. "Yes but ... as you say, I'm a greedy girl." I sit up and let the covers fall away. Birthday suit for the birthday girl. Leo goes off to a side table. I hear the distinctive snap of a match being lit, and then he's walking towards me carrying a tray laden with all the things. Coffee, warm croissants and fancy pots of jam to go along with them, a selection of berries, cheese, toast, poached eggs, and smoked salmon. And a cupcake with a birthday candle in it.

"Make a wish, butterfly." He spreads out beside me propped up on an elbow.

I freeze, unsure what to wish for. Seconds pass by, and Leo doesn't miss my hesitation. He tilts his head. "Do you need some ideas?"

"No." I frown. Why is this so hard? Suddenly it comes to me.

I want you.

I want this.

I want things to go back to how they were before you broke me apart.

When I open my eyes, Leo is staring at me. "Are you going to tell me what you wished for?"

But there's no point in sharing that, so I stick to safe territory. "I wished for more orgasms."

He smirks. "Well you know what they say ..." He leans in and nips at the sensitive spot behind my ear. "Be careful what you wish for. But first ..." Leo plucks the cupcake from my hand. "Open up." I do as he says, opening my mouth and taking a bite, moaning in pleasure.

"This is delicious," I say between bites.

"I agree. Delicious." He feeds me every single bite, right up until the last morsel. When my lips wrap around the final bite of sweet goodness, I draw his finger into my mouth, sucking the chocolate residue clean off it. "Good girl," he growls. "I like to see that mouth put to good use."

I laugh and grab a pillow to toss at his head, but he's too quick and ducks out of the way. Smiling, I lean back on the bed, needing a moment to digest the hit of carbs and sugar. Just as I close my eyes, Leo's cell phone rings.

"I should take this," he murmurs, picking up the phone.

"Who is it?" I ask. Leo's selective with the phone calls he answers, so this has piqued my curiosity.

He pauses for a moment. "It's your brother. He's video calling me."

"Oh, fucking hell," I exclaim, jolting up from the bed. I'm excited about Yulian calling, but this seems like a really bad moment to see him. "You should take it. Just ... go somewhere private," I plead, acutely aware of my lack of clothing.

Leo gives me an indulgent smile. "He's going to want to speak with both of us. We should get it over with now. Together."

"No, that's a terrible idea," I yelp, frantically rummaging for something to wear while grappling with my bird's nest of hair.

"Relax, would you. He's not going to suspect anything. If that's what you're worried about."

I shoot him a death glare. That is *exactly* what I am worried about. The last thing I need is my brother thinking there's something going on between us. It would just lead to a bunch of questions I'm not prepared to answer.

I also don't need Yulian all up in my business, but it's too fucking late, because Leo has accepted the video call and is smiling into the phone. At least he moved to the sitting area, rather than sit propped up in bed.

"So, did you make a baby or what?" Leo says by way of greeting, eliciting a growl from Yulian.

"I go off the grid for two damn weeks and all hell breaks loose."

Leo, unbothered, just shrugs while I scramble to find any clothing that's neither a bikini nor a negligee. Leo catches my eyes and lifts his brow suggestively. *Argh.* I madly gesture for him to quit ogling and address my brother.

"That's right," Leo states matter-of-factly. "But your sister is safe. And by the way, you're welcome."

"*Khuy*," Yulian bites, calling Leo a dick. His way of saying thanks I suppose. "Where are you now?"

"Off the coast of Italy on a yacht. Maybe you could visit. It's quite beautiful here. Where are you?"

Yulian sighs as I locate a crumpled T-shirt and hastily pull it over my head. It'll have to do. "On a plane. I sent Rowan to the estate to be with Bianca and Georgia, and I'm heading to Russia to join the others. We need to regroup before strategizing."

Leo nods, like that plan makes perfect sense. "Good. Andrei and Daniil can fill you in on the latest developments." I get the sense that Leo is being purposefully vague because of me, and I make a mental note to press him for details. I deserve to know what's going on.

"Where is Alyona? I'd like to speak with my sister."

I straighten my T-shirt and quickly run my hands through my sex hair to flatten it out. I settle on the sofa beside Leo, making sure to keep a decent amount of space between us. "Yulian," I say, tucking my hair behind my ears. "I'm okay, don't worry."

His eyes soften the moment they land on me. "Thank fuck. When I heard ..." He doesn't finish that sentence, but I get it. I can see the worry in his eyes. "I'm so sorry I wasn't there for you, Alyona. I'll regret that—"

"Stop," I say. "I'm glad you were able to get some time with Rowan. You deserved it, and I don't want you feeling guilty for one minute." He doesn't look any less tortured, but he nods. "And thankfully, Leo was close by when it happened and was able to help."

Leo and I have never talked about why he was in Europe or how he found out about my situation, though it's pretty obvious Gianni spilled the beans. I was infuriated at the time, but I can't deny how much scarier this would all be without Leo.

More than that, his protection might be the only reason I'm still here.

Leo squeezes my thigh, as if he can hear all the wild thoughts running through my head.

"You're safe now, even if it is with this *svoloch.*" Yulian's lips curl upwards into a smile, and he leans his head back against the airplane headrest. Seeing my brother relax a little, I'm able to relax, too. Even if he is taking shots at Leo, I know there're few people in the world he trusts more. "And by the way, happy birthday, sis. I'm sorry I can't be there to celebrate with you. We'll have to throw a big fuck-off party when this is all behind us."

"Of course. I look forward to it." I offer up a weak smile. Because who knows how long it will be before this is actually behind us.

"I had no idea you could fight like that. When Andrei told me, I was so proud of you," Yulian says, referring to my abductor. "Did you take a self-defense course when you moved to Paris?"

"Something like that," I murmur, resisting the urge to look at Leo. "I had a very good teacher."

Leo's fingers start a slow drag along my inner thigh. I seize up, he wouldn't do anything while we're on a video call with my brother, would he? It's just a gentle touch, a tickle even, but it's enough that my body tightens with desire. As happy as I am to see my brother, I need to end this call, right now.

"Well, bro, as you can see, I'm alive and well. Let us know when you arrive in Moscow." My voice is a little lower, hoarse. Nothing Yulian would notice, but if Leo keeps tracing those damn circles on my inner thigh, we are going to have a problem.

"I will," he responds, eyebrows pressed together. "Leo, let's talk when I'm settled. I imagine you've been keeping an eye on the web chatter." The two men exchange a look—a whole conversation not meant for me.

"Of course. And Yulian ..." He has my brother's full attention now. "Aly is safe. I'm making sure of it. She is in good hands—you know she's like a sister to me."

What. The. Hell. I rip his hands from my inner thigh. Who touches their sister like *that*!?

Yulian's face visibly relaxes. "*My brat'ya naveki.*" We are brothers forever.

Great, we're one big happy family.

With that, the call ends, and I turn to Leo, my nostrils flaring with irritation. "I'm like a sister to you!? Of all things, why would you say that? Especially after we spent the last week—" Fucking like rabbits. Having mind-blowing sex. "In bed."

Leo's lips draw into a tight line. "I was reassuring your brother. He's worried—you know how he is with you. What was I supposed to say? I'll protect her like a boyfriend, like a lover."

"Well, no, but you didn't have to say *that*."

A muscle in his jaw flexes. "You are the one who laid out the ground rules. This is only a hookup, a short-term thing, so what does it matter?"

I huff out an irritated breath, but I don't know why I'm pushing the issue. Is it because his words made me feel like the girl who had a misplaced crush on her older brother's best friend and got burned?

But Leo's right. Yulian needed reassurance that he will keep me safe, like a brother would. I'm silly to be feeling anything but grateful towards him.

"Forget it," I insist. "I'm just feeling a bit emotional about the birthday stuff. Anyhow, I need a shower," I add, trying to keep my tone light. I don't look back at him as I head to the bathroom, and I'm relieved he doesn't follow me.

As I step into the steaming hot shower, I vow to wash his scent off me. If I could go back and erase his touch, I would, because somewhere during our time on this yacht, it's like my body forgot that it hates him, and my mind is so damn turned around, it feels like I might still love him ... which is *insane*.

I cannot still be in love with Leo.

I press my palms into my eye sockets and try to slow my racing breath. All my carefully laid plans feel like they are going off the rails. I'm hurtling towards the danger zone and have no idea how to put on the breaks.

Or even if I want to.

21

7 years ago

ALYONA

"Can you pass the bread, please," Andrei says from beside his father near the head of the table. I smile politely and pass over the basket. Across from me, Leo makes a noise of strangled pleasure, but covers it up under a cough.

Pakhan gives him a stern look. "Leonid, do you have something stuck in your throat?"

"I'm fine," Leo grits, stilling my foot with his hand under the table. But I'm only getting him back for last night, when he fingered me and demanded I come for him in the cloakroom at a fundraising gala that we all attended. Anyone could have walked in on us, making it both thrilling and terrifying, but damn, did I come hard.

Leo shoots me a look from across the table, one that says *I'm going to get you back, and it's going to be so sweet.* Since I've tortured him enough for one night, I lower my foot from his raging hard cock pressed tight against his jeans. Coming in his pants at a family dinner wouldn't be a good look.

I spear a roasted carrot with my fork as Yulian and Daniil discuss who they want to win the World Cup this year, with Andrei jumping in to offer his opinion. It's nice to have everyone home to enjoy a normal Sunday dinner, even if it's just for a short while. They all return to Russia next week. Andrei and Yulian to finish their training, and the pakhan to attend to various business matters.

From across the table, Serge Kozlov regards me while slowly chewing a piece of steak. Although my father was the right-hand man to the pakhan, the two couldn't have been more different. Serge is severe and stern, unlike my father, who was always ready with a smile. Maybe it was their contrasting dispositions that made them work well together.

"Alyona," he says in that intimidating voice of his, and I sit up straight in my seat. "I'm happy to hear you're taking time to seriously consider your options. Your future." He reaches for his wineglass before adding, "Your father would have wanted you to get a good education."

Bitterness catches in my throat at the mention of my father. His absence from my life burns deep even six months later. More so watching my mother fade away. She doesn't get out of bed some days, and when she does, it's like a ghost is in the house. The pakhan is kind to allow her to live here, though I imagine it has to do with the guilt he feels that my father took a bullet meant for him, or at least that's what Leo tells me.

In my parents' absence, no one is too focused on what I'm doing. I'm free to live outside of the bratva, which is what I want—to distance myself from this world of violence and power games, and all the stupid pointless deaths that are the result of it.

I plaster on a smile and nod politely. "Yes, I am thinking carefully about what's next for me. There are a few options I am exploring." Truthfully, while I've been accepted into several colleges, I've yet to make a decision. With my summer wholly consumed by Leo, thoughts of school and internships have been pushed to the back burner.

Serge gives me a curt nod. "And what is it that you are considering?" he asks, sitting back in his seat, intense dark eyes drinking me in.

I take a small sip of water, the cool liquid steadying my nerves. "I am interested in a career in fashion. I'm deciding between Parsons School of Design in the city or doing an internship with a designer in Paris before I commit to a two-year degree."

My eyes dart to Leo, who seems to be hanging on my every word, a frown on his lips. We haven't really talked about what happens after this summer, but there's nothing much to discuss. He'll take the oath and earn his stars, and I'll move on to the next phase of my life.

"Go to Paris, sis," Yulian says between sips of wine. "You're young and you have your whole life to live in New York. A year or two in Paris will be fun. Exactly what you need." What he means is that I need to escape the sadness that has hung over our family for the last six months. But he doesn't know that life hasn't been all sad for me. Leo is the ray of sunshine poking through the clouds. He's kept me going through the hardest period of my life.

"Yeah, maybe," I respond, shrugging. "I'm going to take a few more weeks to decide."

"No need to rush your decision," Leo grumbles, glaring at Yulian, who seems completely oblivious. "You don't even like French food anyways."

Huh? Is Leo bothered that I might be moving on soon?

Moving far away? The thought that he might see me as more than a summer fling sends a spark of excitement through me. My feelings for him have intensified too, in these last few weeks he's become my everything. The idea of leaving him behind rips at my chest, even if I know it's necessary.

"They have American food in France, idiot," Daniil snorts. "They even have McDonald's in Paris."

"What do you consider American food?" Andrei smiles, turning to Daniil. "Like french fries?"

"Nah, like Big Macs. French fries are obviously French."

Yulian rolls his eyes and fixes me with a look. "The point is food should be your last consideration. You're young, not tied down to anything or anyone, you should be experiencing life. Pursuing what you love."

"Of course, I know," I say a little too quickly. I'm distracted by the intensity coming off Leo, like a storm brewing. I give him a quick shake of my head. He's being obvious, getting all sulky like this.

"Daniil, put your phone away," Serge snaps. It's a pretty hard-and-fast rule that there are no electronics at the dinner table. Naturally, Daniil is always the one to break that rule.

"I was just looking up the McDonald's menu in France. Jeez."

The pakhan ignores him, still focused on me. "Alyona, your brother is right. Paris is a fine idea. And if that's where you choose to go, I have connections. I'll make sure you get into any school, or secure any internships you're interested in."

"Thank you, pakhan, that's very kind." But when my eyes track up to meet his, Serge's gaze is lasered on Leo, who is too busy studying me with a clouded expression.

My stomach drops. Leo is being so obvious; if he's not careful, his father will suspect something's going on between us.

He's already warned Leo against distractions before taking the oath.

Even I can admit I'm a distraction. Not just the sex. The way he sneaks out of training early so we can go on a bike ride, or the fact that we often stay up all night, talking and exploring each other. But I'm also not convinced that this is a bad thing. It's like his last taste of freedom before he takes on the heavy responsibilities of being a vor.

Leo stands abruptly, his shoulders tight as he says, "I need to take care of something. I'll be gone for a few hours."

"Leo, you haven't finished your dinner," I hiss. Storming out of the room now will make it obvious he's upset about something, which will lead to questions. But when I look around the table, our brothers are already deep into their own conversation. The only one paying attention to Leo's outburst is the pakhan.

"Go," his father directs, an icy calm coating his words, "you clearly need to blow off some steam." I don't dare steal a glance at Leo or anyone else for that matter. Instead, I focus on the food in front of me.

"What crawled up his ass?" I hear Yulian mumble to Daniil.

"Girl trouble, I bet. Dude hasn't gotten any in a while."

I swear a pea gets lodged in the back of my throat, and I start to cough, pounding on my chest. All eyes track to me as my face turns red. The pea dislodges in no time, but I still use it as an excuse to get the hell away from everyone's curious glances.

"Just need some more water," I choke out, jumping from my chair and heading to the kitchen. No one questions why I didn't just gulp the water in front of me at the table, and for that I'm grateful, because I honestly don't know what I'd say.

LEO COMES to me that night as I hoped he would. It's past midnight, but I can't sleep. I'm sitting up in bed reading, though my eyes continually dart to my phone, hoping for a text from him. I'm worried sick, wondering where he is and what's going through his head.

I've prepared myself for all possibilities. Maybe he wants to break things off with me. Or maybe he's ready to confess his feelings for me have grown stronger, and he can't ignore them anymore. I think the most-likely scenario is that he's just as lost and confused as I am, looking for answers that neither of us have.

Suddenly, the door to my room swings open, and Leo is there. His eyes immediately lock onto mine from across the room. There's a rawness about him, a vulnerability in his expression that I've never seen before.

I can tell he's been on his bike. The wind has styled his dark hair into unruly waves, and his leather jacket is slung over his shoulder.

I slide the covers off me and kneel on the bed, an invitation to step inside. Without missing a beat, he tears off his shirt, striding towards me. I follow his lead, hurriedly stripping off my tank top and sleep shorts.

"Fuck," he breathes, pushing me down flat on my back. "I need to taste your pussy right now." I get it, he needs to feel the physical connection between us. I do too.

He leans over me, dropping a trail of kisses down my body, between my breasts, over my belly, straight south until his head hovers between my spread legs. He glances up at me one final time before he hooks his arms under my thighs and spreads me wide.

"Look how wet you are," he comments, eyes glued to my

bare pussy. And then he spits directly on my clit, his warm saliva coating my sensitive flesh, bringing it to life in an entirely new way. "But now you're truly dripping."

I. Am. Dead.

He gives one slow lick from my entrance to clit, releasing a low groan of pleasure. I gasp, twitching under his firm grasp on my thighs as he goes back for a second swipe. It feels incredible as he circles my clit with his hot powerful tongue. Seriously, his tongue is like the rest of him. Big and *strong*. Made for licking pussy, not that I have past experience to compare it to, but I can't imagine anyone else being better at this.

His hands tremble as they grip my thighs, but his movements remain unhurried. Licking everywhere except where I need him the most. Doesn't he know how bad I need to come?

"Leo ... my clit," I gasp, grabbing a handful of his hair. "Suck on my clit."

He looks up at me, amusement dancing in his eyes. "Oh, is this what you need?" He gives one hard suck of my clit, and then releases it from his mouth. "That's all you get for now."

"What! Why!?" I nearly spring up, but his hands keep me firmly rooted on the bed.

Why is he teasing me like this? Is this punishment for considering moving to Paris? I mean, punishment in the best possible way, but it definitely seems like something else is fueling his actions.

He begins flicking his stiffened tongue into my hole, drilling it inside of me as if it's his cock. "Oh my god!" It feels amazing, even if I'm desperate for him to help me come.

"Look how needy you are." He chuckles. "Should I let you come? Give you the relief you're so desperate for?"

"Yes!" I raise my upper body so I can watch him. His fingers bite into my thighs, dragging my body even closer to his mouth, like he can't get enough of me. Like he needs to drink me in, lick up every last drop.

With a throaty groan, he finally sucks my bundle of nerves into his mouth. Ecstasy courses through my body as a scream rips from my throat. My back bows upward, thighs clamping down around his ears as he licks me like a madman. I twist beneath his mouth as I fall over the edge, but he doesn't let up until I'm a boneless, incoherent mess.

"Holy shit, you destroyed me." I lie panting in a heap as Leo kisses a trail from my belly, between my breasts, and over my neck and jaw. Finally, he gathers me against him as I come down from the crazy high.

"Hey, what happened tonight at dinner?" I ask softly. "It seemed like something was bothering you."

He runs his hand through his chin-length hair, like he's wrestling with his thoughts. "I don't like this. I don't like any of it."

"What?" I ask, more confused than ever. "What is it you don't like?"

"The fact that we have an expiration date. That you're going to move on, move far away from here, and my future is all laid out for me. Set in stone," he says, with a bitter edge. "I don't even get to question what I want or don't want."

I look up at him. "Who says you don't? Your father?"

He gives a derisive snort. "The entire fucking world. The son of a mob boss doesn't go straight simply because he decides to. I'm entrenched in this world, it's all I know. What would I even list on a resume? Good with guns? Twenty kills by the time I was fifteen?"

My stomach twists into an uneasy knot. I never think of Leo like that—a killer, a bad man, a mobster. But there is another side of him I don't get to see, his shadow side. Like my papa. Even though the man he presented to his family was sweet and gentle, his job required him to be a savage killer. I knew that, even if I never saw that part of him.

Still, people can change.

"Being born into a bratva family is not a life sentence," I say, running a hand over the wide expanse of his chest. "You have choices, even if your father doesn't like it. It's your life, you don't have to be sworn in at the end of the summer."

His eyes flicker up to the ceiling and stay there. I don't mean to be naive, but Leo is the third son. How can the expectation for him be the same as Andrei or Daniil?

"What would I do, anyhow?" he asks, with a deep sigh. "This is all I know."

"You've said it yourself—you're good at computers and all that techy shit. I'm sure you could do something with that, go to college for computer science or something."

He chuckles lightly. "Quite the optimist, aren't you? Little Miss Sunshine, always looking on the bright side of things."

"Are you making fun of me?" I slap his bicep. "Seriously, at least talk to your father and tell him how you feel. That you'd like to choose another way." I pause for effect. "I know it's different because I'm a girl, and I'm not the pakhan's child, but the bratva is the only life I've known, and even still, I'm walking away."

I interlace our fingers, feeling oddly hopeful. I haven't allowed myself to think much beyond the next stolen kiss or orgasm, but this makes me think maybe things could be different. Because my feelings for Leo run far deeper than a casual summer hookup. And judging by his frustration about our expiration date, maybe he feels the same way, too.

He takes my chin in his hand and kisses me. Really kisses me. I can still taste myself on his lips, and it's so damn hot. With a groan, he holds my face and winds his tongue with mine. We get lost in each other, in a perfect kiss, but before long, he pulls away, his forehead touching mine.

"I don't know what the right thing is anymore. But I know I can't let you go." His fingers press into my skin, holding me closer. "One summer, one year, one lifetime won't be enough, butterfly." My breath catches. Is he saying what I think he is? His words trigger a wave of emotion. "I've wanted you for so long, and now that I have you ... shit. I can't let you go."

I prop myself up on his chest so I'm staring into his eyes. "I feel the same. You've become my everything." We're in uncharted territory here, but there is one thing that I need to say. A point I can't be flexible on. "If you're willing to walk away from the bratva, I'll be here. We can do it together. Start fresh together."

"I know," he murmurs, his eyes dark and brooding. "I know." A shadow crosses his features like a storm rolling in. As much as I want a future with Leo, it's a big decision to turn your back on the family business. He has to make the decision for himself, not because I'm forcing his hand.

"Hey," I say, angling his face towards mine. "We don't have to figure it all out right now. You need time to think. I know this is a big choice."

He swallows heavily. "It's the story of my life. Torn between duty and what I truly want. But there is one thing I am clear about—I want you."

"And I want you," I whisper.

Wanting to distract him from whatever dark path his thoughts have ventured down, I get back up and straddle him. I'm totally naked, but his jeans are still on. "You're still my teacher, and our lessons are far from over." I grind down on his dick, loving the feel of him hardening underneath me.

His eyes meet mine and my breath falters. His gaze is charged with an intense need. Desire. All for me. Leo's strong hands encircle my waist, holding me in place as he bucks up, giving me a taste of what's to come. I give him a show. With one hand, I reach down and rub my clit; with the other, I trail a path up to my breast.

He groans, barely able to control himself. "I love watching you touch yourself, giving yourself pleasure. But if you keep doing that," he rasps, "I am going to pin you down to this mattress and fuck you like my life depends on it."

"Yes please," I say, slowly inching down his body, releasing his cock from his pants. "But first, I want to take you in my mouth."

"Fuck ye—" But he doesn't even get the full sentence out before I wrap my lips around his hard cock and nearly swallow him whole. I may be new to the whole sex thing, but I can deep throat like a demon.

And the way Leo is practically levitating off the bed, I think he agrees.

22

LEO

"Your move," Aly says, her lips tilting into a sly grin.

I squint at the chessboard, a sea breeze tousling my hair. Sunlight dances off the plastic pieces, turning them into glistening figures on a miniature battlefield. It's a massacre. My king is backed into a corner, threatened by her ruthless queen.

A queen like Aly.

A queen I'd happily bow down to.

Biting the inside of my cheek, I move a rook, a futile attempt to divert her attack. Aly's eyes flash with amusement. She takes a slow sip from her wineglass, sun reflecting off her sunglasses.

"Well," she drawls, setting her glass back onto the table with a clink. "It was a brave attempt."

The corners of her mouth curve upward as her hand hovers over the board, fingers brushing her queen with a confident touch.

I still her hand with my own. "Aren't you going to take pity on me, butterfly?"

She leans forward, interest flaring in her eyes. "What's in it for me?"

I give her a sinful smile. "I'm sure I could think of something. Maybe I can bend you over this table, and fu—"

"As fun as that sounds ..." She shrugs and moves the piece, taking out my rook. "Checkmate."

I clutch my chest. "No mercy, woman."

She sits back, lifting her wineglass in a silent toast to herself. I can't help but raise my own glass, clinking it against hers. "I'm still happy for you to bend me over the table, though."

I chuckle. "Not sure if you deserve it." Truthfully, I'm just giving her time to recover from this morning, when I got acquainted with Bob. With my hand wrapped around her long hair, I'd fucked her from behind, pushed up against the bathroom mirror. Instead of using my fingers on her clit, I had the inspired idea to bring Bob into the mix. As a wingman, he did his job just fine. She came so hard and fast, her pussy spasming around my dick so intensely, I nearly saw stars.

This is how it's been for the last few days. Getting lost in each other. The cold divide that had stretched over our time apart has dissolved, replaced by something warmer; something that's kick-starting my heart back to life. But we're living on borrowed time. Sooner than later, reality will come crashing down on us. Yulian's call a few days ago was a stark reminder.

"Why do you look so serious?" Aly teases, feigning a frown. I suspect she's already buzzed.

I wink at her. "I'm not. Just my resting bitch face."

She crumples up and throws a napkin at me. I'm just about to duck when someone beyond Aly catches my eye, prompting a real resting bitch face. Behind Aly, Jack appears on deck. He's talking with a few other crew members, but his attention keeps veering towards her, his glances not all that subtle.

An unpleasant knot forms in my gut. “Has that mudak bothered you again?” I ask, gesturing behind her with my chin.

Aly turns around. When Jack notices her looking, he has the audacity to lift a hand and wave, the insolent prick.

I return his friendly gesture with a middle-finger salute, which he pretends to not see. “Leo!” Aly hits my arm, shaking with laughter. “Leave him alone. I talked with him and made it clear I’m not interested. He’s kept his distance since.”

My jaw ticks. “Yeah, but I still don’t like the look of him. Or how he looks at you for that matter.”

“Forget him. I have. I’d much rather think about you.”

“Oh really?” I sit back and reach for my beer. “Are you thinking about my magic dick or how hot I look naked?”

“You wish.” But before she can say more, my phone dings with an incoming text. Pulling my phone from my pocket, I see Dima’s name flashing on the display.

Dima: I have the information you wanted.

And there it is. Reality comes crashing down.

I CALL Dima as soon as I enter the office.

He picks up after the fifth ring. "Apologies, boss," he pants. "I lost track of time with the punching bag." I discovered Dima when he was just a pimple-faced teenager hacking into government databases for fun. Recognizing his raw talent, I took him under my wing before he could land himself in jail.

Now, he’s more than just a hacker. He’s become a trusted lieutenant.

With a crack of my knuckles, I ask, "What do you have for me?"

"Marko Horvat. That name ring any bells?"

I pause in thought. "The Croatian arms dealer? He was one of the shitheads Alexander Lukov was locked up with."

"That's right. The two other shitheads Luzkov was in prison with are out of the picture. The Russian drug dealer was killed two months ago, and the Albanian is back behind bars. Which leaves Horvat, and he's certainly been busy," he adds with a low whistle.

"Tell me," I say, dragging my knuckles down my face.

"Days before Alyona's near-abduction, Horvat received a $20 million payment from a company called Transglobal Holdings. He's an arms dealer, sure, but this kind of money? Doesn't make sense, and his arms business has been relatively quiet of late."

The gears in my mind start spinning with all sorts of possibilities, none of them good. "And Transglobal?"

"That's the thing," Dima sighs. "Transglobal is nothing but a cover for a network of shell companies. So far, it's been impossible to figure out who is actually behind it."

The revelation makes me sit back, my throat tightening. Could Horvat be the middleman between whoever is after Aly and Luzkov, the man he hired to do the dirty work?

Figuring out the players behind Transglobal could take weeks, months even. "It'll be faster to track down Horvat and interrogate him," I say, "Find him for me."

"I have a lead. Give me a few minutes, and I'll confirm his location." Just as I'm about to disconnect, Dima adds, "One more thing. You asked me to dig into that crew member, Jack Martin."

I stiffen. I had pushed that to the back of my mind. "What about him?"

"Guy's hiding behind a fake name. Came up empty on my initial search, but once I dug deeper, I found out his real name is Jaxon Marley. Has a criminal record, but since it was before he turned eighteen, it's been expunged in Australia. I'm working on getting it, though."

"Keep on digging. I'm stuck on a yacht with this fucker, I need to know what he's hiding."

Disconnecting, I stare at the blank screen of the phone in my hand. An uneasy knot twists itself in the pit of my stomach. This revelation about Jack is fucked-up, if not entirely surprising, but he isn't my only concern right now. Getting to the bottom of who is after Aly is.

Only minutes later Dima texts:

Dima: Marko Horvat is at his estate in Dubrovnik.

He follows it up with the necessary details about Horvat's location.

Well, shit.

I smile at my dumb luck.

We aren't too far from Dubrovnik, a port city in southern Croatia on the Adriatic Sea. Tonight we'll be restocking and refueling in Bari, Italy, but if we leave just after midnight, we can be in Dubrovnik by late morning.

Satisfied, I send a message to my brothers to meet me in Dubrovnik tomorrow with the basics of what they need to know.

Settling back in my chair, a bitter taste fills my mouth. The harsh reality is once we step off this boat, my time with Aly is up. We'd agreed on that, even if I now regret it.

I barely survived walking away from her once, and the thought of doing so again feels like swallowing shards of glass. But it was part of our deal—she insisted—and I won't go back on my word. I don't know what tomorrow will bring, but Aly and I still have tonight. And I intend to make every moment count.

I pick up the house phone and call Genevieve. "What can I get for you, Mr. Walker?"

"I'm giving you and nonessential crew the night off. Go out and enjoy yourselves on my dime, but be back on the yacht by midnight. We leave for Dubrovnik shortly thereafter."

"Oh wow, thank you." Genevieve sounds beyond excited.

Other than the captain, the crew is young, most of them are in their twenties or early thirties. They work hard and deserve to play hard tonight. Just like I intend to.

23

ALYONA

THE WARMTH of the pool cradles me, my limbs splayed out like a starfish, as I float beneath the dusky Mediterranean sky. Leo had to take a call a few hours ago, and he still hasn't reappeared on deck. I'm trying not to think about what it means, but deep inside I know—he's getting closer to finding who is after me.

Our time floating in paradise is coming to an end. The realization brings a dull ache to my chest. But what did I expect? That I could spend all this time with him and not have those long-buried feelings roar to life again? Silly me. There's no such thing as casual sex where Leo is concerned. We couldn't keep it casual the first time, and it sure doesn't feel very casual now. Which is a problem.

As the saying should go, break my heart once, shame on you. Break it twice, shame on me.

Wrapped up in my thoughts, it takes me a minute to catch Leo's powerful figure standing at the edge of the pool, the setting sun casting a golden aura around him. As usual, the sight of him takes my breath away.

Lord help me, I'm a simp for this man.

"How's the water?" Leo asks, toes curling over the edge.

I take a moment to drink him in. His short hair is disheveled, like he's been constantly running his hands through it. "Perfect. Why don't you come in and see for yourself."

He rips off his clothes and dives into the water grazing my arm. "Leo," I yelp, "You got me wet." I laugh when I realize how stupid that sounds because yeah, I'm already wet. Now I'm just ... wetter.

"I plan on getting you really, really wet tonight." His arms encircle my waist, and my legs instinctively coil around his hips. Our bodies fit so well together, like ivy winding around a tree trunk. His breath warms my neck as his hands glide up my body. I can't help it. I lean into his touch, savoring the feeling of being wrapped up in his arms.

His hand reaches out and gently brushes away a droplet of water from my cheek. "What's up, Aly-cat?"

"Seriously, haven't we put that name to bed?" I tease. He chuckles, guiding me to the edge of the pool. With surprising ease, he lifts me onto the ledge, our eyes meeting at a rare level. "You tell me what's up," I say. "Seems like something's on your mind."

He heaves a sigh, using the heel of his hand to swipe his dripping hair back. "I've got a solid lead on whoever's after you."

"Oh." I had anticipated this moment, but still, the revelation hits me like a lead anchor, directly in the chest.

"The situation's about to get more dangerous." The crease between his brows deepens, as he reaches out to cradle my face, his fingertips delicately grazing my skin. "I promise you, butterfly, I will keep you safe no matter what. I won't rest until I find the *pizda* who's been tormenting you. They will pay for every sleepless night, every moment of fear they've caused you."

My breath catches in my throat while I fight to keep a neutral expression.

"Aly, say something. Talk to me, baby." He swallows hard, the quiet intensity of his voice speaking louder than any of his words.

"I'm fine," I assure him, swallowing down the knot of emotion forming in my throat. "It's a lot to take in, but I'm fine."

Still cradling my face, he leans in and kisses me so tenderly, with so much emotion biting at the edges, it's clear that I'm not the only one falling here. We're both standing on the edge of a cliff, one we've tumbled down before, and we need to back the fuck up before we make the same mistakes again.

Leaning away from his touch, I break contact, needing space to think clearly. "Who is it? Who is after me?"

He drops his hands and lowers his body back into the pool. "I don't know for sure, but it seems a Croatian arms dealer named Marko Horvat is involved."

"Do you think this is about Yulian? Or my connection to the bratva?"

A shadow crosses his face, like he's spent a long time considering that possibility. "Anything is possible. It'll make a hell of a lot more sense soon. Tomorrow we head to Croatia so I can question Horvat ... we'll part ways there." The lines of his face are etched with grim unhappiness as he looks towards the dusky horizon.

My throat tightens. This is it for us. It's what I wanted, but also not what I wanted at all. Because now that I'm faced with our end, it hurts more than I'd imagined. The possibility of a future has finally eclipsed the hurt of the past, but ...

No, I can't allow myself to think of another way. We made

a deal, and it's not like Leo has ever questioned our end date. In fact, this is probably what he wants.

I take a deep breath, steeling myself for whatever comes next. "If tonight is our last night together, let's make it count," I murmur. Slipping back into the pool, I swim towards him.

His lips form a faint, melancholic smile. "Funny you should say that. I gave the crew the night off."

"You did?"

"I did."

I lose my bikini top, flinging it out of the pool, followed by the bottoms. I dance around him in the water, loving the way his eyes track my movements like a predator waiting for the right time to pounce.

"Fuck, butterfly, I don't know where to start with you," he rasps. My core clenches as he bridges the distance between us. His hand disappears beneath the water to gently part my thighs, running a finger between my folds. His eyes, a sexy smolder. "This fucking pussy," he says, and his breath grazes over my ear, sending a shiver down my spine. "How am I ever going to live without it?"

I don't answer because what is there to say? Instead, I weave my fingers through his hair, pulling him towards me, desperate to hold onto this moment a little longer. I want to get lost in him, in the here and now, and ignore what comes next.

"Take me to our room," I say. Despite the storm brewing inside of me, my voice is steady. I need tonight to mean something. I need him to take me fully so there's no doubt I'm his, even if we can't be together.

With a nod, he hauls himself out of the pool, water sluicing off his muscular body. Reaching down, he scoops me up in his arms. My body feels cool from the night air against his warm, wet skin. He kicks the door to our stateroom open with his foot and sets me down carefully on the plush bed. But I have other ideas.

"Lie back on the bed," I say, taking charge. "Hands behind your head, no touching."

Surprise flickers in his eyes, quickly replaced by hot anticipation. He does as I say, lying back, his impressive cock already standing tall, daring me to take control. I scramble to my knees beside him, giving him a show. Jutting out my breasts, my nipples stand at attention.

The smoldering look he gives me makes my skin hum with desire. I feel confident and bold—not the virgin I once was—but his equal.

Tracing my way down his hard body, my tongue softly paves a path from his chest, down his chiseled abs, until I reach my destination. His dick stands at attention for me, and I give it a gentle kiss, admiring the glint of his cock piercing, before wrapping my hand around his balls. His eyes slip closed, and he grunts his pleasure as I lightly tug and cup them in my palm.

"Are you still trying to kill me?" he chokes out, as I continue to gently knead him, mesmerized at the way his dick hardens from me playing with his balls alone.

"Nah," I whisper. "Gave that up a while ago. It was clear you weren't going down that easily." I grin up at him, remembering the day I woke up angry and confused on the yacht. It feels like a lifetime ago.

My hand sweeps upwards, and I palm his thick length as he groans like he might be in pain. As I slowly jerk him, a single bead of moisture clings to the head like a diamond beckoning me forward. My tongue flickers tentatively over the tip before taking his crown into my mouth, circling the piercing with my tongue. It must feel pretty damn good judging by the way he throws his head back and the muscles in his chest ripple with strain. This is the power I craved, the ability to make him squirm in pleasure.

"Don't play with me, butterfly. I don't have that much control right now, and the sight of you on your knees for me is too much, too fucking hot." To drive his point home, he arches his back, pushing his hips up so I am forced to take him deeper.

He continues to rock his hips, slipping his shaft deeper between my lips until I feel his piercing hit the back of my throat. My eyes widen at the intrusion, but I'm hungry for him, so I force my throat to relax around his girth, dragging in breaths through my nose. I swallow, my throat muscles hugging him before I pull back, and run my lips down the side of his hard cock.

He's losing control; I feel it in the way his body trembles with need. All for me. It's a huge turn-on, and my body reacts in kind, slickness dripping down my legs. All I can do is press my thighs together, desperate for relief.

"Such an eager mouth," he rasps. "But that pussy is dripping for me—I can smell you from here. Let me give you some relief. I know you're dying for it."

I am absolutely dying for it. As if he can sense my weakness, he lifts me up, turning me around so my pussy is above his face and his hard length is bobbing in front of my mouth.

"What are you doing?" I cry, but a response isn't necessary. Not when his fingers are already spreading me wide, opening me so he can drink his fill.

"I dream of this cunt," he says before diving in, licking me in one straight line from clit to ass. "I'll never get enough." I nearly scream as his fingers pump inside me in time with his tongue lashing my clit. It's almost too much, but not enough at the same time. I don't even mind that he's taken control, because this is pure fucking bliss.

"Did I say you could stop?" His palm comes down across

my ass hard enough to get me moving in the right direction. He fists his cock, holding it out for me as I hollow my cheeks. Bobbing up and down in a steady rhythm, he grabs my ass cheeks and lowers me down onto his mouth. He feasts on me, his tongue barreling into my pussy like he's a dying man, and I'm the only cure.

It's almost too much. Having him fill my mouth and cunt at the same time. He's giving me no choice but to sit on his face, to really sit on it. His attention is focused on my clit, and he circles it with his tongue, finally sucking it fully into his mouth. My god, my legs tremble, and I have to pull off his shaft to force air into my lungs. Unable to hold back for another second, I go off.

My pussy spasms. Each wave that rolls over me steals my breath, leaving me sensitive and achy. Overwhelmed. But he doesn't let up.

"Please," I beg. "I can't take it anymore."

"You did so good Aly," he croons, planting delicate kisses all over my slick entrance. "Now that I've swallowed all your cum, you're going to swallow mine."

I groan at his filthy words, wanting everything he has to give as I wrap my lips around his length. With one hand around the base, I work him hard and deep until his body tenses beneath mine. His cock seems to grow between my lips, and with a tortured cry, he stills, his body tense as hot cum spills into my mouth. He tastes salty and perfect—like Leo—and I don't waste a drop, sucking him down and licking him clean.

"Holy shit" is all I'm able to say as I crawl off his body and sag beside him. He reaches for me, pulling me tight against his chest. I've come to think of this as my favorite place. It's a dangerous thought, but at this moment, I can't deny it's the truth.

Like me, he seems to unravel at the edges, drawing ragged

breaths and gripping me tight as if I might disappear. "You were perfect, butterfly, that was everything." His tone is so tender, so caring, it fractures something within me.

It's a tone that seals itself within my heart, marking me unmistakably as his.

Again. Still.

LEO

I'm motionless with Aly sprawled atop me as both of us catch our breath, muscles still trembling from the intense high. Her fingers lazily trace a path across my chest, stopping at the butterfly tattoo on my chest. If that's not a declaration of my love, I don't know what is, but she doesn't see it that way.

Aly has made her decision: she doesn't want me—a vor, a man who has already caused her enough pain to last a lifetime. As much as it tears me apart, I'll let her go. All I can do now is leave her with better memories than the first time we parted ways.

I wrap myself around her and whisper into her ear, "What do you need, butterfly?"

"To be close to you one more time."

I turn to lie on my back, offering my body to her. "Take what you need."

She slides her leg over my hips, straddling me as I trail my fingers down over her breasts, over her nipples, to finally wrap around her ribs. Her wet core grazes my cock, teasing it, and it only makes me hungrier for her.

"Put it in," I beg, because I can't take another minute not being inside of her.

Her gaze holds mine as she lines my cock up with her

entrance. With a wiggle of her hips, she slowly sinks down on me, inch by inch, taking my entire length inside of her, a slow stretch. She's so tight I feel like I'm taking up all the space inside her.

"Fuck, Leo, it feels so good," she whimpers. The sound of my name on her lips, the feel of her pussy walls gripping my dick, it's too perfect. She's ruined sex for me. Might as well become a priest after this.

"You fit me perfectly," I tell her. Arousal slices through me as she lifts off me and then slams back down. She closes her eyes and tosses her head back, a long moan escapes from between her lips.

I seek out her clit with my fingers, rubbing in circles, then flick it hard as she begins to ride me slowly, grinding her pelvis with mine.

My hand moves up, grasping her wrist. Her gaze locks with mine, her striking blue eyes carry the same heartache that's suffocating me. But she has to hear this. "I'm not going anywhere. I'll always be here waiting for you."

She nods, biting her lip. Even in the dark, I can see her eyes glistening. My hands cradle her face, drawing her lips to mine, a way to ease this ache. She leans in, and I crush my mouth to hers.

The kiss communicates everything I can't say. How much I want her. How much I still love her.

It's long and slow. Intimate. Our mouths fused together, sharing the same breath, as she churns against me, her clit grinding into my pubic bone with every swivel of her hips. The delicious friction sending white-hot sparks of pleasure through my veins.

"That's it, butterfly. Use me to get off. Use my dick. 'Cause it's yours, baby."

When she pulls away, the raw hunger in her expression

fuels my own lust. My hands clasp her hips, stilling them as I lift off the bed, pounding into her with everything I have. She's so wet; the sound of me sliding in and out of her is so obscene, so hot, tingles build at the base of my spine.

Her breath quickens and her eyes flutter closed. She's close. I know her body as well as I know my own. She's teetering on the verge of an orgasm, and I am desperate to get her there. I press my thumb into her mouth, and she welcomes me inside, her tongue laving my digit as the walls of her pussy begin to pulse around me.

"Eyes on me," I remind her. If this is our last time, she's not robbing me of the pleasure of watching her fall apart. Her burning gaze meets mine. "You'll stare into my eyes as you come on my cock." Her hands grab at my shoulders, nails digging into my skin as her inner muscles contract. She comes apart, her back arching as she releases a tortured sob.

My own orgasm follows, washing over me like a tidal wave, undulating currents that wipe away all else. I flood her pussy with my cum, my fingers digging into her hips to hold her tight against me until my body sags with me still inside of her.

But neither of us move. I'm biting down the emotion in my throat as we catch our breaths. My palms run over her hair and back, and even as she lays on top of me, her limbs loose and tired, I still want more from her.

"Lie on your back," I instruct her as I slowly, achingly slow, pull out of her.

"Like this?" she asks quietly, sprawling on the bed beside me.

"Yes. Such a good girl," I rasp, running my thumb over her lips. Sitting back on my haunches, I pull her legs apart so I have an unobstructed view of her dripping cunt. "Just. Like. That."

I can tell she feels self-conscious, even after what we've shared, but I need to see my seed mixed with her pleasure seeping out of her. "Fuck, Aly, I'm getting hard again from this view."

Holding her thighs wide apart, I position my body between hers as if I'm about to surge back inside of her. But I don't. I swipe the head of my penis along her slit, gathering my seed leaking out of her. Then I kneel in front of her mouth. "Sit up and drink what's yours."

Her eyes go wide, but she scrambles forward. I don't miss the way her breath catches and how her nipples tighten to points. She licks me clean, her eyes holding mine with a wicked gleam in them as she savors every last drop.

She's perfect for me. She has to know that. There will be no one else but her.

"Do you like how we taste together?" I whisper, my hands wrapped around the base of her neck.

"I love how we taste together."

And I'm not sure if we're really talking about the taste or something more.

24

ALYONA

I WAKE up in the middle of the night. It's not any one thing that wakes me up but the sad realization this is the last night I'll sleep beside Leo. The last night I'll breathe in his scent or feel his arms wrap around me or hear his soft rhythmic breaths in his sleep. At that realization, a profound emptiness swells within me.

I can't stay in this bed any longer. Not as thoughts continue to spin through my half-asleep brain. Carefully slipping out from beneath the covers, I grab a robe and head towards the sundeck. The fresh air is welcome.

Leaning against the railing, I stare out into the calm sea spread before me. It's so quiet up here that I can hear the gentle lapping of the waves against the hull, the dark sky above speckled with stars.

We set sail for Dubrovnik not too long ago. As soon as we make landfall, the magic bubble we've existed in goes *pop*. It's what we agreed to from the start.

Still, a thousand doubts plague my mind, each one questioning whether I'm making the right decision by walking away from Leo. By not telling him how I truly feel. I can't lie to myself anymore. I love Leo, and maybe I never stopped, but it doesn't mean we are meant to be. Even if I could get past how he hurt me, I can't get past what he is. A vor. A high-ranking member of his family's bratva.

Time hasn't softened my stance. I won't get entangled with a man who has sworn the oath. Not even one who has captured my heart as thoroughly as Leo has. He made his choice a long time ago, and it can't be undone. I take a deep breath and try to push down the sorrow, but I'm so lost in my thoughts I only hear the footsteps moments before hands grab my waist and spin me around. But it's not the rough hands I've come to crave.

It's Jack. His flirty smile replaced by hard eyes and lips curled into a snarl.

"Jack?" I say, confused. "What do you want?"

A slow evil grin builds on his face. "I think you know what I've wanted the whole time." Terror floods my veins as he grabs my wrists, restraining them behind my back in one hand while the other wraps around my neck.

"Let me go, or I'll scream," I threaten, unable to keep the quiver out of my voice.

He chuckles, and the smell of booze wafts off him, turning my stomach. "Go ahead. Scream and see what happens. See what I do." His hand tightens around my neck in warning, a reminder that I'm all alone out here with a deranged man.

I'll need to fight him on my own. I just have to wait for my opening. Until then, I'll play along. "Please," I whisper, my voice wavering. "You've had some drinks. You're not thinking clearly. This isn't you—"

He jerks away, anger twisting his expression. "You don't

know anything about me. Neither does your fiancé. But I know you're not who you claim to be." His voice drops lower, a dangerous edge creeping into it. "I've got friends in high places, you know. People who were quite interested to hear about a mysterious American couple showing up unannounced, renting this yacht indefinitely."

My stomach knots. "What are you saying? What did you do?"

"Shared your picture with a few interested parties, let them know we're headed to Dubrovnik in a hurry. I wonder why?"

The smile I return to him is just as cold. "I think you'll find that you fucked with the wrong family." Adrenaline courses through my veins, as I twist against his grip, adrenaline fueling my fight. He rocks on his feet, and I seize the moment of opportunity, yelling at the top of my lungs as I crash my knee into his balls.

He doubles over and I take off running, but I don't get far. He lunges and strikes me on the side of my head. Gasping for breath, I let out another scream, but it's swallowed by the warm night air. There's no one else around, no one to hear me, no one to come to my aid.

Not even Leo.

And so I shake off the pain and fight with everything I have. I jab my elbow backward, striking his gut. He wheezes, the breath knocked out of him, but he soon regains his footing, tackling me to the ground. Desperate, I lash out, trying to shove him off me, but he's relentless. Straddling me and pinning me with his weight, my wrists are clamped together in his iron grip, and I'm trapped. My vision swims, but I continue to thrash.

"No," I choke, but he's deaf to my pleas, consumed by his own darkness.

Bearing down, he hikes up my nightgown, settling between

my thighs. Panic floods my senses, but I fight like hell, summoning every ounce of strength. I will resist until my last breath. I owe myself nothing less.

25

LEO

I wake up gradually, the world slowly coming into focus. It's the middle of the night, I can determine that much by the moon still shining in the sky. Which is good. It means I still have another few hours alone with Aly.

My hand instinctively reaches for her warmth, eager to roll over and sink between her legs. Instead, I find her side of the bed cold and empty, like she's been gone a while. Sitting up, I blink against the darkness, confusion clouding my mind.

My hand gropes for my phone, the faint light from the screen illuminating the cabin as I check the time. Three in the morning. I set the phone down only for it to vibrate with an incoming message. Dima's name flashes on the screen. He's sent a file.

Opening it, I find unsealed records from Jack's time in juvenile detention. My eyes flicker over the words, my stomach clenching with a growing sense of dread as a certain phrase stands out.

Sexual assault.

Disgust settles in my stomach. He's the absolute worst kind of scum. Once we arrive in Dubrovnik, he'll get what's coming to him. But right now, all I can think about is finding Aly.

My bare feet hit the floor, and I pull on a pair of boxers before I leave the stateroom. I move through the dimly lit hallway up to the mid-level deck, scanning the space for signs of her. Nothing.

A distant noise from the deck above snags my attention—a muffled thump, heated voices echoing in the stillness. Heart pounding, I race up to the top deck.

The vision I'm met with is worse than what I could have conjured in my nightmares. Alyona, trapped beneath Jack's weight, her limbs thrashing, attempting to push him off her.

Rage pulses through me, and I charge at Jack with a guttural roar. My fist connects with his jaw, and the sound of bone cracking strikes like thunder. "You mudak. You will die for this."

Alyona has scrambled to the side as Jack recovers and comes at me. Our bodies tangle in a vicious dance of punches and blows. Despite reeking of alcohol, he holds his own, but I am relentless, driven by a primal need to protect Aly.

I growl, landing a punch to Jack's gut that makes him double over. "You're a rapist. And I will personally make you pay for your sins."

"She's a whore." He spits blood, venom dripping from his words. "You're both scum, not worth all this shit."

My fury reaches a boiling point, and I send Jack flying with a devastating punch. "You think you can hurt what belongs to me and get away with it?"

He's not so quick to get up this time, and I take a brief moment to enjoy the sight of him sprawled flat on his back, struggling to breathe. I seize Jack by the collar, drag him to his feet, and haul his upper body over the edge of the railing. "You're going for a swim, you miserable fuck!"

He starts bucking and snarling, desperately trying to get out of my hold. "You're fucking crazy. I'll die—"

"That's the point," Alyona's voice rings out, cold and vicious. Our eyes meet across the deck, and she gives me a nod, her eyes flashing with resolve.

Jack's screams rip through the air as I heave him overboard. With a satisfying splash he's swallowed up by the murky waters of the sea.

I have Aly scooped up in my arms within seconds. My chest heaves as I struggle to catch my breath. "Are you okay? Please tell me you're okay," I whisper into her hair.

She nods, a sob slipping past her lips. "I'm okay," she reassures me, though she's still quaking like a leaf in my arms. "I tried to fight him off, but ..." Her voice trails off into a whisper. "He's a monster."

"Was a monster. Was." I kiss her hair, holding her tight. "Fuck, Aly, that scared the shit out of me. Finding you here, with his hands on you ..." My voice cracks as I start towards our room. "I would die to protect you. You need to know that."

"I know," she whispers, face buried in my chest.

In the stateroom, I lay her down on the bed and hold her, trying to erase all his ugliness with my tenderness. "Fuck, baby, tell me how to make this better. What can I do to erase his marks?"

"*You* make it better. Your touch can erase the darkness."

With her permission, I strip her and tenderly examine every inch of her body. Kissing each and every bruise, cursing every red mark and painful welt. When her eyes finally shut and her breathing evens out, I lie down beside her.

"I need to tell you something." She turns to face me, her eyes wide with worry. "He's told people, Leo. Sent our picture out to his contacts. He doesn't know who we are, but it's only a matter of time."

Motherfucker. Ice freezes in my veins but I don't want to worry Aly, so I say, "I'll look into it. Right now, just sleep."

"Don't leave me," she murmurs, but she's already drifting off.

"I'll be right here." I stroke her cheek and kiss her forehead. "I'm not going anywhere." Her breath evens out, and although she can't hear my words, I whisper into her hair, "I love you."

WITH ALY still out to the world, I leave her a note and head to the office. There are things in need of my attention that can't wait. Like figuring out the damage that Jack wrought. I blame myself for not seeing what he was earlier. A sick man, a predator, the lowest of the low. Anger claws up my throat every time the vision of Jack on top of Aly enters my brain. It'll haunt me to my dying day.

But he's left us with a much more urgent problem.

Dima already hacked into Jack's phone and email accounts and learned that he made high-level connections working on the yacht—politicians, CEOs, mob bosses. He sent them our photo, taken in secret like the twisted fuck he was, and exposed us. Our true identities will soon be revealed, if they aren't already.

Time has never been on our side, and now it's become our mortal enemy. Soon, those hunting Alyona will find us.

"Andrei," I say, answering the phone that buzzed in my hand. The fact that my brothers, Kira, and Yulian landed in Dubrovnik a few hours earlier and were able to get a head start on hunting Horvat might be our only saving grace. "What's going on? Do you have Horvat yet?"

"We're watching him. He's in the back room of a nightclub getting his dick sucked. Him and his men are coked up, sloppy. It should make our job easier." Andrei's voice is somber, the weight of the situation evident. "When are you set to arrive?"

"Next few hours," I confirm. "We'll avoid the main port and head to Mlini, a small fishing village a few miles from Dubrovnik. I need a car ready and waiting for me."

"I'll make it happen. Kira secured a safe house. She's grabbing supplies and will meet Aly at the house."

I sigh, running an agitated hand through my hair. "Horvat better have some fucking answers," I growl. "I can't take much more of this shit."

"He'll know something, I'm sure of it." Andrei pauses. "But this goes beyond Horvat, beyond any single brotherhood or mafia. Whoever is behind this has the resources to keep themselves well-hidden. Our contacts in Moscow had no intel. That's rare."

My nails dig into the palm of my hands. My brother's not telling me anything I don't already know, but fuck, it's hard to hear. How the hell am I supposed to protect the woman I love when our enemy is a nameless, faceless force?

This is a nightmare, that's what it is.

But now, it's time to wake up and fight like hell.

26

LEO

Aly looks pale as a sheet as we say a final goodbye to Genevieve, the only crew member present to see us off. After shit went bad with Jack, I met with Captain Hansen and told him about the attack. I also let him know that we would not be getting the authorities involved. We would handle it all on our end.

Being a smart man, the captain understood not to ask too many questions. I've let it be known that the crew will be taken care of and paid handsomely for their silence.

One hand resting on Aly's lower back, I lead her off the yacht towards Mlini's harbor, scanning for any sign of danger. It's quiet here, just a few fishing boats bobbing in the water and locals going about their daily business. Her body is rigid as we approach a sleek black luxury sedan parked a few feet from the main road. I'd like to tell her that it will be okay, that there's no need to worry, but we both know I can't promise that.

I input the code Andrei provided into the car door's

keypad. After the doors unlock, I assist Aly into the passenger seat and then slide into the driver's seat. Swiping my finger across the dashboard, the GPS system awakens, already programmed for our destination.

"Where are we going?"

"A safe house. I'm going to take you there, and Kira will stay with you." I place my pistol in the cupholder between us. Aly eyes it warily, and I hate that she has to see this side of me. The cold, calculating mobster, born of the underworld.

"And what about you?" she asks, her voice quiet with worry. "What will you do?"

I merge into traffic, glancing in the rearview mirror, searching for tails.

"I'm going to find out what the fuck is going on once and for all. I promise, baby, I will hunt down and destroy whoever is after you. I will tear them apart with my bare hands, fucking bury them alive if I have to. You don't deserve this."

"Yeah, well ..." Her laugh is tense. "Deserved or not, it's happening."

An awkward tension fills the car, thick with all the things left unsaid. Even if she won't admit it, I know that Alyona and I are meant to be. She is my destiny. Wholly mine. And I'll bare my soul, confess every sin until she understands, without a doubt, that there will be no one else in her future—or mine. We are the beginning, middle, and end of each other's stories.

But now isn't the time to say all this. Not when she sits next to me, hands nervously twisting in her lap, face etched with worry. So I force the words back, and focus on the road ahead. The navigation system guides us to a nondescript two-story house tucked away in a quiet neighborhood. From the outside, it appears ordinary—weathered stucco walls, a tile roof that has known better days. But as we pull up to the property, I see all the details that make it secure. Thick steel doors, biometric scanners, reinforced windows fitted with metal shutters.

Inside, the safe house is simply furnished but comfortable. The ground floor consists of a living room with a suede sofa, coffee table, and TV. The kitchen is basic with a small stove, refrigerator, and dining table for four.

"I know it looks basic," I say, "but that's the point. To fit in, be unassuming. It has everything we need to keep you safe." I point to motion sensors mounted on the ceiling and the small camera in the corner.

"Are you leaving now?" Aly asks, her mouth pressing into a grim line.

I close the distance between us, taking her in my arms. "Kira will be here soon. She's armed and trained, you're in good hands. But, butterfly, you need to listen to her. Avoid windows, avoid going outside. Stay safe. I can't do my job if I'm worried about you." I let out a ragged breath, grabbing her chin between my thumb and forefinger. "And for the love of god, don't forget to turn on the alarm system like you always do at home."

As soon as the words are out of my mouth, I realize my error. She tilts her head, parting her lips as she processes my words. There's a palpable silence, the wheels of her mind turning.

"How do you know how often I forget to turn on my alarm system?"

I could lie, it's what I've been doing for years. Or I could bring the truth to light once and for all. "Because I'm the one who had it installed. I bought the building, made sure no one else moved in or got too close."

She freezes to stone in my arms, blinking up at me. "What are you talking about? Yulian had the alarm installed, and Yulian bought the—"

I shake my head, cutting off her words. "It wasn't Yulian. It's been me this entire time."

She blanches, her eyes growing wide. "What!? Why would you do that?" she snaps, her voice trembling. She backs up until she is flush against the wall.

Fuck it. There couldn't be a worse time to have this talk, but she deserves the truth. She deserves to know how deeply embedded she is in my soul. In my very being. "I never stopped loving you. Not for one fucking minute did I feel like a whole person without you by my side. Maybe what I did was wrong, but I couldn't bear the thought of someone else having you. I needed to know you were safe and that no unworthy fucker was going to get close to you. Not when you were mine."

"What are you saying? You scared away the men I dated? Is that why— Holy shit." Her palm connects hard with my cheek, but I don't flinch. I don't react. I deserve it. "How dare you? You're the one who threw me aside. You rejected me, remember? You chose the brotherhood over me!" A sob rips from her throat, raw and pained, and it nearly fucking brings me to my knees. Because she's right. I did this. I am the source of her hurt and suffering, when all I wanted to do was protect her.

I bow my head, pain slicing through my chest, straight down through the center of my soul. "It's the last thing I ever wanted to do. I love you, I never stopped loving you, not for one damn second."

"I heard you, you know. On the phone with Kira on the yacht." She paces, her voice has an edge of hysteria as all the puzzle pieces fall into place. "Why don't you man up and tell me the truth, explain why you walked away. Why you had no other choice."

This is what I've spent years running from. My weakness, my vulnerability, my deepest shame. "The truth is ugly," I tell her. "It's ugly and twisted, and it will change things forever." I bow my head, gather my courage. "But I will tell you. I'll do anything for you."

A chime rings out and the front door lock disengages. "It's me," Kira calls, entering the house. Her footsteps are light as she enters the kitchen, grocery bags in hand. She takes one look at us and freezes. "Am I interrupting something?"

Frustration nearly bursts like a dam inside of me. I love Kira, but she has some shitty-ass timing.

Aly swipes away a hot tear that rolls down her cheek. "It's fine," she says, even though it's not.

Kira drops the groceries, her wide eyes drinking us in. "I'm sorry to do this, but you need to leave now, Leo. We have Horvat, but time is running out. The city is swarming with his men, and they're out for blood."

Leaving Aly is the last thing I want to do, but she makes the decision for me. "Go," she says, giving me her back. "I can't stand to look at you right now."

Her words pierce through me, my heart splinters into a million fragments. But if there is one thing I know for sure, it's this. "We're not done, Aly. Not even close. You and I—we will never be done."

27

ALYONA

After Leo leaves, I turn into a blubbering mess on the kitchen floor. Kira holds me, lets me cry, lets me rage, and then makes me a stiff vodka soda as I tell her everything. All the dirty details of our time on the boat and everything Leo just admitted to me. When the words run out and my body slumps forward, she puts me in a steaming shower, the pounding spray helping to calm what's left of my nerves.

Shivering, I can't tell if it's the water or my tears messing with my vision. Definitely tears. Crying in the shower has become a regular thing since Leo stormed back into my life and turned everything upside down. These are not tears of sorrow; they burn with fury. I let him in, opened my heart to him again, only to find out he's been fucking with my life from a distance, as if he had some sort of right over me.

If this is what he calls love, he sure has a warped definition. It's twisted. Sick. Even if he was shielding me from some dark, terrifying secret, manipulating my life from the shadows is nothing but crazy.

Stepping out of the shower, I wrap myself in a towel and make my way into the small bedroom. Kira's perched on an armchair in the corner with a pint of ice cream and two bowls set on a table beside her. A change of clothes waits for me on the bed.

"I apologize in advance." Kira frowns, gesturing to the ice cream. "Vanilla was all I could find on such short notice."

I manage a weary smile as I sit down on the bed across from her. "Beggars can't be choosers."

She hands me a bowl and then serves herself one. "Feeling better?" Kira asks after a while.

"A bit." Not really, but I'd rather Kira not see me like this. A stupid girl who fell for the wrong guy ... twice. "I feel like an idiot," I admit. "I said it would just be sex, nothing more, that I could keep my feelings locked down. How fucking wrong I was."

Kira's gaze softens. "It was never going to be that simple."

"Yeah, maybe not." I look down at my nails, absently picking at my cuticle. "I feel so vulnerable ... like he has some sort of hold over me. Like I can never think straight when it comes to him."

"Listen," Kira says, leaning forward. "I know this is not my business, and Leo was clearly misguided, but maybe you need to hear him out. He loves you, I know he does, and I think on some level you love him, too."

I scoff. "He sure has a fucked-up way of showing it."

"Yeah, they all do, these bratva men are emotionally stunted assholes. That's why we ladies need to put them in their place." She shrugs, taking my empty bowl and stacking it on top of hers.

"That's why we ladies should avoid them altogether."

She gives me a sly smile. "How's that working for you?"

"Not all that well." I stand and grab a towel to dry my hair. And then, because I need to not think of Leo and the fact that I'm locked in a safe house right now, I ask, "And what about you? Who are you seeing these days?"

She pulls a face. "Just hookups. I don't have time for anything more."

"What!? Is Andrei working you to the bone?"

"Nah, it's not that. It's just been a bit hectic lately, nothing we need to discuss at the moment." She shrugs, a small smile tugging at the corner of her mouth. "Besides, I've yet to find a guy that holds my interest. New York is overflowing with entitled trust-fund brats in search of arm candy to feed their ego. That's just not my scene."

"Fair enough." I can tell she doesn't want me to push the issue, so I let it drop. "What is there to do around here?" I ask.

"Nothing. That's the beauty of being locked in a safe house. How about we curl up on the couch and watch a movie? Nothing romantic, I promise. Maybe we can find a *Die Hard* DVD or something."

"DVD? Now that's a throwback," I chuckle.

"Yeah, that's all they have here. It'll be quaint, like a '90s sleepover."

"Right." I nod, a grin tugging at the corner of my mouth. "DVD it is."

28

LEO

I ALMOST DRIVE past the decrepit building nestled in an industrial part of the city. It looks abandoned, which makes it perfect for what we're about to do—torture information out of a man. A man who is our only lead right now. Whatever Horvat knows about the men after Alyona, he won't go to his grave without telling me.

Danger is closing in on us, I can feel it in my bones. Aly is not safe, and until she is, nothing else matters. Even the fact that she'd rather eat dirt than see me again. My heart pounds at the image of her pain-stricken face. I broke her, I did that, and it hurts something fierce. I'll grovel. I'll walk miles on broken glass. Do whatever it takes to earn back her trust. But for now, I need to morph into the ruthless killer I was molded to be.

The rhythmic sound of my footsteps brings me back to the present. "The present" being the sickening sound of hard bone connecting with soft flesh reverberates through the basement.

A familiar sight greets me: a man, in this case Horvat,

strung up by his wrists, his naked body suspended in the center of the room. My brothers hang back, monitoring security feeds outside of the building while Yulian, whose hands are already stained with blood, unbuttons his crisp white shirt and drapes it over a nearby chair.

"Looks like I came right in time for the fun," I announce darkly, striding past my brothers towards Yulian. He braces his palms on the chair he just deposited his shirt on and grits his teeth. Horvat, already battered and bruised, doesn't even lift his face to acknowledge me.

Yulian is the best at what he does—thorough and as brutal as necessary. But this time, it's personal. It's his sister's life hanging in the balance, his only blood relative. If Horvat has any sense, he'll give up the information we need quickly.

"We've already had some fun here, haven't we, *ublyudok*?"

He's a bastard all right. Yulian roughly smacks Horvat's already broken body, and he rears back in response. His eyes are dark and hateful when he spits at Yulian. He misses. Not that it makes a difference, the intent was there.

Yulian retaliates with a brutal punch to his gut.

"Fuck you," Horvat sneers, his breaths coming fast and shallow. "I already told you, I know nothing about Alexander Luzkov abducting anyone. We were in prison together a long time ago. I haven't seen him in years."

"Well, that's simply not true," I say, keeping my voice soft. "I have pictures that show the two of you together right before Luzkov attempted to kidnap Alyona Nikitin. He's dead by the way, although I'm sure you know that. Alyona killed him. Not much of a professional in my opinion. But that's neither here nor there." Crossing my arms, I lean on the blood-flecked wall facing Horvat, allowing him to see the feral glint in my eyes. "We know you're the middleman, nothing more," I say lightly.

"You don't know shit," he wheezes.

I shrug. "I know that you brought Luzkov in on the job. Just tell us who hired you, and we can put an end to your suffering."

"You're wasting your breath," Horvat croaks. "If I knew anything, I'd never tell it to American trash like you. Fucking bratva scum."

A knife sails across the room, landing clean in Horvat's shoulder. He howls in pain. "That's for insulting my family," Andrei roars from across the room before a second knife slices through the air and implants into Horvat's opposite shoulder. "And that's because you're wasting our fucking time."

Yulian stalks forward, his mouth tipped up in a deceptively friendly smile. I should know; the man never smiles like that. "Shit. That looks painful, let me help you with that." One sharp tug on the knife in Horvat's left shoulder, and the blade falls, spilling blood like dark red wine.

When Yulian reaches for the other knife, Horvat begins to thrash and convulse, his cries turning ugly as Yulian proceeds to twist the blade. The cold, damp air in the room fills with the stench of copper and Horvat's howls.

"Listen," I say, stepping forward to play the good guy. "We're just getting started here, next we're going to hack away at you, limb by limb, finger by finger. You don't want that, do you?" I pick up one of the knives that Yulian removed from Horvat's body and trace it up the side of his leg, landing just above his dick. My intent is clear. "I usually like to start here. I find men without cocks get real chatty."

Horvat sucks in air, sobbing and wheezing. His whole body is a heaving, trembling mess. "He'll come after my family," he screams, his voice tortured. "You don't know what kind of man he is."

"You clearly don't know what kind of man I am," I say in a dark whisper. "Or he is." I point to Yulian. "'Cause right now, they're coming after my family. Someone I love more than anything, someone I can't live without." Yulian freezes behind me, but I don't care. The words are out in the open, and I won't take them back. I've kept a secret from my friend for a long time, and now that time is over. No more secrets, no more lies.

I press into the knife below his pubic bone, barely a prick, but it's a warning of what's to come. "I will hunt down and murder each and every person that means anything to you if you don't spill. Just tell us what we want to know, it's so simple. Transglobal Holdings paid you $20 million for a job that you contracted to Luzkov. We need a name."

"You ... you don't want this man's name. Trust me."

"That's where you're wrong." I sink the knife deeper, and Horvat releases an ungodly sound. If I've learned one thing in this life, it's that slicing off a man's dick breaks even the toughest of souls. "Just a name, then all of this ends. All of it."

"Maxim!" he screams, pain filtering through his voice. "Maxim Belov."

Yulian's eyes cut to mine, and the confusion swirling in their depths mirrors my own. Jesus fucking Christ.

"I told you, now kill me. Be done with it."

"I lied." I shrug and cut off his dick anyhow, because no matter which way you slice it, *ahem*, this man was key in hurting Alyona, and hell is too good for him. So I make sure he suffers on his way out.

Behind me, a chair scrapes across the floor. Daniil's voice carries over Horvat's piercing screams. "We need to go. There's company buzzing around."

Yulian shoots Horvat square between the eyes as we move towards the exit, taking the stairs two at a time. We burst outside, but there's no time to talk about what we just learned. There's only one thing to do.

"Back to the safe house," Andrei grits. "We need to get Kira and Alyona and leave the country ASAP."

"I'll travel with you," Yulian says, jumping into my passenger seat while Andrei and Daniil head towards their vehicle.

I have a feeling Yulian has some questions for me, and although I'm ready to tell him the truth, I don't really feel like being punched out by my best friend right now.

That shit could wait till we're on the plane.

29

ALYONA

My eyes shoot open, the movie that was playing is now finished, the screen of the TV black. Kira is asleep on the other end of the couch, but when a searing explosion rips through the air, her eyes fly open, and she springs to her feet.

"What the fuck was that?" she grits, fear lacing her voice. Drawing a pistol from her waistband, she disengages the safety and whirls around, scanning the room, her body taut and poised for action.

"We can check the cameras," I suggest, my voice trembling.

"No time," she snaps, her tactical training evident as she stealthily peers around the corner of the room. "We need to get to the safe room in the basement. Let's go."

I follow her down the long hallway that leads towards the basement, sticking close to her side. An eerie silence has fallen. Maybe this is all a dream. We're inches from reaching the basement when another explosion thunders behind us, its shock wave accompanied by a blinding flash of light. The house shudders, as if its very foundation is quaking.

Terror grips me as chaos descends. Arms wrap around me from behind, jerking me to a stop. "Kira!" I yell, but someone has her too—a nameless, faceless man in a mask. I'm dragged out of the house, flailing and fighting the entire time until my captor shoves a sharp object into my ribs and hisses a warning to stop resisting.

I don't listen, because I know this is it. If I don't fight with every fiber of my being, I'm as good as dead.

One thought emerges above all others.

Leo.

And despite everything—his betrayal, the secrets and lies—the idea of never being wrapped up in his strong arms, never feeling the warmth of his gaze, is something I can't bear.

So I fight.

I fight until I can't fight anymore.

Until the world fades to black.

30

7 YEARS AGO

ALYONA

The room smells like a mix of antiseptic and stale air, the heavy scent of sickness clinging to every surface. The walls seem to close in on me, suffocating and oppressive. I look at my mother's frail form in her bed, her once proud self now reduced to a mere shadow.

How did it get so bad?

Since Papa's death, Mama has been on a slow, heartbreaking slide, lost in a fog of grief and narcotics. Along with the doctor and shrinks, I've tried to help her, but it feels like a losing battle. Truthfully, there was always something inside her that seemed restless and unhappy. I couldn't place it as a little girl, but I knew it was there, periods of melancholy and depression when she couldn't get out of bed.

I sit at her bedside, her cold, trembling hand in mine. Her

skin is sallow, stretched tight over her bones and her gaze is unfocused. It got so bad that I called Yulian to come home. He's still completing his training in Russia, but I need his help. She can't go on like this.

"Yulian is flying back from Russia. Pakhan and Andrei, too. They'll be here by morning," I assure her.

Her eyes, usually glazed over from the sedatives, are suddenly too sharp and clear. "Russia! No, not Russia. Alyona. You need to stay away from there."

I squeeze my mother's hand, trying to bring her back to the here and now. My parents are from Russia, they only moved stateside when Mama was pregnant with me. I've suspected her home country holds bad memories for her. "I'm not going there, trust me. But Yulian went there for his training."

Something has agitated her, and she attempts to sit up. "Your father ... Alyona, you need to be careful of him. Stay away from Russia."

I blink back tears, biting my lip. It's difficult to hear her speak so poorly about the husband she lost, the man she never really recovered from losing. "Mama," I say softly, trying to keep my voice steady. "Papa's not here anymore. You know that."

"Please listen to me," she insists, clutching my hand with surprising strength. "You need to be careful."

Her words send chills down my spine. What is she talking about? Her warning doesn't make sense, and I wonder how deeply the narcotics have messed with her mind. "You're ... confused," I say, swallowing the lump in my throat. "Everything is fine."

She shakes her head. "I'm so sorry, Alyona. So sorry." Her words sound so genuine and desperate, it breaks something inside of me.

I lean in, pressing a soft kiss to her forehead. "Go to sleep, Mama. You'll see your son soon."

She gives me one more pleading stare before her eyes flutter closed, and the room is filled with an unbearable silence.

LIGHT STREAMS into the training room, casting streaks of buttery sunshine that highlight the play of muscles in Leo's broad shoulders and chiseled back. I lean against the back wall, the rhythmic thud of his fists striking against the heavy bag filling the space. It's hypnotic, a beautiful dance of precision and force, but that's Leo. He wields his power carefully, almost gently. And he's sexy as all get-out when he does.

The sex lessons have evolved into something much deeper. Although we've both danced around the topic, the intensity between us is palpable. The truth is, I'm desperately in love with him. But ultimately, that doesn't matter.

Leo will take the bratva oath soon, and that is our end date. I have to decide what's next for me, even with my mother being ill. Pakhan has hired the best care for her. She'll be looked after no matter what.

As if he can hear my thoughts, Leo turns to face me. His dark eyes lock onto mine, as a bead of sweat rolls down his temple. I don't know what he sees in my expression, but he drops his gloves and wordlessly crosses the room, gathering me into his naked chest. He's sweaty and hot, but like everything else about him, it just turns me on.

"How was it?" he asks, lips pressing against my temple.

"Not good," I say sadly. "She's slipping. Started talking about my father, getting all confused. It's so hard."

Leo lifts me into his arms, setting me down on the edge of the boxing ring. He spreads my legs and stands in between them. His thumb softly brushes down my cheek, over my lips. "Hey," he murmurs, his deep voice soothing, "it's going to be okay. Yulian will be home soon. It won't all fall on your shoulders."

"Maybe not," I murmur, "but it won't be easy for us to be together anymore. With my brother around, you and I ..." The words stick in my throat. We haven't talked about our looming expiration date for weeks, not since the last time his father, Andrei, and Yulian were home and Leo went a little crazy. But now the summer is coming to an end, and everything will change between us.

"Finish that thought, butterfly." He presses his lips together, nostrils flaring. Did I misunderstand something?

"You're taking the oath in a few weeks, and you know where I stand on that." I take a fortifying breath, gathering courage for what needs to be said. "I think we should end things now. Before Yulian finds out. It'll just make it all the more complicated when we ..." The words catch in my throat and pain radiates through me like a physical sensation.

"You think I want to end things with you?" he asks, incredulously.

"I don't know, it's complicated ..." I start to say, but then he's in front of me, one big hand wrapped around my jaw, his forehead pressed against mine.

"I'm not ending things with you, butterfly. Not even close." His breath is hot against my mouth, tension radiating from him. "You think I could ever let you go? I can't. I've thought about it long and hard, questioning my sanity, because this decision, being with you, changes everything."

"What are you saying?" I ask, heart in my throat.

His hand buries my hair, tugging my head back so I'm forced to look into his eyes. "You belong to me. You've always been mine, even if you didn't know it, I knew it. Deep inside.

And now everyone else will know it, too. Tomorrow, I'll tell my father. He deserves to be the first to know that I won't take the oath. Then we will sit down with Yulian and tell him together." He plants a sweet kiss on my lips. "I love you, Aly. I fucking do. And the only thing that matters is being with you. I don't care about all the other shit. I just want you. I've never been so sure of anything in my life."

Happiness surges through me like a tidal wave. Ending things with Leo was the last thing I wanted to do. It would have shattered me to walk away from him, even if it was necessary. But he's made his choice, and he chose me.

We're not taking the easy way out, that's for sure. Yulian is going to freak, and the pakhan—lordy, I can't even think of that right now. But Leo has, and together, we'll deal with the consequences.

"I love you, too," I say, claiming his mouth with my own. "So damn much."

From now on, it's him and me against the world.

31

LEO

The drive is tense. Both of us are silent, grappling with the news we've just received and the weight of its consequences. I keep my eyes on the road and my hands on the wheel, racing through the outskirts of Dubrovnik. It's supposed to be beautiful here, but this coastal city is ruined for me. Forever tainted with the ghosts of betrayal.

I glance over at my oldest friend, his Sig poised and ready for action, held taut between his knees. Like me, his eyes are constantly scanning the mirrors and windows for possible tails. Just as we approach the house, his ravaged voice breaks the silence. "What's really going on with you and Alyona?"

My jaw clenches, and I grind my back molars together. "I think you know. I think you've always known."

"Fuck," he bites out under his breath, and the click of the safety catches on his gun before a 9mm is pointed at my head. "Did you hurt her?"

My eyes flick to his, but other than that I don't move a muscle. "Yes."

"Khuy." He calls me a dick and presses the cold metal against my temple. "When? Tell me. What did you do to her?"

If I tell him the truth, maybe he'll pull the trigger and put me out of my misery. Because the look on Aly's face when I admitted to playing puppet master with her life, that look was nearly my undoing. "Just do it," I goad Yulian. "Pull the trigger, because you won't like what I have to say."

"Are you fucking serious?" With a thud, his gun crashes down on the dashboard in front of him. "A bullet to your head isn't good enough. You deserve my hands around your neck!"

I'm not going to argue that; when Yulian finds out the truth – how long it's been going on for, everything I've done to her – he'll want to extract every ounce of my misery.

"Let's get her to safety, and then you can pummel my face in or kill me." My ragged breaths fill up the space between us. "Whatever you see as a fitting punishment."

"I can't fucking believe you. I knew something happened between you. Aly always told me to mind my own business. I figured it was a childhood crush that went sour, because I stupidly believed my best friend would never get involved with my sister behind my back. And now this ..."

The looks of hate he flicks my way makes my chest burn with shame. The truth is so much worse. And there is no hiding it any longer. But there is another truth he also needs to know. "I love her. Not like a sister. I fucking love her with every fiber of my being." His nostrils flare as he slowly shakes his head. "And even though I've hurt her, I'll make it right, I'll do anything to make it—" My voice falls off as we pull up to the safe house. Or what's left of it.

"Fucking hell," Yulian growls. Before the car has even

stopped, he jumps out, sprinting towards the charred remains of the structure.

I throw the car in park and dive out as well, only to be stopped by Daniil blocking my path. "They're not here." I hear the panic in his voice before I fully understand the words.

"What do you mean? Where are they?"

"The house, it's empty. Someone blasted their way in." My heart pounds so loudly I can hear it in my ears, each beat feeling like a hammer against my ribs. I need to see the destruction for myself.

I enter through the huge gaping hole in the back of the house. Explosives were used. If Kira or Aly were in the kitchen at the time of the bomb, fuck me, they'd be ...

A beastly sound rips from my chest just as Yulian ascends the stairs from the basement. His face is grim, ashen, he looks like I feel. Ruined. He just shakes his head, indicating they didn't make it to the basement's safe room.

"No." I refuse to believe it. "We need to search this whole house. Every square inch."

Andrei and Daniil join us in the blown-out kitchen. Andrei is talking on his phone in rapid-fire Russian, Daniil is staring at his phone.

"They were taken," Daniil assures us. "There's footage." He holds up his phone, but I can't bear to look at it. I don't know if I should feel relieved that they are still alive or terrified.

Honestly, I feel both.

Yulian punches a wall, and plaster rains down on him. "We were fucking played. Maxim Belov knew we were coming for Horvat. He waited until we were distracted, and like fucking idiots, we played right into his hands."

Daniil shakes his head. "We had no way of knowing. We did what we had to."

Yulian's head snaps up, and they share an intense look. "Back home? Our girls—"

"They're safe, I promise," my brother assures him. They are talking about their wives and Andrei's daughter, safely holed up at the Kozlov estate. "An army of our best men are protecting the home. Drones. Explosives around the perimeter. It's impenetrable."

Andrei hangs up the phone and holds up his hand to get our attention. "That was Dima. He thinks he can get us a location on where Belov's men took them, but with no registered tail number and no official paperwork submitted to the aviation authorities, it's going to take some time."

"Thank fuck," I exhale, even though I don't feel very thankful, because a man like Maxim Belov has the ways and means to cover his tracks so efficiently that even the best of hackers might not be able to find him. But I don't allow my mind to slip down that rabbit hole, because if I do, there's no coming back.

I holster my gun, and spit on the floor beside me. "We need a plane, stat. As soon as Dima has the answers, we need to be on our way."

Daniil mutters something about reinforcements, but there's no time to gather more men, barely time to gather more weapons. No matter what, we'll never overpower Belov's militia. All we can offer him is us—our loyalty, a cut of our business, the brotherhood in the palm of his hands. Because whatever Maxim Belov wants, he gets, and for some reason, he wants Alyona. And that's the one person I'll never let him have.

At whatever cost.

At whatever sacrifice.

32

ALYONA

THERE'S nothing like waking up and not knowing where the fuck you are.

The last time, I woke up on a yacht. This time, I'm in a room that looks like it belongs in Buckingham Palace with its crystal chandeliers and gold trim. Kira still sleeps soundly in the bed beside mine. I'm nearly jealous that she's still shielded from reality by the comfort of sleep.

Fragments of memories come back to me—the explosion, forced into a vehicle by strong, unyielding hands. A hood pulled over my head before my whole world went dark.

Cold dread percolates in my stomach. The bad guys got me after all.

But who are they?

And why aren't I being held in a dungeon or something?

Soft, thick carpet cushions each of my steps as I make my way to the door. Locked. Expected that one. The windows are also locked. Peering through the glass, I find an endless sea of emerald-green treetops stretching into the horizon, and just beyond that, a massive body of water.

Something tells me we are far from Dubrovnik.

Which means we're far from Leo and the others.

Kira stirs and her eyes flutter open. The same fear and confusion I feel is mirrored in her gaze. I want to say something to assure her, to tell her that everything is fine, but she's too smart for me to feed her lies, so I say nothing, but fetch a glass of water from the bathroom and bring it to her as she sits up.

"What in the ever-loving fuck?"

"Exactly." I hand her the water, which she gulps down before rising from the bed. She completes a full 360, absorbing every detail of the room. "The door is locked, and so are the windows," I inform her, "But it wouldn't matter. We're pretty high up."

"This is not good." Kira approaches the window, resting her forehead and hands on the glass. "I know where we are," she says.

The tiniest match of hope flares inside me. "Well, that's a good start."

She spins on her heels. Her eyes wide with horror. "No it's not. We're in Russia."

"How can you tell?" I ask, joining her at the window.

"I grew up here, I know a Russian estate when I see it." She gestures around the room. "The over-the-top opulence. The Russian realist art. Also, those are boxwood trees. They're native to the Black Sea region."

My mouth goes dry, as Kira sits down on the bed, her head in her hands. "Okay, so, we're far from where we started, but it can't be that bad," I say, running a hand over her hair. "We haven't been separated. We're in a lovely room. I'm sure the food is excellent," I say trying to coax a smile from her. "I'm sure it gets a five-star review on Yelp."

"How can you joke about this? I failed you," she moans. "I was supposed to protect you and I failed."

"There was nothing you could do. They—whoever *they* are —came in with an army, blew the back off the house. These assholes are persistent."

At this point, I'm just mad. I've wasted too much time being scared for myself and the people I love. Now, the worst has happened: I've been taken, and Kira's been dragged into this mess. Well I refuse to turn over and play dead. Heads are going to roll. "We need to find a way to escape," I tell her.

"Did you not see the guards patrolling the perimeter? And even if we somehow managed to elude them, we're surrounded by forest and sea. Where would we even go?"

"We could hide in the woods. Eventually, we'd come across someone who would help us."

Kira shakes her head sadly. I hate to see my usually feisty friend, so defeated. "We'd just get ourselves killed trying to escape here. We'll have to be craftier than that."

"I suppose the smarter thing would be to figure out who has us and what they want." My eyes go wide with alarm. "Do you think we're being sex trafficked!?"

This finally elicits a humorless smirk. "Er, no. I don't think it's worth the trouble of sex trafficking a Kozlov and Nikitin. You know our brothers are going to move heaven and earth to find us. God, I hope they don't do anything dumb."

A knot forms in my stomach because I know without a doubt Leo won't rest until he finds me. Yulian, too, but he has Rowan to think about, and maybe a baby on the way. He'll do everything in his power to rescue us, but he'll at least be smart about it.

Not Leo.

The thought of him dying to save me hits me like a gut punch. My anger from yesterday has dissipated, replaced with a tangle of emotions I can't quite sort out. But I do know one thing—I can't stand the thought of never seeing him again.

Before we can say anything further, there's a click of a lock and the door opens. A sour-faced guard with white-blond hair stands in the doorway.

"Thanks for knocking," Kira bites out. I elbow her because this guy doesn't look like the friendly sort, but I'm secretly relieved to see some of the fight back in her.

But he doesn't spare Kira a glance. He points at me. "Make yourself presentable. You have a meeting in half an hour," he says in heavily accented English.

I rise from the bed. "Who will I be meeting with?"

"You will see."

In an instant, Kira is next to me, her customary sass making a comeback. "What do you mean 'make yourself presentable'? All we have is the clothes on our backs, and we haven't brushed our teeth in way too fucking long. My mouth tastes like I've been drinking swamp water."

His eye twitches at Kira's outburst. "Everything you need is in the bathroom. Fresh clothes in the closet. I'll be back soon. Be ready," he commands, closing the door behind him with an efficient click.

"*Yob tvoyu mat,*" Kira yells at the closed door.

"What does that mean?"

"It means ... ah, it's probably better if I don't tell you." A worried sigh escapes her lips. "Are you going to be okay alone? I can throw a hissy fit and demand to come with you?"

"I don't think Ice King out there responds to hissy fits. Anyhow," I say, pulling my shoulders back, "this is my fight, and I'm going to go down swinging."

She nods in agreement, but there's doubt in her eyes because whoever I'm up against is nothing like anyone I've faced before.

MY HEELS ECHO on the marble floors as I follow Sir Scowls-A-Lot, whose real name I've learned is Pavel, toward the other wing of this mansion. It's deathly quiet here, as if speaking in anything but hushed tones is a federal offense. The silence does little to steady my nerves, which have been on edge since I stepped out of the room.

I distract myself by smoothing the fabric of my dress, focusing on the task to help steady my racing mind. The guard stops in front of an ornate set of double doors and knocks once. He waits until a deep resonant voice invites us in.

The door swings open and my attention is immediately drawn to the powerful outline of a man standing with his back to me, looking out the window. As he turns, I'm struck by his appearance. I'd put him in his early forties with dark hair streaked with silver at the sides, framing a stern jaw. High cheekbones and his deep-set blue eyes give him a distinguished look. But the thing I most notice about him is the air of authority he projects. Beyond his lean, muscular frame and ten thousand-dollar Savile Row suit, power seems to radiate off him in waves.

Who is he?

As if he can hear my thoughts, he tilts his head and asks, "Do you know who I am?"

"Yeah," I huff. "The asshole who abducted me."

This seems to amuse him for some reason. "Yes, I suppose that's true." He studies me intently, his eyes roaming over my face as if he's trying to figure out a secret. I hold my ground, refusing to let him see the fear churning inside. "But there is more to the story. If you'd care to sit down, we have much to discuss."

"I don't care who you are. You've made my life a living nightmare, and I have nothing to—"

"Sit." His voice is like a sharp whip, and I do as he says.

Once I am seated, he clears his throat, breaking the tense silence that has settled between us. "My name is Maxim Belov. Have you heard of me?"

The ground beneath me shifts, threatening to swallow me whole. Belov's name is known all across Europe—no, more than that, the world. He's what would be called an oligarch. He has his fingers in all the major industries—oil, power, telecommunications. And in hushed whispers, it's said he's a major player in international organized crime.

I believe it. Because for all his perfectly tailored suits and sophisticated veneer, the man sitting across from me has the eyes of a cold-blooded killer. I should know, I've known more than my fair share.

While I've heard of Maxim Belov, I've never actually seen the man. He's notoriously private and has somehow managed to keep his face largely out of the papers and off social media. Probably because he'll kill anyone who dares disobey him.

"Of course I've heard of you, but that's not the point." I squirm in my seat. "Why am I here?"

"I think it is." His eyes bore into mine, demanding my full attention. "I knew your mother many years ago. We had ... an affair," he confesses. "And you, Alyona, are the result of that union."

I blink. Once. Then again. A bitter taste rises in my throat. This can't be real. He must be lying.

"No ... you're not. I had a father and he died. He's gone."

A muscle in Belov's jaw ticks as he holds up an envelope between two fingers. "I have proof."

"Save the story, I'm not interested in an explanation." He

might be intimidating, but I won't allow him to sit here and feed me lies.

"Alyona," he commands. "Look at me. Can't you see the physical resemblance?" I slowly lift my eyes to meet his, taking in his features. Really studying them.

Our eyes are the same deep shade of blue, but that doesn't mean anything. And yes, we both possess dark, straight hair—but it's a common Russian coloring.

A little voice reminds me that Papa had light-blond hair and dark-brown eyes, coloring that sharply contrasts with mine. Neither my father nor my mother was particularly tall, but I am ... and so is Belov. But it's his jawline and chin which are strikingly like my own. Sharp and well-defined.

A wave of nausea rolls through me, bile clawing at my throat.

I don't want what he's telling me to be true. He is not someone I want to know, let alone call Dad. Anyhow, I had a father who I loved. This man can go to hell.

"No matter the proof you have, I have no interest in getting to know you. So can we please wrap this up so I can get back to my life?"

Belov reclines in his chair, crossing his legs nonchalantly as if my words mean nothing. "I had an affair with your mother when I was eighteen. I was a guard in your parents' home. Your father worked for the Inanov Bratva at the time and was never home. Your mother was lonely." He shrugs. "The affair was brief. Shortly after it ended, your parents moved to America."

My brows crease together. The timeline tracks. My parents moved to Brooklyn when my mother was newly pregnant with me. My father was supposed to expand the Ivanov Bratva into the US, but instead he met Serge Kozlov and helped him establish the Kozlov Bratva.

"I didn't know Mina was pregnant, if I had ..." Belov's

expression tightens as if he's grappling with something. "I only learned of your existence when you were seventeen, shortly after Kiril died. I met Serge Kozlov at a party, he was showing me pictures of his boys, and you were in one of those photos. The moment I saw you, and realized your age and your mother's identity, I knew you were my own flesh and blood."

"No." I shake my head furiously. "Why wouldn't my mother tell me?" Suddenly, an old memory comes to me, a memory of sitting by my mama's sickbed, when I thought she was delusional.

"Your father ... Alyona, you need to be careful of him," she'd whispered. "Stay away from Russia."

I stand and pace the room. My dress clings to my back, damp with sweat. Questions flood my mind. Did my mother know there was a chance I was Belov's? Did my father know?

Maxim gets up and opens a window, perhaps sensing my rising anxiety. Perched on the edge of his desk, his voice is steady as he continues. "I approached your mother, asked her if there was a chance you were mine. She denied it, but I am a powerful man, and I found a way to confirm it by DNA." Belov hands me a sealed envelope. "The proof," he says simply.

The envelope sits heavily in my grasp. It's like Pandora's box. Once opened, there's no returning to blissful ignorance. But living in denial is an ugly thing. With shaking hands, I rip open the envelope. The first piece of paper is the result of the paternity test. One phrase sears into my brain as I scan the page —*positive match.*

Betrayal rips through me, the truth now undeniable. Gritting my teeth, I move on to the other document, a letter in my mother's unmistakable handwriting.

Maxim,

As you have now discovered, Alyona is your daughter. I genuinely believed that her not knowing the true nature of her paternity was for her ultimate benefit. However, since you have forced my hand, we must establish an understanding.

Kiril cherished Alyona deeply and raised her as his own. Alyona reciprocated this love for her Papa—his passing has left her emotionally shattered, and I am deeply concerned that any further disruptions in her life could significantly impact her mental and emotional health.

Hence, I ask you to respect my wishes and refrain from any contact with Alyona until she reaches the age of 25.

Please understand that my request is not meant to deny your rights as a father. Instead, it is an effort to protect our daughter from any unnecessary emotional turmoil until she is old enough to understand and handle the impact it may have.

I trust that you will respect my wishes and put Alyona's interests above all else.

Regards,

Mina

Tearing the letter into shreds, I let the fragments scatter onto the floor. Belov watches me, his face stoic. Fury blazes through my chest, hot and consuming. Anger at my mother for allowing me to live a lie, at Papa for letting my mother slip into another man's arms. But above all, I'm angry at

Belov for hunting me down like I'm an animal, only to unload this shit.

"Even if you are my father, I don't want you in my life. If you had approached me differently, maybe I would have thought about it. But this? No. Thank you for respecting my mother's wishes, but I want to go home now."

Lines deepen in Belov's forehead. "I am afraid that is not possible."

I cross my arms over my chest. "Why?"

"Like you said. I abided by your mother's wishes. I waited until you were nearly twenty-five, allowed you to have a full life on your own terms. But now it's time to take your rightful place as my daughter. You are my only heir, and as such, you will help lead my empire. And one day, it will be yours."

Hell no. "Consider finding a wife and producing another heir, because this one isn't interested."

I start towards the exit, but Belov's words stop me. "You misunderstand me. I'm not asking, I'm telling you." His voice is low and calm, but it's laced with a lethal edge.

"You can't force me to be your daughter, to join your world!" I snap, my voice trembling. Belov is not a man used to hearing the word *no*, but I plan on holding my ground, despite my fear.

"That's where you're mistaken." He seems to rise up before my eyes, the room shrinking around his commanding presence. "I'm not saying this as your father. I'm stating this as a man with the power to halt the world on its axis if I so decide. You *will* join this family and take your rightful place by my side."

My eyes narrow to slits. What a soulless bastard. He's nothing like my gentle, loving Papa. Belov is devoid of humanity. I'm ready to tell him where he can shove his ultimatum, when his next words pierce the air like an arrow.

"Choose your response carefully," he warns. An ugly smile

spreads across his face. "I'm aware of everyone in your life that you care about, everyone that you hold dear. Your brother, Kira ... Leonid Kozlov."

My throat clenches, fear and fury battling within me as his words settle into the pit of my stomach. "What are you saying?"

"You're a smart girl. Don't make me spell it out."

Holy shit. He's threatening my family, the people I love. *Leo*. "You wouldn't!" I gasp. "If you hurt anyone in my life, I will—" What? The truth is I have no power over Belov.

He sighs heavily. "It seems you need time to come to terms with your new reality. Take a few days. Enjoy all the amenities my home provides—there is a bowling alley on-site, an ice rink, a vineyard. But make no mistake, Alyona, your place is by my side."

I press my lips together, hatred burning in my gut, but I know better than to lash out. The threats he made hang in the air between us.

There is only one acceptable choice here, and Maxim Belov just made it for me.

My life in exchange for the people I love.

Even if it eats my soul.

Even if it kills me.

33

ALYONA

The sun is high in the sky, casting its bright rays over the vineyards as Kira and I navigate our way through the rows of grapevines. The leaves rustle gently in the midday breeze, their shadows dancing on the warm, earthy path beneath our feet.

As beautiful as it is here, neither of us can muster much enthusiasm for our midday walk.

It's been two days since Belov revealed he is my father, and it's taken me nearly that long to process everything. To pick through my thoughts, wrestle with the sadness, with the lies. I've mourned Papa all over again, raged at my mother, then mourned her, too.

But mostly, I've mourned Leo and what we could have been. I was conflicted about our future together—if we even had one—but now that the choice has been taken from me, it feels like I can't breathe. Because to keep Leo alive, I must convince him that I *want* to be in Belov's world. That this is my choice. If he believes otherwise, he'll die fighting for my freedom.

Kira is the only person who will ever know the truth. And that's only because it's impossible to keep it from her. She was as stunned as I was to learn it's Maxim Belov who is not only holding us captive but also my father. After the shock wore off, she moved on to outrage, prepared to fight him in any way necessary.

But there is no fighting a force as powerful as Belov. I've let her know she can't risk her life. This is my burden to bear.

"Let's sit," Kira says, pointing to an ancient oak tree on the edge of the vineyard. "I'm getting hot."

I settle beside her, our backs against the tree trunk. Despite Belov's noticeable absence these past few days, we're both tense, waiting for him to summon me.

Sure, we're treated like esteemed guests here. If it weren't for the heavily armed guards patrolling the vicinity, we could almost be fooled into believing this place was some sort of luxury resort. Almost.

"Alright, new idea." Kira turns to face me, her cheeks flushed from our walk in the sun. We've been playing this game for days. It's called 100 Ways to Kill Belov. So far, we have seventy-nine. "You poison his food. Easy. Everyone will think he died of a heart attack."

I smile, letting my head rest against the tree behind me. "I'd probably screw it up and poison myself, too."

She stretches her legs out in front of her, staring off into the distance. "Okay, how about this? You get close to him, earn his trust, and then start feeding him misinformation. You create enough chaos that his empire crumbles from within, and he's left powerless."

I laugh. "Sounds complicated. I'd much rather push him off a tall building. Although I doubt he goes anywhere without guards." I throw my arm around Kira. "You're full of good ideas."

Kira shrugs. "I wish I was. Then at least I could get you out of here."

The sweet scent of ripening grapes fills the air, and a gentle breeze brushes against my skin. I always thought of Russia as a harsh and cold place, but it's beautiful here. Could I get used to a life by Belov's side? He is my father, even if he's a power-crazed psychopath.

"Maybe it's for the best," I blurt. Kira's head snaps my way. "Having my future laid out for me. A destiny. Even if it's not what I want, it's not like my life was so great ..." My chest tightens; being with Leo on the yacht, no matter how brief, gave me a glimpse of happiness. It was everything I ever wanted. Until it all came crashing down.

"Don't say that," Kira responds, her mouth turning downward. "Belov is a psychopath. I don't care who he is, I won't let him steal your future, and neither will our family."

"That's the problem," I say, my voice rising. "Leo is going to get himself killed coming after Belov and his army. I can't allow it."

"What are you saying?"

"I need him to believe that this is my choice. That this is what I want."

"He'll never believe it," Kira argues. "Leo knows you better than anyone. That man loves you. He won't give up easily."

I clench my fists in frustration. "And I love him, too. That's why I need your help. He'll only believe me if you back me up. If you help convince Leo, Yulian—*everyone*—that this is what I want."

She huffs out a breath. "I think you're making the wrong choice."

"There is no choice. Look around." I gesture in front of me.

"Belov's power is beyond the Kozlovs', beyond any single faction. He exists in a league of its own. He may be involved in legitimate businesses, but he's a gangster through and through. He wouldn't hesitate to kill anyone that got in the way of his plans. Including you."

Kira is quiet, weighing my words. "I could talk to Leo, explain the situation."

"To what end?" I take her hand in mine. She needs to hear this. "I've accepted that Belov has the power here, and the best thing for me to do is play nice. Hopefully when I'm by his side, I can negotiate small freedoms."

Even if it means walking away from the man who will hold my heart forever.

In the distance, an imposing figure walks between the vines, heading towards us. Kira motions ahead. "Is that a guard?"

I wish it was. "No," I say, rising to my feet and dusting off my pants. "That's Belov." He moves with a commanding presence that's hard to miss.

"Jeez." She rises to stand beside me. Running a hand through her shoulder-length waves and straightening her shirt. "You didn't tell me he's so ... striking."

"Guess I forgot to mention it with the five million other things we had to discuss."

He holds up his hand in greeting, like we're old friends. I'd like to tell him to go to hell, but I can't. So I smile and wave back. If this is what is required to keep Leo alive, so be it.

"Good afternoon, ladies," Maxim greets us, his voice deep and resonant. "Kira Antonov, I don't believe we've had the pleasure."

He extends out his hand, and Kira sneers at the gesture. She has some serious lady balls. I'm just not sure giving Belov the big old *fuck you* is very helpful. I shoot her a warning look, but her focus is locked on the man before us.

"I go by Kozlov now. Since you seem to know who I am, you probably know why I don't want anything to do with my father's name."

Belov doesn't appear fazed. A wry smile touches his lips. I wonder if he intentionally used Kira's father's name. A man who never loved her, who was willing to sacrifice her for his own gain.

"Ah yes, I can't blame you for that. Your father was a vicious man."

"Not unlike you," she shoots back. Her voice is dark ice.

"Kira, behave," I hiss in warning. I know firsthand that Belov's patience only lasts so long.

"No need," he says, holding out his arms wide. "We're all friends ... and family. Let's speak openly."

Kira's hands clench into fists at her sides. Like it's the only thing stopping her from gouging Belov's eyes out. For a five-foot-nothing pixie, she's as fearless as it gets. She literally staged a coup to take down her father. No one could accuse her of being timid.

"In the spirit of speaking openly, what you're doing is wrong. Even if you are her biological father, you don't get to abduct my friend and snatch her life away."

Maxim regards Kira with a sneer, the predator within him surfacing. "I'm sorry you feel that way. I'd like to think I'm giving Alyona an opportunity to do great things. To be rich beyond her wildest dreams, powerful. Her career was middling at best. She has no husband, no children ... I am giving her the life she was destined for."

Ouch.

"Excuse me?" Kira springs up, bristling like an angry cat, which is my signal to intervene.

"Kira, calm down," I say softly. I then turn to Belov, my hands on my hips. "You've left me with no choice in the matter. I don't want your life and everything it represents." My shoulders slump. "But I also don't want war."

My father narrows his gaze on me. "And what is it that you do want, Alyona?"

Leonid Kozlov. All I've ever wanted. But the only thing in my life that's an impossibility. "I'm still figuring that out," I admit.

"You love fashion, I'll buy you a fashion empire to run. I don't want you to be unhappy, I just want you to be by my side. Involved in my world. Ready to take the reins when I'm no longer able to."

"You can hire someone for that, ya know," Kira mutters, forcing Belov's eyes back on her.

His smile is arctic. "I'm aware. But that's not how this works." His eyes linger on Kira, scrutinizing her, but Kira boldly holds his gaze. "I knew your Aunt Masha," Belov adds, shattering their silent battle.

Kira's whole body tenses. Her aunt was her rock, the one person who loved her unconditionally. Kira's father, Oleg Antonov, ordered his sister's execution when she conspired against him. Kira rarely speaks of it; the memory is too raw.

"You knew Masha?" she rasps.

"I did. She was an acquaintance. You remind me of her," he says, his lips tipping up just the slightest bit. "Hot-headed. Would never back down from a fight. Didn't know how to hold her tongue." He pauses, sincerity in his tone. "But I liked her, and I was sorry to hear of her passing."

Kira's mouth twists, and she looks away. "If you knew my aunt, then you know she didn't *pass away*. She was murdered in cold blood."

I hold my breath, but Belov doesn't flinch. While Kira's father was supposedly responsible for Masha's death, Kira has hinted there's more to this story. More that she intends to discover one day.

Belov's mouth settles into a grim line, but he doesn't say anything more. I lay a hand on Kira's shoulder. "Why don't you go back to our room? I'll meet you there in a bit."

She delivers a final scathing look at Belov before squeezing my hand in a show of support.

"Shall we walk?" Belov asks, and I gesture for him to lead the way.

As we stroll through the vineyards, Belov pauses to tenderly touch a plant, drawing my attention to the green bud emerging. "People don't often associate Russia with wine making, but the Black Sea region has a rich, diverse soil, allowing us to produce exceptional wines." He leans down to inspect a cluster of grapes, assessing their ripeness. "Soon it will be harvest time. I think you'll enjoy being involved in that process. I do."

"Like you spend much time harvesting grapes," I snort. "You must have more important business to attend to."

"Of course I do, but this is my hobby." He tips his head to the side, a smirk tugging at the corner of his lips. "Even bad men like me have hobbies."

"I never said you were a bad man." At least not aloud.

"You didn't have to. I know what you're thinking. And it's true, I'm not a good man. But I'm fair, in my way."

Hate to break it to him, but threatening to kill the people I love is far from fair. Still, we're past the point of a lecture. So I ask him the only question that truly matters. "If I agree to your terms, will my family and friends be safe?"

He studies me, his gaze unblinking, before he finally nods.

"I never go back on my word. Let's hope you have as much honor."

Sadness settles like a stone in my chest. I take a deep breath, choking on the heaviness of my decision. "I'll do it. I'll lead by your side."

34

LEO

I CAN'T SIT STILL. My legs carry me back and forth across the plush carpet of our suite at the Ritz in Moscow. The weight of worry inside me is a leaden anchor, dragging me down. It's been two days since Alyona and Kira disappeared, and there's still no sign of them.

Dima tracked their flight route—they were definitely heading for Russia—but as soon as they crossed the border, the trail vanished. It's no surprise, Belov has the clout to wipe the paperwork clean.

"You need to stop pacing," Andrei snaps, his attention fixed on his laptop. "It's distracting. Go outside, take a walk. Get some fresh air. Something."

I'm about to snap back that I'm trying to be useful, but ... well, am I? I've been a snarling animal locked up in a cage while my brothers and Yulian work around the clock to piece together any scraps of information that could give us a clue as to where they are. But I'm more concerned—no, obsessed—with the *why*.

Alyona is gorgeous, of good breeding, practically mafia royalty—I know very little of Belov, but I don't believe he is married. Could he want a wife? Fuck, just the thought has fire ants crawling under my skin. I pick up the closest valuable—a glass vase and smash it into the wall.

It's official.

I'm losing my shit.

Daniil emerges from the shower, a towel slung around his neck. He whistles when he sees the damage done. "I thought we hid all the breakables?" he shakes his head. "Dude, I'm either going to book you a massage at the hotel spa, or we need to find one of those axe throwing places."

"Drink. I need a fucking drink," I grumble, but I'm quite sure Andrei hid all the booze in the room. Either he doesn't want an angry stumbling giant to deal with, or he doesn't want me to smash the bottles to pieces.

Yulian, who has been standing by the window watching my outburst with distaste, approaches. "Come with me," he grumbles, striding past me towards the door.

He leads me down to the hotel bar where, minutes later, we're side by side, nursing matching scotch whiskys. Yulian hasn't said much to me since we learned of the girls' disappearance, so I'm not sure if this is him calling a truce, or what. Though he hides it better, he's as fucked-up as I am. I can see it in the tense lines of his shoulders, the dark circles beneath his eyes.

"Better?" he asks, as I throw down my first shot of hard alcohol in days. The amber liquid hits the back of my throat with a sharp burn that I welcome before warmth spreads through my body, loosening my limbs.

"It's a start. I'm gonna need more." I throw a handful of fancy bar nuts into my mouth. "A lot more."

Yulian stands up and reaches behind the bar to grab the full bottle of Macallan M. The bartender frowns and opens his mouth to contest, but one look from Yulian and he backs the fuck up. Neck tattoos always send a certain message.

"Well, aren't we two sacks of useless shit." Yulian huffs, a smile building. "You more than me."

An unexpected laugh bursts from my chest. "I deserved that." I throw back the last of the whisky, the burn igniting my throat, and lower the glass onto the bar with a satisfying thud.

Yulian grunts and tops off my glass before raising his own to his lips.

I snatch up my drink, eyes fixed on the liquid in my glass. "You still planning on killing me?"

He smirks. "Nah, I figured I'd let Alyona have the honor. At least give her first dibs."

I find myself grinning, although I'm not entirely convinced he's kidding.

He tilts his head. "When did it start?"

I need another gulp of whisky before we go down that road. This is the bombshell. "The summer you and Andrei were in Russia training. But if I'm going to be honest, it started long before that. Or at least my feelings did."

"Why didn't you ever tell me? Either one of you." He shakes his head, his lip curling in annoyance. "If it was real between you two, I deserved to know, didn't I?"

I run an agitated hand through my hair. "We planned to tell you, but I fucked it up before we could."

"Fucked up how?" His eyebrows lower, and if I'm not careful, I'm quite sure he'll take a swing at me.

All the air leaves my lungs in a rush. "You deserve to know the truth—all of you do—but Aly deserves it first." I just hope I get the chance to tell her everything, explain myself, that it's not too late for us.

Yulian drags a knuckle over his jaw, studying me as if for the first time. "I never knew you were so adept at keeping secrets, bratan."

"It's nothing I'm proud of." I shrug, running a finger over the scar in my chin. "How should we play this? I know Andrei is all for diplomatic maneuvering, but I say when we have a location, we go in with an army, guns blazing."

Yulian snorts into his drink. "There are times to be aggressive, but this is not one of those times. This is about being smart."

I close my eyes for a brief moment, tension gathering in the base of my neck. "I'll behave. As long as that *svoloch* hasn't hurt her or Kira, I'll be on my best behavior. But if he has, if one hair on either of their heads is out of place, I can't be held responsible for my actions."

Yulian slams back the rest of his drink, his face lined with tension. "Me neither, *bratan*. Me neither."

I DON'T KNOW what time we make it back upstairs to the suite, but we're in rough fucking shape. I needed this though. A little booze to soften the edges. As soon as we walk into the room, we're met with a hive of activity. Both Andrei and Daniil are talking loudly into their phones, each of them pacing.

Something has changed.

Andrei finishes his call and approaches Yulian and I, both a little worse for wear.

"Looks like you motherfuckers are back just in time. Grab a coffee and shower, you'll need to sober up."

"What's going on?" I bark.

"We have a location for Belov. He owns a secret estate on the Black Sea coast."

I spring into motion, but Daniil stops me with a hand to my chest. "Where are you rushing off to?"

"Where do you think? We have a location on Belov."

"Not so fast. First off, you smell like a distillery." His eyes flick to Yulian. "You too. And second, we have to do this right. Which means coming up with a plan."

Yulian is practically vibrating with impatience. "We can develop a plan en route. Let's move."

Andrei and Daniil exchange a heavy look, one that says there's more to this story. "You tell them," Daniil mumbles. "You're the pakhan."

Unease creeps under my collar, as Andrei, possibly for the first time in his life, looks just a bit unsure of himself. "We've learned Belov is throwing a ball tomorrow night. It's to introduce the world to his daughter."

My head snaps up. "I didn't know he had a daughter." But then again, Belov only reveals what he wants to the world.

Andrei eyes flick up to the ceiling before landing on Yulian and I. "Alyona is his daughter."

What!? My jaw drops open, as Yulian rears back like a spooked horse. And just like a spooked horse I'm pretty sure he's about to bolt, but Andrei presses on. "Dima found the proof. A paternity test." Andrei's face softens. "I'm sorry."

I can't draw a breath. Everything feels wrong, upended. I look over at Yulian and see the same pain and confusion etched on his features.

Silence descends. A few moments pass before Yulian releases a string of Russian expletives as he storms from the room. Daniil makes a move to go after him, but I stop him with a shake of my head. I had my time to rage, this is his.

I sit down heavily on the couch, my mind churning with

everything Andrei's told us. Alyona is Belov's daughter? Shit, I don't even know how to make sense of that. I'm relieved Belov wasn't hoping for a wife, but also damn confused why he'd abduct her rather than reaching out another way.

But fuck it, there's only one way to find out. Andrei mentioned that Belov is throwing Alyona a ball tomorrow for all his cronies. That gives me an idea. One I'm sure no one will like, but one I'm convinced could work.

35

ALYONA

I TILT MY HEAD, studying my reflection in the mirror. I look like I just stepped off the cover of *Vogue*, draped in a Givenchy gown of sapphire silk, my dark hair is tamed into soft waves cascading down my back. Not that I'm complaining, it's just surreal being all dressed up for a ball in my honor when I'd rather pluck my eyelashes out one by one.

Kira joins me in the mirror's reflection, her honey-colored hair is pinned up with delicate silver hairpins. Like me, she's immaculately styled, wearing a ruby red off-the-shoulder couture gown that Belov somehow scared up in twenty-four hours.

And in the same amount of time, he's managed to pull together a ball or whatever we're calling my introduction to high society. Power players and Belov's political cronies from all over the world are flying in as we speak to take part in tonight's festivities.

It's all too much. My head is already spinning, and I swear

a migraine has been thumping my skull all day. Sensing my inward spiral, Kira delivers a glass of champagne into my hand.

"For your nerves," she says, before settling onto an ottoman. "This is nuts," she adds, tipping her head toward the window. "With all this fuss he's making, you'd think the Queen of England herself was getting married." She's right. There's a glittering fountain at the front of the palace, lit up with spotlights as if it were an old-school movie premiere. A slew of guests continue to arrive by luxury car and helicopter.

"It would be a dream come true for some women," I murmur. "Just not this one."

Kira sets her drink down on the dressing table and sighs. "I worry about you."

"I'll be okay. I've accepted it, really," I lie, my stomach twisting in a knot. In truth, I've accepted nothing. I've barely slept since my meeting with Belov, the father I never wanted. But I'm putting on a brave face for Kira because as soon as I've settled into Belov's life, I'll petition him to let her go. And I don't want her thinking she's leaving me here miserable.

"You're one of the toughest chicks I know. You take no shit from anyone, but for some reason, you're not fighting back. Negotiate with him. Don't let him take all of your power, even if he thinks he's god."

"What choice do I have?" I voice sharply. "What choice did he give me!?"

Kira responds with a sigh, her fingers pressing against the bridge of her nose. "I wasn't going to say anything, but I'll regret it if I don't." She hesitates, her eyes softening. "Are you sure you're not agreeing to Belov's terms because you're scared of what will happen if you actually fight for Leo? If you give him a chance, for real."

My first instinct is to flat out deny it, but the words stick in my throat. Kira knows me better than most, and she's sure to see through my lies.

"I don't know." I lower onto the edge of the bed and bury my head in my hands. All the emotions I've kept at bay for the last few days comes rushing at me like a dam unleashed. I reach for a tissue and dab at my eyes. "When we were on that yacht together something shifted. It's like ... like every single feeling I'd buried came back, but this time more intense, all-consuming. I'm mad at him, but I'm also so in love with him it hurts."

Even now, Leo is the first thing I think about when I wake up, and my last thought before I go to sleep. He's consumed me, broken me in ways I can't even fathom yet, but I still ache for him. Leo might forever have my heart, but the world has conspired against us.

Kira pulls me in for a fierce hug, her arms wrapped around me like a protective shield. When she pulls back, her gaze is gentle. "Why don't you try reasoning with Belov. Talk to him. I get it, he's not just going to let you go, but maybe you can work something out. Some middle ground where you get to maintain some control over your life."

"Maybe," I say, but I'm doubtful. Why would Belov agree to any of my terms? He may be my flesh and blood, but he's shown me no mercy, no kindness. And he's clear about the role he wants me to take in his world.

A knock at the door to the room startles both of us. It must be one of the millions of staff members ready to escort us downstairs.

"Come in," I say, rising and smoothing my dress. The door opens to reveal not a staff member but Belov. He's the picture of perfection in his slim-cut black tux, his hair slicked back, drawing attention to his chiseled features.

He leans against the doorframe, one hand in his pocket. His dark eyes scrutinize me. I'm sure it's to ensure I look flawless, as required of his daughter. He must be satisfied with what he sees because he nods approvingly. "You look beautiful, Alyona."

His gaze flicks to Kira, who meets his stare with a scowl. Kira's appointed herself my guard dog, snarling at Belov every chance she gets, even though I've told her it's not necessary or helpful. Instead, it creates an electric tension every time they are in the same space.

I don't miss the way Belov's gaze drifts appreciatively down Kira's body before snapping back to her face. "Kira," he says, with a hint of a challenge. "You look lovely as well."

She responds with a vicious eye roll as he steps further into the room. "And you look like the devil incarnate."

A muscle ticks in his jaw. "If you can't play nice, you can spend the night in the dungeon. I'm sure you'll find it lacking compared to the accommodation upstairs, but I won't have you ruining tonight for her. Or for me."

Kira's eyes narrow, her ruby-red lips press into a thin line. If there weren't half a dozen guards milling about, I bet she'd break a champagne flute and use the broken glass to shank him.

"Whatever," she says, crossing her arms and looking away.

Belov turns towards me. "It's time to come downstairs and greet your guests."

My fingernails cut into my palm. *My guests*. They are hardly my guests, but there's no point in a rebuttal. I made a deal with the devil and now I must see it through. Kira and I exchange a final look before I follow Belov out of the room, towards the destiny I never asked for and don't want.

One day at a time, I remind myself. I just need to get through tonight and not think about everyone and everything I am leaving behind.

Not think about Leonid Kozlov, and what we could have been.

What we almost were.

36

ALYONA

"What a wonderful surprise it must have been to learn about your father," the wife of the interior minister says to me, a blank smile on her face.

Her husband chortles his agreement. "And what luck," he winks. "You certainly won't want for anything ever again."

I choke back a sarcastic reply. "Yes," I say between clenched teeth, "a happy surprise."

The whole night's been like this. Distinguished guests whose names I forget the minute I'm introduced fawn all over me, telling me how damn lucky—*lucky*!—I am to be Belov's heir. To be brought into his strange and suffocating world. The guest list is a testament to the spheres he straddles— business tycoons, politicians, and organized crime heads mingle like it's the most natural thing in the world. And maybe it is.

But fuck, it's not a world I want to be part of. As the couple drones on, I scan the opulent ballroom, searching for Kira, my anchor in all of this. I need to feel like myself again, even if it's just for a moment. It's not hard to find her, not with that vibrant-red dress, the color of blood. A *fuck you* to Belov if I was to guess.

She's in a corner of the room, talking to my father, and it doesn't seem to be a friendly chat. Belov appears irritated, his hands gesturing, brows pressed together.

This again.

Even though I've told her to drop it; I have no doubt that they are arguing about me. She's on thin ice here. Because if Belov is pushed too far, he will come out swinging, and I don't want her to be on the receiving end.

"Would you excuse me," I say to the older couple. "I need to have a word with my father."

They wave me off, and I head in their direction, sticking to the edges of the room to avoid being sucked into any more useless conversations. Just as I make it to the edge of the room, a big male body carrying a tray full of hors d'oeuvres steps into my path.

"Shrimp toast, madame?"

"No thanks," I say, and then stop. Because that voice, I know that voice. That body, the broad shoulders and hulking frame a head taller than almost anyone else in here, it's more than familiar.

It's mine.

"Leo, what the fuck are you doing here?" I whisper-yell. Dressed as a server, he's wearing a ridiculous blond wig and thick black-rimmed glasses, a tray delicately balanced in his enormous hand. And even though I'm horrified that he's here, I also desperately want to fall into his arms.

"I'm offering you an appetizer."

"Jesus, you're going to get yourself killed." Desperate not to attract attention, I pull him further into the corner. "You need to leave. Turn around now and go." Fear curls low in my belly.

I'm terrified what will happen if Belov's guards see him, if they realize who he actually is. Belov will interpret this as a declaration of war.

"That's right, I do need to leave. With you and Kira. My brothers and Yulian are all here and we're not leaving without the both of you."

"I'm serious," I plead. My voice edged with hysteria. "You can't be here, Belov ... You don't know what he's capable of. He won't take kindly to you crashing this party."

"Has he hurt you? Are you okay?" He scans my body, looking for welts or bruises but there are none. Because Belov didn't have to use physical force with me. He used a much more persuasive method. Threats that I have no doubt he will make good on. Which is why Leo, my brother, the Kozlovs, they all need to go.

And there is only one way for me to make sure that happens.

"I'm all right, I promise. He hasn't hurt me. In fact," I take a breath, gathering steel for the acting job of the century. "This was my idea. It's what I want. A life with my father."

"Bullshit," Leo explodes, loud enough that heads turn.

"Shhh," I beg, fear clawing up my throat. "Please—"

"Belov abducted you, and he's forcing you into this," Leo continues, his voice unwavering. "I know you. All you've ever wanted is to live a normal life. Even if he is your father, you'd never choose to run his empire alongside him."

Unwelcome tears burn behind my eyelids, but I fight them. Just as I fight to maintain my composure. "My father is ... surprisingly flexible. He cares about my happiness." The words ring false, and Leo's doubtful expression is proof that he's not buying it. Before I can try for a more convincing tone, his head jolts upwards as his hand grazes his ear.

"*Chert*" he bites. "Andrei gave me the signal, we need to move."

"Take Kira," I plead "but I can't leave." Not without serious repercussions.

"Please, baby. I'm not leaving without you," he insists, his words thick with raw emotion. "I can't live without you, Aly. I won't."

"You have to, Leo. You have to." A lone tear escapes, which I quickly brush away. Then from behind Leo, I see my father heading towards us, a smile on his face, his arm outstretched like he's been looking for me.

"Go," I beg under my breath. "Belov is coming."

"There's a wine cellar in the basement. Meet me there. Down two floors to the right. If I don't see you in ten minutes, I'll come back up and look for you. There's nothing you can say that will make me leave without you. Nothing."

I can't respond, not with my father's eyes on me, so I take another toast off the platter, and breeze past him like he's actually just a server and not the man I love.

"I'm glad you had a chance to grab a bite. It's a long night, and the champagne continues to flow," Belov says, grasping my elbow.

My nerves are frayed, but I force a serene smile onto my face. "Me too. The food is delicious," I say, walking in the opposite direction of Leo. "You've really outdone yourself." I'm laying it on thick, but I want to put Belov at ease. If he thinks I'm happy, maybe he'll lower his guard.

"Could it be?" He gives me a wry smile. "You're not actually enjoying yourself, are you?"

"Maybe a little."

"How about a dance?" he gestures towards the middle of the room filled with couples swaying to the music of a string quartet.

"Of course," I say, because there's really no other acceptable answer. I take my father's hand and allow him to lead me to the dance floor. Placing his hand at the small of my back as we begin to dance, he projects the air of a perfect gentleman.

But I see through his act. For all the wealth, prestige, and confidence he displays to the world, I see the beast lurking within him—hungry and fierce.

"I need to confess something," Belov starts, his voice unsettlingly soft. I stiffen, my nerves wound tight as a coiled spring. "I was married once. It didn't go all that well, to be honest, and I had no interest in trying again or having children. But when I learned I had a daughter ... it shifted my perspective. There's no point in any of this if I have no one to share it with." He falls silent, his gaze drifting into the distance. "As you grow older, you start to grasp the value of family. When all is said and done, blood is the only bond that truly matters."

I suppose this is Belov's idea of a father-daughter bonding chat, though if anything, it just highlights how delusional he is. But I don't have time to engage; I need to wrap this up and meet Leo in the basement before he does something reckless.

Well, more reckless.

So I force a smile and murmur, "Sure, Dad, that would be nice."

He stops dancing and gives me a quizzical look. "*Dad*?"

"Since we're bonding and all ..." I lift my shoulders but can't look him in the eye.

He seems satisfied with my response, and we soon fall back into step, even as I will this song to end so I can make a break for it. "I know this isn't the life you'd necessarily choose, but I'm confident you'll find your place. You were impressive on your own, but alongside me, you'll be unstoppable. The world will be yours to command."

"I was doing just fine until you came along," I say, unable to hold back the words. Because this man has his head so far up his ass if he thinks I'll ever find happiness by his side. I found my happiness, and I'm about to lose it a second time. Belov doesn't respond, but the pressure of time weighs on my shoulders. "Have you seen, Kira?" I ask Belov, in what I hope is a casual tone.

His jaw tightens at the mention of her name. "Not for a while."

Could she have pissed him off enough that he did something to her? "I saw Kira talking to you earlier. I hope she wasn't giving you a hard time. She's protective of me."

"Yes, I can see that. She's ..." His eyes darken. "Stubborn. But no, we weren't discussing you."

Strange. What else could they have been arguing about if not me? But before I can ask, the song ends and a group of men close in on Belov, clearly desperate for his attention. "I'm going to visit the ladies' room," I say before I step aside.

I take advantage of his distraction to make my escape. My eyes bounce all over the room, but Kira is nowhere in sight. Leo or one of the others must have gotten to her already ... I hope. I keep my eyes lowered and my steps measured as I make my way to the basement. One wrong move could alert Belov's guards that something is going on.

The wine cellar isn't hard to find. Stepping inside, I'm enveloped by the cool, musty air. The room is dimly lit with flickering sconces casting shadows on the walls. Tall wooden shelves are lined with wine bottles that are, I'm sure, equivalent to the GDP of some countries.

Leo is leaning against one of the shelves. When his eyes meet mine, he straightens, his face a mix of relief and concern. "We don't have much time," he says, stalking towards me. "We've jammed the signal to the security cameras down here, but someone will notice soon enough. Kira and the others will be here any minute, there's a back door that we need to—"

"No, Leo. You're not listening. I'm staying here. It's my choice." The lie tastes bitter on my tongue, but I swallow it down, willing him to believe my words.

His hand curls around the back of my neck, his face so close to mine that his heated breath brushes against my lips. "I don't know what game you're playing. What shit Belov is coercing you into saying, but I'm telling you now,"—his grasp on me tightens—"I'm not leaving without you."

A sob rises in my throat, and my hands curl around the collar of his starched shirt, pleading with him to listen. "Please, you have to."

His warm palms cup my cheek, and his lips lower onto mine. The kiss is deep and all-consuming, sending an electric shiver down my spine. "Fuck, Aly, I'm a wreck without you. You are the light that guides me, you are the reason I breathe. I know I've fucked up so many times you've lost count. Let me make it right, let me love you the way you deserve to be loved."

His words are charged with so much raw emotion it's nearly my undoing. But I can't lose focus, because what happens next determines whether he lives or dies. And since I've failed to make him believe my lies, it's time to deliver the truth.

"If Belov thinks you are standing in the way of me leading his empire with him, he will kill you, he's said as much. It doesn't matter what I want ... just ... fuck, Leo, I love you. I love you so goddamn much it hurts. Even if I can't be with you, I need to know you didn't die for me."

His hands wrap around my waist, holding me against him. "I won't lose you again. Once nearly destroyed me. I'll do whatever it takes to make Belov see reason. I'll stay here and fight for you, fight for us—"

His words are cut off as the door swings open and my brother barrels into the room, trailed by Daniil, Andrei, and Kira. Yulian doesn't seem to notice or care about the fact that I'm in Leo's arms. He just pulls me away and hugs me tight. "Thank fuck you're okay."

"I am," I say, squeezing my brother back. I've missed him, but this is no time for a reunion.

"We need to get moving," Yulian says. "Van's out back."

"I can't," I tell him, my voice shaky. "You go, I need to stay for now. It won't be forever, but—"

"What are you talking about?" Yulian says, his eyebrows pressed together. But before I can explain myself, Leo steps between us.

"If you stay, I'm staying. I'm not leaving here without you."

I feel like knocking my head against the wall, this man is making what I have to do near impossible. I take a deep breath, prepared to plead my case, when the lights flicker on and off, plunging the wine cellar into utter darkness.

"Shit," Yulian hisses. Leo finds my hand in the dark as panic claws at my chest.

The cellar door creaks open, followed by the heavy thud of footsteps. The lights snap on, revealing Belov with a cold snarl painted on his lips. His guards flank him, their guns drawn and aimed in our direction. Belov also had a weapon pointed square at Leo's chest. "A family reunion. And I wasn't invited?"

Leo puffs out his chest. "You're not her family, even if you do share blood with her."

The atmosphere in the room thickens. My worst nightmare is unfolding before my very eyes. All the people I care about in one room, vulnerable, surrounded by Belov's evil army. Body trembling, I throw myself in front of Leo. Belov needs to understand I'll take a bullet for Leo without a second thought. If he hurts Leo or anyone in here, he hurts me.

"Let them go," I plead with Belov. "We had a deal. I'll stay, but you have to let them all go."

The words are barely out of my mouth before Leo pushes me behind him. Looking up, I'm met with the sight of Leo, pistol in hand, pointed at Belov. Defiance burns in his gaze even though we're clearly outnumbered, and from what I can tell, no one else on our side has a weapon.

What is Leo doing?

Belov's henchmen all train their guns on Leo, but he doesn't blink an eye. My heart hammers in my chest, a deafening drum that drowns out all other sounds, but I don't dare move a muscle or say anything. One wrong move could tip this all in the wrong direction.

Belov lowers his gun and perches on a cask of wine, his posture relaxed, as if this isn't a tense as fuck standoff. "What's your endgame here, Kozlov?" he asks Leo. "Do you think you can rescue Alyona and gallop off into the sunset as a happy couple? You—the man who abandoned her for the brotherhood—you're suddenly the knight in shining armor?"

What!? How does Belov know our history? Judging by his self-satisfied grin, he knows he hit his target. Leo's hold on the gun tightens, his aim shifting to target Belov's head. "You know shit about what happened in our past."

"That's where you're wrong. I knew your father well—not exactly friends but business associates." A jolt of surprise shoots through me as this revelation. "He would come to Russia often, as you know. He was even a guest here a few times. We drank cognac together well into the night. Well, he would drink, and I would listen. After a few drinks and a bump or two of cocaine, Serge was quite talkative. My daughter—the daughter I was sworn by my honor never to contact—lived under his roof. I had a vested interest in keeping tabs on your family."

If looks could kill, the combined looks of venom directed at Belov would have him dropping dead to the floor. But that's not what happens. Instead, Belov goes in for the kill. His voice is deceptively light when he adds, "Alyona doesn't know the truth, does she, Leonid? Why don't you tell her. In fact, tell everyone in the room. I imagine your brothers don't know the full story, either."

All attention shifts to Leo. He's still like a statue, his heavy breathing the only outward sign that Belov's words have unsettled him.

"Leave him alone," I snap back. "You have no right to interfere like this. What happened in the past is between us. Not you."

"He's right," Leo says, voice hoarse. He lowers the gun in his hand. "You deserve to know the truth."

"But not like this," I argue. I pull him towards me, but he won't look me in the eyes.

"Yes, Aly, because you may not want anything to do with me after you learn the truth. When you learn how weak I was."

"That would never happen," I insist, but it's as though my words bounce off a wall. Leo's trapped in his own thoughts.

With a gesture, Belov clears the room, sending all his guards to wait on the other side of the door except Pavel, his right hand.

My eyes dart to Yulian, then sweep over Andrei and Daniil—all wear expressions of shared confusion. Kira shoots me a worried look. She understands what's coming next.

I don't know what Leo is about to tell me, but I do know there is no turning back from here.

Kneeling down, he grabs my hands in his and proceeds to shatter my world.

37

7 YEARS AGO

LEO

WHEN ALYONA'S BREATHING STEADIES, her body soft in sleep, I ease out of bed. It's just after midnight, Papa will be awake, and I know exactly where to find him. I move quietly through the halls, having rehearsed this conversation in my mind over and over. He won't be happy, but my decision is firm. There's no doubt or second thoughts.

Alyona is all I'll ever want and need. She showed me there was another way. That I can create my own destiny. That I can live in the light. She believes in me, believes I am capable of so much more, and I will prove her right. I'll make us a life beyond the brotherhood, with her by my side.

The dim light under Papa's office door tells me he's still working, the life of a pakhan is a 24/7 gig. Not that he minds. Papa *is* the

Kozlov Bratva. It wasn't a legacy passed down to him, it was a legacy he created, that he fought for. Hell, he moved continents knowing his business could only thrive on American soil since the bratva in Russia was too entrenched to make room for an upstart like him.

But leading a bratva to greatness is his dream, not mine. I knock softly. The shuffling of papers on the other side of the door ceases. "Enter," Papa's booming voice rings out.

My father sits behind his grand mahogany desk, a king perched on the throne. There's not a computer in sight. Papa doesn't believe in electronics to run a business, not an illegal one at least, he's a gentlemen's handshake kind of guy. What good is a contract when a bullet can drive the point home much more effectively?

"What is it, son?" Papa asks, lowering his bifocals down his nose.

"We need to talk. It's important. It can't wait until morning."

"Very well." He gestures to the seat across from him, and I sit. Abandoning his glasses on the desk, he rubs the bridge of his nose. "What is it?"

The confidence I'd felt earlier is a little shakier now. "It's about Alyona. Alyona and me." I take a moment, debating how to tell him. But with my father it's best to be direct. "We're together, Papa."

He raises his eyebrows, not in surprise, but in confirmation. "I know," he finally says.

"You know?"

"I know everything that happens in this house, Leonid. Why would you think differently?" His face turns stony, an unsettling stillness settles around us.

There's a cruel edge to Papa. I've always known it—the terrifying way he'd yell at my mother when they fought, or the way he'd punish soldiers when they disobeyed him. But I've never had it directed at me. Not like this.

Until now.

I do my best not to flinch under his scrutinizing glare, because my father can smell weakness from a hundred miles away, and he detests it. So I harden my resolve, and press on. "Ever since Kiril was killed, Alyona's chosen to distance herself from the bratva. This life is not for her. She's accepted Yulian's choice, of course, but she doesn't want it for herself, or for the man she is going to spend her life with."

My father picks up a small clock on his desk, polishing it with a handkerchief from his pocket. "I don't care what Alyona does. She's useless to this family."

I wipe my sweaty hands on my pants, trying to find the right words. "I love her, Papa. I've probably always loved Alyona, but we've become close this summer. She's the woman I want to be with for the rest of my life. I know I'm young, but I'm clear about what I want."

The sneer on my father's lip is the only indication that he's heard me. He continues to polish his timepiece, not even sparing me a glance. "What are you saying? That you don't want to be a vor?"

I shake my head slowly. "You know I have a good mind for computers and technology. There are things I can do. Ways I can help the family without being sworn in as a—"

The sound of shattering glass drowns out my words, and the once-elegant clock now lays in splinters on the wooden floor. "You would shame yourself like that? Shame our family?" His words are low and venomous. I almost wish he was screaming, because somehow this is worse. But I won't be bullied by him. Not for something as important as this.

"There is no shame when it's a choice. You have Andrei

and Daniil, even Yulian. I'll still be here, the only difference is I won't have my stars."

Rising to his feet, my father rests his two hands on his desk and leans forward. He's not overly tall—I have a few inches on him—but he's a former boxer, built wide and sturdy and he knows how to use his size to intimidate. "I tolerated your dalliance with Alyona. You were meant to fuck her out your system and move on with your life. The life you are destined for, by your brothers' sides. Not as a pathetic subcontractor that plays with computers all day." His next words leave his lips on a snarl. "I won't have it."

Determined to hold my ground, I rise and unflinchingly meet his vicious glare. "I'm sorry you see it that way, but I don't need your blessing. I've made my decision. Even if I don't have your support, I stand by my choice."

The slow grin that builds on my father's face is unsettling. "And what about sweet, innocent Alyona? Do you think your decision doesn't affect her?"

Fuck, why does my father have to look so smug right now? Like he's holding all the winning cards. "Of course, it does. We made this decision together. It may not be the easiest path, but this is what we both want. It's our choice."

"You keep on talking about choice. 'My choice, my freedom,'" he mocks in a whiny tone. "You sound like a bloody American brat." His eyes sharpen into slits. "Since Kiril passed, I've made sure Alyona wants for nothing, I've treated her like my own. I arranged for her schooling and brought her into my home. I have a team of doctors and nurses looking after her mother under my roof." Terror skitters down my spine. My father is not just making idle chitchat, he's going somewhere with this, and I have a feeling I won't like it.

"Leave her out of it, Papa," I threaten between clenched teeth.

"How can I do that? This is all because of her. You are days away from being sworn in as a vor, and now some stupid bitch is going to come in here and ruin the future you were destined for? I don't think so, Leonid." His lips curl with disdain. "If you reject your stars, I'll have Alyona killed in the ugliest way possible. I will give her to my men, and after they pass her around, I will strangle her with my own two hands, then run her organs through a meat grinder before feeding her to the dogs."

Bile fills my mouth, and the room spins. "No. No!" I yell uselessly. "How could you? You said it yourself, she's like a daughter to you."

"But she's not my daughter, is she? And she's threatening to take away my son, to strip him of his honor. The honor of a Kozlov. I won't have it!" he yells, slamming his hands down on the desk so hard it reverberates through the room.

"How dare you! How fucking dare you!?" I come at him, but I'm too worked up, emotion robbing me of my aim and precision. The punch he lands on my jaw is swift and brutal. I hold my face as blood pools in the corner of my mouth. "How could you do this? To your own flesh and blood? To Aly?"

"One day, when you're a father, you'll understand." But I'll never be like him, I'll never be dead inside. I'll never be a cold shell of a human. "You leave me no choice, Leonid. I won't have the family legacy sullied by the stupid caprices of a twenty-one-year-old boy who's seen nothing of this world. Knows nothing about life. You think love is enough, but one day you'll learn that love is not forever. The brotherhood is forever. Honor is forever." He beats his chest to punctuate every word. "But Alyona, she will move on. And what will you have then? You'll be a glorified IT specialist for your brothers with nothing else to show for it. Shameful!"

I wipe the blood from my mouth and spit on the floor. "Just because Mama grew to hate you, doesn't mean that will happen with Alyona. You drove Mama into your enemy's arms—she was desperate for a scrap of warmth and affection. *You* are the reason she turned cold. *You* are responsible for her suicide. I hope it haunts you every night for the rest of your life."

If I wasn't in such a state, I would have anticipated the punch, but I don't. I just feel the snap of his gold ring as his fist connects with my temple. The thud of my head on the floor. My vision swims as a gray cloud grows at the edges, moving outward.

And I hear his final words to me. "Choose wisely, son. Choose wisely."

I DRIVE AROUND in the dark for a long time. My head still throbs like a motherfucker, but I'd take that pain over the pain in my chest, because that doesn't just throb, that feels like I'm being ripped open from the inside out.

Two hours on the bike hasn't brought me any more clarity. The only thing that seems clear to me is that I am screwed no matter what I choose to do. I pull off the main highway, driving over mottled leaves and overgrown greenery and pull up in front of a little abandoned fishing hut. Not sure when or how I first found this place, but every once in a while, I find myself back here. It's a shack, not much in terms of shelter, but it's on the water, and it feels far from civilization. No one can find me here unless I want them to.

I take a seat on the battered porch and drop my elbows onto my knees, resting my head in my hands. God, to give Aly up ... it's unimaginable. She is my person, I know it with a bone-deep certainty. Before her, I was willing to blindly take the oath, walk the path that someone else drew for me. She made me realize I can be my own person, determine my own path.

Or at least, I thought I could. How wrong I was.

My father, my own flesh and blood, is leaving me no choice. If I choose Alyona, I'm signing her death warrant. It's as simple as that. For better or worse, my father always makes good on his word.

How can I look Aly in the eye and tell her my father is willing to sacrifice her in the cruelest way possible? She'd be devastated, but more than that, she'd be stubborn, she'd want to run away together or find another way to make it work. Even though it's hopeless.

There's also Yulian to consider. If he learns the depth of my father's brutality, he'd go ballistic. He'd start a war, turn against the brotherhood—and although he'd have every right to, it would only serve to get him killed.

And my brothers? I honestly don't know what they'd do. Yes, they'll be horrified by Papa's actions, but would they turn their backs on the Kozlov Bratva to side with their oldest friend? To side with me? That I can't say.

Grief mounts, and I'm on my feet before I can process it, ripping out a wooden board from the floor and hurling it against the wall of the shack. I rip out the next beam, and the next one. By the time I'm done, my hands are bloody and ravaged, and the hut is no longer intact.

It's the actions of a crazy man. And I've gone crazy, there's no question because as I stand on the muddy ocean banks—my hands on my knees, doubled over, trying to catch my breath—clarity comes, and it is devastating.

The only way I can protect Alyona is to push her away. Tell her I never loved her, that she meant nothing to me.

As much as it will destroy her, the truth is even more devastating.

ALYONA

I wake up alone in an empty bed and smile up at the ceiling. Today is the day that Leo and I become official. No more sneaking around, no more hiding.

Yulian will be home from Russia this afternoon, and Leo and I will sit down and tell him everything. Man, he is going to be shocked, and probably more than a little pissed that we've been carrying on behind his back, but he wants the best for me, I'm sure of that.

And Leo is the best. He's my everything.

Leo must have snuck out of bed early this morning so as to not wake me up.

Today is a big day, and I'm sure he's taking some time to figure out how to tell his father. Although the pakhan might oppose Leo's choice, he'll accept it in time. How could he not? Leo is his son, and he loves him. Don't all parents just want their children to be happy?

I eat breakfast, work out, read a bit, do my nails, and then finally turn on a movie, but by the time 4 p.m. rolls around and there's still no sign of Leo, I'm feeling a little anxious. I text him, letting him know that I'm in my bedroom, and that Yulian will be home soon.

Minutes pass, but still no response. He leaves me on read, which is strange, but I'm not going to start obsessing over this. If Leo needs time, I'll give it to him. We can wait until tomorrow to talk to Yulian, nothing will change between now and then.

Hours pass, and still nothing from him. Now the worry starts to set in. What if he's been in an accident? What if his talk with Serge didn't go well? What if ... any number of scenarios play through my mind, but I refuse to panic just yet.

I call Daniil. The phone is ringing, pressed against my ear, when the door to my room flies open and Leo stands on the threshold.

"Thank god." I hang up the phone, tossing it onto the bed, and hurry towards him, but just as I'm about to fling myself into his arms, I stop myself. Something isn't right. "Are you okay?" My eyes rove all over his body. His muddy boots, his bloody hands, his bruised face, he has a crazy shiner on his left eye. "Holy shit, what happened to you?" But his face remains deadpan. My pulse roars in my ears, something is wrong. I've never seen him like this.

"We made a mistake," he says coldly. His expression is remote. Like a stranger has taken over his body.

"Leo, I don't understand." Panic unfurls in my belly, its icy tendrils extending out to wrap around my lungs. "Is this about telling Yulian? Are you getting ner—" He holds up a hand to stop me.

"No, Alyona, we are the mistake." His voice is hoarse, like he's forcing out the words. "I was wrong to think this could be anything serious. That we could actually have a future together."

The room spins, and I nearly fall to my knees. Is this really happening? "Like hell we are a mistake!" I rage. "Are you getting cold feet? Is that what's happening? You!? The bravest man I know. Don't take the cowardly route, Leo, it's not who you are."

Raw devastation passes over his face, but he blinks, forcing his features back into that fucking blank mask. This is not the man I fell in love with. This is a poor substitute. "You're wrong. What we have—no, what we *had*—was nothing but lust. I was your first fuck, so you mistook it for love. It's not that, only lust." He takes a shaky breath, his chest rising and falling unevenly. "You're just a kid, Yulian's little sister. I can't give up my future as a vor. It's my honor. My family's honor."

It's like someone hurled a stake at my chest, that's how blinding and raw the pain is. This is not Leo. He's not this person, this monster, his expression shuttered. Closed off.

But maybe he is. I just never saw it before. My knees give out, and before I know it, Leo has me in his arms, but instead of comforting me, all he does is deposit me on the bed and stand over me.

"I ... I never meant to hurt you, but I don't want to lead you on any longer. We need to end this."

Some things in life carve wounds too deep to heal from; I should know. My father's death was one, but this ... I don't know how I'll come back from this. I turn over to face the wall so I no longer have to look at him. "Get out," I manage to whisper. "Get out, Leo. I never want to see your face again."

He hovers over me for a second longer before clearing his throat. The door clicks shut as he leaves. My breath hitches, but no tears come, the pain is so immense it's physical, it hurts like someone cracked open my chest and ripped out my beating heart.

A minute later, a devastated howl rips through the house. It sounds like a beast ensnared in a trap. I recognize the voice behind the anguish, but it's an echo in the void. Everything is lost, nothing else matters.

"ARE YOU SURE ABOUT THIS? Going to Paris alone?" Yulian pulls up to the arrivals curb and switches off the engine. Sitting back in the driver's seat, he takes me in, a frown marring his usually handsome face.

"I'm sure, Yulian," I say, plastering yet another fake smile of reassurance on my face. "It's really what I want. You know I've always been interested in fashion."

"Sure. It just seems so sudden." He runs his hands through his hair. "I'm just going to ask you this once." He swallows and flicks his gaze out the window. "Did something happen between you and Leo? Because for the last few days, you've barely left your room and he's ... god, he's a fucking wreck. I haven't seen him like this before. He's been on a three-day bender."

Pain slashes through my chest, followed by a much stronger emotion. Anger. I grit my jaw, but I know I need to tell Yulian something. And it can't be a bullshit excuse, either, because my brother will see through my lies.

"Something did happen," I confirm. Yulian's body tenses, his hands curling into fists. "Something that was a long time coming. But it's not going to work out for us. It's better if I go to Paris and he joins the brotherhood."

That will always fucking burn. That Leo chose the bratva over me. But what did I expect? The Kozlov Bratva is his family's legacy, it was the only future Leo ever imagined for himself. Maybe for a time when we were together, he entertained the idea of a different way of life, but in the end, he was too chicken shit to follow through.

Yulian's jaw hardens. "I didn't see that coming." His nervous fingers drum out a beat over the steering wheel. "Do I need to kick his ass?"

I shake my head sadly. "No, it's fine. Pakhan made a few calls ... I have an internship at a prestigious fashion house starting in a few days. This is what I want, Yulian. A fresh start."

He pulls me into his chest, wrapping both arms around me. "I'm going to miss you. And I'm going to visit the first chance I get."

"Sure." I pull away, offering him a small smile. "The bratva keeps you busy, bro. Promise me you'll be careful. Promise me."

My words catch in my throat and if I want to avoid soaking his leather seats in tears, I need to leave his car right now.

"I will. You know I will."

"I better go." He makes a move to help me, but I stop him with a hand on his chest. "I'll hire a porter. I just ... need to leave now. On my own."

Yulian seems torn. But in the end, he only gives a nod. "Take care of yourself," he says, his voice heavy with restrained emotions.

38

LEO

They say the truth will set you free. I'm not so sure about that. Standing here with my confession echoing in the stark silence, I don't find freedom, only a hollow numbness in my chest.

Yulian reacts first. With a muttered curse, he tears off his wig, flings it on the cellar floor, and stalks out. I knew this would be hard for him to stomach, having worked closely with my father for years. To learn that the man your father trusted, the man your father died for and that you were loyal to, would have your own blood killed. It's devastating.

Aly calls after him, but she doesn't move. I can feel her gaze on me, but I can't bring myself to look her in the eye, afraid of what I might find there: a mirror of my own shame, a sting of disappointment. I wish I could have said all this to her privately, but Belov forced my hand, and now there's no stuffing the genie back in the bottle.

Belov watches Yulian's departure with a hint of amusement. The mudak is clearly pleased with the unfolding drama.

He forced this confession from me to divide our family. If we're at odds, Aly is easier to control. Well, that motherfucker can burn in hell, because I won't let it come to that.

It's Kira who closes the distance first, wrapping her arms around me. "I'm so sorry you had to go through that. What your father did was—" She shakes her head. "There are no words."

Before I can argue, before I can explain that I took the coward's way out, Andrei wraps a hand around the back of my head and presses my forehead against his. "Why didn't you tell us? This shouldn't have been your burden to bear alone."

A lump forms in my throat. "What purpose would it have served other than to start a civil war? Force people to take sides?"

"We would have had your back no matter what," Daniil assures, his hand resting on my shoulder. "What you did wasn't shameful, it was honorable."

My gaze flicks between my brothers, both of them wearing solemn expressions. "Is that what you believe? What honor is there in destroying the person I loved the most?"

I can't help it now, my eyes seek out Aly's. Tears glisten on her cheeks as she steps towards me, raising her hands to gently hold my face. Her voice, full of emotion, ricochets off the stone walls. "You did it to save me because it was the only way. That's an act of courage, not an act of cowardice." Her words rock me to my core. I don't know what kind of reaction I expected—revulsion, disappointment, disgust, maybe—but it wasn't this. This ... understanding. "I just hate that you've kept this to yourself for so long. It must have eaten you up inside."

"More than you'll ever know," I answer honestly. It nearly destroyed me.

Her face falls. "The truth is I'm horrified, yes, but I'm not shocked. Serge was a brutal man who lived in a brutal, ugly world."

"I wish I had found another way to stand up to him," I say, my hands clenched into fists as I admit my biggest regret. "I wish I didn't have to hurt you like I did."

"You made the only choice you could have at the time. You were young, he was your father, the pakhan." Her arms drop around my waist, and she pulls me close, like we're the only two people in the room. "Your father manipulated you, whether he would have made good on the promise or not, he messed with your head."

I have no doubt he would have, but it's not a point worth making. Instead, I press a soft kiss to her lips and murmur a thank you, because her words crack me open, sparking something inside of me back to life.

Behind Aly, Belov shifts position, locking onto me with a heavy stare. "This doesn't change anything," he says tersely. "Alyona is still needed by my side."

Anger threatens to burst from my chest, but Aly speaks up before I can reach for my gun. "I know this whole father-daughter relationship dynamic is new to you, but if you actually care, if you actually want to know me as a person beyond someone you can order about, don't force this on me."

He gives us a slow, calculating perusal—the sign of a man who makes all his decisions with his head, not his heart. "It's the way of the world, Alyona," he adds with a heavy sigh. "But I do have a counteroffer. If this is the man you want to be with, it will be on my terms." He addresses me now. "Come and work for me."

My eyes track to my brother, and Andrei gives me a small nod of approval before I continue. "No," I say simply. "That's not happening. I'm cutting ties with all organized crime. For Aly. For us to be together. You may not be bratva, but you play in the same underworld."

"You seem to think it's a choice," he spits.

"It is a choice. Her choice," I roar. "And I'll do whatever it takes to secure Aly's freedom. What I should have done from the start. But we won't be joining you, Belov. Kill me if you must to make your point, but it will only drive your daughter away and deepen her hatred for you."

Aly's eyes are wide with alarm, but she needs to know I won't back down. I wasn't able to stand up to my father, but I sure as hell will stand up to hers. Even if right now he is bristling with the intensity of a bull in the ring ready to charge.

Andrei steps forward in an attempt to diffuse the situation. "Let Aly go, and I can offer you a partnership, an alliance," he says, his voice carrying through the silent room. "Your power is concentrated in Europe, but we have the East Coast of North America—the most valuable American market—locked down. Working together will benefit you financially and in other ways."

If there is a shred of humanity left in Belov, he has yet to show it. His laugh is chilling, as he starts a slow walk around the room. As if summoned, his men filter back into the space, making it feel all the more suffocating.

"More money, more power, that means nothing to me," he says with a dismissive wave of his hand. He comes to stop in front of Aly and me, his face hard as granite. "While I applaud your loyalty to my daughter, I require an heir, a blood relation to lead by my side. And make no mistake"—his mouth settles into a hard line as he tilts his head towards Aly—"you may not want this, but you will learn to be a leader. As my daughter, it's in your blood. Are you willing to walk away from our agreement, Alyona?"

There's an underlying threat to his words, and the irony isn't lost on me. My father would have killed her, and now Belov is threatening the same to me.

"Maxim, please," Alyona begs, releasing a tight breath.

"Don't do this." The anguish and despair in her voice is so palpable it tears at my soul. But I've had enough of this khuy and his veiled threats.

Despite the fact that we are surrounded by his men, I step forward, ready to fight, not with weapons, but man to man. The air thickens around us at my implied challenge.

"Stop, Leo." Kira's voice cuts through the air, halting my movement. She strides past me and positions herself directly in front of Belov, who peers down at her with barely contained interest. "You want an heir, you want someone to rule by your side ..." The room takes a collective breath. "Then take me. I will marry you. I will become your wife and lead by your side but let Alyona go."

My head shoots up, shock blasting through me.

"Kira, no!" Aly nearly jumps out of her skin, but Kira holds up her hand, continuing to face-off with Belov. I don't like how he looks at my sister, his eyes roam over her body like a wolf eyes his next meal.

"Now, why would you want to do that?" he questions, the edges of his lips tipped up into a grin.

She holds her chin high. Even with her back to us, it's clear she's not intimidated—or if she is, she hides it well. "Because I want to be in power. I was born to rule. Even if I despised my father, royalty is in my blood, it's my fate. This will be nothing more than a business arrangement. No romantic entanglements, nothing that could get messy." She pauses for effect. "And I will give you heirs if that's what you want."

Belov's jaw is tight, his hands clenched by his side. Even holding stock-still, I can tell Kira's offer piqued his interest. He's considering it carefully.

Aly tenses, as if she's about to jump into the fray, but I stop her with a hand on her forearm. Whatever is happening now needs to play itself out. And while I have no idea what Kira's endgame is, I am sure she has one. Because one thing about my sister—she is crafty and cunning.

I expect Belov to dismiss her, but he doesn't. Instead, his eyes seek out Alyona's. "What do you have to say on the matter?"

A scowl etches across her face. "I'd like to speak to my friend alone. Without you and your guards breathing down our necks."

"You have five minutes." With a sweep of his arms, Belov and his men clear out of the room.

Kira turns around to face us—her three brothers and her best friend—looking every inch the bratva princess she claims to be.

"Are you crazy!? I won't let you do this," Alyona explodes, stomping her foot. "You can't bear him a child, you're twenty-three and hate him! I won't allow you to sacrifice your happiness for mine."

"You're not *allowing* me to do anything," Kira says gently, grabbing Aly's hand. "It's my choice."

"*Sestra*, it means the world that you offer yourself like this," I echo, emotion building in my chest for my sister's selflessness, "but there is another way."

"Leo is right," Andrei says. "I can't stand the thought of you tying yourself to that monster for the rest of your life. We'll figure something out."

"I don't get it." Alyona shakes her head. "You hate him. You hate him more than I do!"

"Oh, I hate him, alright." Kira sighs. "But he's a means to an end."

"To what end?" I ask, genuinely confused. "Money and power we have ... what could he possibly give you?"

She rubs her temples, her face a mask of weariness. "Trust that I have my reasons. I can't tell you what those reasons are right now, but I'm going into this with my eyes wide open."

"There is no 'wide open' with a snake like Belov," Daniil says through clenched teeth. "At least take some time to consider. You can't decide your entire future under pressure like this."

"Aly and I can stay here while we try to work things out with Belov," I offer. Not that I have high hopes we'll come to an agreement with him, but no matter her reasons, she needs time to think. "I can't allow you to throw away your future on a whim."

Kira smiles sadly. "This isn't a whim. And this is not a case of altruism, although, Aly, you know I would do anything for you." A meaningful gaze passes between the two friends. "This is for me."

"I don't know what to say." Aly shakes her head gently and bites her lip. "'Thank you' doesn't seem sufficient."

"Not 'thank you.'" Kira embraces Aly. "How about 'good luck.'"

Fuck, that's ominous, but my sister is an adult, she's brilliant and tough as nails. If she has her reasons, I won't undermine her. There's no chance to push the issue anyhow, because Belov and his henchmen reappear.

"So?" he asks, raising his eyebrows at Alyona.

Her tone is bitter when she replies, "What do you want me to say? You've left us with no choice."

Belov approaches Kira, standing so close they are breathing the same air. One of his fingers tips her chin upwards, their eyes clashing like titans.

"Is this what you want, little dove?"

"*Want* is a strong word," she fires back, eyes narrowed, "but I accept this arrangement."

His shrewd eyes travel over her face, like she's a code he's trying to decipher. "I look forward to learning exactly what it is you're really after, Kira. And make no mistake, I will find out." His gaze sweeps the room, his smile wolfish. "It's settled, then. Kira and I will marry. And that makes us all family."

Coming from his mouth, it sounds more like a threat than an invitation, but the deal is done. And now I have to call the man who was prepared to kill me less than an hour ago, both brother-in-law and father-in-law.

That is, if I can convince Aly to marry me.

39

ALYONA

LEAVING KIRA WAS HARD. Not just for me, for all of us, judging by the tense silence on the journey back to Moscow. Belov arranged for his private helicopter to transport us. Tensions being what they were, I didn't think it was wise for us to spend the night.

Anyhow, Kira was adamant that we leave. It was only after we said our final goodbye and the bird lifted into the air did her face fall. Doubt creeping in. But by then, it was too late. She'd made a deal with the devil.

And the devil happens to be my father.

Belov was surprisingly easygoing about swapping me out for Kira, and honestly, it makes me uneasy. Why did he go along with her plan so readily? I get that Kira has her motivations, though those are still a mystery to me, but Belov? He's an enigma wrapped up in a mystery, wrapped up in a ten-thousand-dollar suit. I don't trust him as far as I can throw him. But he's my biological father who is (weirdly) going to marry my best friend, so I can't shut him out of my life completely.

But as we left his compound tonight, I warned him he better treat Kira like the fucking queen she is. Biological father or not, I will kill him by my own hand if he hurts one hair on her head.

Behind me, Leo carefully runs a loofah along my arm, trailing it up to my neck before gliding it back down. A pleased hiss escapes me. "I can practically hear your mind working," Leo says, releasing a small chuckle.

"I'm still shell-shocked," I admit. "I never imagined that tonight would end with us together and Kira being tied to Belov for life."

"It's crazy." He sighs. "And if I thought for a second Kira sacrificed herself for us, I wouldn't have allowed it. But she offered herself up for a reason."

In the end, this here is all that matters—Leo and I, moving forward without secrets and lies. It broke me to hear the truth that Leo had buried for so long, knowing how it ate him up all this time. But would it have been better if he'd told me the truth all those years ago? I honestly can't say.

Knowing the ugliness Serge was capable of is still a bitter pill to swallow and not just for me, but Yulian too.

After we got back to the suite, we all sat around and talked well into the night. Some things can't easily be fixed. Some pain takes him to heal. It's the way it is. But Leo and I, we've agreed to leave the darkness in the past and move towards the light. Together.

Leo's warm breath cascades over my neck, causing my eyes to flutter closed. "What are you thinking?" he whispers, dropping small kisses along the nape of my neck.

I glance out the window at the sun rising above the horizon.

"I'm thinking it might be time for some sleep." We've been wrapped up in each other since we got back to the suite and haven't had time for much else.

"Sleep is for the weak," he jokes, allowing his hands to wander over my breasts and under the water. I sigh, warmth growing in the pit of my stomach. "Before we go for another round, tell me what's going on in that pretty little head of yours."

"My head is ..." I close my eyes and marvel at the truth. "Quiet, actually. It's my heart that's making a racket. I didn't think I'd ever see this day."

He lets out a deep sigh of contentment, and I can feel the steady rhythm of his heartbeat against my back. "Neither did I. But fuck, I feel like I'm getting a second chance at life." I turn to him and see a mischievous glint in this eye. "And I want to say ... I'm 'sorry, not sorry' for fucking with your love life in Paris."

"There was never going to be anyone else for me," I admit. "Even before you scared them away. It didn't help that I was still in love with this one man from my past."

"Oh yeah," he purrs in my ear. "Tell me about him."

"He's six three, hot as sin, tattoos everywhere. Although he has this one tattoo of a butterfly that I think is really sweet. He has great hair—thick, dark—looks best when he grows it out to shoulder length ... hint, hint ... and"—I raise my left hand out of the water—"I'm already wearing his ring."

He threads his fingers with mine, his thumb brushing over the diamond glinting on my finger. "It's very convenient indeed. Know why?"

"Why?" I ask, playing coy.

He turns me around so I'm straddling him, looking into his soulful brown eyes. "Because I'd really, really like it if you married me. How about it, butterfly. Are you gonna say yes and make me the luckiest man in the world?"

"Yes! Fuck yes!" I laugh and kiss him, my chest feeling like its going to burst with all the happiness in the world. "The only thing I care about is being with you. But there is one more thing." Because this time, it needs to be his choice. "If being part of Kozlov Bratva is what you want, if it makes you happy, I won't take that away from you. I can make peace with it."

"No, butterfly, I'm ready to cut the ties. Andrei is not my father, he doesn't see the honor in forcing a destiny on someone who never wanted it in the first place. My brothers will always be my brothers, that will never change, but you and our future is all that matters to me now."

Emotion clogs my throat as I wrap my arms around his neck. Our tongues meet and intertwine, break apart and meet again. I can't get enough of him. His taste, this touch, his scent. Not only in this moment, but forever.

I want to uncover all the layers of him I didn't know about —the good, the bad, the messy—all of it. As long as he is by my side for this crazy journey of life.

When I finally pull away, he grins and cups my jaw, guiding my gaze to his. I can feel the head of his cock nudging against my opening under the water, and I adjust my hips, my core lined up perfectly to take him in. His voice is hoarse when he says, "You look damn hot with my ring on your finger."

He groans, his fingers digging into my hips as I slowly sink down on his hard length, loving the way he fills me up to bursting. "And you feel damn good with that piercing in my cunt."

"Butterfly," he whispers, his voice thick, "there's nothing I wouldn't do for you. Whatever you need, whatever you want. You are my fucking queen, and I will obliterate anything that stands in our way."

I writhe against him, barely able to form the next words out of my mouth, lost in the rising tide of pleasure. I raise my hand, covering the butterfly right above his heart. "I'm ready for forever with you, Leonid Kozlov."

"Fuck, you've stolen the word right from my lips."

EPILOGUE - 3 MONTHS LATER

ALYONA

"Ah-ah," gurgles Anya from her blanket on the sand, her little hands reaching out towards me. I bend down to pick her up, her gummy smile warming my soul as I spin around just to hear her giggle.

"Thank you for being my flower girl," I tell her, pressing our foreheads together. "You did a wonderful job."

Still a baby, her role as flower girl consisted of her wearing a wreath of flowers while Georgia walked her down the aisle, but she was adorable, and waved to all our guests like the little princess she is.

As swiftly as she's come into my arms, her attention shifts towards her papa, who is approaching us. "Congratulations Alyona," Andrei says, kissing my cheek. "You were always my sister, but now I also get to call you my sister-in-law."

"You sure do," I smile, passing Anya back into her father's capable arms. "Now I just need to remember that Georgia,

Bianca, and I are all Mrs. Kozlov. That's going to get confusing."

Andrei grins, bouncing Anya gently in his arms. "Seems like a good problem to have."

"Agreed," I say as Andrei gently heaves his young daughter onto his shoulders.

I never imagined I would see this man barefoot in the sand playing with his baby, but Andrei continues to surprise me at every turn. This includes dressing in a pair of jean shorts and a Hawaiian shirt to embrace the casual beach style of our wedding.

Our wedding in Lipari.

Because the irony was too rich to resist returning to Italy and exchanging vows on the exact island where I once declared to Giuseppe that we would never tie the knot because I was just using Leo for his body.

Joke is on me.

Although ... sometimes I do use Leo for his body.

Turning towards the sea breeze, I find Yulian perched on the edge of a sun-warmed blanket, watching me with a small smile on his face. I grab two beers from a cooler and make my way towards him. It's our first chance to connect after a hectic few days, and I'm glad we have a moment to ourselves.

"Congratulations, sis," he says, throwing an arm around my shoulder as I settle beside him on the blanket. "You make a beautiful bride."

"Thank you, and you make a handsome best man. Just not as handsome as my husband," I joke, my eyes seeking out Leo as they always do.

I still feel an electric thrill every time I look at him and realize that he's mine; that somehow we found each other again after all the insanity and chaos. And damn, he is handsome. Standing tall by the water's edge, his broad shoulders and muscular arms are accentuated by his worn-in jeans and linen shirt, rolled up to reveal veined, tattooed forearms. His hair is pulled back into a ponytail, well on its way to shoulder-length.

In the past three months, it's like he's shed the weight of the world. He's happy. And so am I.

This is the man who captured my heart, mind and soul. The man who loves nothing more than a worn-in pair of jeans, a leather jacket, and to hop on his bike and take me on adventures.

The man I now get to call mine. My husband. Forever.

Leo approaches Andrei and plucks his little niece off his brother's shoulders, spinning her around while she shouts with glee.

"That's going to be you soon enough," I say to Yulian, gesturing towards Leo and Anya.

"I can't believe it." He shakes his head, grinning widely. I nearly can't believe it either. Rowan and Yulian's baby-making holiday was successful, and in a little over six months, a bambino will arrive. They don't want to know the sex of the child, which makes it hard to buy cute baby outfits, but I've already threatened to go hog wild shopping after the little one arrives. "I'm a bit freaked out," he admits after a while. "I hope I'll be a good father ... but I worry I'm going to fuck it up, that I'll make mistakes."

Resting my head on my brother's shoulder, I consider his words. "There's no such thing as perfect. We all stumble and make mistakes along the way, but you and Rowan will love your child unconditionally. You'll be a great father. I know you will." I take a sip of my beer and gesture towards our friends. "Andrei wasn't exactly the poster boy for fatherhood before Anya but having a little person to care for and love, it changes you."

He nods, but his mouth stays flattened into a straight line. The revelation about Serge Kozlov threatening my life still haunts Yulian. Serge was a father figure to him, took him under his wing after our father died and Mama was sick. We've spent a lot of time these past few months processing and talking about it, all of us, especially Leo and Yulian.

While I can't say any of us feel closure, we've accepted that Serge was from a different time, a different world. The man was deeply flawed but it doesn't erase some of the good he did. We are all yin and yang. A flare of light in the darkness.

"Thanks, Aly." He sips at his beer, watching a seagull swoop overhead. "I wish our parents were here today."

I smile wistfully. "Me too. I still miss them every day." Papa will always be my father, blood relative or not. My relationship with Belov is still a work in progress. Leo and I have been so busy settling back in New York these past few months, as well as planning this wedding, we haven't had time for much else.

It pains me that Kira couldn't be here today, but she thought it best if Belov wasn't present—not yet. Maybe I can have a relationship with him someday, but now it just feels too soon. Too raw.

I still talk to Kira regularly, but she's guarded about her life, particularly anything to do with Belov. Is she actually happy? I have no idea. Kira is the queen of putting on a brave face. For now, I accept that she did what she had to.

Leo appears, carrying two plates piled high with a full Italian antipasto spread. He passes me one plate and keeps the other for himself.

"Hey, where's mine?" Yulian whines.

"Dude, get your own. Since when do I fix you a plate?"

"Since you put a ring on my sister," Yulian teases, eyebrows raised.

Leo snickers and takes a big bite of focaccia. "Being my brother-in-law doesn't buy you special privileges."

"I'll remind you of that next time you ask me to help you rebuild the engine of your Harley."

"Would you two cut it out," I interject, though I secretly love it when they bicker, because it means things are back to normal. It took Yulian a hot minute to get used to the fact that his best friend and baby sister are head over heels, but I think he gets it now. "Do you ever tire of needling each other?"

"Never," Yulian says, a big smile on his face as he gets to his feet. "Congrats again, both of you." He plants a kiss on my head before wandering off towards Rowan. Coming up to her from behind, he places his hands over her growing belly and kisses her neck.

Leo watches them wistfully. "I wouldn't mind that," he says lightly. "Seeing you swell with my child. Fuck, it's giving me a semi just thinking about it."

"Down boy," I chide, but truth be told, I want that too. We haven't talked much about children, but now that we're married, it might be time to revisit. Or maybe there's no need for a discussion at all.

"Well, it is our wedding night," I whisper in his ear. "And you know what that means." I look up at my husband through my lashes.

"Does that mean I can have my way with you, Mrs. Kozlov?"

"Always," I whisper against his lips.

I don't think I'll ever get my fill of this man. My soulmate. My everything. I've tried living without him, and it was impossible. He makes my life sweeter in every way. He makes my life worth living.

THE END

BONUS EPILOGUE

Thank you so much for reading Fierce Vow!

Want to spend Christmas with the Kozlovs? Check out this free bonus epilogue, set two years into the future, featuring the full Kozlov clan! It's a perfect mix of naughty and nice. Download here:

https://monicakayne.com/bonuses

ALSO BY MONICA KAYNE

KOZLOV EMPIRE

Merciless Heir

Cruel Deception

Fierce Vow

Shattered Crown

BRTAV KINGS

Ruthless Reign

Savage Reign

Brutal Reign

ABOUT THE AUTHOR

Monica Kayne is a former documentary TV producer turned proud romance writer. She writes dark and swoony romance novels with a liberal dose of sass and humor. Her favorite characters to write are sweetly possessive bad boys and the feisty, smart-mouthed heroines they can't resist. When she's not dreaming up sexy plots, she can be found searching for the perfect Negroni and her next K-drama fix. She lives with her family in Toronto, Canada.

Connect with me!

www.monicakayne.com

TikTok

@monicakayneauthor

Instagram

@monicakayneauthor

Facebook reader group

Monica's Mafia Queens

Printed in Dunstable, United Kingdom

64134169R00201